One Scandalous Kiss

Also by Christy Carlyle

Coming Soon:
One Tempting Proposal

One Scandalous Kiss

AN ACCIDENTAL HEIRS NOVEL

CHRISTY CARLYLE

AVONIMPULSE
An Imprint of HarperCollinsPublishers

This is a work of fiction. Names, characters, places, and incidents are products of the author's imagination or are used fictitiously and are not to be construed as real. Any resemblance to actual events, locales, organizations, or persons, living or dead, is entirely coincidental.

Excerpt from *Right Wrong Guy* copyright © 2015 by Lia Riley.
Excerpt from *Desire Me More* copyright © 2015 by Tiffany Clare.
Excerpt from *Make Me* copyright © 2015 by Tessa Bailey.

EPub Edition SEPTEMBER 2015 ISBN: 9780062427991

Print Edition ISBN: 9780062428004

10 9 8 7 6 5

To my best friend and husband, John.
None of this would be possible without
your love and support.

Acknowledgments

My deepest gratitude to my wonderful editor, Elle Keck, who saw promise in my story and has shepherded me through every step of this exciting new journey. Thank you, too, to Collette and Kerensa, who provided feedback on this manuscript when it was still a seedling that hadn't bloomed. And thanks to my Insomnia Coffee write-in gang, who encouraged me through my first submission process, and to my friend Jon, who was with me when I got "the call" and completely understood my exuberant, teary, stunned reaction.

One Scandalous Kiss

Chapter One

London, September 1890

SHE'D NEVER IMAGINED wealth would be so uncomfortable. Nearly every aspect of the Marquess of Clayborne's Belgrave Square drawing room made Jessamin Wright uneasy. There were no books stacked in piles, no candles whose wax had run down their sides in haphazard sculptures, and not a spot of ash dusting the hearth—nothing inviting about the room at all. How could any lived-in space be so clean? The slippery damask settee felt stiff and unyielding beneath her body. Nothing about it urged you to sit and stop awhile. Even art was lacking from the walls, except for a series of watercolors of what must have been a terribly boring fox hunt. A fire burned low in the grate and offered a bit of warmth against the autumn chill, but the cool beiges and tepid pinks of the wallpaper and furnishings made Jess feel slightly queasy, as if blood had been drained from her body as thoroughly as color had been drawn out of every surface in the room. Even the wood was light-colored or painted white and lacquered to a high sheen. It was all wrong. No room should be so spotless. As she and Alice had yet to meet their host, she began to doubt that anyone lived here at all. Then again, she'd never before set foot inside a fine London town house. Perhaps they were all this stark and unpleasant.

Jess didn't have to look down to know the room's pristine neatness contrasted sharply with her scuffed boots, soot-dusted cloak, and unfashionable work clothes. She found it impossible to settle herself in such elegant surroundings. Sitting, then standing, then sitting again, she rearranged her limbs and scratched her neck in a most unladylike manner. Finally finding a spot on the settee that suited her, she stripped off her twice-mended gloves but kept her hands clasped, careful not to touch anything for fear she might leave a mark.

Her cluttered thoughts offered as little comfort as the room. She fretted about leaving the bookshop managed solely by her assistant, Jack. He was a longtime employee and utterly trustworthy, but he'd never been fond of dealing with customers. He simply loved books—acquiring them, reading them, repairing them—and that was something she understood. He hadn't stayed on after Father's death for her, but out of loyalty to Lionel Wright. She understood that too. One of Father's gifts had been the ability to inspire a bone-deep sense of obligation in others. Since Jess had taken on the shop, other employees had been hard to come by—few men wished to take their wages and direction from a woman.

As she slipped Father's old watch from its place in her skirt pocket, Jess's mind sifted through what she had yet to accomplish before resting her head for the day. It was a long list and—*ah, that too*—now included an article she'd almost forgotten to write for the Women's Union journal.

"I hope Lady Katherine hasn't forgotten us. To be honest, I won't be sad to see the last of this room. It's all rather cold, even with the fire. Makes you afraid to touch anything or even breathe."

Alice McGregor had an uncanny talent for reading one's mind and could always be counted on for blunt and insightful commentary. Of all Jessamin's friends at the Women's Union, Alice was the most practical and plain-speaking. Delicacy was overrated as far as Alice was concerned. She said what everyone else was thinking but knew it impolite to mention.

"No, it's not terribly inviting, is it?"

If Jess could decorate such a room, the colors would be bold and full of life. Red would do very nicely. And she'd decorate the walls with art so vivid you'd believe you could smell the pot of basil in a Holman Hunt painting or hear the swish of silk and satin as one of Mr. Tissot's beauties crossed the room. She closed her eyes and imagined crimson walls covered with art in rich, vibrant colors.

"Miss Wright, have I caught you napping?" Lady Katherine Adderly's giggle was like the clash of two crystal glasses meeting in a toast. Sharp and clear, it instantly snapped Jessamin out of her fantasies.

As she swept in, a maid followed close on her heels

with a tea tray. Lady Katherine smelled of flowers, but far too many, the scent cloying and sickly sweet.

"Forgive me, my lady." It was easier for Jessamin to apologize for drowsing than acknowledge how she loathed the decor.

Jess and Alice exchanged raised-brow glances as their hostess handed each of them a fine porcelain teacup and began the process of pouring tea and offering them confections from plates laden with biscuits and tiny pastries. It was an elaborate ritual, much more fuss about tea than Jess had ever made in life. But the rich tang of jasmine in the brew was delicious and she was grateful for the distraction of the warm refreshment, even as she sensed the persistent tick of Father's watch against her skirt pocket. She had to get back to the shop and hoped their meeting with the marquess's daughter wouldn't take long.

"I'm pleased to make this donation to the Women's Union. You know how I enjoy the lively meetings."

Lady Katherine had attended only three of the group's weekly meetings over the course of four months, but she'd been eager to make a financial contribution, and Alice, as the union's treasurer and cofounder, was all too happy to accept. Jess wasn't certain why Alice had asked her to come along to collect the money, but as editor of the group's printed journal and author of many of the speeches given at gatherings, she supposed she was a visible member of the organization.

"We are most grateful for the funds, my lady." As always, Alice spoke with sincerity, gratitude clear in her tone.

"Oh, please call me Kitty."

Alice took a sip of tea, attempting to hold the cup with all the dignity Kitty seemed to manage effortlessly.

"I understand there's another worthy cause to which I may also contribute."

"I'm sure there are many in London," Jess offered, thinking of a dozen ways she might spend charitable funds, not to mention the money needed to salvage the indebted bookshop her father had left her.

"I was referring to you, Miss Wright."

Jessamin shot Alice a look, wondering just what her scrupulously honest friend had revealed to Lady Katherine.

"I understand you have a bookshop and lending library here in town."

"Yes, my lady," Jess bit off, unable to keep the irritation from her voice. Alice shouldn't have mentioned her situation to anyone. Kitty might be feeling benevolent, but the amount needed to clear the shop's debt was more than any wealthy aristocrat's daughter would wish to spend, no matter how generous she was feeling.

"Would one hundred pounds be useful to you?"

A shiver tickled Jessamin's spine as she contemplated the amount, a sum she couldn't earn at the shop in months, perhaps not even in a year. It wasn't nearly enough to clear the entire debt, but it would bring her payments with the bank current.

Jessamin studied Kitty's feline smile and tried to unravel the mystery of the young woman's wish to help her. She knew Kitty was wealthy, the daughter of a marquess, and perhaps a bit bored, but she'd never even conversed with her before today. Kitty was mentioned off and on in the scandal sheets Jess admitted to no one she indulged in reading, but the lady was hardly known as an outstanding philanthropist.

Charity tasted sour, yet how could she refuse the sum? "Neither a borrower nor a lender be" had been one of Father's favorite lines from *Hamlet*. But it was an adage he'd failed to uphold. His gambling had turned him into the worst sort of borrower, taking loans from friends and money from the bookshop he'd worked so hard to build up. For Jess's part, she'd become a lender soon after her father's death, finally instituting the lending library she'd been envisioning for years. It seemed neither of them had heeded the Shakespearean admonition at all.

Kitty watched Jess closely and appeared to notice the moment she'd almost made up her mind to accept the money.

"I am so pleased you'll allow me to help you, Jessamin. And in return, I'm certain you won't mind assisting me with one tiny request."

Alice frowned and set her teacup on the table between them, edging forward on the settee as if she meant to get up and leave. "I'm not sure that's quite right."

"What is the favor, Lady Katherine? Please, let's speak plainly with one another." It didn't surprise Jess in the least that Kitty expected something in return. No one offered such a sum without expecting something in return.

"Kitty, please. Do call me Kitty. It's a simple favor,

really. As simple as a kiss."

Jess choked. "Pardon?" she squeaked, when she'd finally managed to swallow her mouthful of tea and could breathe again.

"Just a kiss, Jessamin. Surely you don't object to kissing." Kitty's teasing tone belied the glint of steel in her gaze. "You're a modern, freethinking woman, after all. You believe in the suffrage and equality for our sex. You should feel quite free to kiss any man you like."

Kissing men had nothing to do with Jess's interest in social reform or gaining a voice for women in the political sphere. If Kitty thought it did, she hadn't been to nearly enough meetings.

"You want me to kiss a man?" Jess spoke the words as if it was an extraordinary feat. And it was. She'd never kissed a man. Not really. A childish, graceless kiss on the cheek from Tom Jenkins when she was twelve years old hardly counted.

"This seems a rather strange favor, Kitty." Alice's precise tone cut through the quiet of the room.

Kitty's tinkling laughter rang out. "Yes, I suppose it does. But it's merely a harmless bit of revenge."

"Revenge." Jess waited. There had to be more.

"Oh, all right. If you must know, the dreadful man snubbed me." Kitty plumped her bow-shaped mouth in a pout.

Was she the shallowest heiress in Belgravia? The thought that Kitty wished to seek revenge because a man did not prefer her company was ridiculous. Her beauty and wealth could secure her any suitor she set her cap at.

In fact, the question of why the man rejected her was as intriguing as her desire for Jess to kiss him.

"Why did he snub you?"

"Why, indeed!" Kitty straightened up in her chair and slid her fingers into honey blond hair, tucking her already neatly pinned coiffure more firmly into place. "Perhaps because he is an odious man. If he wasn't a viscount, soon to be an earl, and so irredeemably handsome, I wouldn't have bothered with him. Never mind Papa's mad notion I marry Lord Grim. Freddie is much more fun, even if he doesn't have a farthing to his name." Kitty turned the full force of her bright green gaze on Jess. "You'll do it then?"

"I'm still not sure I understand."

Kitty's tone became pedantic, as if she was speaking to a child who needed to be set aright.

"My dear, it couldn't be simpler. Viscount Grimsby snubbed me at a soiree last week and I would like your help to put him in his place. He's a dour man, as cold as marble. Some call him Lord Grim. And so he is. Grim and heartless. He needs a little comeuppance." As an afterthought, she added, "He's against the vote for women, of course."

As if that made the whole ridiculous scheme noble. As if kissing him would change his mind about women's suffrage.

"And where does kissing come into play?" It all sounded wrong to Jess, like the discordant notes of an untuned piano playing over and over in her mind, but Kitty waved away her concern dismissively.

"It won't be a real kiss, my dear. Not the kind that

matters. Just a kiss that knocks him off his pedestal a bit. It will cause him a trifle of social bother. Stir up some tittle-tattle."

For a moment Kitty's expression altered, the corners of her mouth turning down as if she'd fallen into troubled contemplation. Jess wondered if she was already regretting her petty scheme. Then she lifted her head, a satisfied cat-at-the-cream grin lifting her cheeks.

"The next time I see the man at a ball, perhaps he'll manage a bit of humility. And since no one else will wish to stand up with him, I suspect he'll be more than happy to dance with me."

None of Kitty's words put Jess's mind at ease. She'd never heard of Lord Grimsby, but from Kitty's description, kissing the man certainly didn't sound appealing.

"I happen to know he'll be at an art gallery in Mayfair this evening."

"And?" Jess was growing impatient. Who had time for games when she had a business to run?

"There will be a gathering at the gallery. Mrs. Ornish is a great fan of art and has sponsored one of the artists whose works will be featured. I do wonder why he always goes to Mrs. Ornish's events. Could he have his eye on Meredith, do you think?"

Of course, Jess had no idea who Mrs. Ornish or Meredith was. She might share their love of art, but they were the kind of women with wealth enough to offer an artist patronage. Jess couldn't even afford to buy a painting. Her walls were decorated with cut-out prints culled from books and newspapers.

"Kitty, please just tell me. What must I do?"

Kitty crooked her mouth alluringly. Jess supposed she used the simpering expression to charm everyone. Everyone except Lord Grimsby, apparently.

"I want you to show up at the gallery event and stride up to Lord Grim. Yes, you'll just walk up and plant a kiss square on that cruel, unsmiling mouth of his."

"I really don't think—"Alice's voice had taken on the same pitch and volume she used to quiet the women's group meetings.

Jess knew what she was going to say and cut her off. "Wait. Let me consider a moment."

Jess closed her eyes and breathed deeply. She had to do it. She needed the one hundred pounds Kitty offered. There was no denying what the woman proposed was scandalous, not to mention farcical and childish. But Jess had no reputation to protect. As Kitty said, she saw herself as a freethinking woman, unhampered by society's strictures and eager for changing women's roles. She had no idea how kissing a complete stranger would strike a blow for women's suffrage, but her desperation for funds made her beholden to Kitty's whims.

"Come, Jessamin." Kitty's singsong voice was cajoling. "I dare you."

Because Jess's speeches encouraged action over words, perhaps Kitty saw her as brave and daring. But if she was brave, it was because Father died and took all her options with him. She'd lost everything—her home, a modestly comfortable lifestyle, freedom to study and spend her days more or less as she wished—and put all her energy into maintaining his business, even after discovering the massive debt he'd accumulated. She was beginning to make inroads toward repaying the debt, and Kitty's funds would be another step toward financial success for Wright and Sons Booksellers.

"Fine. I'll do it."

Kitty gasped with delight and clapped her hands together.

Alice shot her a look as if Jess had taken leave of whatever sense she'd been given.

Jess couldn't match Kitty's enthusiasm or acknowledge Alice's concern. She was too busy fighting off the sense of dread that settled in the pit of her stomach at the prospect of what she'd agreed to do.

"Where is this gallery and what time will he be there?"

Chapter Two

The room was sweltering. Who knew a gallery event in Mayfair would attract such a crush? Lucius Crawford, Viscount Grimsby, darted his gaze from framed portraits to lush landscape pieces, fully expecting the paint to start melting off the canvases. No one could deny the colors were extraordinary and the compositions pleasing, but couldn't they have found someone with a better eye to hang the pieces? The arrangement of art was irritatingly haphazard, small and large side by side, some frames just inches apart and others an arm's length, or two, away from each other. Despite the impulse to find a ladder and impose order on the chaos, Lucius found focusing on the paintings preferable to meeting the eyes of those around him.

Glancing around a crowded room could be dangerous. Too often he'd find himself snared by a questioning look here, a disapproving frown there. They wondered about his father, of course, especially now that he had withdrawn from London society completely.

Lucius was prepared to admit his own lack of aristocratic tendencies—he was far more interested in discussing business than horse racing, technology than teacakes—but none of his faux pas or successes since becoming heir to his father's earldom eclipsed Maxim's infamy. The man had been so querulous and apt to initiate feuds with fellow noblemen that they'd dubbed him the Dark Earl of Dunthorpe.

Would the gossips be any kinder if they could see the frail, doddering man Maxim Crawford had become? Lucius doubted they would, and he had no intention of giving anyone the opportunity for either pity or pardon. Sheltering the earl from rumormongers was one of the duties that had fallen to him.

So he would learn to tolerate the speculative gazes and whispers. Eventually. But they still set his nerves on edge and made him wish for the haven of his study back at Hartwell. Never mind what else awaited him at Hartwell. Leaky roofs and crumbling masonry didn't daunt him. And regardless of the pain he'd experienced within its walls and the resentment that swelled and ebbed between him and his father as regular as the tides, the family estate in Berkshire was home now.

He'd accepted that it was no longer the home of his childhood, that idyllic Hartwell he'd longed for and missed with a searing, stubborn ache all the years he'd been away. The real Hartwell, a pile of wood and stones—some rooms as old as the Dunthorpes' Tudor ancestors, others as new as those Lucius had refurbished the previous year—was a bit of a mess. A mishmash of architectural styles, just as the estate itself had seen a mix of care and indifference over the years. Father's neglect had caused the most damage, and neither his ailments nor his obsessive love for Mother excused his poor stewardship. Lucius was determined to do better by the estate than his brother, Julian, or his father ever had.

Turning his head, he snagged the gaze of an elderly matron, her eyes as beady and hungry as those of any crow he'd ever seen. He acknowledged her with a minute nod, and she reared her head a fraction, as if utterly taken aback. And that, exactly that, her reaction and his failure to exude one tenth of the charm required to engage in any sort of social repartee, was why he came into town and mixed in society rarely. Even without an infamous father, he would have found the social rounds daunting.

So let them talk. Let them watch him tug at his neck cloth like a man on the gallows might claw at the noose and straighten and re-straighten his waistcoat, running a finger down the four buttons at the bottom to make sure they formed a perfect line. This visit to London was necessary and would, if his aunt could be believed, allow him to settle his future—to meet Father's demands that he marry a woman with money and impeccable breeding and ensure the estate's future with an heir. Stability had always eluded him, and the notion of a settled future seemed as unlikely as a happy one, but if anyone could achieve such a coup, it was Aunt Augusta.

She'd been the one constant in his life, writing and

visiting after Father shipped him off to Scotland, guiding him after Julian's death and the news he'd become heir to Hartwell, and comforting him when his own mother could not. She'd been as much a parent to him as either of his own.

"You look a bit seasick, my boy. But unless someone has failed to inform me, I don't believe Mayfair has set sail."

Aunt Augusta tucked herself into the space between him and the scowling crow woman. She lifted a glass and he took the crystal flute with a nod of gratitude.

"How long must we stay?"

"I believe the hostess is going to give a brief speech. It would behoove us to linger until then."

He sensed her eyes on him, assessing his discomfort, looking out for him as she always had.

"You will be attending many more social events once you marry. Get in as much practice as you can."

"Didn't you promise to find a candidate who'd be content to do the social rounds on her own?"

"Independence is one thing. Being forever without one's husband is another matter entirely."

Lucius closed his eyes a moment and imagined a life of house parties, elaborate dinners, and sitting room musicales. The prospect made him shudder. He opened his eyes, still avoiding Aunt Augusta's inspection, and took in the canvas before him—a man on horseback with a verdant English landscape stretched out behind him. It looked a bit like Hartwell's meadow, and though he'd been away only a week, longing for the place gnawed at him. In this hot, congested space of too many colors and a cacophony of voices, he missed Hartwell's spacious rooms, familiar scents and textures, and labyrinthine floor plan, so well-known to him he could navigate it blindfolded.

"She certainly enjoys London more than you do."

She? She was very specific. Far too specific. He'd come to London to discuss the possibility of marriage. No, more than that—the necessity of it. And to seek Augusta's help in securing the perfect candidate, a woman with an ample dowry to keep Hartwell afloat, enough connections to earn his father's approval, and such a rabid desire to be a countess that she might not notice how ill-suited he was to be an earl.

The notion that she'd found a match so quickly, and that the young woman might be here among the crush of attendees . . . that he did not expect. And in Lucius's experience, the unexpected never heralded a pleasant turn of events.

"Does she? I wasn't aware you'd settled on anyone. Is she here tonight?"

He looked around, scanning one perspiring feminine face after another. None of them stood out. None of them stopped him short and made him wish to continue to look, to learn what lay beyond a flushed cheek or bright, smiling eyes.

"Not tonight, no. She is traveling at the moment."

That finally earned his attention and he turned to question Augusta further just as an older woman approached and embraced her, gushing about how long it'd been since they'd last seen each other.

As Aunt Augusta allowed herself to be pulled away to join a lively conversation, his sister, Julia, and brother-in-law, Marcus Darnley, approached. Marcus and Lucius exchanged nods. Julia merely sipped at the liquid in her glass as she watched him, much as his aunt had moments before. But Julia's was a different gaze. Her eyes narrowed, not out of concern, but in judgment.

"Do stop glaring at everyone, Lucius. People will think you as frightful as Papa."

His sister's tone held a note of irritation along with the command, and he allowed himself a slight twitch of his mouth that none but those who knew him best would ever mistake for a grin.

"He must continue glaring, love. I believe he enjoys nurturing his grim reputation." Marcus Darnley leaned in to whisper the words to his wife, though Lucius didn't care who heard him. His sister's husband tweaked him as often as she chastised him. And though he would never admit it, he found as much enjoyment in Marcus's teasing as he did in his sister's scolding. He and Julia had missed out on years of sibling squabbles as children, and he didn't mind catching up now.

But Lucius would never apologize for being discerning about how he spent his time and whom he took into his confidence. His reputation as one of society's most dour bachelors served him well. It kept giggling debutantes, scheming mothers, and nearly everyone else at bay. Marriage was necessary—he accepted it as his chief goal for the year. But not the game, the silly business of inane conversations, coy flirtation, and stolen kisses on balconies. Lucius was quite content to leave such carrying on to rogues like his friend Robert Wellesley and allow Augusta to find him a sensible, practical, and exceedingly wealthy bride.

Time was too precious a commodity to waste on games. Managing Hartwell, a task he loved but had never been groomed for, consumed his days and nights. But Julia played on his sense of obligation and had urged him to help make Delia Ornish's gallery gathering a success. Mrs. Ornish's friendship with their late mother had indebted them both to the wealthy social butterfly.

Marcus stood close to Lucius and leaned in to speak confidentially. "There are some lovely young women in attendance tonight. Don't you agree, Grimsby? Surely one of them must strike your fancy."

His sister and her husband were unaware of Augusta's matchmaking efforts.

"Yes and no." Lucius lifted the flute of champagne to his mouth and sipped.

Marcus quirked a brow at him, begging explanation.

"Yes, there are lovely women in attendance. No, none of them strikes my fancy."

The women in the crush of attendees were stunning in their finery. Every color and shape one could desire. But none of them stirred him.

Marcus wouldn't be deterred. "Are you never lonely, old chap?" His brother-in-law turned his eyes to Julia as he spoke.

Lucius caught the look, and an ember of loneliness kindled in his chest. He didn't desire any of the women before him, yet he did envy the easy companionship that his sister and brother-in-law shared. He could envy it but never imagine it for himself. Even if Aunt Augusta's scheme was successful, it wouldn't be a love match. He'd seen the results of what such an attachment had done to his father, a man whose adoration for his wife became a destructive obsession, sparking jealous rages that drove her—and Lucius—from their home.

He wouldn't lose himself in that kind of passion. Now, with the responsibility of Hartwell laid on his shoulders, he couldn't spare the time for it. Let his father indulge in maudlin sentimentality; Lucius had an estate to run.

"I haven't the time for loneliness." He lied easily and ignored the look Marcus shot him, fearing he'd read pity there.

A fracas near the gallery's entrance offered a welcome distraction. Turning away from Marcus, Lucius craned his neck to spot the cause of the ruckus. The room was so full of bodies it was difficult to see the front of the building, despite his height. But whatever the commotion, it caused a few shouts mingled with cries of outrage.

Then he saw the trouble. A woman. A bluestocking, more precisely, wearing a prim black skirt and plain white shirtwaist, spectacles perched high on her nose, pushed her way through the throng of ladies in colorful evening gowns and men in black tails. She looked like a magpie wreaking havoc among the canaries, though her hair was as striking a shade as any of the finery around her. The rich auburn hue shone in the gaslight, and though she'd pinned her hair back in a severe style, several rebellious curls had escaped and hung down around her shoulders.

As he watched the woman's progress, a gentleman grasped her arm roughly, and an uncommon surge of chivalry made Lucius consider interceding. But in the next moment the woman proved she needed no rescuer. Stomping on the man's foot, she moved easily out of his grasp and continued on her path—a path that led directly to Lucius.

FOR THE HUNDREDTH time, Jess called herself a fool for agreeing to Kitty Adderly's ridiculous plan for revenge against Viscount Grimsby. Kissing a viscount for one hundred pounds sounded questionable at the time Kitty had suggested it. Now Jess thought perhaps the jilted heiress had put something in her tea.

Initially she made her way into the crowded art gallery unnoticed, but then a woman dripping in diamonds and green silk had questioned her. When the lady's round husband stepped in, it all turned to chaos before she'd even done what she'd come to do. The deed itself shouldn't take long. A quick peck on the mouth—Kitty had insisted that she kiss the man on the lips—and it would all be over. She'd already handed the money over to Mr. Briggs at the bank. Turning back now simply wasn't an option.

She recognized Lord Grimsby from the gossip rag Kitty had shown her. The newspaper etching hadn't done him justice. In it, he'd been portrayed as dark and forbidding, his mouth a sharp slash, his black brows so large they overtook his eyes, and his long Roman nose dominating an altogether unappealing face. But in the flesh every part of his appearance harmonized into a striking whole. He was the sort of man she would have noticed in a crowd, even if she hadn't been seeking him, intent on causing him scandal and taking unimaginable liberties with his person.

He was there at the end of the gallery, as far from the entrance as he could possibly be. Jess continued through the gamut and a man snatched at her arm. Unthinking, she stepped on his foot, and he spluttered and cursed but released her.

Lord Grimsby saw her now. She noticed his dark head—and far too many others—turned her way. He was tall and broad shouldered, towering over the man and woman beside him. And he did look grim, as cold and disagreeable as Kitty had described.

Jessamin turned her eyes down, avoiding his gaze. Helpfully, the crowd parted before her, as if the respectable ladies and gentleman were unwilling to remain near a woman behaving so unpredictably. Every time she raised her eyes, she glimpsed eyes gone wide, mouths agape, and women furiously fanning themselves.

Just a few more steps and Jess stood before him, only inches between them. She met his gaze and found him glaring down at her with shockingly clear blue eyes. Furrowed lines formed a vee between his brows as he frowned at her like a troublesome insect had just spoiled his meal.

She opened her mouth to speak, but what explanation could she offer?

Every thought scattered as she studied her objective—or more accurately, his lips. They were wide and well-shaped but firmly set. Not as firm as stone, as Kitty claimed, but unyielding. Unwelcoming. Not at all the sort of lips one dreamed of kissing. But Jess had given up on dreams. Her choices now were about money, the funds she needed to keep the bookshop afloat for as long as she could.

Taking a breath and praying for courage, Jess reached up and removed her spectacles, folded them carefully, and hooked them inside the high neckline of her gown.

His eyes followed the movement of her hands, and the lines between his brows deepened.

Behind her, a woman shouted, "How dare you!" A hand grasped her from behind, the force of the tug pulling Jessamin backward, nearly off her feet. Then a deep, angry male voice rang out and stopped all movement.

"Unhand the woman. Now, if you please." He'd spoken. The stone giant. Lord Grim. He glared past her, over her head. Whoever gripped her arm released their hold. Then Lord Grim's gaze drilled into hers, his eyes discerning, not cold and lifeless as she'd expected.

For several heartbeats he simply watched her, pinning her with his gaze, studying her. Jess reminded herself to breathe.

"Are we acquainted, madam?"

The rumble of his voice, even amid the din of chatter around them, echoed through her.

She moved closer, and his eyebrows shot up. Oh, she'd crossed the line now. Bursting uninvited into a room filled with the wealthy and titled was one thing. Ignoring a viscount's question could be forgiven. Pressing one's bosom into a strange man's chest was something else entirely.

A surge of surprise and gratitude gripped her when he didn't move away.

Assessing his height, Jess realized she'd have to lift onto her toes if the kiss was to be accomplished. She took a step toward him, stretched up tall, and swayed unsteadily. He reached an arm out, and she feared he'd push her away. Instead he gripped her arm just above her elbow and held her steady.

A woman said his name, a tone of chastisement lacing the word. "Lucius."

Then she did it. Placing one hand on his hard chest to balance herself, Jess eased up on the tips of her boots and touched her lips to his.

A shock of sensation snaked through her. *Kitty lied.* His lips weren't made of stone. They were warm, smooth flesh. For a moment he didn't move, merely stood stiffly, his hand still heavy on her arm. Then his breathing hitched and his mouth moved beneath hers as he responded to the kiss. His free hand slid to the small of her back and tightened there, inching her toward him. His palm was warm and firm through the layers of her clothing, and she let him take her weight. He smelled delicious. Like clean, crisp linen and some exotic spice. She tasted liquor on his breath when she felt his tongue slide between her lips, but her sense of intoxication had nothing to do with the brief taste of spirits. He enveloped her now, his mouth moving over hers, his arms and scent surrounding her. For a moment she felt protected. More than that. She felt desired, wanted. For one moment she forgot that she was so terribly alone.

A woman shrieked, the sound high, ear-piercing, and blessedly brief. Just long enough to break the spell and snap Jess back to the moment, the scandalous scene she'd created. She pulled away from Lord Grimsby and he instantly loosened his hold, though he seemed unwilling to release her arm. To steady her or to steady him? His expression remained as humorless as before she'd kissed him. Only his eyes revealed how she'd affected him. A flame there singed her, warming every inch of her body before settling deep in her belly. She wanted to lose herself in that heat, sink into it, let it unfurl her knots of worry and melt away every fear.

His quickened breath gusted against her face and Jess breathed hard too as they stared at each other. Those around them clucked and fussed, but she heard the crowd as if from a distance, her awareness centered on the inscrutable man whose flavor still clung to her lips.

Jess never dreamed a kiss could be so potent, never imagined a man's gaze could set her on fire. No man had ever looked at her with the blatant yearning she saw in Lord Grimsby's eyes. Had any glanced at her with an ounce of interest at all? If they had, she'd been too busy running the shop to notice. And she wasn't prepared for it now. To acknowledge that she felt it too and imagine her eyes reflecting the same need and desire as his—that frightened her most of all.

A blond man at Lord Grimsby's side whispered to

him, placing a hand on his arm as if to lead him away. But the viscount didn't move, didn't release her or meet anyone else's gaze.

When the blond man turned a withering glance her way, Jess knew she had to leave and extract herself from the scene she'd created. Dizzy and a bit off balance, she rallied the strength to break away, to pull her arm from the viscount's grasp and walk out of the gallery on wobbly legs. The din of the crowd rose as she strode away, and she heard a lady hiss as she passed by.

Turning from the sound, Jess lifted her gaze and glimpsed a familiar face. Golden hair dappled with diamond pins, Kitty Adderly stood amid the crush. She lifted her glass a fraction, simulating a toast, but there was no victory in her gaze. Eyes wide, dainty mouth slack, she looked as shaken by the whole debacle as Jess felt.

Focusing on the front of the hall, Jess pressed on, ignoring the stares, blocking out the voices. When she was finally free of the gallery, a burst of chilly September air enveloped her. Cheeks stinging, eyes watering, she inhaled deep, gulping breaths. Her frantic heartbeat refused to steady, but her breaths came less frequently as they billowed out before her.

Why had she agreed to Kitty's scheme? There had to be consequences for striding up to a viscount and taking liberties with his mouth in front of everyone. The thought of his mouth and that awkward, wonderful kiss made her breathing hitch again. Shaking the thoughts away, Jess began scanning the street for a hansom cab.

She spotted one, its lantern glimmering in the fog,

and stepped across the pavement to hail it. Before she could take two steps, someone approached from behind. Lord Grim. She already knew his scent, the same distinctive spice that still clung to her clothing.

Tensing, cringing inwardly, she waited for harsh words. Of course he'd come out to curse her or demand some explanation for her scandalous behavior. Drawing a deep breath, Jess turned to face the viscount just as a carriage, its black sides so well polished they gleamed even in the fog-shrouded night, drew up near the pavement in front of her.

"My carriage."

Jess jumped as his deep voice rattled through her. With a hand at her back, he steered her with gentle insistence toward the carriage. Out of nowhere, a cloaked man appeared, opened the carriage door, pulled down the step, and stood aside.

"I can make my own way home." The wind whipped around her, stealing her breath as she spoke, but it wasn't enough to make her forget who she was. Who he was. Through chattering teeth, she added, "Thank you, my lord."

Either he hadn't heard her or the man was used to getting his own way. He pressed his hand more firmly against her back and moved toward the carriage, sweeping her along with him.

Jessamin stepped back, turning out of his grip. Snapping her head in his direction, she tried to make out the harsh planes of his face in the shadows and fog. She could only see those light blue eyes, glowing in the muted gaslight.

Long, gloved fingers wrapped around her wrist, not gentle but far from bruising.

"I have questions that require answers." He tugged at her arm and she stepped toward him. "I prefer to ask them away from prying eyes." She saw his head jerk back and only then noticed a small crowd gathered in the gallery's entrance hall. Jessamin could see the group was atwitter with shock and outrage—one man pointed toward Lord Grimsby and another shouted futilely through the woolly fog.

Jess imagined what they were saying, curses and condemnations about her outrageous behavior. Getting into the man's carriage would only fuel the gossip, of course, but it was preferable to being left to the crowd's mercy. And Lord Grimsby didn't seem inclined to allow her out of his sight until she'd offered some explanation.

Wobbling as she took the carriage step, she whispered her address to the silent footman who'd lifted a hand to steady her.

Lord Grim seemed to rise and seat himself across from her in one swift motion.

She hesitated before facing him, chafing her frozen fingers together and pointlessly arranging her skirts. Anything to avoid those eyes that had nearly melted her into a senseless puddle in the gallery. When she could finally look at him, her heart kicked against her ribs. *Mercy.* He was a handsome man. Kitty hadn't lied about that. The warm glow of the carriage lanterns revealed all the details of his face. Sharp edges and flat planes, it was as perfectly chiseled as a statue and just as still. She could almost believe he was carved of marble, except for those eyes. They glittered like ice in the golden light. It was daunting to be the object of his scrutiny, particularly as she'd just embarrassed the man in front of everyone he knew.

With the heated spark between them cooled, guilt crowded in to mar all the pleasure of that moment when she'd pressed her mouth to his.

"I'm sorry." She whispered the words so quietly Jess wasn't certain if she spoke to herself or to the man seated across from her.

He didn't respond, just continued to stare at her, and she looked away, nervousness making her pulse race. When she lifted her eyes again, she caught him studying her oft-mended skirt hem, her ink-stained fingers, shamelessly bare of gloves, and then slowly perusing the buttons of her shirtwaist before assessing her face. The intensity of his gaze unnerved her.

Then the marble shifted. Lord Grimsby pursed his lips, grimacing, and she wasn't certain if he found her distasteful or was considering precisely how to devour her. He spoke low, one syllable slipping from his lips.

"Why?"

Chapter Three

In the silence between his question and her answer, Lucius acknowledged to himself that the woman seated across from him was lovely. The observation had nothing to do with attraction. It was a cold, hard fact, one even the most cursory observer would be foolish to deny. There was no romanticism in the deduction. It was simply true. It was just as true she wore unfashionable clothes, kept too long and mended too often. It was equally undeniable that the striking shade of her hair held appeal, though she wore it in the most unflattering arrangement he'd ever seen. Only the stray curls escaping from pins here and there, despite evidence of her efforts to force them back into place, hinted at the lush beauty she hid with her scraped-back style.

Yes, most decidedly lovely. The cool air had put a rosy glow in her cheeks and reddened her mouth. With a jolt of shock, he realized he knew those lips—the pointed bow of her upper lip, the plump pillow of her lower—and could still recall the cushion of their fullness. He twisted his own mouth in derision. The lips might be familiar, but he knew nothing of the woman. From her behavior, he could only surmise her poor judgment and moral laxity.

He looked away, turning from the sight of her, tamping down the memory of their kiss. It was too ridiculous to contemplate. But the glass of the carriage window conspired with the night sky to offer him a mirror. Turning away from her, he found only her reflection as she huddled in the corner of the carriage, chafing her hands and avoiding his eyes.

He lifted the carriage blanket from the space next to him and thrust it toward her. "Here. Warm yourself."

As she accepted his offering, he licked his lips and then cursed under his breath at the taste of her lingering there.

Damnation. He would not savor the taste of a reckless bluestocking. When he wished to sate his baser needs, he accomplished it as every unmarried gentleman did—with discretion. Mistresses weren't hard to come by, though lately the very notion of a paramour seemed more bother than indulgence. And now, with Aunt Augusta on the hunt for a suitable bride, a mistress was a complication he did not need.

The scent of starch and violet water tickled his nose and he wanted rid of the woman. Her silence irritated him. Why act as if she feared him? The brazen creature had just stomped up to him in public and put her mouth on his.

What on earth could possess a woman to commit

such a scandalous act? Infatuation wasn't even a consideration. He would remember if they'd ever met before. No one could forget the unique shade of her hair. Surely she didn't hope to initiate an acquaintance in such an outrageous manner. Never mind that her unexpected kiss had jolted through him like an electric current, that he'd stood staring at her like a fool, unwilling to release her arm and break the connection between them.

He'd never see her again after this night and it irked him. And the fact that it irked him stoked his irritation.

"Will you offer no answer, madam?"

She jumped at the sound of his voice, the small confines of the carriage making it louder than he'd intended.

Softening his tone, he tried again. "I must know why."

"Why?" Before he could consider whether she mocked him by returning his own question, he was struck by her voice. It was strong and rich. As distinctive as the color of her hair. And it belied the embarrassment in her eyes and the way she tucked herself in the corner, as far from him as possible.

"Do I not have the right?" As he watched the emotion in her eyes shift from embarrassment to acknowledgment, he noted that their color was inscrutable. Gray? Green? Good grief, what did it matter?

"Yes, my lord." For the first time since entering the carriage, she settled back against the leather seat. "You deserve an explanation."

His eagerness to hear her speak again made him lean forward, an elbow on each knee, hands clasped before him.

The maddening woman tortured him with more silence and by sinking her teeth into her bottom lip. He stared at the pierced pink skin until she let out a pained little groan of frustration and finally turned to him.

"It was a mistake." Her husky voice released the words with a kind of finality, as if the whole matter was suddenly clear. She even had the temerity to lift her chin a fraction.

Lucius took it as a challenge.

"I see. You mistook me, then. It was another man you intended to accost with your mouth."

"Did I accost you, my lord?"

Her eyes widened and he was gratified to finally identify them as green. The darkest of greens, like the murky depths of a winter pond. He quirked his eyebrow and saw her deflate.

"Yes, I did. Forgive me. It seemed such a small thing, but I see now that it must have caused you a great deal of mortification in front of all your friends."

Lucius was torn between allowing himself a moment of righteous indignation and assuring the strange young woman she'd done him no real harm.

"They aren't my friends." He didn't bother to add that his aunt, sister, and brother-in-law had been in attendance. Marcus and Julia had never caused a bit of scandal and held their position in society securely. Aunt Augusta was beloved as a confidante and renowned as a hostess. Being associated with this event would only cause a bit of gossip, surely. The wags would be malicious, perhaps, but not destructive.

Because he kept to himself and had only come into his title following Julian's death two years before, the gossips had little to say about him, and Lucius was grateful for it.

The bluestocking lifted a hand to her mouth, drawing his attention there, and he noticed her dark eyes had taken on a glassy sheen. He shivered at the notion that she might actually start weeping. He couldn't abide a tearful woman. Clearing his throat loudly, Lucius waved a hand toward her in a gesture of absolution.

"You have my forgiveness, Miss . . . ?"

She took a deep breath before answering his implied question.

"Wright, my lord. Jessamin Wright." He knew the impropriety of such an introduction, but Miss Wright seemed to take no notice.

"Miss Wright." He weighed her surname on his tongue, but it was her first name that he repeated in his head. It was far too sibilant and ornate for such a shabbily dressed woman, but he sensed this woman was much more interesting than her layers of plain cotton and wool suggested.

"Will this cause you a great deal of scandal, my lord?"

He opened his mouth and then caught himself on the verge of reassuring her. What power did this woman wield? In the space of seconds she'd once again turned his—quite justified—ire into an urge to put *her* mind at ease. And was he truly to believe the effect of her actions concerned her now? She should have thought of that before letting him taste the sweetness of her mouth.

No, this bluestocking wasn't at all what she seemed.

Lucius's desire to suss her out grew with every moment that passed between them.

"No, Miss Wright. I'll be returning to the country soon. I haven't a care for what they say about me in London."

It wasn't true, but he wished it was.

He'd spent the last two years attempting to put Hartwell's finances in order and secure the future of the estate. Preferring the rational, logical rows of figures and facts in his ledger books to London society didn't mean he was immune from scandal. Though he could easily ignore what the gossips might say, he couldn't deny that any kind of ignominy would reflect on the earldom, and his own future heirs. He did not yet hold the title of Earl of Dunthorpe, but protecting the family name had now fallen to him.

She didn't look like she believed his lie anyway. He'd never mastered the art of falsehood.

"What of you? What will your family have to say about your behavior this evening?"

She swallowed hard, dipping her head, and then blinked up at him. She seemed confused, as if she didn't take his meaning. Or perhaps it was too difficult to contemplate. Shouldn't she have considered her family before behaving in such a shocking manner?

"Come now. Your family. Your father. Perhaps an older brother. Tell me I won't be receiving a call from them demanding I marry you to save your reputation?"

"No, of course not!"

Her exclamation bounced off the carriage walls, and it

was Lucius's turn to blink. He'd meant the comment as a jest, infusing his tone with as much mirth and irony as he could muster. But he joked and teased rarely. Apparently he was as ghastly at it as he was at acknowledging beady-eyed women in a crowd.

"My father and mother are dead. I have no brothers or sisters."

The words were plain, simple. Perfectly understandable. Yet there was more behind them, a well of loneliness and need that resonated in Lucius, as familiar to him as his own name.

"You're an orphan." Lucius rarely spoke words with the sort of care he took in stating the truth of Miss Wright's circumstances. A foolish impulse made him wish to confess that he was an orphan too. Not in the same way, of course. His father was alive. But if your mother was dead and you'd been estranged from your father most of your life, did that not qualify you as an orphan?

Miss Wright seemed to take his words as gently as he'd intended. She glanced down at her hands before reaching out to run a long, slender finger over the beveled glass of a pocket watch she'd pulled from her skirt. When she finally met his gaze, she seemed as resolved as she'd been the moment she'd walked up to him in the gallery.

"Yes, I suppose I am, though I'm not a child. And my father only died a few years ago."

"I'm sorry."

"Don't pity me."

The fury in her gaze was familiar. He'd stared back at it in his own looking glass for years.

"I require no one's pity, my lord."

No. When you'd lost everything, pity was the last thing you desired. He'd learned that truth at nine when his mother ventured out on a trip, leaving him behind because he was ill, and a carriage accident took her life. His world became bleak, colorless, and in his child's mind he believed fate had dealt him its worst. But being banished to Scotland two months later because his father could not bear the sight of him—that had been worse. And the pity he'd seen in the faces of his mother's family, worse still.

The carriage slowed to a stop too soon for Lucius's taste. He'd asked the coachman to take the longest route to the address Miss Wright had offered before returning him to his sister's house in Belgrave Square.

As soon as the carriage stopped moving, Miss Wright looked about her like a wary bird, just landed on a foreign branch. She leaned forward to get a glimpse out the carriage window.

"This is the address you gave, Miss Wright. But there is still the matter of providing the explanation I require."

Indignation wasn't there when Lucius searched his heart and mind. He didn't pity Miss Jessamin Wright. He'd abide her command on that count. But her honesty and unfortunate circumstances called to him, triggering emotions that had nothing to do with discovering why she'd approached him, why she'd given him the most singular experience of his life.

His desire to hear her explanation came from a different impulse now, a curiosity about her life and history.

"I have already explained, my lord. It was a mistake. I

behaved rashly. Abominably. I've apologized and you've accepted. Will that not suffice?" Her uniquely appealing voice turned petulant for a moment, and Lucius had the distinct sense it was not a manner she often assumed.

"No." It gave him a perverse satisfaction to see her eyes widen again, and then something like fire begin to kindle there.

"Well, I beg your pardon, my lord, but it must. I can offer no further explanation for my actions." She turned away from him to emphasize her refusal.

He expected her to grasp the knob on the carriage door and disappear from his life just as abruptly as she'd entered it. But then she turned back and leaned toward him, her voice quiet and pleading.

"Can you not forget this night, my lord? Or if not the night, just that moment. That . . ." She struggled to form the word. "That kiss. Can you not forget?"

He moved toward her, their bodies inches apart in the confines of the carriage. He felt her breath whisper across his face, just as he had in the gallery.

"I am not certain I can, Miss Wright. Can you?"

Chapter Four

"Mr. Briggs, I don't understand. I presented you with payment toward the debt just yesterday afternoon." Jessamin struggled to keep the panic from her voice. It wouldn't do for the banker to see her as an overemotional woman. Throughout their dealings, they'd never managed to develop a truly pleasant rapport. Perhaps he just couldn't stomach the notion of doing business with a woman. He hadn't been terribly fond of her always-in-arrears father, but who could blame him? To a banker, there was no greater sin than failure to pay one's debts.

Yet despite his frustration with Lionel Wright's deficiency as a borrower, Briggs had always dealt fairly with her father. More than fairly. He'd frequently given him an extension or accepted partial payments, even past the due date. He was a good man. Which made his angry tone and refusal to take her payment even more of a mystery.

Mr. Briggs hadn't set foot in the shop in years. She

usually delivered her payments in person and had even met the man's wife and daughters when one of their visits to the bank coincided with her own. But he never came in person to the bookshop, and she'd never seen him as unsettled as he appeared today. A sheen of perspiration glistened on his upper lip, just below his quivering mustache. A shiver chased down her back as she noted additional signs of anxiety in the man. He was avoiding her gaze, and he fumbled with the latch on his leather folio before wrenching it open.

Jess swallowed against the flutter in her throat, the anxiety bubbling up in her chest, as she watched the banker reach into his case and lift out the very check she'd given him the day before. He laid it on the desk between them and slid the slip of paper toward her as he spoke.

"Miss Wright. As you can see, I am returning your check." The man's whole demeanor had changed since she'd delivered the payment toward her father's loan the previous afternoon. The banker had seemed pleased then, happy enough to take the amount and happier still for a respite from dealing with the perversity of a woman who'd chosen to take charge of her father's business and its debt. Jessamin imagined them well rid of each other for a while. The last thing she expected was to find him on her doorstep the next morning.

Placing her hand over the check, she fought the urge to thrust it back at him.

"I don't understand, sir. Is this not the proper amount to bring payments current? You accepted it just yesterday. How has it come to be inadequate today?"

There was no stopping the panic now. Jessamin felt the morning air chilling the sweat on her neck, and a sickening weight settled in her belly. If Mr. Briggs refused the money, all her recklessness of the night before had been in vain. If such an enormous sum wasn't sufficient, she'd never pull the bookshop out of debt. What would she tell Jack? The prospect of putting a loyal employee out of work troubled her more than the thought of closing the shop.

"Miss Wright, our bank is one of the most respectable in London." He looked down his pince-nez at her, arching his bushy gray eyebrows above the golden rims. He paused for a beat, as if expecting her to take his meaning. When she said nothing, he added, "And we mean to remain respectable. In all of our dealings."

Jess opened her mouth but no words came.

Briggs turned away from her dismissively, huffing out a grumble of frustration.

Then realization hit with the force of a strike, and she covered her mouth with her hands to keep from crying out. That kiss. That bloody foolish kiss. Had one act—a choice made out of desperation to stave off this very moment—cost her everything?

Jess closed her eyes and struggled to settle her whirling thoughts long enough to find her voice.

"Mr. Briggs, were you by any chance at an art gallery in Mayfair last evening?"

Please say no. But he didn't have to say anything at all. Though she'd often suspected his disdain for her, whether because of her father or her own failures as a bookshop owner, it was clear now. His mouth tilted in a sneer, and then he looked away, as if disturbed by the very sight of her. At the gallery, after she'd kissed Lord Grimsby, many of the men and women around her had done the same.

She'd disgraced herself, plain and simple. And somehow Mr. Briggs knew of the incident.

He'd brought a toady along with him, and the two of them wandered about the shop, no doubt assessing and planning how to dispose of her stock. After they whispered together, heads bent, Briggs glanced back at her, and the look of disgust in his bulbous eyes was the only answer she required.

The man who accompanied him, a younger, lankier version of Briggs himself, stepped forward and handed her a neatly folded document. Her hands shook as she tried to open it, but the gentleman spoke up in a surprisingly pleasant voice and said, almost regretfully, "Miss Wright, the bank has not acted on your overdue lien for years. Now that there is no viable means for you to settle the arrears, we have come to inform you that we will take possession of your inventory in one week in an attempt to settle the debt."

"It won't be enough." Jessamin heard her voice as if it was another's, an echo from far away—lifeless, hopeless. "You can sell every book, the bindery equipment, everything, and it still won't be enough to repay the debt."

When she looked up at the young man with tears blurring the corners of her vision, she imagined the regret she'd heard in his voice reflected in his pale gray eyes. But he merely stared down at her and said, "No."

He glanced at a sheaf of document in his hands, and then looked at her again with his cool, direct gaze. "Your lease. I see here it is—"

They wanted her out and would no doubt be pleased to know she was already halfway there.

"My lease has been up for months. The landlord has allowed me to pay month to month, but there's the matter of . . ." The bank men knew more about her father's money troubles than anyone, but acknowledging that he had even failed to pay the rent, that it was another debt she had yet to bring current, seemed like a final betrayal. "There was a previous arrears. Landlord wished me to clear it before he would allow me to sign a new lease."

He nodded as if that bit of information was very interesting indeed. The fact that she didn't have the certainty of a roof over her head was simply a fact to him, as if a life wasn't attached to it at all.

"Mr. Briggs has noted here that you started a lending library on the premises. You should make arrangements to retrieve any of the books currently lent and—"

"No."

Finally that sparked some emotion. Mr. Briggs's assistant narrowed his eyes, and his smooth-shaven cheeks began to bloom with color.

"No, Miss Wright?"

"No, sir. Those books are not part of what is owed to the bank, nor to anyone. They were donated or purchased with charitable funds."

"I see."

"Did you charge your borrowers a fee?"

"Whatever fees I collected were used to purchase more books. In that way, I hoped to make the lending library self-sustaining."

The young man glanced around her shop and expelled a pitying sigh.

"If only you'd put the fees toward saving your shop, Miss Wright."

The coins she'd accumulated from the borrowers would never have made a significant impact on her father's debt. But she wasn't going to argue with Mr. Briggs's assistant. The young man believed he'd won the point, and Jess was too busy willing herself to stop shivering and worrying over her future to mind conceding it to him.

"Yes, perhaps you're right."

Fisting her hand, she crinkled Kitty's check, still folded in her palm. If Mr. Briggs wouldn't accept the payment, she'd have to return the funds. They'd been given to support her father's shop, and there wouldn't be a bookshop anymore.

There won't be a bookshop anymore.

It couldn't be true. Father's bookshop had always been here. She'd spent nearly every day of her life in it. An infant when her parents rented the space and started their bookselling venture, Jess didn't remember a single day before Wright and Sons Booksellers existed.

And she promised her father she wouldn't let it founder. His last words to her had been about the shop, urging her to stay on, to keep it going, and to succeed in all the ways he'd failed.

I trust you'll fare better than I ever did, my girl.

In four years she'd barely managed to keep the shop afloat. A bit had been paid to all of Lionel Wright's creditors, but none of the outstanding debt had been cleared. Some days her burdens all seemed so heavy she would stand in front of her mirror, feet sore from standing, head sore from worrying, and swear she'd shrunk an inch under the weight. Now it was collapsing around her, the sense of loss a hollow, gaping pain. She'd felt it only once before—the day Father died after urging her to keep up his shop.

"Miss Wright?"

Jess looked up to find Mr. Briggs and his assistant staring at her. She'd forgotten they were still in the shop. The mild expression she'd come to expect from Briggs had settled on his whiskered face, but his assistant watched her warily, as if she might break into a fit of hysterics.

Her mouth had gone dry but Jess managed a few words to send them on their way.

"As you've requested, gentlemen, I'll be out in one week. Would you mind seeing yourselves out?"

Turning her back on the men, Jess approached the door of the small back room she used as an office. It was as much rudeness as she'd ever shown to anyone who'd visited Wright and Sons Booksellers. But she couldn't face them, not when tears welled up and began sliding down her cheeks faster than she could swipe them away.

The moment the bankers were out the door, Jack

Echolls emerged from the back room and thrust a well-used scrap of cloth into her hand.

"Dry your eyes, miss. We both knew this day was coming."

Yes. She'd feared it, dreaded it for years. Even while she'd been working to stave it off, the inevitability of the shop's failure had always loomed over her. For the past four years, she'd only held it at bay, toiling as futilely as Sisyphus forever pushing a boulder up the hill.

Jack pulled a straight-back chair from the office and Jessamin sat down hard, deflated, her whole body sagging despite the restraint of her corset, as if the weight of all that her father had left her—his poorly managed business and completely neglected obligations—had finally flattened her.

"I thought we could get out from under the debt."

Jack made a tsking sound. "By borrowing more?"

The word *borrow* brought Kitty Adderly and her ridiculous bargain to mind. Jess closed her eyes to block out the memory of her foolishness, but shutting her eyes only heightened the memories. She saw the gas lit swatches of bright color in the gallery, the ladies and gentlemen in all their finery, and the black-haired figure in the midst of it all—a man with the coldest eyes and the warmest lips.

"Did you hear me, miss?"

Jessamin pushed the memories away and looked up at her employee.

"I'm sorry, Jack. What was it you said?"

"You're not going to faint on me like some proper lady, are you?"

"I don't faint. And I'm sitting down. Now, what was it you said?"

Jack averted his eyes and scuffed the toe of his boot across the floor. "It was hard enough to say the first time."

"Out with it, Jack. I can take it." If bad news had to come, let it all be at once.

"Mr. Harker's offered me a position."

Jessamin gasped, and Jack's next words tumbled out quickly.

"I would never have considered it, you understand. Not unless I knew there was no chance of work at the shop. I would have stayed loyal to you, miss, just as I was to your father."

Jess didn't wait for him to finish before wrapping the older man in a quick embrace. When she pulled back, it was clear she'd embarrassed him, but her joy at his news was too much to contain.

"Jack, that is the best news you could have given me. Nothing worried me more than the thought of leaving you without employment."

A bit of the morning's tensions began to seep away. A bit of the hollowness had eased. She could breathe again, and she sucked in a greedy breath, letting the relief of knowing Jack would be all right ease a bit of the guilt she felt over losing the shop.

She beamed at Jack and pressed a palm against her chest, attempting to quell the ache there. *Breathe.* Focusing on the rhythm of her slow-to-steady heartbeat, Jess noticed another sensation—a fluttering, a lightness, as if a pressure on her chest had subsided. It was anxiety, surely. Her future had never been more uncertain.

With his usual practicality, Jack fixed on the biggest question of all.

"I'll be fine, miss. Please don't worry yourself about me. But what about you? What will you do now the shop is closed?"

Chapter Five

THOUGH THE WEATHER had been dreadful during his entire stay in London, on the morning following the incident, it suddenly turned warm and unseasonably bright. The sun rose with an extraordinary show of color and hung in a sky as clear and blue as a robin's egg. Sleep had eluded him, and Lucius witnessed every moment of the sunrise's bold display and had been awake, turning and tossing and checking the mantel clock far too often, during all the hours of evening's dark before it.

He'd returned to his sister's town house and consumed more than enough brandy to assure a sound slumber, but the moment his body was prone and his eyes slid shut, the scent of violet water assailed him. His thoughts kept tangling in strands of auburn hair. Auburn hair released from its pins and cascading in waves over the shoulders of Miss Jessamin Wright. Miss Wright, whose mouth was full and delicious and had moved so sweetly against his own.

He blamed his ruminations on the brandy. Romanticizing the woman was utter folly. She'd behaved outrageously. Appallingly. Yet as Lucius considered just how outrageous she'd been, his arousal grew in equal measure. And the relentless ticking of the clock did nothing but set his mind turning. And despite admonishing himself, reviewing the whole scandalous matter with logic and reason, and vowing to set it aside, Miss Jessamin Wright remained vivid in his mind's eye—with her wire-rimmed spectacles, shabby clothes, pretty hair, and floral scent.

He'd intended to remain in London for a fortnight but when he'd finally given up on sleep and risen early, he yearned for nothing more than to prepare for the journey back to Hartwell. Distance from the incident in London and a return to the responsibilities of the estate would cure him of the fanciful notions running through his head.

His valet, Mather, assisted him to dress, but in his usual slow, precise method. Lucius bit his lip, praying for tolerance to bear the man's snaillike pace. It didn't work. He pulled his neck cloth from Mather's gnarled hands and began tying it himself, ignoring the fact that he was making a mess of the thing.

In his low drone, Mather said, "Are you in a very great hurry, my lord?" He spoke the word *hurry* as if it was a distasteful and a quite unexpected possibility.

Why *was* he suddenly so keen to be away from London? Surely the scent of violet water and the memory of Miss Wright's kiss would have the power to haunt him as far as Berkshire. And departing early might provide more fodder for those who'd make much of the incident at the gallery. Not to mention that he'd yet to speak to Aunt Augusta at any length about her short list of marriageable young ladies. It had been the main impetus for coming to London. The need to marry well, to refill the estate's coffers and see to long overdue repairs weighed on him more and more. Yet this morning, for reasons he refused to ponder too deeply, the notion of marriage held no appeal, practical or otherwise.

"No, Mather. Carry on." Lucius thought he saw amusement lifting the elderly man's mouth but couldn't be sure. Mather generally disdained displays of emotion as much as he loathed hustle. The man resumed tying Lucius's neck cloth, slowly and precisely, and heaved a sigh when a knock sounded at the door. Mather loathed interruption too.

"Beg pardon, my lord." The housemaid pushed through the door almost as soon as she rapped. She bustled forward and held a letter out to Lucius. "A messenger from the Countess of Stamford just delivered this, my lord. He waits for your reply."

Unlike Mather, his aunt wasn't known for rising early, and Lucius feared she might be unwell. Her note was short and to the point.

Lucius, come at once. A.

For such a talkative woman, his aunt was an unhelpfully vague correspondent.

"Let the messenger know I will come at once." His aunt wouldn't settle for anything less.

The young maid bobbed a curtsy and made a hasty retreat, nearly slipping on the polished floor as she pulled the bedchamber door shut with an unpleasant bang. The sound echoed painfully in his brandy-soaked head. Perhaps Mather had a point about the undesirability of haste after all.

"LADY STAMFORD IS well?"

Nothing about the demeanor of his aunt's energetic butler, Noon, seemed amiss, but Lucius needed to hear from the man's mouth that his aunt wasn't ill.

"Quite well, my lord. Lady Stamford is expecting you. She asked that you join her and her guests in the drawing room."

"Guests?" Lucius pressed his lips together to stifle a yawn. He never minded time spent with his aunt but, still bleary-eyed from his sleepless night, he didn't fancy being sociable. And why must it be now, so early in the far too sunny morning?

"Dearest nephew!"

Lucius arched a brow, instantly awake. His aunt's use of such a sugary endearment put him on high alert. He knew she felt a great deal of familial warmth toward him, but she'd never express it in such terms, especially in front of others. The crafty woman was warning him. Even her constant companions, twin pugs Castor and Pollux, their stout, biscuit-colored bodies tucked on either side of her, looked unsettled.

Lucius leaned in to place a kiss on his aunt's cheek and

whisper near her ear, "I feared you were unwell. Tell me why I'm here so early."

She patted his arm and whispered back, "You shall soon see. Gird your loins."

Pulling back to squint at her, Lucius had only a moment to ponder why she'd advised him to prepare for battle before turning to face the two guests she indicated with the sweep of an arm.

"I believe you're all acquainted with my nephew, Viscount Grimsby."

She spoke his title with special emphasis. Lucius couldn't remember the last time she'd bothered to do so. But as he took in the two ladies perched on her settee, he understood. Both of the women had been at the gallery the previous evening.

"Lucius, you know Mrs. Ornish, of course."

He nodded to his late mother's friend and she returned a tight smile.

"And her sister, Mrs. Briggs."

Before he could perform the niceties of *Pleased to meet you*s and bowing and placing chaste kisses in the air above hands, Delia Ornish spoke up.

"Lord Grimsby, I do hope you are well after last evening's . . . Well, the dreadful incident with that . . . that horrible woman."

Lucius had spent the most of the evening thinking about that particular woman. *Horrible* wasn't a word he would use to describe her. *Lovely, inscrutable, frustrating*—all that, but never *horrible.* He took a breath to state that he was quite recovered and that no lasting harm had been done, belying his restless night, but Mrs. Briggs preempted him.

"You should know that my husband has taken direct action as a result of that woman's behavior."

"Has he indeed? What sort of action might that be, Mrs. Briggs?"

"Lucius, do sit down."

His aunt's tone made it sound as if he'd been remiss, absolving her two guests of their rudeness in bombarding him so early in the morning.

"Tea?"

She didn't wait for his reply before ringing a crystal bell that rested on a side table next to her chair. A maid entered the room in the next instant bearing a tea service. After receiving her teacup and a scone-laden plate, Mrs. Briggs didn't bother partaking before offering her reply.

"He's ruined her."

Lucius nearly choked on the hot liquid he'd begun to sip, and the teacup and saucer rattled a moment in his hands before he got the porcelain under control. The notion of Mr. Briggs, whoever the blasted man was, ruining the woman who'd haunted his thoughts was more outrageous than anything she'd done. More outrageous than his own wicked thoughts about ruining her, certainly.

"I beg your pardon, madam?"

"She owns some miserable little bookshop and has incurred more debt than she can ever repay." Mrs. Briggs fussed with her dress, sniffing haughtily as if that was an end to the matter. Lucius had the impulse to take her by her puffed sleeve–covered shoulders and shake the rest of the story out of her.

Closing his eyes, he only just resisted pinching the bridge of his nose where his head had begun to throb—too much brandy and too little sleep were a wretched combination.

"And how does this involve your husband, Mrs. Briggs?" he bit out slowly, giving each word its due and tempering the tone he truly wished to use.

His aunt finally chimed in. "He owns the bank that made the loan, you see. He has foreclosed on her. Or he will do soon, according to Mrs. Briggs."

He could see Miss Wright in a bookshop, her wire-rimmed spectacles perched at the end of her nose. The young woman had already lost her family. He couldn't abide the notion of her losing anything else.

"For this? Because of some foolish nonsense that no one will remember in a week?"

He took a swallow of tea, the flavor suddenly bitter, after barking out the words. Perhaps he'd been too loud, too vehement. It certainly hadn't done the drumming in his head any good.

Augusta was staring at him, her eyebrows peaked high on her forehead.

He too wondered why he was suddenly defending Miss Wright's actions. It most assuredly had nothing to do with that extraordinary kiss. Or at least that's what he'd say to his aunt if she pressed him on the matter.

Mrs. Briggs shot to her feet, and her tight-fitting, puffy-sleeved gown rustled with the effort.

Lucius stood too. Etiquette demanded it despite his frustration with the woman's husband.

"My husband could not allow his bank to be associated with such a trollop! Sh-she humiliated you in front of everyone. One would think you might be pleased that Mr. Briggs acted in your interest, my lord. We all feel your embarrassment as one." Her little speech started out on a strident note and then trailed off into an obsequious whine at the end.

"Forgive me, Mrs. Briggs, but it seems your husband acted in his own interest, not mine." When the woman's lower lip began to tremble, Lucius bit back his irritation and tempered his tone. "I do appreciate that Mr. Briggs acted on his moral principles, but what of his compassion? No real injury was done to me. Certainly none that compares to what has now been done to this young woman."

If the bluestocking had humiliated him, he had yet to sense an inkling of it. Perhaps the pleasure he'd taken in the kiss was blinding him to the damage she'd done and he'd wake up in a week to find he was the laughingstock of London. At least he'd be in the countryside by then.

Mrs. Briggs looked momentarily confused and then seemed to comprehend that regardless of his gentler tone, she was being chastised. She slumped back down onto his aunt's damask-covered settee as if, with all her superiority gone, she had no strength left to hold her up.

"No one should lose everything over one kiss." Whatever the truth of his declaration, no one seemed to be listening. It was almost as if he'd said the words to an empty room. None of the ladies responded. Mrs. Ornish was busy fanning her sister, who seemed on the verge of tears, and Aunt Augusta looked down at her pugs with a tiny grin on her face.

Lucius cleared his throat before standing and straightening his cuffs, settling each shirtsleeve button at precisely the same position on each wrist.

"If you'll excuse me, ladies. I'm returning to Berkshire and would like to make a start."

His aunt followed him to the foyer and spoke in hushed tones while the butler fetched his coat and hat.

"You haven't been in London for more than a week. And we've yet to discuss the list of eligible matches. Why such haste to return? Is it Maxim?"

Lucius's aunt was many things: clever, irreverent, and fiercely loyal. He was glad to be counted among her allies and shuddered at the thought of being her enemy. And she was loyal to no one as much as to her elder brother, Lucius's father, Maxim Crawford, Earl of Dunthorpe.

Lucius gave his aunt's arm a reassuring squeeze. "No, I had a telegram yesterday from Higgins. Father is well. He's in one of his melancholy moods."

"Are they more frequent? And what of his memory? I fear another spell."

Lucius's father was ill, though it was a sickness of the mind more than the body. He'd always been a volatile man, but in recent years his memory had begun to fail. Names, incidents, even lifelong servants were at times as unknown to him as strangers. He had good days when he was lucid and as indignant as ever, but more often he halted in the middle of a conversation, uncertain of what he'd meant to say in the first place. On days when his memory didn't fail him, his father's emotions swung from energetic highs to lows when he was barely interested in rising from his bed.

"His melancholia comes and goes and there've been no more spells like the last." Lucius had grown used to his father calling him by his brother's name or mistaking his nurse for the housekeeper, but several months before, the earl had a spell when he woke frightened and disoriented, unable to recognize those around him.

"There are days when I'd swear he's the same man who drove Mother and me away, as angry and bitter as he was all those years ago. But more often he's a kinder version of that man, with his good humor and even a bit of compassion restored."

"That's the Maxim I knew as a child. If only you'd experienced more of that aspect of his nature."

But he hadn't. Lucius's childhood memories were of a man embittered by paranoid jealousy and a love for his wife that consumed and twisted him. Though Lucius had lost his mother too early, he recalled her as sweet-natured and intelligent, quick to laugh and more interested in books than in entertaining—a loving antidote to his father's wrath. Even as a child, he'd wondered what had drawn the two together and vowed never to let himself drown in the sort of love they shared.

"It must be what my mother saw in him."

Augusta's expression gave nothing away. She rarely spoke of the difficulties of his parents' marriage.

"Yes, I'm sure it was. Do give him my love when you return to Hartwell."

"Of course."

Maintaining the estate and caring for his father had consumed the last several years of Lucius's adulthood. Though Augusta marked the change in her brother from the day Lucius's mother died, Lucius recalled his father's extremes from much earlier and suspected they'd always been a part of his character. And whatever the cause of his failing memory—the village doctor ascribed it to Maxim's age—Lucius's one avowed goal was to keep him at Hartwell and provide whatever care he needed. Rancor aside, Maxim was his father.

"What of our discussion of eligible young ladies?" Augusta was a master at drawing him back to the matter at hand whenever his mind wandered elsewhere.

"Are there so many on the list?" The prospect had never seemed more daunting.

Aunt Augusta chuckled. Matchmaking tended to make her giddy.

"There is one young lady in particular I'd like you to meet."

"Is she in London?" If she was, it was only reasonable to extend his stay another day and allow his aunt the introduction. He didn't wish her efforts to be in vain.

"As it turns out, no. She's in Saratoga, New York, apparently, and decided to extend her stay. She means to make a visit to Marleston Hall within a fortnight."

"Saratoga?"

"A bit like Bath, I understand."

"Very well, send for me after she settles in, and we'll see if your machinations are as effective as you claim."

His aunt loved a challenge nearly as much as a matchmaking opportunity. Where his future was concerned, she'd found both.

Nothing in his life had ever gone as he'd planned. His late brother, Julian, should have been heir to Hartwell. Lucius had considered studying law in Scotland or joining his Scottish uncle's shipping business in London. He'd never wished to be lord of Hartwell. And he'd certainly never expected to be in search of a suitable woman to become Countess of Dunthorpe.

"What shall we do about the other young woman?"

There was no doubt about to whom she referred. He hadn't thought of Miss Wright for a handful of minutes, but his aunt's question brought her vividly to mind—and to his senses. His mouth and other southerly parts of his body tingled at the memory of her lips. Then he recalled how they'd parted company, how she'd scampered out of his carriage as if the hounds of hell nipped at her heels.

He cleared his throat, forcing the memory from his mind.

"I don't believe she wishes to continue our acquaintance. And it would hardly be appropriate for me to do so."

Seeing the woman again was too absurd to contemplate. Never mind that an impractical urge to meet her in the light of day ticked at the back of Lucius's mind like an overloud clock. Never mind that he'd spent the better part of the night tormented by thoughts of her, or that she'd apparently lost her shop because of a kiss he feared he'd never forget.

"Then perhaps I shall see about her." With a beaming smile, Aunt Augusta lifted Pollux—or was it Castor?—as if Lucius should offer the creature some parting words.

The butler helped Lucius into his coat and held the door open for him, letting in a breath of the unseasonably warm air. Lucius knew he was only imagining the scent of violets that hung on the breeze.

"You will see about her? What exactly do you intend to do?"

Pollux stared up at him with innocent eyes, but his aunt wore a grin so full of machinations and mischief that it would have made a vicar blush.

The ticking at the base of his skull built to a crescendo. Jessamin Wright was an orphan, without family, with perhaps no other means of support than the bookshop she'd just lost. He owed her nothing. The woman had publicly disgraced him, if Mrs. Briggs was to be believed. Yet despite his aunt's desire to see about her, he could not imagine returning to Berkshire without seeing about Miss Wright himself.

Even if the impulse was an ill-conceived one. And it most certainly was.

Even if it would be the last time he ever saw Jessamin Wright again. And it definitely would be.

The distraction of donning his hat and offering Castor, or perhaps Pollux, a farewell pat on the head allowed him a moment to silence the doubts and make his decision.

He wouldn't be leaving London straightaway after all.

Chapter Six

"MISS WRIGHT, THERE's a gentleman here to see you."

Jess jumped at the sound of Jack's voice. She'd been staring for nearly an hour at the faded photograph of her father she kept in the bookshop's back office. In her mind, she was turning over what to tell their patrons, their lending library borrowers, and, mostly, what she would say to her father if he were still alive. How could she explain that she'd lost a business he'd managed to hold together, even through years of mismanagement?

Jack's words pulled her back to the present and reminded her explanations were unnecessary. If Father hadn't died, she wouldn't be in this predicament in the first place. Then again, if she hadn't kissed a viscount on some silly woman's whim, Mr. Briggs might have had a bit more mercy.

But there was no use worrying over the past and what might have been. Her main task now was settling their patrons' accounts and finding some form of gainful employment.

"Did you tell him the shop is closed? Permanently."

"Seems he's here to see you, miss."

Jessamin stood and arched her back, working out the stiffness the straight-back chair had caused during her pointless, dejected woolgathering.

"Please tell me it's not Mr. Briggs again."

Jack quirked a queer little grin, which only piqued her interest.

"Well, who is it?"

"Didn't give a name. Just asked for you."

It couldn't be good news. The way the day was going, Jess felt certain it could only get worse. After pushing a few stray hairs into pins and straightening her skirts, she took a deep breath and prepared to meet *worse* head-on.

She took three steps and halted so suddenly that Jack, who'd been following behind, bumped into her and nearly knocked her off her feet.

"It's all right, Jack. Will you work on the borrower letters in the office?"

Jack made a noise that reeked of disapproval, but he obediently retreated. He peeked out at her through the office door before shutting it behind him, as if to signal he'd be available should she need saving.

Here, in the middle of her sunken business, stood the one man in England she was certain she'd never see again. It was the tall, dark viscount. The man she'd been hired to kiss—that rash and ridiculous kiss, the very reason for the second worst day of her life.

"Lord Grimsby." There was nothing else to say. At least nothing civil or polite, nothing pleasant. She doubted very much that he'd wish to hear how her life had just broken into pieces.

Jess clasped her hands behind her back. In the awkward silence, she could think only of what she wished to say but couldn't. Based on her station in life, she shouldn't even know a viscount, let alone be familiar with the taste of his mouth.

"Miss Wright."

Such a lovely voice. In the night, she'd remembered his voice and the few words that had passed between them. She'd convinced herself its deep, seductive appeal was half imaginative fancy. But, if anything, it was more seductive in the daylight. Indeed he was more extraordinary in the daylight. His hair was pitch dark, truly black, and his eyes were the lightest, clearest blue she'd ever seen. Beautiful eyes, though their color did nothing to detract from the air of coolness about him. He cleared his throat and she felt a blush heat her cheeks. She'd lost track of how long she'd stood studying him.

"I heard some troubling news this morning, Miss Wright."

"Did you, my lord?"

"Did a Mr. Briggs visit you this morning?"

"How could you know that?"

Why would this man know about her problems and the very changeable Mr. Briggs? Then it struck her.

"Did you send him here to close my shop?"

"No. Certainly not." His denial was emphatic and his

voice almost intimidating when matched with volume. "I was appalled when I heard the news."

"And so you came to see the wreckage."

He looked away from her then, as if he couldn't bear to meet her eyes.

"Or did you come here to save me?" As soon as the words were out of her mouth, Jess knew it was why he'd come. In his aristocratic way, he probably believed he could throw money at the situation and it would all be neatly resolved. Perhaps he meant to pay her off—or make a much more inappropriate offer. She had to know.

"I don't require saving, my lord."

The fact that she would have no place to live within the week, owned only two decent dresses, and had approximately eleven pounds and nine shillings to her name wouldn't make her accept the man's charity. She'd taken Kitty Adderly's offer of charity just last night and look where that had landed her.

He didn't respond to her strident declaration, but he looked at her again, watching her awhile before turning his gaze to the bookshelves.

Jess allowed herself a moment to study his far too appealing profile before emphasizing her point.

"I have no wish for *your* charity, my lord."

She'd been working in the bookshop most of her life, aside from the few years her parents saved enough to send her to a boarding school she loathed. The notion of work didn't frighten her. Now it was a simply a matter of finding new employment.

Her words failed to earn her his undivided attention.

He'd turned to inspect her books more closely, tilting his head to read the spines.

Jess lifted her hands to her hips.

"My shop is closed, my lord."

He was behaving as if he'd come to pick out a new book. Yet he'd admitted knowing about Mr. Briggs and had to realize the books were no longer hers to sell.

"How many do you have here?"

Goodness, that voice. Her ears warmed at the sound of it. She opened her mouth and then bit her lip, trying to recall what he'd asked her.

"Books, Miss Wright? How many would you say are here in the shop?"

"We've maintained a smaller stock of late."

He turned an irritated glance her way, narrowing his eyes before lifting a black brow over his right eye.

She wasn't prevaricating. She just couldn't fathom what the number of books in her shop had to do with the viscount she'd kissed standing in the middle of it. Surely he had no desire to purchase a bookshop. He must know involvement with her or her shop would only stoke the rumor mill. It made her wonder why he'd risked coming to see her at all.

"There are a little over eight hundred books."

He pursed his mouth and continued glancing up at the shelves.

"Everything is quite tidy and meticulously organized. It must have been a great deal of work to run a shop on your own."

She was grateful he didn't look at her when he said it.

Heat crept up the back of her neck and Jess suspected her cheeks were flushed too. She could count on one hand the sum of compliments she'd received from gentlemen in her life, and certainly none had anything to do with her skills as a businesswoman. It was shockingly gratifying and yet, considering that she'd just lost her business, did she truly deserve it?

"I do have an assistant. Mr. Echolls."

"Ah, yes. The gentleman in the back room."

She nodded her head, but he'd turned his back on her and missed the gesture.

Standing near their oldest bit of shelving, his shoulders aligned with a barely discernible series of notches on the side of the bookcase. It was where Father had marked off her height as she grew year after year. Lord Grimsby's shoulders crested the highest notch by several inches. No wonder she'd had to crane her neck and stand on the tips of her toes to kiss him.

The memory of their kiss set loose the warmth in her cheeks and it flowed to her limbs in a pleasurable rush.

Foolish woman. That kiss had been her downfall. She'd lost her father's shop over that kiss. It was madness to recall it with anything but regret.

"Why are you here, my lord?"

He looked at her again, capturing her gaze in a glance that made her shiver. He stalked toward her in two long strides, and it took every bit of strength she had left to stand her ground. Like the night before, he was so close she had to tilt her head to look up and meet his eyes.

She thought he might touch her. A kind of blue fire burned in his gaze.

"Don't you know, Miss Wright? Don't you know why I'm here?"

"I . . ." She meant to offer up one of her theories, but his tantalizing scent sent her thoughts scattering. It was a familiar scent to her now. Just that morning she'd imagined she could smell it lingering on her clothes.

"I could give you money."

Tension coiled in her belly at his words. Money was what she needed most, though she doubted Mr. Briggs would accept any amount from her now. But why would Lord Grimsby offer her money? Charity? She'd never take that again. And there could be no fair exchange. She had nothing with which to bargain.

Was he asking her to be his mistress? Did he respect her so little?

She thought of her behavior the previous evening and a wry grin twisted her mouth. She'd already kissed him, brazenly, without permission or even an introduction. Why wouldn't he expect her to do much more for money now that she'd lost her business?

"Why, my lord?" She wanted to hear him say it, to admit his desire or that he thought her as dishonorable as those who'd witnessed her foolish act.

But her words seemed to douse the fire in him. He blinked and took several steps back. She thought he'd turn and walk out. The blaze had gone and there was only finality in his gaze.

He'd go and leave her to face the results of her actions alone. Just as her father had left her alone to deal with his debts and bad choices. Though now, this trouble, this had been her choice. She found a strange sort of comfort in that. That made it easier to face somehow.

She lifted her chin and looked Lord Grimsby square in the eyes. "I do not wish to be a charity case, my lord. There are many other worthy causes if you wish to give your money away. Thank you for calling. Good day, my lord."

But he wasn't finished with her. He didn't respond, but he took two steps toward her, nearly as close as they'd been the night before.

"I can't forget." He touched her the moment the three words were out of his mouth. No bargain. No gawking socialites. Just the warm press of his fingertips against her skin. He was gentle, his touch reverent as he explored the curve of her cheek. He touched her as if she were precious, as if she mattered, even now when she'd lost everything.

Jess swayed toward him, and he reached for her, wrapping one arm around her waist as he dipped his head. If he wished to kiss her, she'd let him. Right or wrong, she'd let him. But he didn't take her mouth. Instead, he moved his head lower, pressing his cheek to hers.

"I can't forget." He repeated the words low, a hot, breathy whisper that tickled her ear and sparked a wave of sensation across her skin. She was already quivering when he kissed her, pressing his lips to her cheek, just at the edge of her ear.

Then it was over. He lifted his head and steadied her

on her feet. There was no fire in his gaze now. Just sadness. Or was it regret?

He stepped away from her once more, stroking his hand down her arm before releasing her.

After placing his top hat on his head, he bowed—to her, a ruined businesswoman and public strumpet—before striding out of her shambles of a bookshop. Out of her shambles of a life. This time, she was certain, forever.

EVER FAITHFUL, JACK stayed on past their usual closing time to help Jess with the borrower letters and tidying the shop's back room. Ever discreet, he'd kept mum about the viscount's visit. Jess was thankful for both.

"We're down to our last few penny stamps, Jack. Should we spend what's left on some more?"

Determined to let all of their lending library borrowers know the shop was closing, Jess also wanted to urge them to keep the books currently in their care. Better that devoted readers have a book of their own than Briggs and his men have the lot or use it as kindling.

She handed the last of the Wright and Sons Booksellers' petty cash to Jack and he donned his coat. The London weather was predictable only in its unpredictability. What began as a day of blue skies and warm breezes had now turned cool and foggy.

She followed Jack to the front door carrying a packet of letters to be mailed to the borrowers. He was on the threshold and she'd nearly closed the door on him to keep out the cold when he turned back to her.

"What will you do, miss?"

The question chilled her more than the biting autumn air. It was the problem she'd been ignoring as she busied herself with what must be done. Her morning listlessness had dissolved with the viscount's visit and she'd been cleaning and sorting and writing letters for hours. The question of her future had been at the back of her mind, but she'd pushed it aside.

"I honestly don't know." Her options were few and her means even less. Service loomed as the most reasonable option.

"Perhaps I shall go into service." It was a relief to simply say the words aloud.

"Well, you should go as a governess, miss. You've more sense and cleverness than most men I know."

She couldn't help but smile at the irony of his words, considering the situation. "Lot of good it did me, eh?"

Jack looked down and studied the letters in his hands. They both knew that the loss of the bookshop led directly back to her father—his drinking, his gambling, all the secrets he'd hidden from her for years.

"I'm freezing, Jack. Hurry back and I'll treat you and Sally at the Frog and Whistle." He offered her a toothy smile, appearing much younger than his fifty years, before dashing off like a man half his age. There was no underestimating the motivating power of good food and frothy ale.

Jess latched the door behind him and made certain their hastily made "Closed" sign was in place. Then she turned and surveyed the shop from that spot, just inside the front door. Tears welled in her eyes. She bit her lip and choked back a sob as her gaze lit on each bookcase, the neat columns of spines, the brass plates indicating topic, and the glint of gilt on the newest, most expensive volumes. Some would simply see it as a collection of paper and leather and binding glue. To Jess it was the world. For as long as she could remember, the bookshop had formed the boundary lines of her life, but through the pages of so many of its books she'd encountered the world. Far-off places she'd never visit, though she could see them in her mind's eye. Some of her favorite books' characters were as dear as friends, their stories and landscapes available for a visit whenever she wished.

And she couldn't look at the bookshop, each element that made it a whole, without seeing Father in her mind's eye. He'd been the one ingredient that bound it all together. It had been his dream, his life's work. With his own hands he'd polished the bookcases, filled them with precious volumes, and carefully formed the elegant script on each brass category plate. She held a vague, fragile memory of Mother and Father dancing a lively jig on a day of bountiful sales, and more vivid memories of how her father would whistle or break into song as he worked, his lively tenor echoing off the towering bookshelves. He was a man who loathed silence, often talking to himself aloud, and she realized what had been missing from the shop hadn't just been his presence but his noise.

The latter days she tried not to remember—the nights he would disappear and she'd find him too hungover or despondent to run the shop the next day. The promises and lies about money, the assurances that all would soon be well, that their luck would change. She didn't wish to recall her father for his weakness of character, but she couldn't deny it. Especially now. Taking Kitty's money and kissing a stranger had been her folly, but he'd sown the seeds of the shop's failure years before.

A rap at the door doused her reverie, and Jess quickly wiped away her tears.

Though it was not yet six, the sky had begun to turn dark and she couldn't make out the figure through the glass.

"I'm sorry, but we're closed."

The rapping sounded again, this time louder and more insistent. Her visitor wasn't going to be deterred, it seemed.

She undid the latch, turned the knob, and was pushed back nearly into the wall. Just on the verge of protesting, she spied two beige creatures sprinting into the shop and disappearing among the stacks. Then a woman emerged through the open door. At least it appeared to be a woman. A hat, the largest, grandest, most ornate creation she'd ever seen, was the dominant feature that moved across the threshold. Then the hat moved and two blue eyes, cool and clear, met hers.

The woman's dress, a deep blue creation with panels of lace and velvet, fit her shapely figure perfectly. She finally tilted her head and the enormous hat receded, feathers and a coil of ribbon still settling into place against her dark hair moments after she'd stopped moving.

"How do you do, Miss Jessamin Wright? You are Miss Wright, are you not?"

Jess could only manage a nod.

"Excellent. I am the Countess of Stamford. I believe you are acquainted with my nephew, Viscount Grimsby."

For a moment Jessamin stared at Lady Stamford much as she'd stared at Lord Grimsby. Both of them looked so completely out of place in the midst of her sagging shelves of books. The oddity and extraordinary coincidence of having two members of the aristocracy visit her shop in the same day made a giggle bubble up. Jess bit her lip and cleared her throat to stifle the impulse.

The lady's pets, two identical pugs, had finished their perusal of the bookshop and waddled over to sit at their mistress's feet. One quickly tired of sitting and folded his short legs to lie down. Both looked up, assessing Jess with bulging eyes. Lady Stamford watched her too, and Jess wondered how she fared in the fine lady's estimation. Not well, she imagined. Nothing she owned was fashionable, and her hair was likely a fright after a day at the shop, not to mention the embarrassment she'd caused the woman's nephew. That, of course, must be why she'd come. *Might as well get the apologies out of the way.*

"My lady, I truly regret the incident of last evening. And any trouble I might have caused your nephew—"

The countess cut her off. "Miss Wright, I am not here to discuss last evening's . . . misunderstanding." *Misunderstanding* was a terribly gracious and inaccurate way of viewing the entire debacle. "Rather, I am here to discuss you and your future."

"My future?"

"I understand your shop here . . ." Lady Stamford took a moment to look around at the shelves of books, as if just realizing their presence. Jess was surprised to see that she didn't look dispassionately but actually took the time to read the titles on a few nearby spines, just as her nephew had done. "Yes. You have quite a selection, I see." She picked up a small red morocco leather folio of poetry. "Would you sell me this one?"

"I'm afraid I won't be selling any more books, my lady. My shop is closed as of this morning."

"Yes, of course. That's why I'm here."

For a moment, Jess had the mad notion Lady Stamford meant to buy her shop. Before she could form a question, the lady's clear, strong voice provided an explanation.

"I mean to offer you employment, Miss Wright. I heard about the closure of your shop and thought you might be in need of a situation. I have need of a companion. When would you be able to start? I'll be returning to Wiltshire soon so I will need your answer straightaway."

Jess told Jack she would go into service, but she'd imagined a place as a governess. She had no idea what being a lady's companion might entail. She only knew that she wasn't suited to it, either by birth or by preparation. Weren't lady's companions usually wellborn young women?

"I am not suited to be your companion, my lady." Did

the woman truly not care about the business with her nephew? "And the events of last evening—"

"—will soon be forgotten, Miss Wright."

"My behavior wasn't that of a lady's companion." Jess couldn't quite meet the woman's eyes as she recalled her own behavior—the kiss she'd shared with Lady Stamford's nephew, the fact that she'd let him touch her again hours before.

Though she didn't know the man's aunt—or him, for that matter—Jess felt an instant liking for Lady Stamford. The notion of bringing her any shame or making her the object of more gossip was wholly unacceptable.

Lady Stamford smiled, and her entire face lit up. Jessamin thought she even detected a glint of mischief in her eyes.

"Well, you weren't a lady's companion at the time."

Jess sensed the firm set of her mouth melting into a grin and felt a bit of the day's disappointments ease. Lady Stamford's mirth was infectious, as if she was inviting you to see the world in the unique manner she did.

"Miss Wright, though I do not begin to know your reasons, I can recognize an act of desperation when I see it."

Jessamin snapped her head up and looked at Lady Stamford directly. She felt raw and exposed. How much did this woman know of her situation?

"Oh yes, I too have been desperate in my life. I've made dreadful choices as a result. I see you doubt me, but I promise you it's true. However, that is past, as is last evening. Now, will you come to Wiltshire with me or not? I need an answer as soon as you can give it."

Jess was tempted to be swayed by Lady Stamford, moving in her mind and heart toward acceptance. The shop was closed and she had no other options for work or lodging. The prospect of leaving London, where the ruins of her failure lay, was extremely appealing. Then a thought struck her with doubt.

"What will Lord Grimsby say to all of this?"

Lady Stamford quirked a grin before answering.

"Hartwell, my brother's estate, is miles away. A whole county, if it puts your mind at ease. My nephew is preoccupied with running it and rarely has time to visit. I assure you, Miss Wright, the two of you are unlikely to cross paths very often."

The assurance should have brought Jess relief, but it only brought an ache, an echo of the sense of loss she felt over her father's shop.

The burdens of the day, of her situation, hit her all at once, and Jess wanted nothing more than to crawl into bed, fall asleep, and hope it had all been a bad dream. But she sensed the grand lady's impatience.

"I will . . . have to think about it, my lady. Thank you for your—"

"I have yet to make an offer, my dear. One hundred pounds per annum."

If there'd been a chair nearby, Jess would have sunk into it. As it was, she held herself quite still to stop from doing something very silly, like fainting.

"One hundred pounds?" To Jessamin's mind it was such an extraordinary sum that it bore repeating—the amount she'd taken to kiss the woman's nephew, the amount of the check she intended to return to Kitty Adderly now that the whole scheme had gone dreadfully wrong. She tried to hide the note of incredulity in her voice but found it impossible.

"Very well. Two hundred pounds. But you drive a very hard bargain, Miss Wright."

This time she couldn't stifle her response. She laughed and immediately raised a hand to her mouth to quell it. If the lady hadn't been standing before her looking as serious as her grim nephew, Jess would have asked if she was joking.

"I don't know what to say."

"I very much hope you will say yes. It is a reasonable salary."

It was an unheard-of salary.

"Room and board will be provided at Marleston Hall, of course."

Lady Stamford watched her closely, and Jessamin suspected she read her troubled thoughts easily.

"It need not be an appointment forever, of course. I suspect you wish to rebuild your shop again. Such a sum after a year would set you up quite nicely, would it not?"

The regal woman in the preposterous hat truly was a mind reader. And a very effective saleswoman.

"May I have at least one day to think on it, Lady Stamford?" Jess feared the confident expression she strove for didn't quite meet her eyes. Fear overrode everything. Fear of the future. Fear that service would become her fate, and not just for a year. Fear that even if she attempted to rebuild the shop and lending library, she'd fail again.

But if Lady Stamford noticed any sign of Jessamin's reservations, she chose to ignore it.

"One day, Miss Wright. I shall expect your answer tomorrow."

Tomorrow was not precisely giving her a full day to ponder the offer, but Jess could hardly quibble with a woman who'd just proposed a salary double, even triple, what most in service expected to earn.

"Tomorrow you shall have your answer, my lady."

As she led Lady Stamford to the door and watched the two small dogs scurry after their mistress, Jess suspected the countess already knew what answer she'd give. She needed a new start, and she'd never find another post that would set up her up so well, allowing her to save for the future, whatever it might bring.

Chapter Seven

"AND SHE INSISTS on your answer today?" Alice tried a sip of coffee and reared back as if she'd been stung. They served their aromatic brew scalding hot at Sampson's, Jess's favorite coffeehouse just around the corner from her father's shop.

"I think she wanted it last night. She seems eager to return to the countryside." Jess blew across the surface of the inky liquid in her own cup before attempting a sip.

"Do you think it's anything to do with the . . . you know?" Alice lifted an eyebrow and glanced down at the scandal sheet Jess had purchased. It was the signal she'd used throughout their conversation to refer to the kiss Jess had given Lord Grimsby.

Though they'd found nothing in the broadside mentioning the incident, Jess would never forget the crush of people packing the overheated space. The kiss had been witnessed by a teeming crowd. Surely it would cause a bit of gossip. Apparently it was so scandalous even Alice couldn't bring herself to speak of it openly, despite her obvious curiosity.

"It makes it worse when you don't say the word."

"I suspect I'll find it easier to say when I've actually done it." Now it was Alice's turn to go red in the face. Since Alice usually eschewed the notion of marriage, Jess hadn't given much thought to whether her friend wished for a suitor or had ever had one.

"Well, *I'd* certainly never kissed a man before last night." Jess said the words a bit too emphatically and glanced over her shoulder to make sure the young men playing chess at a table nearby hadn't overheard.

When she turned back, Alice leaned forward, her face inches away.

"What was it like?" she whispered.

Jess took a long draw of her now pleasantly warm coffee and looked Alice squarely in the eyes.

"Astonishing." She swallowed and continued, determined to be just as honest with Alice as her friend had always been. "I was nervous and very nearly turned back. But I'd already taken Lady Katherine's money and even delivered it to Mr. Briggs at the bank. I couldn't turn back."

"Yes, but the act itself. Was it very awkward? You'd never met the man."

None of what she'd done had been proper, and parsing the details made it seem much worse. Discussing it, even with someone Jess trusted completely, had her squirming in her chair and sipping her coffee too quickly. She told herself that was why her cheeks burned as if she'd been sitting in the sun overlong.

"It was awkward at first, but then . . . it wasn't."

Alice looked awestruck, as if Jess had just imparted a newly discovered law of the universe.

"I always imagined it would be wretched at first, and one would improve with practice."

Jess frowned. "Perhaps I was wretched, but I suspect he's had a good deal of practice."

Alice choked out a laugh before falling silent, waiting for Jess to continue.

"The kiss was electrifying. I didn't expect that. And I probably shouldn't even admit it. But it's true, even if it cost me the shop. I should regret it more than I do."

Though she wasn't usually given to physical gestures of affection, Alice reached across the table and patted Jess's hand.

"What's done is done. I've always appreciated your honesty." Alice sat up straight and circled her warm mug of coffee with her hands. "But what will you do? His aunt is offering you a remarkable salary, but what will the viscount have to say about it?"

Alice's reassurance settled her nerves a bit, and Jess was grateful to broach the topic at hand. Should she accept employment with the aunt of a man with whom she'd shared that electric kiss?

"Lady Stamford promised I'd see him rarely, and she didn't seem concerned with his reaction."

"She's quite the Good Samaritan. Perhaps she'd like to contribute to the union."

Jess grinned before lifting her cup again. "I'll be sure to tell her about the union."

"You've already decided, then?"

Jess cocked her head and released a breath. She had decided. When she'd asked for Alice's advice, she'd already been halfway to accepting Lady Stamford's offer. Now she was certain, and that certainty eased her heart and mind.

"Yes, I suppose I have. It's just for a year and it will provide sufficient funds to set me on a new path."

"More than sufficient, especially with Lady Katherine Adderly's contribution."

Jess set her cup down harder than she intended, nearly upsetting it and spilling the dregs of her coffee.

"No, Alice. I have to return that money to Kitty."

Alice tipped her mouth wryly. "I don't think you do."

"I do. It would be wrong to keep it." One hundred pounds was a sufficient sum to tempt anyone, but whether Kitty truly intended the money to aid Jess's shop or buy her complicity in a harebrained scheme, every penny of it seemed tainted now.

"Because you enjoyed it?"

When Jess glared at her, Alice added, "When you . . . you know with the dandy."

As if she needed that additional bit of explanation, especially with Alice's refusal to even speak the word. As if it was the ultimate sin. As if it was wicked. And while kissing a stranger had felt a bit sinful and, if she considered it too long, yes, wicked, it had been so much more. A revelation, a rare moment of bliss.

Jess pushed her empty cup away. "Yes, maybe. I don't know. I kissed him. All right? I kissed him!" Confession was shockingly liberating, and yet the leers from the gentlemen seated at the table next to them quelled the pleasure of it.

"Do you want me to go with you to see Lady Katherine?"

"I'm not afraid of Kitty Adderly. Besides, I'm returning her money. She'll surely be pleased."

Alice looked dubious. "I hope you're right."

THE ADDERLYS' DRAWING room was as cold and miserable on her second visit as it had been on her first. More so because Jess hadn't allowed Alice to accompany her. But she couldn't involve her in this business. Kitty might have presented it as charity, but her one hundred pounds represented a good deal more now.

Reaching inside her pocket, Jess pulled out the check and smoothed it across her lap, attempting to work out all the crumples and folds it had acquired since Kitty placed it in her hands two days before.

"And who might you be?"

Jess jumped and her back stiffened at the man's imperious tone. She turned to glance at her questioner, but three heavy footsteps brought the older man into view. He was tall and elegant, handsome and beautifully attired, and he exuded an unmistakable air of authority. She'd expected Lord Grimsby to be intimidating, but he'd been encouraging compared to the man standing inches away, examining her and looking increasingly impatient for an answer.

"My name is Jessamin Wright, sir."

She shot to her feet and nearly dropped the check before clutching it ungracefully against her skirt and remembering it was men who were to stand when women entered a room, not the other way around.

"And I am Lord Clayborne. This is my home, and I am not a sir. But you couldn't have known that as we've never met." The high-handed tone faded from his voice as he spoke, and he ended with a smile so warm and seemingly genuine that Jess almost forgot his earlier bluster.

"Please retake your seat. My guess is that you're here to see one of my daughters."

"Yes, my lord, Lady Katherine."

He sat and crossed one slim leg over the other while he studied her, narrowing his eyes and reaching up to stroke his neatly trimmed beard.

"May I ask your business with my daughter?"

Jess began tapping her foot and pressed down on her knee to stop herself. What could she say? Before taking Kitty's money, they'd barely exchanged glances at the Women's Union meetings.

"We are members of the same ladies' organization, my lord."

The information seemed to shock him, though if Jess hadn't been watching closely, she might have missed the twitch at the edge of his mouth and the moment of confusion that shadowed his gaze.

"I see. And what is the purpose of this ladies' organization? Charitable ventures?"

Charity was certainly among the union's initiatives,

but they'd first come together over the cause of women's suffrage. Based on the man's surprise about Kitty's involvement in the group, Jess hesitated to mention its political aims.

"We wish to see all women given the right to vote." Speaking as she glided into the room, Kitty's voice trailed like a ribbon of sound behind her.

She perched on the edge of a chair and beamed at her father, who'd begun to go slightly pink along his neck and forehead, as if he'd taken too much pepper in his soup, or swallowed a hot coal.

Kitty held her smile until her cheeks looked tight and unnatural. Her father's color heightened, but he too tipped his mouth in a perverse semblance of a smile. Jess shifted her glance from one to other, wondering if a skirmish was about to commence in the middle of their pristine drawing room.

"I'll leave you two ladies to carry on with your visit." Lord Clayborne stood and patted his waistcoat before spearing his daughter with a final glance. "And do come and speak to me after Miss Wright departs, Katherine."

"Of course, Papa." Kitty watched the doorway for several beats after her father strode away before finally easing back into her chair and exhaling a long breath.

"Looks like I've frightened him off. Now we can breathe."

She'd had her fair share of disagreements with her father, but Jess didn't think they'd ever generated the sort of palpable tension she'd just seen flare between Kitty and Lord Clayborne.

When she met Kitty's gaze, she felt a new understanding for the young woman, and a bit of sympathy she suspected Kitty would loathe.

"Thank you for seeing me, Lady Katherine."

She shot one slim finger in the air. "Kitty, please. My father's the one obsessed with titles, not me."

"Kitty, then." Jess no longer felt animosity toward Kitty. She attempted to convey warmth in her gaze, and Kitty's mouth slid up into a tremulous almost-grin, as if she wasn't trustful of kindness. "I've come to return your check to you."

Kitty began shaking her head so emphatically the pearls around her neck clicked as they slid against the beading on her gown.

Jess pressed on to get past the most difficult part. "I've lost my shop, and I'll be leaving London."

"Lost your shop?"

Tears, little pinpricks of moisture at the corners of her eyes, welled up, and Jess sniffed them away.

"Because of . . . what happened at the gallery." She'd apparently caught a bit of Alice's timidity and couldn't bring herself to say the word, despite the fact she'd just shouted it several times in her favorite coffeehouse.

"You lost your shop because you kissed a man?"

It did sound implausible in Kitty's incredulous tone. And yet Jess felt the truth of it, the grief of it fresh and heavy, like a substance she carried with her, weighing her down.

"Well, then you can't give back the check. You'll need those funds now more than ever."

"No." Jess thrust the check toward her, willing to leave it lying in the middle of the Adderlys' beautiful Aubusson carpet if need be.

When Kitty hesitated to reach for the slip of paper, Jess leaned forward, lifting it up like an offering, flat in the palm of her hand. Other than the summer she'd caught the chicken pox, she'd never been more eager to be rid of anything in her life.

"Please, Kitty."

The plea seemed to strike a chord. Kitty's eyes softened and she finally lifted her hand to retrieve the check.

"What will you do now?"

Jess sighed, relief lightening her, before focusing on Kitty's question. There was genuine concern in her tone, but Jess was reluctant to reveal the identity of her new employer.

"I've accepted employment with a noblewoman."

"Goodness. You do rebound quickly." Kitty looked truly impressed and Jess sat a little straighter in her chair.

"I'm made of stern stuff, or so my mother used to say."

Kitty scrutinized Jess, assessing her much as Lord Clayborne had moments before.

"So it seems. Well, good luck to you. We'll miss you at the meetings."

Jess doubted Kitty would attend any more meetings than she had before their strange bargain, but she nodded and thanked her for her well wishes.

As she stood to depart, she gripped the chair's arm, momentarily dizzy. Returning the check to Kitty was the last item ticked off her list before departing for

Wiltshire and a different sort of life. The prospect of leaving London, the Women's Union, and even Kitty, whom she barely knew, seemed daunting, heart-wrenching, despite her boast about being strong.

If Kitty noticed her distress, she didn't let it show. She merely led Jess to the front door, where a maid appeared to help her into her coat.

The maid opened the door and Jess took the first step out before Kitty clasped her arm.

"Jessamin, I can trust your discretion, and Miss McGregor's, regarding Grimsby, can't I?"

Revealing her part in the scheme would be as mortifying to Jess as it might be damaging to Kitty, and that alone ensured her silence.

"Yes, of course. Who would I tell?"

Kitty's full mouth tipped as if she was satisfied with Jess's answer.

As she walked away from Clayborne House, one thought stalled in Jess's mind. Would Kitty have looked as serene if she knew Lord Grimsby's aunt would soon be her employer?

Chapter Eight

Somewhere between the platform at Paddington Station and the doors of Hartwell, Lucius finally untangled himself from thoughts of Miss Jessamin Wright and fell asleep. When the train's whistle roused him at Newbury, he couldn't recall his dreams, though his overwhelming sense of frustration indicated they'd probably involved the one woman he had to forget.

He hadn't been away long, not nearly as long as expected, but his telegram must have put Hartwell's staff in a dither. None but the estate's long-suffering butler appeared to greet him. The man bowed as low as his years would allow and followed Lucius inside. Considering the hour, Lucius knew his father would have already dined.

The great house was dark. There was no one in the main living area to require light or warmth. Many rooms were shut up and rarely used. Lucius had tired of the pretense, not to mention the expense, of running the estate as if it was a happy home. He kept to his living quarters and his father to his own. Though he missed Hartwell when he was away, there was nothing particularly welcoming about the house when you first approached, even for Lucius, who'd finally come to think of it as home over the previous two years.

A hazy, remembered image, of windows aglow with light and laughter and color infusing every room, tickled at his memory, but those days were long gone. They'd fled Hartwell when his mother died so many years ago. The relationship between his parents had been so volatile that his mother left Hartwell on any pretense she could devise—a trip to the continent, a visit to family in Yorkshire or Scotland, a jaunt down to London, even when the season was over. More often than not, Lucius had accompanied her and enjoyed their travels as any child relishes adventure. But her attempts to cool the conflict with her husband with brief separations had only fired his suspicion and fueled his jealousy.

"How is my father, Melville? Would you ask Mrs. Ives to come to my study and give me a full report in a quarter of an hour?"

"Yes, my lord."

Lucius didn't miss how Melville answered his last question and ignored his first. Open discussion of his father's condition seemed to make the staff uneasy, though some had endured his unpredictable moods for much of their working lives.

"Will you take a supper tray in the study too, my lord, or in your rooms?"

"My study, I think. Excellent idea." Lucius divested himself of hat, gloves, and coat as he spoke, and Melville dutifully built a pile of his master's outer garments in his arms.

Before the man could depart, Lucius tried again.

"How is my father?" Worry for his father mounted with each moment Lucius spent within Hartwell's walls.

Melville's pause told Lucius what he needed to know and he guessed what the old man would say next.

"He was moved to the blue room this afternoon, my lord. Just this afternoon."

What Melville avoided saying was that his father was worse and in the midst of one of his spells. The blue room was one of the rooms his father used in Hartwell's east wing. It had been emptied of most furniture, save for a couple of chairs and a bed, a few books his father loved, and thick quilts hung from the walls. It was the room his father occupied when his nurse feared he might harm himself, as he'd done on several occasions when his forgetfulness was most acute.

"Thank you, Melville."

After the butler left him, Lucius sensed his body giving in to the need for sleep. If not for the estate's accounts to review and his father to visit, he would have happily sunk into the comfort of his bed. His empty bed. Though it had been empty for months—no, for over a year—its emptiness was suddenly unappealing.

He made his way to his study and had just crossed the threshold when Mrs. Ives stopped him with her usual effusive greeting.

"My lord, how wonderful it is to have you back at Hartwell. We did not expect you quite so soon, so it is an extra pleasure."

How could anyone resist such a greeting, not to mention the smell of lemon oil and clean linen that always seemed to cling to the woman?

"Mrs. Ives, I trust you've been well and all has been as expected in my absence."

Other than the nurse Lucius had hired to care for his father, the estate's staff rarely involved themselves with his father's illness and unpredictable moods. They were content to pretend for Lucius's benefit that all was well, and he was usually content to play along.

"His Lordship has been quite well, though he took a little turn today. No rhyme or reason why. But he is tucked in bed now and ended the day quite well. Perhaps he will return to his own rooms more quickly than the last spell."

Mrs. Ives was a dutiful caretaker and always strove to return his father to his fully furnished rooms, his books, writing implements, and the specimens he'd collected from around the estate as quickly as possible. His rooms encompassed the increasingly dilapidated family wing where Lucius's mother and father had lived in happier times. His father refused to move from the space he'd shared with his wife, but Lucius was content to sleep in the renovated portion of the house usually reserved for guests. Back in the days of the country house parties his parents hosted, the many bedrooms had been filled. Now they stood empty, furnishings covered with dust cloths, except for the spacious dark-paneled suite Lucius had selected for himself.

"I hope you're right."

"The spells don't seem to last quite as long lately, my lord. Have you noticed?"

The truth was he had not. The pattern of his father's highs and lows seemed as unpredictable to Lucius as they ever had. It wasn't surprising, however, that Mrs. Ives, perennial optimist, would think so.

"Perhaps I should take closer note. They seem quite consistently inconsistent to me."

Mrs. Ives was too polite to contradict him. "Yes, my lord."

Melville scratched softly at the open doorway and then proceeded into the room to place Lucius's supper tray on his desk. Despite his fatigue, the food smelled delicious. Mrs. Ives saw him eyeing him the meal and seemed to take pity.

"I shall leave you to your supper, my lord. You must be famished and exhausted after your journey."

"Indeed. Tell my father I'll visit him in the morning."

"Yes, my lord. He'll be pleased to see you."

When his father was in the midst of his worst spells, he wasn't particularly pleased to see anyone. If he found any pleasure in visitors, he only took umbrage with them moments later. The extremes of his emotions were dizzying. Lucius couldn't imagine the misery of such riotous feelings. Observing his father's highs and lows and the travesty of his parents' marriage drove Lucius to control his own emotions. And it usually worked.

Men should be guided by logic and reason, and reason should always rule over the deceptions of the heart.

He'd read it once, but Lucius couldn't remember where. Marcus Aurelius, perhaps? Some rational, stoic man who'd never allowed himself to drown in emotion as his father had. Whoever'd written it, Lucius was only certain the man had never been kissed quite unexpectedly by a beautiful bluestocking.

JESS WOKE ON her twenty-third day at Marleston and found her surroundings familiar for the first time since arriving. Every other morning she'd woken early, expecting to be in her tiny room above the bookshop. She missed the smell of book leather and the bustling sounds of London beyond the window glass, but the music of birdsong and the scent of fresh-cut grass was an undeniably pleasant consolation.

As her first weeks at Marleston Hall flew by, Jess and Lady Stamford managed to settle into a comfortable rapport and predictable daily routine. They met in the countess's sitting room late in the morning to go over the previous day's post, plan the next day's meals, and write letters to the countess's many correspondents. Castor and Pollux had taken to joining their morning sessions, one balancing happily on the countess's lap and the other dozing at Jess's feet.

In her evening hours, Jess continued to work on speeches and articles for the Women's Union, as she'd promised Alice she would. Some days, between Lady

Stamford's extensive correspondence and the writing and rewriting of speeches, her wrist ached and her fingers went numb. At those moments, she'd find a quiet nook and read one of the handful of beloved books she'd brought with her to Marleston. Settling on just a few had been one of the hardest parts of leaving the shop behind, but they were favorites she'd never tire of reading again and again. And the familiar words never failed to soothe her.

Among the staff, she'd encountered a frustratingly mixed reception. For the most part Marleston's employees welcomed her with kindness and a willingness to impart the rules of correct behavior at a grand estate. It seemed she needed reminding about a few points of etiquette nearly every day. But she was an oddity to some, a working-class woman raised up to be a countess's companion. If *she* still questioned why Lady Stamford had given her the position, Jess could hardly blame the lady's maid, Miss Dawes, for snubbing her at every turn, or the butler, Mr. Noon, for slanting a gaze at her now and then as if she might abscond with the silver.

Her mood soared on days she managed to remember which spoon to use, how to properly address each of Lady Stamford's correspondents, and how to be more help than hindrance to the other staff. But she missed Jack and Alice and her circle of friends in the Women's Union so fiercely that the hours filled with foibles, missteps, and the chastising glance of Mr. Noon made her itch for her first month's wages so she could buy a ticket and take the next train back to London.

Tilly, Marleston's between maid, had found Jess

tucked in a library alcove on her fifth day. She'd already swiped away her tears and settled her breathing, but Tilly gently prodded her to confess the rest—her anxieties about being a lady's companion and a longing for London and the few friends she'd left behind. It helped, especially when Tilly assured her Noon distrusted everyone and Dawes found favor with few.

Tilly queried Jess about the volume of *Oliver Twist* clutched in her hands like a precious talisman, and it eased her mind to talk about books. When Tilly confessed her inability to read and asked if Jess might teach her, Jess had been eager to help. Their lessons enriched her days at Marleston, and despite continued blunders in etiquette, Jess was growing accustomed to the grand house.

The loss of the shop, the scandalous kiss in Mayfair, the man with a voice as smooth as melted chocolate all receded in her thoughts, an occasional twinge in her heart, and she busied herself with teaching Tilly and learning how to be helpful to a countess.

During her hours with Lady Stamford, the countess spoke of Lord Grimsby often, mostly recounting tales from his boyhood. She described her family as full of men, mentioning one son and two nephews. Of the three, it seemed Lord Grimsby held a special place in her heart. Her stories painted a picture of an admirable man—one with a ravenous curiosity, kind toward others despite his quiet, taciturn nature, and whose most reliable trait was a fierce loyalty to his family. He seemed quite a precise gentleman too. Lady Stamford smiled when recalling Lord

Grimsby's insistence that everything on his desk remain in exactly the same position, that chairs in the sitting room be a specific distance apart, and that the art on the walls of the dining room be hung equidistant from one another. The countess spoke of her late husband too and occasionally of her son, who'd inherited his father's earldom and was on the hunt for a suitable bride to become the next Countess of Stamford. It seemed to Jess that her employer was looking forward to becoming a dowager countess, and even more so to grandchildren.

Jess listened quietly, only interjecting questions when it seemed appropriate, and above all attempting to appear as interested in stories of Lady Stamford's son as she was in tales of her favorite nephew. It was silly to feel any kinship with the man she'd met on only two occasions and in the most awkward of circumstances, yet Jess found herself smiling more and fidgeting less when Lady Stamford described Lord Grimsby's boyhood adventures. It was difficult to reconcile the serious gentleman she'd met with the young man the countess described so lovingly.

"Anything interesting in yesterday's post, Jessamin?"

Lady Stamford spoke to her in familiar terms and had invited Jess to call her Augusta in return, but she'd yet to manage it.

"Yes, actually there is, my lady. A letter from America that smells of roses."

"Do let me see that one, my dear."

Lady Stamford held out her hand and Jess glanced at the return address before handing the sealed letter to her. The name Sedgwick was embossed on the paper, and someone with a looping, feminine style of handwriting had addressed the letter. The script was so ornate, Jess struggled to decipher the words.

Lady Stamford unfolded the letter and made a tsking noise as she skimmed the paper.

"Oh my, this will be a challenge."

"A challenge?" Jess continued to slice open each letter in the small pile on the desk, though the dismayed tone in the countess's voice set her on edge. In the short time she'd been in her employ, Jess had never known Lady Stamford to be anything but cheerful and carefree. The woman seemed to take everything as a pleasure to be enjoyed or a minor conundrum to be efficiently unraveled.

Jess lifted a cup of tea to her lips and watched as the countess began to pace the length of the intricate floral rug that decorated her sitting room. Her peach-colored gown was a similar hue to one of the half dozen she'd ordered from her dressmaker for Jess. She'd insisted a lady's companion must have a fashionable wardrobe, though her duties of fetching, writing, and reading to the countess required no such thing. Still, she couldn't deny the pleasure of sorting through fabrics, sifting the luxurious textures through her fingers, and picking colors that reminded her of flowers she'd seen at the Botanical Garden or the riotous shades of a London sunset.

"This letter is from Miss May Sedgwick. She's the daughter of an old acquaintance and one of the richest heiresses in America. I met her father in London many years ago. I've yet to meet his daughter, but she's reputedly quite lovely, and apparently very changeable. I expected her for a visit here at Marleston, but she says her heart is set on going straight to Hartwell."

Jess assumed Hartwell might be another of the countess's estates, though she had no notion why anyone would need another. Marleston was lovely and spacious, so beautifully constructed and well-appointed that she couldn't imagine anyone craving another home.

Augusta looked at her expectantly.

Jess raised her eyebrows, uncertain what to say.

"Hartwell is my brother's home."

"Ah, I see. Is it as lovely as Marleston?"

Augusta sat down in the armchair nearest Jess.

"It used to be. It could be again, though I suspect my nephew would deny the claim."

Heat warmed Jess's cheeks and she had to stop herself from nervously tapping her pen against the desk. Lady Stamford had at least two nephews. Perhaps more. Though she hadn't mentioned any others, there was no reason to assume she'd detailed her entire family tree. It was presumptuous to assume she referred to the same dour viscount Jess had been paid to kiss.

Lord Grimsby was there in her memory, too vivid and quickly brought to mind. His voice, his scent, the shape of his mouth—the more she tried not to ponder each detail, the more fixed they became in her mind's eye. Jess remembered him far too often, and the man invaded her dreams with impunity.

"We must prepare to depart for Hartwell, Jessamin. I'll speak to Dawes about what to pack, but could you oversee the preparations? And we should craft a letter to my nephew. He won't welcome a house party, but that's what he must have. We can invite Matilda and her granddaughter, perhaps Dr. Seagraves from the village, Julia and Marcus. And Lucius will no doubt wish for Mr. Wellesley."

Augusta continued to tick off names of guests, most of whom Jess had never heard her mention, to be invited and tasks to be completed before their departure. Jess stalled on one name. *Lucius.* At the gallery, a woman had called Lord Grimsby by that name.

That moment—the disdain in the woman's voice, the weight and warmth of Lord Grimsby's hand on her arm—came back as if she stood again in the overheated gallery. Jess bit her lip to stop it trembling and clasped her hands to stop them shaking. She'd never expected to see him again, and now she was to visit his home. In just a few days, she might lift her gaze and look into his eyes, stand close enough to him to see the flecks of silver in the crescent of blue. Excitement and fear tangled in a breath-stealing mass that seemed to center in her chest, and she pressed the flat of her palm against her breastbone in a futile attempt to ease the pressure.

I can't forget. His three words never left her, as if the heated breath of his whisper had seared them into her skin. Yet she'd spent hours tormenting herself with theories about his meaning. Was it a curse? An accusation? A plea?

That day in the shop, he'd come and offered her charity, yet the night before he'd accused her of accosting him.

She'd undoubtedly scandalized him. But in the gallery, he'd held on to her as if she were his lifeline, his glacial blue eyes burning her with the intensity of his gaze. The man was inscrutable, confusing, and took up altogether too much space in her head.

"Lord Grimsby." Jess wasn't certain she said his name aloud until she noticed Lady Stamford had stopped speaking and sat watching her with interest.

"Yes, my nephew is at Hartwell. Maxim and Isobel's eldest son died two years ago, and Lucius is now my brother's heir." Augusta answered the questions Jess hadn't asked.

And, always sharp-eyed, Lady Stamford noticed the trembling Jess attempted to hide. Reaching out, the countess took Jess's hands in her own. "All will be well, my dear. Please don't worry."

"Yes."

It would have to be. Lady Stamford was her employer and she insisted on going to Hartwell. Lord Grim would simply have to accept Jess's presence, though she vowed to herself she'd steer clear of him.

For the next hour they made plans, assembled lists, and addressed several invitations to those the countess wished to have at Hartwell's house party. The letter she dictated to Lord Grimsby was brief and to the point.

L.—

I will arrive at Hartwell within the week, and Miss Sedgwick will follow shortly thereafter. Prepare

Hartwell for a house party. I have invited Lady Turbridge, Marcus and Julia, Robert, and a few others.

I pray Maxim is well.

We shall be with you soon.

—A.

"We must leave tomorrow and begin preparations for Miss Sedgwick's arrival." Augusta reached out and patted Jess's arm before giving it a gentle squeeze. "I'm so grateful to have you with me. There is much to do."

Jess smiled at her employer even as her stomach churned. She could only imagine Lord Grimsby's reaction when he found the woman who'd accosted him taking up residence in his home. Would he curse her? He certainly wouldn't kiss her, though she couldn't resist imagining it. Lifting her hand, she stroked the flesh near her ear, tracing the spot where he'd pressed his mouth to her skin and whispered those three haunting words. *I can't forget.*

She shivered and anticipation rushed through her, as if he might walk into his aunt's sitting room at any moment. As if he would greet her with pleasure. As if the man had given her two minutes of consideration since walking out of her failed bookshop.

Despite his parting words, he would have forgotten her. Surely he'd forgotten. He was a viscount with an estate to run and an ailing father to care for. If he simply didn't loathe her, that would be enough. But more likely, he'd demand his aunt dismiss her on the spot, and Jess wouldn't blame him for it. After hearing of his protective nature, especially when it came to his family, she envisioned a dismissal as the probable outcome of her trip to Hartwell.

Then a thought struck her. "My lady, why is Miss Sedgwick so keen to go to Hartwell?"

The countess didn't meet her gaze, merely slid her hand across Castor's fur, as if contemplating how to respond.

When Lady Stamford looked up, her mouth was tight, mirthless, but her lips trembled as if she was attempting to force a pleasanter expression. "She intends to marry my nephew, my dear."

Chapter Nine

"MY LORD, WE'LL do all we can, but it will take weeks to prepare all of the rooms and stock the kitchen. We'll make do with the suites in the west wing. Cook wishes to know how many we can expect."

Hartwell's housekeeper, Mrs. Penry, spoke in her usual pleasant tone, yet even that sound grated on Lucius's frayed nerves. His first cup of tea had done nothing to clear the fog from his brain. Nor had his second, or the third. His eyes itched when they weren't blurring the figures before him, the joints of his arms and legs protested when he moved after too long a spell at his desk chair, and every noise set him on edge. Sleep continued to elude him, coming only in miserable fits and starts after weeks back in his own bed, and all the usual duties and minor troubles associated with running the estate seemed suddenly insurmountable. Focused thought eluded him too, unless it involved contemplation of a certain young woman's lips.

And now his aunt proposed a house party the day after Mrs. Penry reported that a part of the east wing's third-floor ceilings had begun to crack and leak. The exterior masonry and slate tile roofs, deteriorating and untended for years, had apparently decided now was as good a time as any to crumble away completely. He told himself that part of the estate, unsheltered by Hartwell Woods on the west, was more exposed to the wind and rain. But less rationally, gut deep, he wondered if the rancor between his parents, who'd slammed doors and shaken the walls with their shouting in that portion of the house for years, had somehow taken its toll. Whatever the cause, the cost of repairs, in addition to the interior updates the house required, was quickly piling up.

A lavish house party, confined to the renovated west wing and public rooms, would further diminish Hartwell's coffers, but it might help him woo the young woman Aunt Augusta thought most promising among his prospects. Miss Sedgwick was the daughter of American business mogul Seymour Sedgwick. As Augusta told it, she'd met Miss Sedgwick's father during her first season, when he'd married one of her dear friends, a viscount's daughter. Since she was the sole heiress of a millionaire and granddaughter of a viscount, Lucius wasn't surprised to find May Sedgwick at the top of his aunt's list.

"The short notice is unfortunate, but we must do what we can, Mrs. Penry. Lady Stamford is due to arrive today, and we should expect eight more guests within the week." Lucius infused his words with as much gentleness as he could manage. He was asking for a bit of a miracle and the housekeeper deserved his respect for undertaking the challenge, despite his black mood.

"I've taken on some additional staff, my lord, as you suggested. Two have arrived this morning. Do you wish to meet them? It shouldn't take but a moment."

Mrs. Penry's good humor and her ability to infuse any situation with the same enthusiasm she'd show a royal visit was enough to draw him out.

"Very well."

"They're just in the drawing room, my lord. Shall I send them to you?"

His father had visited the study in the morning and still sat dozing in a chair by the fire. It was one of his mellow days, when Maxim seemed the affable father Lucius always wished he'd been. On such days Lucius could almost forget the animosity between them and simply enjoy the older man's company. Disturbing the calm by waking him was out of the question.

"No, let us go to them. This will only take a moment, as you say."

"Yes, my lord."

As Lucius made his way through the great hall to the drawing room, he was stunned to see the progress the staff had already made. Every piece of furniture shone with polish, and even the gilded frames around portraits of long-dead Dunthorpe ancestors glinted in the morning sunlight dappling the room. The staff had opened the drapes and he glimpsed a cloudless autumn sky through the gleaming windowpanes. He insisted on order, and the staff were diligent in their care of the family rooms, but the public rooms were so rarely used, he'd grown used to seeing dust motes dancing in the gaslight and stifling a sneeze. This morning fresh-cut hothouse flowers scented the air.

"I'm impressed, Mrs. Penry." He glanced back as he spoke to his housekeeper, who followed close on his heels. The look of shock on her face lightened his mood. He'd have to remember to compliment his long-suffering staff more often.

"Thank you, my lord. Hartwell does look well with a bit of polish and light."

He heard the note of castigation in her tone but chose not to respond. Perhaps Hartwell did deserve to have a bit of the old liveliness and cheer infused back into it.

As he approached the drawing room threshold, he saw a young woman sitting on one of the settees, her back straight and stiff and her gaze focused warily on the door where he approached. Another young woman stood looking out the window onto Hartwell Woods, her back to him.

The figure of the woman at the window made him stop in his tracks, his boot heels scuffing the no doubt freshly polished floor. He heard Mrs. Penry make a little oomph sound as she came up short behind him.

The young woman's hair was a unique shade of auburn. The light from the window caught highlights of red and gold, bronze and crimson. He'd only ever seen hair that color once in his life, and now in his daydreams, when he longed to touch it, thread it through his fingers, feel it slide across his skin.

All his dulled senses stirred to life and a kind of humming awareness buzzed through his body. It was impossible. Miss Wright was back in London. He'd spent long nights considering what she might be doing. With no family, whom had she turned to after losing her shop? How many times had he paced the length of his study, denouncing the scruples that had prevented him from offering her some arrangement when he'd visited her? However many times it had been, it was always followed by a bout of self-loathing. Whatever drove Jessamin Wright to accost and kiss him, it had nothing to do with desire.

Logic told him she'd been desperate. The only desire between them had been on his part.

Yet as he stood looking at the woman at the window, reason and logic lost their potency.

She'd come all the way to Hartwell to find him. An absurd notion struck him—that Hartwell was just where she belonged.

"Miss—"

Before he could say her name, Mrs. Penry spoke at the same moment, drawing the young woman's attention. Miss Wright turned from the window to look back at him, but it wasn't Miss Wright at all. Once he examined the girl more closely, she didn't even truly have auburn hair, just brown with a hint of burnish afforded by the light from the window. He felt dizzy, disoriented. He'd been so sure it was Miss Jessamin Wright before him that he could smell her scent and had licked his lips, recalling the taste their kiss.

My God, did whatever ailed his father plague him too? Not even Maxim experienced hallucinations, just the occasional delusion that he was younger and stronger than his years would allow.

"My lord, may I present Miss Hobbs and Miss Stephens. Miss Hobbs." Mrs. Penry indicated the young woman seated before him, and she stood and bent a hasty curtsy. As the other woman strode forward, he closed his eyes for a moment, pushing away his illusion that she bore any resemblance to the bluestocking who'd kissed him in London. When he opened his eyes, a plain, brown-eyed woman stood before him. Her cheek bore none of the color of Miss Wright's, her lips didn't approach that woman's lush, full mouth, and the intelligence and spirit he'd glimpsed in Jessamin's eyes didn't spark in the gaze of Miss Stephens. He felt a ridiculous vein of loathing for the woman who fell so short of the one who featured in his fantasies and would never again enter his life.

"I am ever so pleased to be at Hartwell, my lord."

He should welcome her and the other young woman. He should do his duty as acting master of Hartwell, as the heir to his father's name and title. He should be grateful for the additional staff to help prepare the house for its upcoming visitors. But everything in him rebelled.

"No." He felt the word as much as spoke it, a ripple of anger tensing through his body and tightening his jaw, negating the reality of never seeing Jessamin Wright again while condemning his foolish desire for her. He should have stamped out thoughts of her weeks ago. *Forget the woman.* He'd never allow himself to sink into the love-sopped obsessiveness that had ruined his father's peace of mind.

He saw the new maid's mouth gape open before turning on his heel and striding out of the drawing room. He bolted back to his study, eager for the comfort of its dark wallpaper and thick drapes to keep out the world—no harsh sunlight there, no cloyingly sweet flowers, and no fantasies of a completely inappropriate woman.

His father was awake and sat at the ornate desk dominating the room, flipping pages in the estate's ledger book. He turned them with a speed that indicated he took no interest in their contents.

"Heavens, has your aunt arrived? You look as if hellhounds are nipping at your heels."

"Not yet, Father. And no hellhounds, only housemaids."

"Ah, just as persistent but a bit less ferocious, I'd wager."

"Mrs. Penry has taken on more staff for the house party."

The earl looked momentarily confused.

"Yes, tell me again about this chit you plan to marry."

Lucius hadn't told him much of anything about May Sedgwick, only that she would be among the guests visiting Hartwell in the coming weeks. And Lucius certainly felt no conviction he'd be marrying the American. But he knew his father and aunt carried on a lively correspondence and wondered if his father might know more about Miss Sedgwick than he did.

"She's American but also the granddaughter of Viscount Siddingford."

"So she's in search of a title."

"Mmm."

"Can't say I fathom much enthusiasm in your manner."

"I've yet to meet her. I shall be full of enthusiasm when I do." Surely he could manage a bit of enthusiasm for a woman who'd traveled across an ocean to make his acquaintance.

His mind wandered to places it shouldn't, to the woman who'd become so fixed in his mind he was beginning to see her everywhere.

"Is she beautiful?" His father's words barely pierced his reverie.

"Quite. And her hair is the most extraordinary shade of auburn." As he spoke his musings faded and Lucius realized his blunder. Father hadn't been referring to Miss Wright. No one knew Miss Wright's identity, except his aunt, Mrs. Ornish, and that dreadful Mrs. Briggs and her husband. The scandal sheets only speculated about the woman who'd outraged society by kissing a viscount at a public gathering.

He met his father's eyes, as blue as his own. Today his father's gaze appeared lucid and unclouded, his memory seemed sharper, and the two of them had taken tea and carried on a conversation as genial companions. But it was almost as difficult to trust the good days as to weather the bad. Lucius couldn't be certain which version of his father he might encounter. And the man he needed to face, with whom he longed to settle old scores, was lost somewhere in the jumble of emotions and demeanors his father wrestled each day.

"Whoever she is, I wonder how Miss Sedgwick will compare."

Lucius needed to clear his head, sweep his mind of its cluttered thoughts.

"I'm going to take a walk."

The estate comprised nearly two thousand acres. As he strode into the meadow, Lucius wondered how far he'd have to walk to finally put the whole London business and one reckless bluestocking from his mind for good.

Chapter Ten

THE CARRIAGE RIDE from Wiltshire to Berkshire was the most bone-rattling experience of Jess's life. Not even the uneven cobblestones of London's streets offered the kind of jarring travel the rutted lanes between England's counties afforded. Jess had secretly hoped they'd travel via train. She thought the notion of a long train journey held adventurous appeal, but Lady Stamford preferred her carriage, despite the bumps and jolts.

Amazingly, Lady Stamford and her pugs seemed oblivious to the bouncing and swaying, all three falling asleep in a compact heap—pugs on top of each other on Augusta's lap—halfway through the journey and remaining so until they stopped at an inn for luncheon. Along with her lady's maid, Rachel Dawes, Lady Stamford had brought Tilly, whom she thought might serve as her lady's maid or assist Jess in case Rachel was required to tend to another guest. Rachel and Tilly, like Jess, sat staring out the carriage windows, unable to nap along with their mistress.

"It must be a very fine house." Tilly's voice made Jess jump, despite its soft timbre.

Rachel turned her hand to some stitching and ignored Tilly.

Jess thought it impolite to ignore her, though she wasn't sure she was the one the girl had addressed.

"Yes, I think it must be."

"I hear he's very handsome." Tilly whispered the words conspiratorially, turning a quick glance toward Lady Stamford to make sure she still slumbered.

"I hear he's mad as a March hare." Rachel managed to sound both resolute and dismissive.

"Is he? What a pity." Tilly looked bereft. "Is he truly mad? Perhaps he only plays at it for fashion."

Jess couldn't imagine what might be fashionable about madness, nor could she imagine the tall, dark viscount as a madman. He'd seemed utterly rational. If anything, her impression had been of a man who kept his emotions in check. Despite the fire she'd glimpsed in his gaze, it had been fleeting, and the stoic expression on his face had never truly wavered.

"Who says he's mad?" Jess couldn't resist attempting to discern if there was any truth to the maids' gossip.

"The earl?" Rachel put down her sewing and turned her full attention to Jess. She was an intimidating woman, with her direct stare and humorless expression.

"I thought he was a viscount." Jess distinctly recalled Kitty and Lady Stamford calling him a viscount.

"Oh, you mean the son. Yes, he is right handsome. No, it's the father what's mad, but it's in the blood, isn't it? The son's bound to go mad himself one day." Rachel spoke without passion, matter-of-factly, as if she knew her beliefs to be utter truths.

Jessamin thought it all sounded a good deal like slander and suspected her employer would be livid to hear her brother and nephew dismissed in such terms, whether there was a shred of truth in the rumors or not.

"What a shame." Tilly sighed out the words as if she felt genuine sadness for her employer's family.

"It's more than a shame, girl. If the son goes mad, no rich lady will ever marry him, and they'll lose their fine estate," Rachel attempted to whisper the words, but her tone was so full of venom most of it came out more like hissing.

"Why do you dislike him so?" The question came out before she could bite her tongue, and both young women turned wide eyes on Jess.

"And why should you favor him? I'd wager you know as much about him as you do about being a lady's companion."

Lady Stamford's lady's maid didn't like her, but Jess couldn't match the woman's hostility. Rachel had been helpful to her, however begrudgingly. And her certainty that Jess knew nothing of Lord Grimsby was just as it should be. At least her involvement in the London incident hadn't become fodder for downstairs gossips. Yet.

"You're right, of course. I have a lot to learn." Jess didn't have a bit of trouble allowing Rachel her moment of satisfaction. It was true. Not a single day went by when Jess didn't discover some new rule, ritual, or standard she'd failed to adhere to.

Rachel sniffed and nodded her head, no doubt pleased to have won this round.

Tilly seemed to realize the inappropriateness of the conversation and kept silent. Rachel continued to sew, her nimble fingers moving silently over the fabric, even as she turned to look at the passing countryside. As Jess watched the woman's hands move, drowsiness drew her down into sleep, but she fought to keep her eyes open, despite the swaying carriage.

It seemed only a moment later the carriage rattled to a stop and footmen began assisting Lady Stamford to separate herself from the pugs. Augusta looked refreshed, but Tilly and Rachel blinked against the bright sun and moved slowly for a few moments before collecting cases and bags. Each woman took a leash attached to one of the pugs.

Neither of the maids spared a glance for the enormous structure before them, but Jessamin guessed they'd seen Hartwell many times before. It was even grander than Jess anticipated, dwarfing Marleston Hall in size. But it possessed none of the simple elegance of Lady Stamford's estate. Marleston Hall's façade had been designed to invite, while Hartwell's architect seemed to have conceived a house that would overwhelm all who gazed upon it.

Jess heard the story of Marleston House from her employer. It had been built within the previous century and reflected the late earl's preoccupation with Greek architecture. Hartwell, on the other hand, seemed to strain at the bonds of being called merely a house. It had an air of the ancient, with Gothic spires and a rounded tower at one end that made Jess imagine it had been a fortified castle at some point in its history. She couldn't take her eyes off it, yet the enormity of the building unsettled her. Marleston was stately but it had quickly become familiar. Jess didn't think she'd ever feel at ease in a place like Hartwell.

Placing her hands on her lower back, she arched, trying to stretch out the stiffness. Her legs felt as heavy as lead, and she wanted nothing more than to walk. In London, walking had been a necessary part of life, her main mode of transport. At Marleston, Lady Stamford kept her near and there was only the occasional opportunity for a stroll around the grounds. She'd begun making Castor and Pollux her excuse to walk out nearly every day, but the two dogs were more used to reclining on their mistress's lap and disdained going far.

As she had a knack for doing, Lady Stamford divined her thoughts.

"Why not take a little wander, my dear? The grounds at Hartwell are lovely, and I can see long carriage rides do not agree with you."

Jess knew she should accompany the countess inside to help her settle into her rooms and then find her own. But the offer to take a walk and have a moment to herself was too tantalizing to refuse.

"Thank you, my lady. I won't be long and I'll come to your rooms directly."

The countess was already ascending the wide stairs toward the doors of Hartwell, though Jess saw no one other than servants ushering her in. The idea of climbing those stairs herself and being confronted by Lord Grimsby made her shudder. Would he would think her a madwoman—accosting him in public and now breaching the walls of his fortress-like home—or just an infatuated girl who'd finagled employment with his aunt in order to see him again? Both notions made her queasy with doubt about her decision to become Lady Stamford's companion.

As she walked, Jess turned her mind to the moment she'd first glimpsed him. So tall and proud, yet completely uneasy. He'd been wearing a frown, his brows knitted and full mouth pulled tight, and he'd tugged at his neck cloth just before she approached. He tugged at it the same way Jess sometimes pulled at the collar of the high-necked day dresses Lady Stamford had ordered for her. Fine clothes were as confining as the many rules aristocrats seemed to impose on every little action, every impulse.

But as Jess had drawn near to Lord Grimsby, there'd been a spark of something more in his ice blue eyes. She still couldn't identify it. Curiosity? Interest? Horror? And then certainly when she'd kissed him, when he'd grasped her waist and pulled her closer—that hadn't been horror. That had been pleasure. She hadn't experienced much of it in her life, so it had made a lasting impression. She'd never forget the moment when the kiss had turned from an embarrassing, perfunctory act into an experience of heat and sensation she ached to sink into, to lose herself in—to forget about money and Kitty and her father's blasted bookshop. In that instant she'd needed something more than money. She needed to be desired. For that moment, she needed to be precisely where she was, there in that gallery kissing Lord Grimsby.

The path under her feet began to change as she walked, the grass becoming denser and unkempt as stones appeared now and then. Jessamin slowed her pace, then stopped and looked back. The ground had descended, taking her down a long sloping hill, and she could barely glimpse the spires of Hartwell in the distance. Turning away from the house, she spied a copse of trees and began to walk toward them. Then a movement caught her eye and made her stop again.

He was there. Lord Grimsby. Striding back and forth so quickly he must have carved a bald patch in the grass under his feet. He gesticulated as he paced. Nothing wild, just the lift of an arm here and the movement of his hands there. His mouth—that lovely, familiar mouth—moved, but Jess couldn't hear his voice. Was the man talking to himself?

It was impossible not to notice how well he looked with disheveled hair and dressed more casually than on the two previous occasions she'd seen him. A honey-colored waistcoat hugged his chest, but he wore no jacket or tie. His black trousers molded to his legs as he marked off a small distance and then turned to travel it again and again.

That fizz of anticipation she'd felt back in his aunt's sitting room welled up. The prospect of seeing him was nothing to this, to standing a few paces away from him, close enough to see the shape of his mouth as he mumbled to himself. Close enough to be grateful for his unfastened top button that allowed her a peek of the line of his neck and the hollow at the base of his throat.

It was too close. So near he might turn and see the woman who'd shocked him and everyone else with her brazen behavior. The woman who was now supposed to be assisting his aunt in preparing for the arrival of the heiress he planned to marry.

She should turn away, move as quietly and as quickly as she could back to the estate and Lady Stamford's room. It was only prudent to allow the man's aunt to be there when they met again. Augusta could explain Jess's employment, her role as companion, and the likelihood she wouldn't remain in her position for long. That might reassure him.

Yet he was just there. So close. In the gallery, she'd pushed through a throng to stand before him. Now there was nothing between them but fresh air, nothing surrounding them but grass and trees as far as the eye could see. Once they were back inside Hartwell, all the rules she was so dreadful at following would dictate every word, regiment every glance.

Some wild impulse in her couldn't resist making a noise. Clearing her throat loudly enough to attract his attention, she took a step toward him. It was as if a force pushed her in his direction, one her body insisted on obeying no matter how much the sensible voice in her head urged retreat.

His head snapped up and he stared at her. Turning

his body, he moved into a solid stance, hands on hips, seeming to brace himself as if she might hurtle toward him and knock him over. He looked down at the ground between his feet and then up at her again.

"Are you flesh and blood?"

His husky whisper carried on the breeze, but Jess wasn't certain she'd heard him properly. She stepped closer, close enough to see the blue of his eyes. His gaze traced her face, paused at her lips, and then skimmed down her body, and Jess would have sworn heat warmed her skin along the trail his eyes had taken. She found herself ridiculously grateful to be garbed in one of the fashionable dresses Lady Stamford had purchased rather than the outdated clothes that had served her well as a failed London bookseller.

"Pardon?" She wanted to hear his voice again. She'd never heard a low rumble quite like his before, and she'd yet to hear it nearly enough.

"The apparition speaks." He closed the distance between them in three determined strides.

Jess noted flowers embroidered on his waistcoat in the thinnest golden thread, a shade that perfectly matched the color of the fabric. She found his fine clothes much easier to study than meeting his searching gaze, which teased at her like the insistent flutter of butterfly's wings.

"I'm no apparition." Her voice was soft, shaky, belying the words coming out of her mouth.

He slipped a finger under her chin.

"You shouldn't touch me." The man really did have an awful habit of touching her quite freely.

Applying the slightest pressure, he nudged her head up to meet his gaze.

"And you shouldn't be here. How did you come to be walking the grounds of Hartwell, Miss Wright?"

Jess didn't see the condemnation she'd expected in his eyes, though some emotion had turned them a shade darker, and the grim line of his mouth and clenched jaw implied anger. Much like the night at the gallery, his eyes and expression telegraphed conflicting emotions. Was there so much dissension in his heart?

Good grief, what does the state of his heart matter?

Unraveling the puzzle of Viscount Grimsby would be Miss Sedgwick's task, not hers. And he was right. Jess knew she shouldn't be here, with his skin pressed against hers, his mouth inches from her own.

Guilt rushed in, and she lifted her chin away from his touch and turned. Tugging the full skirt of her dress up a fraction to make walking easier, she began striding away. Then she stopped, closed her eyes, and drew in a deep breath. She owed him an explanation, but accepting employment from his aunt—*his* aunt—now seemed ridiculous when considered from his perspective. It smacked of a woman far too eager to remain near him, connected to him by any means possible.

When she looked back, he'd returned to his wide-legged, hands-on-hips stance, his golden waistcoat straining its buttons as it stretched across his broad chest. A breeze kicked up and riffled the black waves of his too-long hair.

Jess had never seen a more appealing man in her life.

"I came to Hartwell in your aunt's carriage. She should explain why I'm here." She called to him more loudly than necessary, considering the distance between them, in a strident voice she'd never used in her life. She lowered her tone before continuing. "I am sorry for intruding on your . . ." What did one call it when a man stood pacing and gesticulating to himself in the open air? "On your walk, my lord."

"Wait, Miss Wright. If you please."

She'd turned back toward Hartwell, determined to stride away as fast as her legs would transport her. But his voice held just the right note of aristocratic haughtiness to make her stiffen and snap her gaze back to him. She was half tempted to tell him he had no right to command her. Yet here, on the grounds of his estate, it seemed a foolish argument.

"You have a most irritating habit of ignoring my questions and running away to avoid answers."

He spoke as if they shared a long acquaintance, as if he made a habit of questioning her and she a habit of avoiding him. The notion of familiarity between them was so silly, it nearly made her laugh. But he looked too serious for laughter.

The only reply on the tip of her tongue had nothing to do with his accusation, but she couldn't hold back from expressing it.

"My father used to do that."

His eyebrows dipped down in a dark vee, just as they had the moment before she'd kissed him. The memory sparked a hum, a vibration of energy in her body, warming her, making her tremble. She prayed Lord Grimsby didn't notice the effect he had on her.

"I beg your pardon."

He wasn't begging at all, and his emotions were no longer difficult to discern. He was irritated. Crossing his arms and tilting his head back a fraction, he put that chiseled aristocratic chin of his on full display. One dark brow jumped up in a gesture that seemed to signal disdain and displeasure all at once.

It made the laughter Jess had stifled moments before bubble up and burst out in a choked sound, resulting in a smile she couldn't contain.

"He talked to himself and paced about flapping his arms while he did it."

Lord Grimsby opened his mouth as if to protest, perhaps to deny her comparison. It was rather daring of her to compare a noble lord to her poor, unlucky bookseller father.

But the memory of her father and the quirk the two men shared inspired a measure of mirth she hadn't allowed herself in such a long time.

"It was a rather charming habit, really."

She turned then and left him, never looking back to see if he was gazing at her in that haughty manner of his as she retreated or if he'd returned to flapping his arms, talking to himself, and pacing. Whatever his reaction, Jessamin suspected their awkward encounter would mean the end of her employment with his aunt. And perhaps that was for the best. As he'd said, she didn't belong here, in his home or his world.

She stumbled on a stone hidden in the deep grass and kicked at it with the toe of her boot. The notion of parting ways with Lady Stamford brought a wave of sadness that made Jess's throat tight and tears gather at the corners of her eyes. The lady had been kind to her, offering an opportunity when she'd needed it most. Lady Stamford had never even asked her to explain the events in Mayfair, and despite Jess's inadequacies as a companion, the countess praised and encouraged her each and every day.

As the tower and gables of Hartwell came into view, another anxiety weighed on her mind. What if Lady Stamford refused to dismiss her? This might be the first of many awkward encounters with Lord Grim during the fortnight house party.

She'd need a new strategy for avoiding him. One that didn't involve giving in to the urge to approach him, no matter the pull, like a magnet drawing metal, that seemed to rise up whenever he was near.

Surely she could survive two weeks near him for a wage that would secure her future.

Chapter Eleven

LUCIUS STOMPED UP the wide staircase leading to the doors of Hartwell, swung the left door abruptly enough to make a housemaid jump like a frightened cat, and nearly slid on the damnably well-polished marble floor before reaching the haven of his study.

But he didn't find solitude beyond its door. One glance at the scene before him and his frustration whooshed out in a deep sigh. His aunt stood embracing his father, a tear trickling down her cheek. Though it was tempting to think of his father as his worry alone—heaven forgive him, his burden—Augusta's presence reaffirmed that his father was more. He was a brother, a man his aunt looked up to since childhood, the eldest son, and the man who bore the titles and owned the estates that had been in their family for generations.

His aunt must have sensed his presence. She turned to

him and hastily lifted a handkerchief to her cheek before releasing his father.

Maxim settled back in his chair by the fire, and Lucius noticed the old man was a bit glassy-eyed too. Though it hadn't been long since the siblings had seen each other, Lucius knew his father's illness caused Augusta to worry unceasingly about him.

Augusta approached and embraced Lucius, kissing each cheek before looking up at him expectantly.

"Is all ready for our visitor?"

"Only one? I thought you had a list. A list I'd like to have a glance at, by the way. And, yes, everything should be ready in time for Miss Sedgwick's arrival. Have you not seen the staff scurrying about every which way?"

She smiled, a bright, charming expression usually reserved for persuasion. She was clearly pleased, and Lucius surged with pride for Hartwell and the diligence of its staff. He allowed himself a momentary quirk of his mouth, but his expression fell as he recalled the matter between them.

"Speaking of guests, I wonder if we might speak of the companion you acquired since we were last in London."

Lucius leaned toward her as he spoke, lowering his voice so his father didn't hear.

Augusta turned to glance at Maxim, but he sat gazing at the low, flickering flames beyond the grate.

She whispered her reply. "Mightn't we save this conversation for later? Let's take tea first. Both of you can come up to my sitting room." She turned to Lucius's father again. "Would you care to join us for tea, Maxim?"

Just as his father opened his mouth to answer, Mrs. Ives appeared in the doorway of the study.

"Sorry to intrude, my lord. I came to fetch Lord Dunthorpe."

Lucius glanced at the clock on the mantel and noted the time of his father's daily nap. Schedules and regularity seemed to ease his condition, while exceptions and change kindled the chaos in his mind. Lucius knew Mrs. Ives was making an effort at discretion by not mentioning her reason for collecting his father.

Lady Stamford looked crestfallen, but Lucius watched as his father dutifully rose from his chair and shuffled toward the door, patting his sister on the arm as he passed. He grinned at Mrs. Ives as he approached her, apparently quite content to stick to his schedule and take his daily respite.

"Ah!"

Lucius and Augusta turned their gazes toward the door, surprised by Maxim's outburst.

His father pointed a finger toward his sister. "Your companion."

"Yes? My companion. What of her?"

Augusta shot Lucius a chastising glance. Clearly his whispers hadn't escaped Father's keen hearing.

Maxim's eyes lit with amusement as if terribly pleased with himself. "I'll wager she has auburn hair," he said as he followed Mrs. Ives out the door.

"What the devil was that about?" Augusta watched her brother exit with a smile on her face.

"The man is far more cunning than any of us suspect."

Augusta let loose a laugh, full-bodied and throaty, the kind she used only among friends and family.

"I've always known his crafty ways. You have no notion how he tormented me as child." She looked wistful for a moment and Lucius found it difficult to be truly angry with her.

But he had to address the matter of Miss Wright.

"How could you bring her here? She shouldn't be here."

Never mind that he'd stared at the back of the new housemaid not an hour ago, convincing himself it was Jessamin Wright, and letting the opposite notion tease at his mind.

Augusta frowned at him a moment as if unsure of whom he spoke, but then she stood up a bit straighter and met his gaze squarely.

"Miss Wright is my companion, my employee, not my captive. I assure you she came very much of her own volition."

Lucius indicated the two chairs arranged before the fire, and Augusta swept toward the one his father had vacated. When they were both settled, Lucius arranged his elbows on the chair's arms and steepled his fingertips under his chin.

"Do you think it appropriate?" Even Aunt Augusta couldn't think it appropriate for the woman who'd kissed him so publicly to reside at Hartwell during a house party designed to introduce him to a potential bride. Distraction didn't suffice to describe how unsettling Miss Wright's presence would be. Hell, she already was.

He picked at invisible fluff on the arm of his jacket, swiping down the fabric before grasping the buttons at his cuff and settling them so that the etched design on each aligned.

His aunt sighed wearily, as if his concern with propriety was a very great bore.

Of course, Augusta did not know, could not know, that Miss Wright had hardly left his mind since she'd marched up to him at the gallery in Mayfair.

"Propriety is more flexible than you might imagine. It often bends to practicality. The girl needed employment. I needed a companion. She's helped me immensely in the last few weeks. I'm not certain I could do without her now."

Now it was Lucius's turn to sigh. His aunt seemed determined to mistake his meaning.

"I am not referring to the woman's suitability as your companion, though many would question it. I am referring to—"

"You kissed her." His aunt interrupted him in a tone implying he could say nothing that she hadn't already considered and dismissed, and she wished to put the whole subject to rest.

"I did not kiss her!"

It wasn't true and his lips burned, accusing him of the lie. Other parts of his body ached too, and he stood up, trying to ease the tension, the frustration thoughts of Miss Wright always inspired.

He turned toward the mantel and arranged the items on the deep marble shelf—framed photographs, porcelain dogs, a beautifully sculpted crystal rose his mother had purchased in France. He spaced the items evenly, turned the photographs just so, and placed the dogs near each other, both facing toward the window on the west wall. Whoever tended the room apparently had little concern for replacing the items with care after dusting.

He sensed the weight of his aunt's gaze and turned to find her watching him with a knowing expression curving her lips. He bristled under the examination.

"My goodness, Lucius. Do you fear the girl? Has she truly affected you so?"

Lucius couldn't answer, could barely consider the question. He turned away, refusing to let his aunt read his thoughts, as she was far too talented at doing.

"Jessamin is an honorable young woman. I'd wager she'd never even kissed a man before. Her skill can't have been so great as to scramble your wits."

It was too much. Hearing her name spoken with such warm familiarity by his aunt—to hear her name at all. And discussing kissing, that kiss in particular, with the woman he held in as high esteem as his own mother. It was all too much, and Lucius wanted nothing more than to head out for another walk, a longer one this time, up hills and over ravines, until he'd exhausted body and mind and couldn't manage a single thought about women or dowries or Miss Wright's auburn hair. But he heard himself speaking, felt the words reverberating in his chest, playing across his tongue—the truth, unvarnished and irrepressible.

"It was an unpracticed kiss. Completely unexpected. It was . . . singular."

He expected his aunt to retort, but she said nothing. Lucius turned to find her staring at him, mouth agape, as if he'd just made an astounding admission.

"What is it?" He was afraid to ask, uncertain he'd like her answer.

Augusta merely shook her head as if to clear her thoughts.

"I've no doubt there have been half a dozen scandals in London since the incident in Mayfair. Infamy is a fickle mistress, my boy. She'll soon tire of you. There are precious few who know that my Miss Wright is the young woman from the gallery, and I am confident of their discretion. And most especially of hers."

His aunt could fight her corner unlike anyone he'd ever known, and her lack of concern about the propriety of the situation reassured him. A bit. But it did nothing to quell the disturbingly satisfying sense of knowing Miss Wright would be at Hartwell for two weeks. He should not be pleased. He closed his eyes a moment and tried to rouse a sense of horror, a measure of indignation. But in his mind's eye, a vision of Miss Wright blotted out all else. He saw her as she'd looked in the meadow, cheeks flushed, green eyes turned to jade in the sunlight, strands of her fiery hair fluttering in the breeze.

"Miss Sedgwick arrives soon. She may be here within three days."

Miss Sedgwick. Lucius's mind was so clouded with thoughts of Jessamin Wright it took a moment to remember who Miss Sedgwick was—who she was and who she might one day become.

"You don't have to marry her. I sense she wished for a trip to England as much as a marriage proposal. Perhaps you will not suit each other." His aunt spoke the words so quietly he could almost imagine it wasn't her voice but his own conscience whispering words he wished to hear.

It was nonsense. Marrying Miss Sedgwick was a practical solution. She was wellborn, well educated, and almost unimaginably wealthy. Her wealth would secure Hartwell's future. With her dowry, there would be no more leaky roofs or crumbling masonry. And the funds would not merely repair Hartwell, they would provide for repairs on the tenant housing, and maintenance of the lands and outbuildings that had been neglected for years.

He would marry her. It was his duty, and producing an heir and restoring the estate would ease Father's mind. Miss Sedgwick's father was a self-made New Yorker but he'd married a viscount's daughter, and May's parents had ensured their daughter received a thoroughly classical education, including travel in Europe and time spent at a ladies' seminary. She was an ideal match. Best of all, Miss Sedgwick reputedly loathed the countryside and wished for nothing more than a title and a London town house.

Lucius counted on her predilection and imagined them spending much of their time apart, she in London and he at Hartwell, preventing her from observing any of his father's more extreme behaviors. In marrying her, he hoped to do his duty and protect his father at the same time.

For the satisfaction of doing his duty and succeeding in the role that had been thrust upon him, surely he could steer clear of Jessamin Wright for a fortnight.

"She seems a perfect choice for a countess."

Perhaps it was some hitch in his tone, a note of insincerity. A lack of enthusiasm, as his father had so astutely observed. His aunt stood and approached him, then laid a hand on his arm. When he looked at her, he read pity in her light blue eyes.

Lord, how he loathed pity. *Don't pity me.* Miss Wright's words that night in the carriage came back to him. On that point, she had the right of it.

"Lucius . . ." Whatever she wished to say was apparently unspeakable. His aunt paused and he waited, but she said nothing more.

"My options are few. We can no longer put off repairs, and even if the income from the estate could bear the cost, there is still the matter of maintaining Hartwell. I've initiated some promising investments, but Father refuses to consider our best option."

She shook her head, and Lucius couldn't divine whether it was a gesture of sympathy or the same disagreement his father had expressed.

"Our father would never consider selling off Dunthorpe lands either."

Tradition, choosing a path because it was the one that had already been worn, was the worst sort of argument and one that didn't persuade Lucius at all. Perhaps he'd worked too long in his uncle's London office, where he'd been encouraged to trust his gut as often as his business acumen to take risks when making investments.

Here at Hartwell, he was essentially his father's steward, and that meant respecting the earl's wishes regarding the estate, even if the man's commitment to tradition seemed outmoded.

Marrying Mother, with her generous Buchanan dowry, had allowed his father to bolster the estate's coffers. Was it any wonder the same was expected of him?

"You've chosen well, Aunt Augusta, as I knew you would. And what else shall I do? What other choice do I have? Miss Wright, perhaps?"

It was the most outrageous remark he'd made in years. It opposed all of his father's expectations, every matchmaking effort on his aunt's part, and every goal he had for Hartwell. But he savored his subversive moment and the sound of her name on his tongue.

His aunt didn't reply in words, but a series of emotions swept over her face—confusion, surprise, pure bewilderment. She hadn't meant he should consider Miss Wright at all.

Then her eyebrows shot skyward as she emitted a squeak.

"Jessamin!"

The woman herself stood just inside the room.

JESS HAD NO notion what Lord Grimsby might be considering her for, but the look of guilt on his face—a sort of panicked grimace as if she'd caught him with his hand in the biscuit tin—made her suspect it couldn't be for any fine purpose.

As Lady Stamford had addressed her, or rather shrieked at her, Jess tried to ignore Lord Grimsby altogether and direct her attention at her employer.

This might be the moment of her dismissal, and she steeled herself to accept it.

"My lady, you asked me to request tea service in your sitting room." Odd how her own voice sounded strange to her ears when spoken under the viscount's scrutiny. It shook and teetered a bit. Very disconcertingly, in fact. She swallowed down the lump in her throat and tried again. "And you wished for me to bring you the guest list for the house party, but I couldn't find it in your rooms."

Lady Stamford seemed to compose herself. "Yes, my dear. Thank you. Actually, there is a new list. I've added one more guest to equal out our numbers. Lucius wished to see it." She reached inside a pocket of her skirts and produced a folded piece of paper, handing it to Jessamin and nodding her head toward Lord Grimsby.

Jess took the paper, but the simple act of passing him the sheet seemed daunting. She stepped toward him, and an echo of the same trepidation she'd experienced in the gallery caused her hand to shake.

Lord Grimsby didn't seem to share her discomfort. He reached out to retrieve the sheet with only the merest glance in her direction, oblivious to the tremor in her hands or any other part of her body.

An awkward moment of silence passed, and Jess became aware of her breath, too rapid and ragged for her short walk down the stairs.

The paper crackled as he smoothed it with his fingers, and she studied the breadth of his hands, the play of sinews as he moved them, before forcing her gaze away. He'd touched her with those hands every time they'd met. Until now. Now, inside the walls of Hartwell, inside the bounds of rules and propriety, he would never touch her again.

That is as it should be. They should never have touched each other at all. She bit her lip and repeated the words in her mind, and again, until she suppressed the urge to look at him.

She forced herself to examine the room. The study was a masculine haven of dark wood, heavy drapes, and a desk larger than the bed she'd slept in over the shop. She darted her gaze from his brass desk implements to the details in the crimson wallpaper above the wainscoting, but as silent seconds passed she heard the quickened inhale and exhale of his breath, noticed the moment he lifted a hand to his mouth while examining the paper she'd handed him.

She focused on the ticking of a clock and examined

the beautifully crafted device on the fireplace mantel. Fixing her gaze on the slowly moving hands, she watched the second hand slide across the clock face, any distraction to keep from looking in the viscount's direction.

"Equal numbers for dining, and dancing, if we wish it."

Lord Grimsby didn't respond to his aunt's words and continued to skim the paper in his hand.

"There's one name I don't recognize."

"Oh?"

None of the names on the list had been familiar to Jess, except for Miss Sedgwick's. She wasn't even aware it was a social faux pas to invite an uneven number of guests to a house party and had no notion whom Lady Stamford might have added.

After another moment, Lord Grimsby's deep rumble sounded. "Who is Lady Katherine Adderly?"

The room went hazy and Jess felt heat rush into her cheeks, flames crawling across her ears, and a trickle of moisture at the nape of her neck. Praying neither of them noticed how her legs trembled, she made her way to the chair next to Lady Stamford and sat.

"The Marchioness of Clayborne has been a friend for years. I met her during my first season. Kitty is her eldest daughter. A lovely young woman, though perhaps a bit too fond of frivolity. You met her at the Worthington ball."

"Did I?"

You refused to dance with her. You snubbed her. The words were just there, ready to burst out, along with her confession about taking money to carry out Kitty's scheme. The prospect of releasing it, of finally explaining her behavior, held tantalizing appeal. The secret had been a burden, pressing down on her, like the stack of books Mother used to place on her head to instruct her in proper posture. She'd never been any good at balancing those books, and she was dreadful at keeping secrets. As an only child and veritable spinster, she'd had few to keep.

It would ease her mind to tell it. But what would they think of her? She'd taken money to kiss a man she had no right to touch, with whom she hadn't even cause for a passing acquaintance, considering their difference in wealth and status. The names for a woman who accepted payment for kissing a man played through Jess's mind. Such a woman certainly had no right to serve as paid companion to a dowager countess. Such a woman deserved to be turned out without tuppence, without even the funds for a train ticket back to London.

And what would she do in London? Who would employ her if the whole ugly truth were revealed? Even with Lady Stamford's generous salary, one month's wages wouldn't sustain her long.

She couldn't bring herself to tell them—to tell him.

Jess sensed Lord Grimsby watching her. Looking toward him, she found his searching inspection held a flicker of what she'd glimpsed the night she kissed him, a heat that warmed and soothed her. She felt for a moment as she had in the gallery, as if all else faded away and his gaze meeting hers was sacrosanct, a private moment, even if others watched.

Jess broke the spell and turned away, focusing on the benign face of the mantel clock.

Would he look at her the same way if Kitty Adderly divulged the part Jess played in her plan to humiliate him? Though Kitty's plot reflected as poorly on the young woman herself as it did on Jess, it didn't excuse her actions.

What had Kitty called her? A freethinking woman? The kiss had been her act, her choice, and these were her consequences. And she would take them, come what may. She had to. If she didn't claim the folly of her actions, she wouldn't own any of the power of that kiss. And whatever kissing Lord Grimsby had cost her, it had given her something too—her own moment of passion, of being desired, the sort of desire she'd only read about in books. She'd never imagined a bit of it for herself, and now that she did possess it, and very little else, she was determined to keep it. Brazen woman, trollop, failed bookseller, unfit lady's companion, whatever they called her in the end, whatever it had cost her, she would cherish that one sliver of passion. At six and twenty, she was keenly aware it might be her life's portion.

"Jessamin?"

Lady Stamford's voice made her jump, and Jess bowed her head, clenching her hands in the fabric of her skirt forcefully enough to tear it. Holding her breath, heart hammering, she waited for her dismissal from service, and lifted her head to stare at Lord Grimsby's back. He seemed a pillar of calm, a soothing contrast to her tangled emotions. He'd turned his attention to the mantel, not to the clock she'd been watching, but to rearranging the knickknacks and framed photographs lining the space.

"Yes, my lady?"

"In other circumstances I would introduce you to my nephew, but I am well aware you have already met in a most . . . singular fashion."

Lord Grimsby turned the moment Jess stifled a gasp.

"Aunt Augusta . . ." Jess detected a thread of the same discomfort in the viscount's deep voice that she felt at his aunt's reference to the moment in Mayfair.

Lady Stamford lifted a hand, her ivory handkerchief fluttering in her fingers, as if to forestall whatever objection he might have.

"Now I do not wish to make a feast of it, but do hear me out. I trust we'll make this house party a success. That shall be our focus, and we'll leave the rest behind us. Agreed?"

Though she spoke the words loudly enough both of them could hear, she directed her gaze at Lord Grimsby throughout.

He pressed his mouth into a grim line before offering her a curt nod of agreement.

Jess wasn't certain if her agreement, or even her presence, was necessary, but when she opened her mouth to acknowledge Lady Stamford's terms, the countess spoke again.

"Wonderful. Oh, isn't it a relief to have a matter settled?"

Chapter Twelve

JESS TWISTED HER hair into a loose chignon, pinned it, and then slid her hands over the velvet panels of her emerald green gown, one of three evening dresses Lady Stamford had commissioned for her. The velvet, cool against her fingertips, soothed her nerves.

Lady Stamford hadn't dismissed her, but Lord Grimsby had stalked off, somber as ever, immediately after the odd agreement between the three of them in his study. She'd made a partial confession to Lady Stamford after his departure, acknowledging the money she'd taken and returned. But when she'd mentioned that a scorned young woman had put her up to kissing the viscount, Lady Stamford appeared more amused than shocked. The moment had reassured Jess regarding her employment with the countess, but it had done nothing to stem the dread of encountering Kitty Adderly at the house party. Her employer seemed oddly disinterested in

Jess's motives for taking money to kiss her nephew, and Lord Grimsby hadn't pressed her on the matter, but the notion he'd learn she had done it for money and as part of a plan to embarrass him churned in her mind.

And the anxiety multiplied at the prospect of taking her first meal at Hartwell with Lord Grimsby. At Marleston, Lady Stamford had occasionally allowed Jess to dine alone in her room, especially if they weren't hosting visitors, but the countess had insisted she attend the first evening meal at Hartwell and dress formally for the occasion. Jess considered it an oddity of nobility to make such a fuss over meals, but she could hardly refuse Lady Stamford.

As she took one last glance at herself in the looking glass, surprised as she always was to find what a difference a bit of effort made, a knock sounded at the door.

Tilly stuck her head around the door frame. "My lady sent me to assist you with dressing," she said as she entered and closed the door behind her.

The maid stopped and placed a hand on each hip. "I see you've gone and done it on your own." The girl's tone was chastising, but then a satisfied gleam lit her face. "Ah, but you haven't finished your hair. I can at least do that for you, miss."

Jess crossed her eyes to focus on the strand of hair snaking down her forehead, already escaped from her inexpertly pinned arrangement. Perhaps she could use Tilly's help after all.

"Thank you, Tilly. I'd be most grateful."

"Sit yourself there, miss. Where's your brush and pins?"

Jessamin showed her the collection of hairpins and the girl set to work. Tilly tugged and twisted and pinned with a speed and skill that caused Jess to wince only once. Whatever the result of Tilly's efforts, it would be far more elaborate than anything she'd ever attempted on her own.

The maid didn't speak while she worked and Jess was grateful. Her nervousness ratcheted up with every passing moment. She imagined the awkward dinner table conversation and vowed to remain as mum as possible throughout the ordeal. What did she have to say to a viscount, and to that inscrutable one in particular? What topic might she broach with any of them? Perhaps if she drew no attention to herself and refrained from conversing any more than necessary, the whole thing would pass by quickly.

She wasn't certain when Kitty would arrive at the house party, but Lady Stamford had indicated they would have a smaller group for this first dinner.

"Not bad if I do say so meself. Not bad at all." Tilly turned the looking glass toward Jessamin. "You do have the prettiest hair, Miss Wright."

"Th-thank you." Tongue-tied with shock, Jess examined herself in the mirror. She looked . . . elegant. Tilly had wrapped certain strands of her hair into curls and woven them to create an elaborate style while allowing a few wavy locks to fall down over her left shoulder.

She'd never had cause to look elegant in her life, and there had been a freedom in it. There'd been no need to fuss over ladies' magazines or keep up with the latest style of gown. Fiction had always interested Jess far more than fashion. But now, it was gratifying to find that she could pull it off, that with expertly arranged hair, a fine dress made to fit, Father's green eyes and Mother's high cheekbones and strong chin, she might just pass as pretty.

It was a bit like acquiring a new skill, and she wasn't certain how to practice. Like the time she'd set herself to learning French, only to find she'd never have reason to use a word of it. But even if no one else noticed, and she had no idea how to wield her modest share of feminine beauty, she was grateful to know she could achieve it at all.

"You're so talented, Tilly. Thank you."

The maid looked abashed. "Nonsense, miss. Downstairs with you now, or you'll be the last in the dining room."

That thought was enough to make Jess scurry toward the hall as quickly as she could with petticoats and the heavy skirt of her gown threatening to trip her. Following on the heels of a footman carrying a steaming of tray of foodstuffs, Jess found the dining room, only to discover there'd been no need for haste. The chairs were empty and the footman looked at her as if she might be lost.

"I believe His Lordship is in the drawing room with Lady Stamford and his guests. Through that door and down the hall, miss."

"Thank you," Jess said, already heading for the door.

The hallway toward the drawing room led back to Hartwell's grand front doors. Some rooms along the hall had doors that stood open and she looked in on one, just next to Lord Grimsby's study, that appeared to be an impressive library. Bookshelves reaching to the ceiling held volumes of books all neatly arranged, the gilt on their spines forming perfect lines across each shelf. Jess longed to explore the room, to find out what titles the Dunthorpes had collected, and pressed a hand against her chest to stifle a pang of longing for the little bookshop in London. Would anyone notice if she disappeared for a few hours in the library rather than take her place at the dinner table?

She forced her feet to keep moving and drew near the drawing room. In Hartwell's entryway, Jess saw a collection of trunks, portmanteaus, and hatboxes. A flurry of maids and footmen were attacking the collection piece by piece.

"Have any guests arrived?"

A harried maid glanced at Jess, swiping stray hairs back under her mobcap.

"Aye, miss, His Lordship's sister and her husband."

Upon hearing the girl's answer, Jess released the breath she hadn't realized she'd been holding. No Kitty Adderly. At least not yet.

"Thank you." Jess nodded her thanks and continued on toward the drawing room.

She heard voices and laughter carrying through the half-open door. Lord Grimsby's tone roared out above them all.

"Give the chin wags a week. Then it will all be forgotten."

Jess cringed, fearing the discussion had already turned to her encounter with Lord Grimsby. No, surely not. A gaggle of aristocrats would have better subjects to discuss.

The maid from the foyer passed behind her carrying three large boxes balanced with precision in her slim arms.

"The drawing room's just in there, miss."

Everyone else seemed to know where Jess belonged. If only she felt as certain.

She slanted a grin back at the maid. "Thank you. Working up my courage."

The girl stopped in her tracks a moment. She looked Jess up and down, assessing her. "You look as much the fine lady as any I ever saw, miss."

Jess leaned toward the maid and lowered her voice to a whisper. "I'm afraid you can't always judge a book by its cover."

The young maid stared at her for a moment, as if pondering Jess's platitude, and then hefted the boxes up an inch in her arms before continuing on her way.

Jess turned back to the drawing room door, took a breath so deep it made her dizzy, and stepped into the room. Perhaps if the discussion was lively enough, they wouldn't notice her at all.

A gasp followed by a shattered teacup reminded Jess of one of her father's favorite sayings.

If it weren't for bad luck, my girl, we wouldn't have any luck at all.

Every head turned her way, and the woman who'd dropped her cup of tea was fanning herself and being assisted to a chair by a man Jess found vaguely familiar.

Actually, both the fainting woman and her husband were familiar. Jess recalled with a jolt where she'd seen them before. They'd been at the gallery. They'd witnessed the incident with Lord Grimsby. The man was the one who'd tried to draw him away afterward, and it seemed he knew the viscount well enough to be invited to this intimate house party.

Jess's head began to throb. The maid said the viscount's sister and brother-in-law had arrived. Had she really kissed the man in front of his own sister?

Breathily, the woman whispered, "You can't have brought her here, Lucius. Tell me you did not."

Lady Stamford bustled over to the woman and patted her on the head as one would a fussing child.

"I brought her, my dear." Augusta turned to Jessamin. "Miss Wright, this is Lady Julia, my niece. Lucius's sister. And this is her husband, Mr. Darnley." Augusta leaned toward Lady Julia and then gestured toward Jessamin. "Julia, my dear, this is Miss Wright, my companion. She is a most invaluable young woman. I can't tell you how she has assisted me in the short time I've known her. I simply cannot do without her now."

Lady Stamford's praise was always effusive, and Jess feared her cheeks would soon be as red as the geraniums in Marleston's conservatory.

Lady Julia seemed unimpressed by Augusta's recommendation and continued to stare at Jess skeptically. Then Mr. Darnley approached and whispered something in the woman's ear. Whatever it was, his words seemed to have a beneficial effect on Lord Grimsby's sister. She stood up, straightened her skirts, and approached Jess.

She forced an expression Jess imagined was meant to be pleasant, but looked more as if someone twisted something very sharp in the woman's side. She gave up and offered Jess the slightest of nods.

"How do you do, Miss Wright? I am pleased to make the acquaintance of anyone my aunt regards so highly."

Jess opened her mouth to reply, but Lady Julia's voice quivered as she said, "Tell me, wherever did she find you?"

Truth seemed best, at least what she could tell of it.

"In a bookshop, my lady. Lady Stamford offered me employment when I was sorely in need of it. I will always be grateful to her."

Lady Julia glanced at her brother before offering Jess another upturned grimace.

"How fortuitous for you."

"Yes."

She wasn't certain how she'd done it, but with the single word, Jess sensed some of the tension in the room ease. Augusta and Lady Julia began speaking quietly to each other, while Mr. Darnley joined Lord Grimsby and a tall, handsome man Jess had yet to meet.

Her breathing steadied and the throbbing in her head began to ease, a slight tapping now rather than thunder. She selected a place on the settee where she hoped to be out of the way and yet available to converse if called upon to do so. She focused on remembering to breathe, attempting to project a bit of the elegance she'd seen in the looking glass, and never glancing in Lord Grimsby's direction.

Lady Stamford gave her an encouraging smile from across the room now and then, and Jess grinned back before forcing herself to examine the room's lovely furnishings while plotting ways to escape and explore the library. The gentlemen gathered behind her chattering about horses and an upcoming hunt. She tried not to fidget, even when she caught a bit of the viscount's spice scent on the air around her. Reminding herself not to glance at him, to turn her attention elsewhere, she noticed the tight press of her corset and bodice and couldn't resist rearranging her skirts and smoothing her hands across the luxurious fabric to settle her nerves.

"Do you always fret over your frocks like that?"

There was no mistaking his voice, especially when he spoke low and set off gooseflesh on her skin. Lord Grimsby stood beside the settee, staring down his aristocratic Roman nose at her.

She whispered back, hoping the viscount's sister, who still speared her with an occasional curious glare, wouldn't hear their exchange.

"I've never worn this dress before. I'm not used to it." She wasn't used to any of the finery of her new life. "Perhaps I'm not suited to it." Her comment encompassed the dress, the company she found herself in, even the distracting man looming over her.

He had to know she didn't belong just as surely as she did. For several heartbeats, he said nothing, just watched her, raking her with his gaze as he'd done when she met him near the copse of trees.

She itched to say something cheeky, to distract him from his harsh judgments and save her pride, whatever was left of it.

Then he laid his hand on the back of the settee, his long fingers gripping the damask.

"It suits you perfectly. The fit, the cut, the color." Then more quietly, just for her. "You suit the dress, Miss Wright."

Jess allowed herself a glance at him. He wasn't even looking at her, but she noticed a twitch of movement along his jaw.

He turned then, his gaze tangling with hers, searing her with an intense spike of heat in her chest, down her spine, lower into her center.

"Do I?"

A curt nod of his head was his only reply. It was such a small, quick movement, she almost missed it.

But then he spoke again. One word, husky, deep.

"Spectacularly."

Chapter Thirteen

"DINNER IS SERVED, my lord."

At Marleston, there'd been a gong the butler sounded before luncheon and dinner meals. It was an exotic and pleasant noise, and Jess loved the sound of it. This gentleman's voice, whoever he was, couldn't compare. Nasally and high-pitched, his tone commanded rather than invited. And everyone in the room responded instantly, men and women pairing off before proceeding to the dining room.

As Lord Grimsby escorted his aunt, his sister and her husband followed, and the man to whom Jess had yet to be introduced approached her.

"May I escort you in to dinner, Miss Wright?"

"Yes, of course."

He smiled and said, "Ghastly improper, of course, since we've yet to be introduced. Robert Wellesley. Grimsby and I have known each other for ages. And you"—he paused and his gaze took Jess in from the top of Tilly's elaborate hairstyle to the toes of her shoes—"are his aunt's most invaluable companion."

Wellesley's manner was far too familiar and his wandering gaze brazen, but Jess felt a sense of instant kinship with the man. The way he held his mouth, something in his blue-green eyes, told Jess he didn't feel as comfortable as he was attempting to appear.

His smile faltered as Jess studied him. Then he lifted his arm and met her gaze with one as searching as her own. "Shall we?"

Jess took his arm and allowed him to lead her.

"Shall I call you Mr. Wellesley or something else?"

He leaned toward her as they walked. "I should very much like you to call me Rob, but that might cause a scandal. So I suppose it shall have to be Wellesley."

"No title then?" Jess wanted to bite her tongue the moment the rude words were out. She sounded as catty as Kitty Adderly. But something about Mr. Wellesley's manner invited her to jest.

And he wasn't cross. In fact, his response—a belly-deep laugh so infectious she laughed too—drew the attention of Lady Stamford and Lord Grimsby as they crossed the threshold into the dining room.

Wellesley cleared his throat and stood up straight, projecting an air of solemn propriety. He whispered so only Jess could hear. "I am the second son of a second son, I'm afraid. But I assure you, Miss Wright, I wouldn't take a title if a dozen were on offer. Too much bother. Too many rules. Doesn't suit me at all."

Jess believed him. Sincerity shaded every word, but then he tilted his mouth mischievously before breaking into a dazzling smile, as if honesty and solemnity were the least of his concerns.

"Besides, a title makes a man the most sought-after fish in the pond. I allow that a day will come when I can no longer slip the hook, but I don't wish to be caught for a title. What man does?"

There were more chairs at the long dining table than seemed necessary for their small group, and Jess had no idea where hers might be. Thankfully, Mr. Wellesley seemed to know exactly where each of them belonged. He assisted her into a seat to Lady Stamford's right and then took a chair directly across from Jess. She could barely see him over the large floral arrangement decorating the table.

Lord Grimsby was already seated near the head of the table, but not in the chair at the head itself. For the first time, Jess wondered about the absence of his father. She had yet to meet the earl. Would the gentleman the maids had spoken of so dismissively be joining them?

By the third course, Jess's corset was protesting, though she knew from formal dinners at Marleston there would be at least two more. She sipped at her wine and listened to the conversation around her, grateful no one had engaged her in more than polite exchanges. A bit of the tension in her body seemed to melt away, and she found it increasingly difficult to resist glancing in Lord Grimsby's direction. He was a broad-shouldered black and white form, enticing her at the periphery of her vision, and if she tilted her head just so, she could watch him as he lifted his glass to the mouth she'd kissed.

Then she'd look away and lifted her own glass, silently chastising herself for such silliness.

The dinner table conversation ranged from people Jess didn't know to soirees she would never attend, and then back to horses. It was the only topic that tempted her to join in. She'd read Miss Sewell's *Black Beauty* with pleasure, and Jess admired horses. They were valiant creatures that pulled omnibuses and carriages through London's muck. Horses were reliable, and after a lifetime with Father, Jess admired reliability in man or beast more than any other quality.

The tower of flowers before her shuddered and Wellesley's face appeared around the far edge of it. He reached out his hand and nudged the tower of blooms to his right. The arrangement now sat between them and the rest of the table, affording them a modicum of privacy, which she suspected was terribly improper.

"Have you given up on that fish?"

"I can't eat another bite."

"You haven't had Cook's custard. It's divine, Miss Wright."

His sincerity regarding the custard made her smile. There was no denying the appeal of good custard.

"Then I'm definitely finished with my fish. It seems I must save room for Hartwell's renowned custard."

"I do adore a sensible woman."

Jess felt herself blush and silently cursed her pale skin that always gave her away, betraying her embarrassment and nervousness just when she wished to be strong and unaffected. She sipped at her wine to cool the heat and hoped no one else at the table heard Mr. Wellesley's teasing flirtation.

Augusta's voice, mock stern, emanated from beyond the floral arrangement.

"Your mother will be pleased to hear it, Robert. She has long believed you had a weakness for all women, but it seems if she wishes to get you married, it is a sensible one who will fit the bill. I shall pen a letter to her straightaway. Miss Wright can help me with it."

She should have known the countess would hear. Jess had quickly learned Lady Stamford had extraordinarily keen hearing and an even more impressive ability to distinguish all the various conversations going on at once, no matter how crowded the social gathering. Jess was certain this small group posed no challenge for her skills.

Mr. Wellesley took a healthy drink of wine before replying.

"You're too good to me, Lady Stamford."

He leaned toward Jess, his upper body looming perilously close to the remnants of fish on his plate.

"Never allow my mother and that woman in the same room together. The way they're always scheming, I call them the Gorgons."

"Weren't there three gorgons, Jessamin?" Augusta's voice was so pleasant, Jess could almost imagine the countess didn't know she'd just been referred to as a monster with hair made out of living snakes. But Jess knew her employer was well read and particularly loved Greek mythology.

"In some of the stories, yes, my lady." Jess sat up straight and turned to look at Lady Stamford as she spoke.

The countess signaled to a footman, who stepped forward to remove the fragrant floral arrangement, opening up the table so that Jess and Mr. Wellesley were no longer cloistered at their end.

"Thank you, my lady. Miss Wright and I were feeling quite left out down here on our own."

Despite his polite words, a touch of sarcasm colored Mr. Wellesley's tone. Jess had the sense he was a bit like her, quite content to converse with one person rather than the group. His conspiratorial wink in her direction convinced her she was right.

With the view opened up, Jess took the opportunity to glance at the rest of those gathered around the table, at Mr. and Mrs. Darnley and then at Lord Grimsby. Mrs. Darnley and her husband were still tucking into their fish, but the viscount's gaze was locked on Jess. She felt a tickle at the back of her neck and shivered.

Did he glare at everyone in that same searing way? And was everyone as unnerved by it?

If he continued to look at her like that for the next fortnight, she wasn't certain she could be elegant or proper or help to make the house party a success as Lady Stamford desired. When he gazed at her, all she could think about was their kiss, a moment when he'd made her feel as if she was the most desirable woman in London.

The footman leaned in front of her to take her plate,

blocking out her view of the viscount. She turned to the young man and thanked him under her breath. But Lord Grimsby remained a distraction in the corner of her vision. She noticed another footman refill his wine glass before he lifted it to this mouth and drank from the cut-crystal vessel until it was nearly empty again.

"But I do admit that if it's a sensible woman you seek, my dear Miss Wright is an excellent example."

At Augusta's pronouncement, Mrs. Darnley spluttered, emitting a sort of wet squeak, and Lord Grimsby quaffed the last of his wine before coughing into his napkin.

Jess took a long gulp of her own wine. Her face was now well and truly red. She knew it must be because her cheeks were as hot as if they'd ignited into flames. Every sense told her to flee, to stand up and run from the room, from this house, from this world where she didn't belong, and go back to London. She might not yet have enough money to sustain herself long, but at least she knew who she was in London. There she had a purpose. Or at least she'd had a purpose once. Surely she could find one again.

"Miss Wright is one of the most industrious and intelligent women I've ever met. And her knowledge of books and literature never fails to impress me. And she's quite political too. She's taught me a great deal in the last few weeks."

Lady Stamford's accolades were doing nothing for the heat in Jess's cheeks, nor her nerves. The woman had been kind to her from the moment they'd met, yet Jess couldn't imagine such a perceptive woman had no notion of the embarrassment she was causing.

"Of course she knows about books. She was a shopgirl." Mrs. Darnley's softer voice had a bit of a whine to it, as if she was bored with the subject of Jess's merits as much as Jess was mortified by it.

"She owned the shop, Julia. She was a bookshop owner." Lady Stamford sounded so proud of the fact. Yet why would she be proud?

Was. Was a bookshop owner. For Jess, the reality of her failure held a potent sting.

"Well done, Miss Wright."

Mr. Wellesley's voice was quiet, though Jess guessed Lady Stamford heard him. Jess risked at peek at him, hoping his gaze wouldn't lock on her flaming red cheeks. Instead, he merely shot her a sympathetic grin and she tried to return it, though her face felt stiff and immobile.

"My goodness. A shop owner. Next you'll be telling us she's a suffragette."

Somehow Mrs. Darnley's voice, referring to Jess as if she wasn't even at the table, was far more irksome than Lady Stamford's laudatory list of her qualities had been.

Jess's irritation turned to action before she could think better of it. She swallowed a bit more wine and then stood up, pushing her chair back, and spoke loudly and clearly, determined to confess her transgressions for all to hear.

"Yes, I'm a suffragist. Women own shops, even if some of them lose their shops because their fathers are incurable and very unlucky gamblers. That doesn't mean they shouldn't have the right to vote."

Jess bent a bit at the waist to resume her seat and then remembered something else that needed saying. "And women run their homes and great estates"—she pointed to Lady Stamford before remembering that pointing was a terrible blunder and letting her hand fall to her side—"as the Countess of Stamford does at Marleston. Shouldn't they have the right to vote and help decide their fate?"

The dining room grew eerily quiet—no sound, not even the clink of silverware against porcelain. All the guests seemed to be holding their breath. Mrs. Darnley stared at her with huge eyes and lips slightly parted. Her husband stared down at his plate. Lady Stamford beamed at her, Mr. Wellesley tilted his mouth in a sardonic grin, and Lord Grimsby pinched the flesh between his eyebrows. His eyes were closed and a grimace marred his handsome face. He finally let out a sigh and she thought she heard him say, "Good God, a suffragette" as he exhaled.

Jess's tongue felt swollen, too large to fit her mouth, and the suffusion of heat in her cheeks had now spread throughout her whole body, particularly the center of her chest. As she resumed her seat, she was grateful for the lack of motion. Even the mere act of standing and sitting made her dizzy.

Mr. Wellesley leaned toward her and whispered, "How often do you drink wine, Miss Wright?"

"Rarely before coming to Marleston. And only one glass with dinner."

"You've had three tonight."

"Have I really?"

"Mmm. It's a defect of Hartwell, I find. These bloody footmen are far too generous."

"Bloody footmen."

Jess thought she was whispering as quietly as Mr. Wellesley, but every time she spoke, she saw Mrs. Darnley's head snap in her direction as if she was a particularly annoying bee buzzing about the table.

Why did the woman loathe her so? Jess had never met her before tonight. Well, unless she counted that silliness at the art gallery. Which, of course, she would.

Would she never overcome that rash and scandalous act? She'd come to think of it as a private moment between them, but of course it hadn't been. It had been contrived to be as public as possible, to cause Lord Grimsby as much mortification as possible. It was a wonder the man didn't loathe her. Perhaps he did.

Jess felt suddenly drowsy, and nothing seemed more appealing than resting her head for the night, forgetting about the viscount, and giving up on trying so hard to be elegant. But even as she considered excusing herself, a footman slid a beautiful dish of custard onto her plate.

"The custard." She smiled across at Mr. Wellesley, who'd already taken the first spoonful and scooped it into his mouth.

Jess lifted her spoon and was just about to dig into the dessert when she felt Mrs. Darnley's chilly glare on her. The woman's wrath spoiled Jess's enthusiasm for the custard, and she dropped her spoon with what seemed to her ears to be a deafening clatter.

Mrs. Darnley's eyes weren't the only ones fixed on her.

Across the table, Mr. Wellesley's gaze had gone wide. On her left, Lady Stamford swiveled toward her and, at far at the end of the room, Lord Grimsby's brow furrowed as he drummed his fingers on the table and watched her. The weight of their stares pressed down on her, chipping at her resolve to behave properly, to keep Kitty's secret. She loathed secrets. Father's secrets had ruined their lives. The truth was just there, longing to escape, and she could only think of the sweet relief it would be to let it go.

She stood again, though she held on to the table edge to stop herself from listing. Goodness, if this was what intoxication felt like, she couldn't imagine why her father had been so keen on it. He'd been a man who prided himself on his intelligence, yet at the moment Jess wasn't certain she could recall her full name if called upon to do so.

"Forgive me, Mrs. Darnley." Or was it Lady Julia? The rules were so confusing. She was an earl's daughter, yet she'd married a mister Darnley. "Er, Lady Julia. Do forgive me. Yes, you saw me kiss your brother in Mayfair. But it was only for money. Quite a lot of it. I tried to give it to the bank, but they wouldn't take it. Wasn't enough. I'm sorry."

Her words sped up and tumbled over one another as she spoke and a great weight, like a heavy drape, drew down around her. She bent to sit, but either the chair had moved or she'd missed it completely. She sank down to the floor, only her stiff petticoat with its small attached bustle and the frame of her corset keeping her from melting into the carpet completely.

She heard, as if from far away, Mrs. Darnley shriek. The woman certainly did exclaim a great deal. And then that voice, as dark and deep as a bottomless pool, the one that haunted her dreams—Lord Grimsby. He was angry.

"No, I shall take her. Eat your blasted pudding, Robert, and kindly take your hands off of her."

"I have smelling salts."

"She hasn't fainted, Julia. Miss Wright has had a bit too much wine." Jess's chest warmed to hear the same note of concern in Lady Stamford's tone she recalled hearing in her mother's voice whenever she'd fallen ill as a child. "Careful, Lucius. Gently."

Jess felt herself lifted, scooped up and collected into arms much bigger than her own, and pressed against a firm chest, a man who smelled achingly familiar. She couldn't resist turning her head toward his shoulder to take a deeper breath of him. Lord Grimsby smelled like cloves. No, maybe not cloves, but some spice, rich and evocative, for which she didn't know the name.

As Lord Grimsby carried her from the dining room, she heard Mr. Wellesley call out. "Do save her some custard. She'll be cross she missed it."

Jess couldn't help grinning.

"He amuses you, does he? He amuses many women."

They were so far away from the dining room when he finally spoke, Jess had already forgotten about Robert Wellesley. She'd nestled her head against Lord Grimsby's shoulder and was enjoying his scent and the warmth of his body, even delighting in the way a strand of his soft black hair brushed against her nose as he moved.

"You smell like spice. And starch. And a bit like leather, like a new leather-bound book."

He smelled delicious, much more appealing than the custard. And she felt safe in his arms, just as she had in the gallery. Even with the glares, condemnations, and gasps of outrage, his arms around her and his gaze locked with hers had insulated and protected her for that single moment of pleasure. He'd managed to exude strength and solidity, even in that heated, reckless moment.

They'd reached the door of her sitting room. Her bedroom was just a few steps away, but it wouldn't have been proper for him to take her there. She could reach her bedroom through a connecting door in her sitting room, if she managed to walk that far.

He turned the doorknob without dropping her and carried her to the long settee in front of the fire. He bent to place her on the furniture gently, almost as if she'd sustained some injury. Then he sorted out her dress, making sure her skirts were settled just right and even slipping her flimsy but fashionable shoes from her stockinged feet. His ministrations felt lovely. Jess had never been fussed over so tenderly in her life.

"I'll have some tea sent up." He'd already stepped away from her and was halfway to the door.

She didn't wish him to go, but she knew propriety dictated it.

"Please." Her mouth felt suddenly dry as dust, but the word came out with a rasp. She had no idea what she was pleading for, didn't want to think about what she might be asking.

He looked as confused as she, but he crossed the room

toward her again. He crouched down, examining her from head to toe in the dim fire glow.

"Are you well, Miss Wright? Were you injured when you fell? There is a doctor in the village—"

"No." Her voice was hoarse, though she couldn't recall saying much of anything in the past few hours. "I am well," she managed, though the edges of the walls tilted around her.

Lord Grimsby seemed the one stable object in the room and she reached for him.

He reached for her too, and she thought he meant to touch her, caress her, that she might get to taste his kiss again. Instead he laid the back of his hand against her forehead as her father had done when he feared she might have a fever. Lord Grimsby's skin felt refreshingly cool against her own. Perhaps she was feverish.

"You're a bit flushed." He turned his hand as he spoke, running his fingers across her temple, down, sliding across her cheek. "Your skin is warm." He cupped her face in his hand, rubbing the pad of his thumb back and forth against her flesh. "And so soft."

Jessamin licked her lips, and he shifted his gaze to her mouth. Surely the warmth he'd felt on her forehead had all rushed to her lips. Her mouth burned in anticipation. She'd kissed him once because she had to, and once he'd touched her as if he wished to kiss her, but now she wanted his kiss, ached for it. His kiss. Only his.

He took a deep breath and pulled his hand away. She spluttered, not unlike his sister. A little moan of frustration erupted from inside and she saw him bite his lip before he stood, turning away from her and toward the fire.

Head throbbing, Jess just wanted sleep. If the spice-scented man wasn't going to kiss her, she wished him gone so she could sleep and, please God, not dream about him.

After several moments of silence, her eyelids grew heavy. Fighting the drowsiness, she watched the dark outline of the viscount, limned by the amber firelight. But the fatigue was winning. She closed her eyes for a few seconds, promising herself she'd open them again. She only managed one, peeking at the viscount as he stood, head down, his palm braced on the fireplace mantel.

Then he turned swiftly, approached, and leaned over her, one hand on the back of the settee, the other on the pillow near her head, capturing her but not touching her. "I have one bit of advice for you, Miss Wright. Heed this. Robert is no man to set your cap at. He is inconstant." He had been watching her, but he bowed his head a moment before meeting her eyes again. "He doesn't deserve you."

If not for the serious look on Lord Grimsby's face, Jessamin might have laughed. She wasn't the kind of woman a man deserved or didn't. She was no great catch, nor did she wish to be. An equal, a partner—that's what she might be lucky enough to find one day. But she wouldn't find him among this aristocratic world of viscounts and earls and second sons of second sons.

Lord Grimsby bent his body closer to hers, leaning toward her so that their chests nearly touched. She could sense the heat and weight of him above her and fought the urge to lift her arms and pull him closer.

He kissed her forehead, his lips firm, his breath warm against her skin. "Remember that next time he amuses you." Never lifting his head, he skimmed his lips down from her forehead and pressed a brief kiss against the tip of her nose. "Remember it next time he flirts with you." He titled his head, his mouth hovering over hers. He breathed in deeply before turning his face to the left, brushing his lips across her cheek, lingering near her ear, nuzzling her there before pulling back. "Remember it when he tries to seduce you." His kissed the corner of her mouth, touching his tongue to the seam just at the edge of her lips.

Then he pulled away slowly, hesitantly, and left without another word.

Chapter Fourteen

JESS WOKE WITH a start, overwhelmed with fear that she'd forgotten to lock up the money box in the bookshop's office. She sat up quickly and instantly regretted it. A thunderous banging echoed in her ears. No, in her head. And when her eyes adjusted to the dim light from the fireplace, she realized she wasn't in her room above the shop at all. She was at Hartwell, and it had to be quite late because she'd already dined and . . . *Oh no. Please no.*

Dribs and drabs of memories came back—mouths drawn down in disapproval and gasps of shock as she'd uttered awful things. She'd said something of her politics and—*why oh why?*—confessed to kissing the viscount for money. She'd fallen, or had nearly done so. Who would have guessed she'd ever feel such gratitude for her corset? In the end, it was the only thing that held her up.

Along with the thumping in her head, embarrassment and regret bubbled like a sickly stew in her belly. Why had she allowed herself so much wine? And why had she let her tongue race ahead of her good sense? Despite all that had happened in the last month, she still believed she possessed a bit of it. Whatever Father's flaws, he'd been a decent man at heart, and though her mother had been with Jess only fourteen years, she'd done all she could to teach Jess how to be a practical, honorable woman.

Neither would be proud of her behavior tonight.

Jess winced at the memory of her graceless tumble, but when she tried to recall how she'd gotten into bed, her recollections went dark around the edges. Then a fragrance—an alluringly familiar mix of starch and spice—tickled her nose. Lord Grimsby. He'd been here, or touched her, or somehow been close enough to imprint his scent on her.

She struggled to recall if he'd spoken to her. Surely she'd remember if he'd kissed her again. Lifting a hand, she traced a finger across her mouth, as if the memory of it might have imprinted itself there. But she felt certain of nothing. Vague images in her head, of Lord Grimsby lit by firelight, and then closer, his mouth gliding over her skin, could as easily have been a dream. Heaven knew she'd dreamed of the man often enough.

Pushing the covers back, she eased out of bed slowly, trying not to rile the orchestra in her head. Someone had removed her dress and gotten her into a nightgown, and she prayed it was Tilly.

With her head thumping, Jess couldn't imagine going back to sleep. More than anything, she longed for a steaming cup of coffee. Father had preferred coffee too, but she hadn't enjoyed a single cup since coming to Marleston. Lady Stamford took tea and only tea, and that was that.

Perhaps if she had a cup of the aromatic brew from her favorite London coffeehouse, she could clear her head enough to get some writing done on the speech Alice would deliver at the next Women's Union event. Jess missed attending the meetings, but not nearly as much as the round of discussions afterward and being able to keep abreast of developments with the group's charitable initiatives. Though Alice sent her letters and pamphlets, even clippings from the newspaper, she missed their face-to-face debates most of all. Perhaps if she survived her two weeks of trying to avoid the viscount, Lady Stamford would allow her a train trip to London, if even for a day. Assuming she could stop blurting to everyone about kissing the man.

No more wine for me. Bloody footmen. Jess grinned, recalling Mr. Wellesley's condemnation. Biting her lip, she recalled more—giggling with Wellesley like a silly schoolgirl and being carried. Carried by a man who warned her off Wellesley. Carried by Lord Grimsby, who'd touched her and pressed his mouth to her skin, and made her wish to be kissed more than she'd ever wanted anything in her life.

No. She had no business kissing Lord Grimsby. She wouldn't regret the first kiss, but that had to be enough. Whether because of his aunt's insistence or his own graciousness, he'd allowed her to remain at Hartwell. And while he might not have loathed her before tonight, what did he think of her now? Now that she'd admitted taking money to kiss him.

That disturbing thought fueled her. She needed to turn her mind to something other than Lord Grimsby. She hooked herself into her corset and searched the wardrobe for the simplest gown Lady Stamford had ordered for her, a blue day dress with matching bodice. It was such an unfussy ensemble, she could easily dress herself.

After lighting a candle, she cupped her hand around the flame and made her way into the hall. She longed to stretch her legs and walk, though she wasn't certain enough of the estate to feel comfortable venturing out of doors. Still, the house was so grand, she imagined she could wander for an hour and still not manage to explore all its corners and corridors.

The stairwell to the ground floor beckoned, lit by gaslights that had been turned low but not extinguished. She made her way toward the main hall. By the time she reached the library door, she realized it had been her destination all along. How could she resist a room full of books?

She turned the latch, pleased to find it unlocked, and inhaled deeply the moment her foot crossed the threshold. The heady scent of books—leather, aged paper, ink—took her straight back to her father's bookshop. Jess bit her lip at the memory of Wright and Sons Booksellers, emotions jumbling in her heart, none of them clear and all of them bittersweet. But then she lifted her candle and took in the view before her. There was no business to run here, no sales to worry over, no ledger books to balance, no debt to weigh her down, just a beautifully appointed room dedicated to one single purpose—the housing of hundreds of expertly bound and tooled books.

The bookcases were so tall, reaching up to the high ceiling, that a carved and polished wooden staircase had been installed. It ran along a track in the wall, and she set her candle on a table and gave in to the impulse to climb the steps and explore the titles far up on the wall. She climbed up several steps and then, with one foot on one step and her other foot higher up, she reached for a copy of Mary Wollstonecraft's *A Vindication of the Rights of Woman*. Kitty claimed Lord Grimsby opposed suffrage for women, but, then again, she'd also said he was an odious man and kissing him would be unpleasant. For a woman willing to pay an enormous sum to humiliate him, she seemed to know very little about the viscount. If a man kept a copy of Mary Wollstonecraft in his library, surely he'd at least give due consideration to the rights of women. Unless it had been a freethinking Dunthorpe ancestress who'd purchased the volume.

Just as she reached out to replace the book, stretching up and to the right to settle it on the shelf, the rolling staircase moved in the opposite direction, sliding easily on its track and knocking the book from her hand. As she shot her hands out to grasp the staircase railing and steady herself, the clatter of the book smacking the hardwood floor below made her jump.

She looked down to ensure the volume was still intact and the staircase began to slide again. Though the bookcases at her father's shop hadn't been nearly as tall, she'd never been afraid of heights or maneuvering on a ladder to place books on the highest shelves. But Hartwell's rolling staircase seemed to have a mind of its own. She attempted one step down, then another, before the contraption began to move again. She reached for a shelf to stop herself, fingertips grazing the gilded spines of several volumes, nearly pulling them over too.

"Bloody bother and blast!"

She felt better for saying it, and with no one to hear her but the library walls, Jess was relieved none would ever know she'd given in to an unladylike swearing fit. Nor how ungracefully she was attempting to descend the rolling staircase. She was close enough now that she could jump the rest of the way, though it had been many years since her tree-climbing, jumping-into-ponds days of childhood summers spent with her mum's family in Dorset. Could she manage a moderately short jump in a long skirt and tight corset without breaking anything essential?

LUCIUS LOUNGED IN his study in a chair before the fireplace, legs stretched out so that his boot heels rested on the hearth. He crossed his hands over his stomach, leaning his head back, and lowered his eyes to continue staring at the remnants of a fire in the grate. He'd be content to sleep like this, in his chair before the fire. If he could sleep at all.

The flames had died down an hour before, but in the black pile of ash, an ember glowed orange now and then, still giving off enough heat to make his nearness worthwhile. He'd given up on finding any rest in his own bed and returned to his study once the house quieted and all the guests were settled in for the night.

One guest in particular eclipsed all other thoughts. With her new frock and elaborately dressed hair, Jessamin Wright had looked so different from the determined, plainly dressed woman he'd met at the gallery in London. And from the tired and disappointed bookshop owner he'd encountered and nearly kissed in her shop. Tonight she'd been as elegant and lovely as any fine young lady he'd ever been introduced to at a country ball or London soiree. Lucius liked being privy to all the forms of her beauty—far too much.

But tonight there'd been more than her beauty to admire. She'd been passionate in declaring her beliefs, bold in admitting that she'd kissed him, and audacious in standing up to Julia, whose glacial stare was known to make the staunchest men shudder.

Miss Wright seemed a woman of endless facets, and he yearned to discover each one.

He closed his eyes and allowed himself the indulgence of remembering the moment she'd leaned into him, the first moment he touched her, steadying her on her feet, before she lifted up and pressed her warm, lush mouth to his.

He lifted a hand to pinch the skin between his brows. It didn't ease the ache in his head, but it offered momentary distraction from the problem of Miss Jessamin Wright. And she was a problem. If one dinner with her preoccupied him to this extent, how would he endure the rest of the house party? She'd no doubt continue drinking and flirting with Wellesley.

If the man touched her . . . Hell, if he continued leering at her every night at dinner, Lucius didn't know if he'd be able to resist throttling his closest friend. No doubt Miss Wright would be more than willing to comfort Wellesley. A few quips and the man had turned the fretful frown she'd been wearing the whole evening into a beaming smile. A few more of those looks in Wellesley's direction and Lucius would be as mad as the gossips said his father was by fortnight's end.

And in the meantime, he was to entertain and woo Miss Sedgwick, whose wealth could save Hartwell. He wondered if the repairs needed to the estate and tenant houses would even make a dent in the dowry she'd bring. If Aunt Augusta knew the lady's intentions as she said she did, Miss Sedgwick would be content with a title, and he'd be content knowing he'd secured Hartwell for future generations. Wouldn't he?

He narrowed his gaze as he stared at the flickering ember among the coals. The heat at its center was waning, the color darkening as its light faded. He reached out for the poker and pushed at the ember, attempting to stoke it back to life. In his fatigued and overwrought mind, it seemed his only chance for heat and he did not wish to lose it.

Nor did he wish to lose the opportunity to make a match with Miss Sedgwick by whiling away in his study, his thoughts fixated on another woman. That reminded him far too much of his father.

He'd spent his youth wondering why his father could find no other pursuit as interesting as his mother, why the man couldn't balance his love for her with this duty to the estate and the responsibilities of his title. Even Lucius's mother had longed for that.

The eldest daughter of a large and well-to-do Scottish clan, Isobel Buchanan had understood duty and expected it of her children. She taught them that they had an obligation to the family and to those on the estate who relied on the earl's good stewardship. It often seemed she cared more for Hartwell and the tenants of the estate than his father ever had.

But Father had been jealous of time Mother spent in anyone's company but his. He'd allowed his preoccupation with her to unhinge him, letting it fester into an irrational jealousy that only served to drive her away.

He would not tread that path. Duty, responsibility, those qualities his mother expected of him, that was where his heart and mind ought to be.

Except for the problem of Miss Jessamin Wright. *Such a damnably tempting problem.*

"Bloody bother and blast!"

His eyes snapped open at the sound of the woman's shout. He might have convinced himself it was a condemnation from the depths of his own conscience, except that he recognized the voice. And the fact that it emanated from the library.

Surging from his chair, Lucius rushed to the door connecting the library and his study.

Miss Wright held on to the rolling staircase with one hand, her body turned away from it, seemingly poised to leap from a disturbingly high step.

Lucius reached out to turn up the gas, lighting up the room and revealing one shocked and disheveled former bookshop owner.

Her mouth opened as if she meant to speak, and he waited, but she merely continued to stare at him.

"Miss Wright, I would have thought you'd had your fill of books."

She frowned as if it was the last thing she'd expected him to say.

"Never. I could never tire of books."

He grinned, unable to hold it back, even if he'd tried. He'd loved books with that kind of passion once, books and learning, the notion that the world was literally at his fingertips within the pages of one volume or the other. Since leaving university and being called back from his uncle's investment office after Julian's death to take over management of Hartwell, some piece of him, that hopeful, curious fragment, had faded. He never dreamed a suffragette bluestocking would stir it back to life.

"Would you steady this staircase, my lord, so that I may climb down? I'm afraid if I jump, I'll rip this dress or scuff your floor."

"Of course."

He moved forward to assist her, but she seemed a woman afflicted with impatience and was trying to climb down herself. She hadn't engaged the latch and the staircase moved in its well-oiled track every time she did. Lucius flipped the lever to engage the braking mechanism.

"Just wait. I've got you."

He reached up to lay a hand against her waist, and she turned toward him, placed one hand on each of his shoulders, and took a step down the ladder. He wasn't truly taking her weight. There was no need to lift her, but he braced his other hand on her waist, encircling her as she took another tentative step down, her skirt dragging against his body as she moved.

Eyes locked on his, she stepped down one more level and they came face-to-face, her bodice pressed against his waistcoat. Her breath came in short, hot wisps against his face, and her mouth was far too close for him to think of anything but kissing her.

"Thank you, my lord."

She took the last step quickly and pulled her hands from his shoulders. He released her with a bit more reluctance.

Then she bent in front of him and lifted a book from the floor. "I'm afraid I dropped this when I was fighting with your staircase."

He lifted a hand out for her to give him the volume, but she shook her head. "I can replace it, my lord." Then she looked up, well above the height of the staircase. "Though I'm afraid it goes up there."

Lucius had the distinct notion she didn't wish him to see which book she'd selected, which made him all the more determined to do so.

"May I see it? I'm happy to replace it for you."

She hesitated, then nodded, as if coming to a decision, and handed him the slim folio.

"It was my mother's." He stroked the aged brown

leather, running his finger along the red Morocco spine. "I'm not surprised you would wish to read Mary Wollstonecraft, but I must say I'm impressed you found it among all of the other books, and on one of the highest shelves."

Jessamin narrowed her eyes, as if uncertain whether he meant to compliment or challenge her.

Lucius started toward the staircase, then turned back. "Are you sure you do not wish to take it to your room? You may borrow any book you like while you're here."

"Thank you, my lord, but I've read it. I was simply curious about that edition and dropped it before I could replace it. I hope it's not damaged."

"It looks well enough to me."

He ascended the wooden staircase and replaced the volume in the gap where it had rested since the days when his mother lived at Hartwell. He noticed the books around it were disturbed and set about righting them, matching their depth, making certain they were perfectly vertical and in line with the books nearby. He lost track of how long he fussed over the shelf until he sensed the press of Miss Wright's gaze on him.

He looked down to find her gazing up at him with an expression of interest, without artifice or coquetry. Just a woman intrigued with a man, and it warmed him as if he'd just settled in before a glowing fire. Had he looked up at her with that same expression? As if she was the most fascinating creature he'd ever seen. Yes, of course he had.

"You like everything to be just so."

"Are you saying I'm overly fastidious, Miss Wright?" Lucius knew he was. He didn't think he'd always been, but the need for order, for precision, to regulate as many aspects of his existence and surroundings as he was able—that compulsion had grown worse over the years. Perhaps his desire for control had grown parallel, measure for measure, with his father's loss of it.

"I don't know you well enough to say anything of the sort, my lord. But I do see that you appreciate organization. There's nothing quite as comforting as imposing order where none previously existed, or at least that's what my mother used to say."

From anyone else, he'd consider the comment suspect, a jibe or backhanded manner of calling him a persnickety fool. But Miss Wright's mouth curved in a warm grin. And he could detect nothing of derision in her tone.

"Did she?"

"Mmm, right before she'd accuse Father and me of creating chaos."

He descended the stairs and took two steps to stand before her, close enough to see the flecks of amber in her eyes. Close enough to smell traces of her violet scent. Proximity to her made him long for what he could not have and, worst of all, it cost him her grin.

"Are you a chaos maker, Miss Wright?"

Of course she was, if one considered the fuss she'd caused in Mayfair and the way she'd unsettled his mind from the moment he'd met her.

She turned her eyes down, her mouth settling into an uncertain line.

"My father and I tended to like a bit of clutter, especially if it involved books or newspapers or anything worth reading. Mother was forever tidying up after us. When we lost her, that duty fell to me. But I was never quite as fond of neatness as she was."

Lucius heard the wistfulness in her tone when she mentioned her mother, and he felt an echo of it in his chest, a twinge just above his first waistcoat button.

"Excellent mothers leave us with a great deal to live up to, don't they?"

Her head snapped up, gaze clashing with his, and an earnest expression lit her face. But there was a hint of sadness in her eyes, and he lifted his hand, no longer able to resist the urge to touch her.

She stepped back, one step and then another. Turning her head, she studied the book-covered library walls.

"I am sorry, my lord. This evening I was . . . I said too much at dinner."

Lucius loathed the way she twisted her hands and ducked her head as if she couldn't bear to look at him.

"*In vino veritas.* We all speak freely when we're in our cups." That didn't help. A crimson blush rushed up her neck and stained her cheeks. Lucius shuffled his feet, placed his hands on his hips, and tried again. "You only said what was true, Miss Wright. And I always suspected someone put you up to that business in the gallery. A prank, I take it. You said they paid quite a sum." He dared not mention that he considered their exceptional kiss worth every penny, however much she'd been paid. "I suppose you can't tell me who arranged it. Sworn to secrecy, I suspect."

He enjoyed shocking her, if only because she opened her eyes wider, allowing him to see the green shade he'd had such difficulty identifying that first night.

"You're truly not angry?"

Of all the emotions she stoked in him, anger didn't even hold rank. He'd touched her, caressed her, come very close to kissing her senseless in her sitting room tonight. But the wine had already dulled her senses, and if they were to kiss again the way they had in the art gallery, it would be because both of them chose it, wanted it in equal measure. After his behavior this evening, how could she think him anything but enthralled with her?

And he was. It was impossible to deny, though he'd try again in the morning, when he woke with thoughts of duty and responsibility, what should be done, what must be done. But here, tonight, with Jessamin gazing at him with an openness that made his body ache, he couldn't deny it.

"You must have heard that I'm quite the grim, ill-humored villain, Miss Wright."

She smiled, a flash of white in the gaslight. Good God, what had she heard about him?

"Nothing quite as dire as that."

Then, as if just remembering who he was, who she was: "My lord."

He shouldn't find pleasure in the fact she'd forgotten, but he did.

"Do you have a favorite? One book you prefer above all others?"

"My goodness, that's an awful question."

Momentarily abashed, Lucius looked away. Would he never learn a measure of the social finesse Wellesley oozed so effortlessly? Then, out of the corner of his eye, he caught her smiling and his blood turned to warm treacle in his veins, a sense of relief flooding him.

"Shall I try another?"

"No, there are moments in life when we must choose. Though I pray I'll never have to do with just one book." She chewed her bottom lip a moment, squinting at the carpet below their feet and then scanning the shelves around them. "All right. I've chosen a favorite. Is there a section devoted to fiction? Let's see if you have it."

"That wall there." Lucius pointed to the western wall of the library and watched as she started her perusal, lifting a finger to trace the spines without quite touching them.

"You do have it." She slid out a volume and lifted it to him.

"*Oliver Twist*. It is a fine tale. I approve."

She beamed at him, and it lit up her face, revealing a dimple, just one, a tiny shadow in her left cheek. His heart stuttered to a stop a moment before thudding wildly to catch up.

"It's not just because Oliver's an orphan. I loved the story long before my father died."

She spoke of her father's death without fully allowing the pleasant expression to fall from her face. It was a fact she'd accepted, clearly, but Lucius still yearned to offer her words of sympathy. To comfort her, if he could. But he held back.

"Why is it your favorite?"

"Because of Oliver, I think. In spite of his burdens, he remains true to himself, good and sweet-natured. He never gives in to bitterness or despair."

Lucius tried not to take the words as an indictment. She had no way of knowing the bitterness he'd harbored for years toward his father, nor the despair in which he'd allowed himself to wallow upon first learning the earldom would come to him one day.

"Are you an admirer of Mr. Dickens's novels, my lord?"

"I am, indeed. Though he's not the author of my favorite book."

She lifted her hands to her hips. "Well, come now. You must tell me yours."

He loved her insistent tone. With her hands emphasizing the curve of her waist, her mouth tipped in a teasing smirk, and her toe tapping impatiently as she watched him, he'd be inclined to give her anything she asked of him.

"It's an author whose surname also starts with a D."

"You want me to guess?"

"If you can."

She liked that. Smiling, she tilted her head and arched one eyebrow to signal she'd accepted the challenge.

"You have it here in the library? Is it a novel?"

He nodded.

She approached the shelves she'd searched to find Dickens, and looked back at him over her shoulder. "Defoe?"

"No. The author's not an Englishman."

As she turned back to the shelves, he gave in to the urge to move forward, to stand close to her. He heard her breathing hitch and forced himself to stay his hands, resisting the urge to reach for her.

She didn't look back at him when she whispered, "Dante?"

"No. Not an Italian either." Dipping his head a fraction, he matched her whispered tone. "He's French."

Turning her head, she met his gaze a moment before looking away again. "Dumas, then. But which one?"

She lifted her hand, hovering over a few spines, very near his favorite book.

He reached up, clasped her hand lightly in his, and pointed to the title.

"*The Count of Monte Cristo*. A man who is exiled and then returns as someone else," she whispered.

Lucius stepped back, unsettled by her words. Miss Wright spoke them lightly, unaware how close she came to describing his life. Though he'd been sent to live with caring relatives in Scotland after his mother's death, as a nine-year-old child he'd only understood that his father couldn't bear the sight of him and had sent him away. And now, wasn't he an impostor stepping into Julian's shoes? His older brother had been groomed for the earldom from birth, and Lucius wasn't certain he'd ever feel he had the right to his father's titles.

The clock in the library chimed to indicate the midnight hour.

"I should return to my room, my lord. I'll bid you good night."

He longed to hear her speak his name—not his title—in her low, resonant voice, but he held back, some sliver of propriety restraining him. Yet here, in the quiet of the small hours of the night, as they stood near enough to reach out and touch each other, he sensed propriety losing its power.

"Do you know my name?"

He drew close to her again, tentatively, fearful he'd startle her if he moved too quickly.

"Your name, my lord? Viscount Grimsby?" She said it as a question, as if he was quizzing her and she worried over giving the right answer.

One more step and her skirt would brush the legs of his trousers. He took that step.

"My given name. Yours is Jessamin." How intimate it was to speak her name with his body inches from hers. "And do you know my given name?"

Her lips parted, and his heart slowed, thick thuds against his ribs, as he waited to hear her say it. But she only nodded her head, setting an auburn wave dancing at her shoulder.

He reached up, easing his hand onto her cheek, barely touching her, yet close enough to sate the desire, the ceaseless need to connect his body to hers. He lifted a thumb and ran it gently along the swell of her bottom lip.

"Say it. Please."

"Lucius."

It was a mistake, complete and utter folly to ask her to say it. She caressed his name as no one ever had, letting the final consonant linger on her lips.

Now that he'd heard her speak the word, he wanted it again. And again. He wanted to hear her chastise him in anger, tease him flirtatiously, shout his name as he brought her to the height of pleasure.

She also seemed to realize the power of what they'd unleashed. She stepped away from him, turned toward the library door, and scampered off as quickly as her long legs would carry her.

Chapter Fifteen

"You didn't tell me she was a suffragette." Lucius spoke the words in a teasingly accusing tone as he entered the morning room. He'd woken after the first restful night of sleep in weeks with the clearheaded conviction that Jessamin Wright should return to London. He could give her the means to rebuild her shop. After seeing her in the library and the pleasure she'd taken in discussing books, he suspected it was what she wished for most of all.

But he anticipated a hearty protest from his aunt, and with each moment that passed, he sensed his own resolve waning.

Aunt Augusta nearly upset her teacup and dropped a fork full of coddled eggs onto her plate as she turned toward him.

"And why shouldn't she be?"

Lucius expected nothing less than fire from his aunt on the subject, one he knew she held dear. He patted the inside pocket of his waistcoat before taking his chair and then reached for his teacup, hiding his discomfort behind his first sip of the morning. He didn't bother answering her question, as he suspected from the way she kept opening and closing her mouth that eventually something more would come out.

"All the best women are suffragists. Every thinking woman certainly should be."

"Miss Sedgwick is not."

He regretted his timing. Augusta had just taken a bit of buttered toast with marmalade and looked as if she might choke on the morsel, but she lifted her teacup, took a sip, and seemed well again. Then she glared at him accusingly.

"What would make you say such a thing?"

She sounded as if Lucius had just accused Miss Sedgwick of the worst kind of sin. And he was prepared for her question. Reaching into his waistcoat pocket, he produced a folded newspaper clipping.

"This."

He held the slightly faded newsprint up, then unfolded the paper and began reading.

"'The better class of women do not hunger after the vote but are satisfied with their sacred place as mother, sister, or hostess within the home. I would much rather host a hundred friends at home than join a throng clamoring in the streets for a duty I do not desire.' Miss May Sedgwick of New York City."

His aunt began reaching for the paper the moment he stopped reading. "Let me see that. Where did you get this?"

"It was among the papers you sent me regarding Miss Sedgwick. Didn't you read them?"

His aunt looked flummoxed.

"I thought the piece was about her skills as a hostess."

Lucius took another swig of tea as his aunt perused the piece on Miss Sedgwick.

"So it is. Hosting and not voting." Lucius felt a moment of mirth at his extemporaneous slogan. "Perhaps she should paint that on a banner and organize a march through the streets."

Aunt Augusta glared at him again, but her glares were always ineffectual. They were belied by the deep smile lines around her mouth and eyes. A woman who smiled so often could hardly pull off a truly menacing glare.

"Well. I'm sure Jessamin and I can avoid the topic of the vote when in Miss Sedgwick's company." She spoke the words as if they didn't please her, but then seemed to have another thought that did and beamed. "Or perhaps we shall convert her."

Lucius didn't return her gleeful expression, though he felt the urge pulling at the corners of his mouth. "I have no doubt. I confess I've never met two more persuasive women in my life. But is it prudent to have Miss Wright here at Hartwell when Miss Sedgwick arrives? Surely, she'd be happier back in London."

Augusta paused in lifting her teacup to her mouth and released a long sigh.

"I thought this matter settled, my dear. If you truly wish it, I am sure we can arrange for Jessamin and Miss Sedgwick to be rarely in each other's company."

No one could persuade like Aunt Augusta could persuade, and his desire for Miss Wright's departure was such a fragile construction, he felt certain she would soon have it down.

"Well, you should devise a strategy soon. Rodgers is on his way to retrieve Miss Sedgwick now."

"Retrieve her? Where is she?"

He reached down for his pocket watch. "She should have arrived at the station a quarter of an hour ago. Miss Sedgwick will be at Hartwell's doors within the hour."

"The train station?"

Though she dressed in the height of fashion and favored reform in her political views, Aunt Augusta generally disdained technological innovation. She'd never taken to train travel, and the very notion of human beings moving faster than four horses could pull them unsettled her.

"She's an American, don't forget. For all we know, she has one of those horseless carriages back in New York."

"Madness."

The moment the word slipped from her lips, his aunt's eyes went wide. It was a word they avoided, a notion they rarely mentioned, a term none of them wished to have associated with the Dunthorpe name.

"I'm sorry, my boy. How is Maxim?"

For a moment he contemplated how much to say. The protective impulse was always first where Father was concerned. But his aunt posed no threat, and she cared fiercely for her brother and the family's reputation.

"If you refer to his memory, Dr. Seagraves says it will

continue to fail as he ages. Nothing to be done on that score. As to his moods, Mrs. Ives thinks he is on the verge of a turn. It's best if he adheres to his usual schedule. Change always seems to unsettle him."

"Miss Sedgwick will bring change, undoubtedly. Perhaps I should have hosted her at Marleston."

Whatever change her visit might bring to the daily schedule at Hartwell, Miss Sedgwick's wealth would sustain the estate for years, and Lucius could think of nothing that would as effectively put his father's mind at ease.

"Nonsense. Miss Sedgwick thwarted that plan. You said she wished to see Hartwell. And it's only a little over a fortnight. All will be well."

Lucius arched an eyebrow at his own assurances. He wasn't known for his reassuring nature, and it felt odd, a bit like an ill-fitting suit. He told himself the flutter in his belly could be dismissed as indigestion, but his conscience rang with the truth of it. The prospect of an elaborately orchestrated introduction to one woman while his mind was full of another was difficult to stomach.

"How was Miss Wright when you took her up last night?"

Her skin is unbearably soft and tastes far better than that custard Wellesley made a fuss about. Lucius imagined the look on his aunt's face if he revealed his wayward musings.

As usual, she had the unnerving ability to read his mind. And, of course, Miss Wright was there in his head, coloring every single one of his thoughts since the moment he'd woken up. He couldn't recall his dreams, but he suspected Jessamin featured in them too, with her petal-soft skin and body-hugging green velvet dress. She'd never gotten a bite of that damned custard and her skin still managed to taste of vanilla.

So he'd concocted a halfhearted plan to send her away, convincing himself she would be happier surrounded by books in London, and he'd be free to carry on with marrying May Sedgwick. He'd struggled to put her out of his mind, even sifting through the clippings his aunt had sent him regarding Miss Sedgwick in an attempt to rouse interest in their imminent introduction. But it was all to no avail.

"Lucius? Miss Wright, my companion. How was she when you took her up last evening? I had Tilly check in on her this morning and she was still abed."

He couldn't talk about carrying her upstairs, touching her, tasting her skin, so he deflected.

"You never told me about the money."

He was curious who'd paid her, but pressing Jessamin about it in the library had been out of the question. Curiosity couldn't induce him to squander those private moments.

"Money?"

"The kiss. She said someone paid her a significant sum. Do you know who paid her? And why she accepted?"

Lady Stamford looked tired and a bit sad. She released another slow exhalation that seemed to deflate her. "I know she was desperate to save her bookshop, and quite devastated when she could not. The individual paid her one hundred pounds, enough to make a significant payment toward her debt."

She glanced at him, but Lucius couldn't read her expression. "We sometimes make surprising choices out of desperation."

Aunt Augusta took a sip of tea before truly addressing his question.

"She's not divulged who offered the money, but she's explained the circumstances of the bargain. I told her the incident would be forgotten. She'll tell me all of it one day. When she's ready to do so."

"Bargain? It's a curious way to earn a hundred pounds."

Aunt Augusta dabbed daintily at her mouth with her serviette before turning to him, her usual conviviality washing away the fatigue and sadness he'd glimpsed moments before.

"She tells me a young woman engineered the incident to repay you for snubbing her."

She picked up her teacup and took a sip, looking away from him as if she'd explained everything and there was nothing more to say on the matter. Yet Lucius found all he had were questions. He opened his mouth to ask one of them, but his aunt cut him off.

"Depending how one looks at the matter, it could be said that you are more responsible for the incident than anyone."

That hardly merited consideration. Whoever this woman was that he'd snubbed—and he couldn't recall a single incident in which he'd done so—her foolish prank was an ineffective retribution. Send a beautiful woman to kiss him? Punishment, indeed.

"I should like to know the name of this young woman I wronged." To thank her, if nothing else. But that wouldn't do, would it? He wasn't meant to enjoy Miss Wright's kiss and care nothing for the scandal it might cause. And he certainly shouldn't be eager for the sight of her this morning after walking down to breakfast determined to ask his aunt to send her away.

After years of loathing his father's changeable behavior, it was sobering to find himself every bit as muddled.

"Would you like me to ask Jessamin outright?"

His aunt respected Miss Wright. No one could mistake the affection in her tone whenever she referred to the young woman, and his own feelings for her were too troublesome to examine. He only knew he didn't wish to distress either of them.

"No."

"You still haven't told me how she was last evening."

In his head, Lucius fashioned a response for his aunt that left out any of his emotions on the matter, but before he could speak, the object of his thoughts appeared in the doorway with Robert Wellesley close on her heels.

Why had Lucius never realized how irritating the man could be? One would think several decades of friendship would have made the fact amply clear.

"I found Miss Wright walking quite slowly down the stairs. I decided to slow my pace in sympathy and escort her to breakfast."

Lady Stamford emitted a girlish titter. The man had the oddest effect on women.

"How good of you, Robert. Jessamin, my dear, come sit beside me and tell me how you're feeling."

"I am well, Lady Stamford. Thank you for your concern. Forgive me for being so late to breakfast."

She wouldn't look at him, and yet he couldn't take his eyes off her. She looked extraordinarily well for a young woman who'd had far too much to drink and been awake into the wee hours of the night. Her skin was a dash paler than usual, but her eyes sparkled, and—

Good grief, what was wrong with him? Cataloging Miss Wright's charms was hardly a useful endeavor, especially with a potential fiancée en route. And judging by Wellesley's leer, admiring Miss Wright was a task someone else already had well in hand.

"My lady, Lord Grimsby, and Mr. Wellesley, I hope you will accept my apologies for last evening. And please extend them to Mr. and Mrs. Darnley. I was—"

"Nonsense, you were the most interesting part of the evening." When Wellesley noticed Lady Stamford shaking her head at his insolence, he didn't bother looking abashed. "Well, she was. And you must tell us more about this 'kissing' incident."

"No!" Lucius spoke the word and heard it echoed and enhanced by the voices of Miss Wright and his aunt. Their chorus was so loud, Wellesley finally looked rattled.

He lifted his arms in surrender, a fork in one hand, a butter knife in the other.

Lucius stood. He'd had his fill of Robert's ceaseless

flirting, the distraction of Miss Wright, and his long-gone-cold breakfast. He stood and straightened his cuffs and necktie, and then his waistcoat, slipping a finger along the buttons to ensure they aligned in an orderly row down his stomach.

"If you'll excuse me, I must prepare for Miss Sedgwick's arrival. Aunt Augusta, would you please come to my study when you're finished?"

He laid his napkin aside and stepped out from in front of his chair. He meant to walk from the room and head straight for his study. He needed to think and the task suddenly seemed unachievable in the morning room. Yet as he took a step toward the doorway, he paused. The impulse to have one more look at her, a single glimpse before everything changed, overwhelmed him.

She was looking at him too. While the others tucked into their breakfast, Miss Wright sat very straight and still and watched him, her cool gaze unreadable.

Emotion hit him, fierce and powerful, too potent to deny. It was desire, yes, and yet more—an ache, a hunger to know every detail about the woman his aunt had chosen as her companion. To know her history, her preferences, her desires and fears, the shape and texture and flavor of every inch of her. To ask about the mother she missed as he did his own and the father who'd shared her love for clutter. He wanted to see her smile again, as she had in the library, artlessly and without a hint of guile. Had he ever wanted anything more?

Yes. Just one thing. To do his duty to his father, whether he'd ever mend the rift between them or not.

To protect his family name and pass it on to Dunthorpe sons and grandsons. It was the one purpose his mother had instilled in him before she'd left Hartwell and taken all of the light and laughter with her. Despite his father's ill treatment, the arguments and accusations between them, she'd loved him. She'd never allowed Lucius or his siblings to speak a cross word about their father in her hearing. And she'd never let him forget that whatever his father said in fits of anger, Lucius was Maxim Crawford's son, and that meant duty to the man as well as to the estate. And now he was his heir, the man upon whose shoulders the future of Hartwell and the earldom rested.

Holding fast to that purpose, he forced himself to move, to look away from Jessamin and break the connection between them, tangled threads of admiration and attraction that seemed to bind him to a woman he'd wanted from the first moment he'd seen her stomping toward him. But she possessed none of the qualities he required in a wife. Or rather, she did not possess the one thing he needed most—funds to repair Hartwell and restore it to its former glory.

Lucius took one step, two, and was finally free of the room. There was no use insisting his aunt send her back to London. Whether she was here or there, he knew her moss green eyes would haunt him for the rest of the day, if not the rest of his life.

Chapter Sixteen

"HARTWELL IS QUITE impressive, Lord Grimsby. Just divine. How kind of you to invite me."

May Sedgwick spun around in a circle, taking in Hartwell's grand entry hall from every angle. She looked like some rich confection in an elaborate bustled day dress of pink and white stripes, her black hair arranged in elaborate, tight curls and coils about her head, and her cheeks glowing as if she'd just come upon them after a vigorous stroll across the meadow. Her eyes were a uniquely bonny shade of blue, but they were busy, darting everywhere, examining everything, from the cornice along the top of the wall to the flower arrangements bursting from vases at her side.

Lucius didn't bother quibbling over the fact that it was actually his aunt who'd invited her. After all, Augusta had merely been acting on his behalf. And Miss Sedgwick came on with enough force and enthusiasm that he couldn't find it in him to disagree with her about anything. He imagined few did.

"My goodness, look at the paintings!"

She spoke as if she had an audience, or was used to having one. His aunt was long familiar with the fresco on the ceiling of Hartwell's main hallway, but she managed to look as if she was seeing it anew.

"It is marvelous, isn't it? How lovely it is to see Hartwell through your eyes, Miss Sedgwick. Your enthusiasm is contagious."

The young woman continued to gaze about as she approached him and lifted her hand for his polite attentions. He took it, a small, dainty thing encased in lace. It seemed far too fragile an appendage to form a part of the formidable woman before him.

He bent to place the expected kiss on the back of her hand and then gazed at her face, but she had yet to meet his eyes. Her gaze was directed over his shoulder.

"Miss Sedgwick, what a pleasure it is to finally meet you." He kept hold of her hand as he spoke, hoping to secure at least a bit of her attention.

"And you, my lord." She leaned down in a motion that approximated a curtsy and then pulled away from him. She moved her body toward the object that held her interest, a large, ornate vase that occupied a nook in the wall.

"Is it Chinese? It's extraordinary."

Lucius gazed at his aunt, trying to signal for help. She knew the knickknacks as well as he did. Better, in fact. She'd grown up at Hartwell, while he'd spent half of his youth exiled with his mother's family in Scotland. He'd noticed the vase rarely and had neither a notion nor a care for whether it came from the Orient or Arabia or any other corner of the world.

"Yes, I believe it is. Are you a connoisseur, Miss Sedgwick?"

"I am becoming one. Father has asked me to find pieces for his museum."

Lucius had never been interested in collecting anything, though his father loved to catalog and gather.

"Starting one's own museum seems an enormous undertaking." Lucius saw Augusta's eyebrows arch disapprovingly and added, "And admirable."

"Oh, nothing scares my father. He can do anything at all. He certainly has the money for it, and he has more energy than most men half his age."

It sounded like a good deal to live up to.

"Lucius is undertaking repairs to Hartwell."

Though he knew his aunt was attempting to increase his appeal, Miss Sedgwick looked far from impressed. Then her bright blue eyes grew large and she shrieked with such volume Lucius had to restrain himself from covering his ears.

"My heavens, no! It's perfect just as it is. Please, do let it be. If it crumbles, it will only make it more romantic. Don't you think? Like something out of one of Mrs. Radcliffe's gothic novels."

She beamed then, smiling as if pleased with herself and everyone, everything around her. Lucius couldn't deny her expression's potency, something akin to being warmed by a ray of sunlight on one of Berkshire's many cloudy days.

"Jessamin, my dear, do come and meet Miss Sedgwick."

In an instant Lucius went from the lazy pleasure of being warmed by the sun to every sense heightening in awareness of Miss Wright's presence. She'd entered the hall from the stairwell behind him, and he found it no loss to turn away from Miss Sedgwick and gaze at her.

As she approached, walking past him, not even sparing him a glance, she wafted her floral scent in her wake and lifted her hand in greeting to Miss Sedgwick.

"Miss Wright is my companion. I thought she could show you to your rooms and see to anything you might need before you meet the other guests."

Miss Sedgwick ignored Jessamin's extended hand, choosing instead to take her in a quick embrace and place a kiss on each of her cheeks.

Lucius could see Miss Wright's face bloom and pink at the American girl's effusiveness, but she smiled with genuine warmth at Miss Sedgwick.

"Perhaps you wish to rest after your long journey, Miss Sedgwick."

Jessamin's rich voice was such a striking contrast to Miss Sedgwick's higher pitch and broad American accent, Lucius found himself soothed by the sound of it. And he hadn't even realized he was in need of soothing.

Though Miss Sedgwick's charms were potent—and she clearly knew it—they were a bit much all at once, like a long quaff of liquor that gives powerful momentarily pleasure only to be followed by drowsiness and regret.

"Nonsense! I wish to move and breathe a bit of this fresh English country air. Would you give me a tour of the grounds, Miss Wright?"

"I've only just arrived a few days ago myself. I am afraid I'm not—"

"Pish posh. We shall explore together. Come, dear."

May grasped Jessamin's hand and began tugging her along.

"We shall see you both at afternoon tea, yes?" Miss Sedgwick called back as she headed for the front door.

Lucius had to remind himself that he was the host and Miss Sedgwick the guest, though it was clear the young woman was used to all around her dancing to whatever tune she set.

Jessamin cast a glance back at his aunt, a question in her eyes.

"Shall we take Castor and Pollux, my lady?"

The two pugs sat at their mistress's feet, warily watching every move the colorful Miss Sedgwick made.

"No, you two ladies go on. We shall look forward to your return within the hour for tea and luncheon."

As he watched Miss Sedgwick pull Jessamin along behind her as if she was leading the tour despite having arrived at the estate only minutes before, he had an urge to follow. If anyone accompanied Jessamin around Hartwell's grounds, it should be he. He wanted to be the one to show her the estate, his favorite paths through woods, and the pond on the other side. And he wanted to take her out to his mother's favorite spot on the grounds again, a copse of alder trees she'd planted from seeds brought from her family's estate in Scotland, the place where he sometimes talked with her as if she was listening and might advise him.

His mouth tickled and twitched a moment before he gave in to a grin at the memory of Miss Wright finding him at the spot and accusing him of talking to himself as her father used to do.

"YOU MUST TELL me all the gossip about the viscount, Miss Wright. And you must call me May. Should I call you Jessamin or do you prefer something else? Jessie, perhaps?"

Jess had never met a more forward young woman in her life. Her first thought was that she would be a powerful member of the Women's Union. Though Alice usually gave the speeches she wrote and had plain-speaking appeal, Jess could only imagine the impact of a speech delivered by the charismatic Miss Sedgwick.

"Call me Jess." It was a nickname only her father and friends at the union had used, but she felt a surge of affection for May Sedgwick. The young woman's openness encouraged openness, yet Jess feared she'd disappoint her in terms of gossip. The notion of discussing Lord Grimsby—Lucius—a man who stirred reactions in her she had yet to sort out for herself—was impossible. She'd learned virtually nothing about him since arriving at Hartwell, unless one counted his favorite author as a revelation, and she had yet to meet the earl. She certainly couldn't tell her about the incident in Mayfair. "I fear I don't know much gossip to tell."

May quirked a disappointed moue. "Are you not long acquainted with Lord Grimsby?"

"No, not at all." A flutter in her throat as she spoke the words made Jess cringe. Was she acquainted with the viscount? Considering each of their encounters, she realized an explanation would be difficult, even if she wasn't attempting it with the man's prospective betrothed. The facts. She clung to them as the only truth she knew for certain. Her feelings were far too messy to sift. "I just entered his aunt's employ a month ago."

"Ah, well surely that's long enough for you to have heard about his mistress."

Jess stumbled though the path before them was clear.

May tugged her close. "Careful, Jess."

"Mistress?" *No.* It couldn't be true. Would a man with a mistress have kissed her as he had? Looked at her as he had?

May made a tsking sound with her tongue. "Imagine my shock. I'd never heard a sour word about the viscount. Papa had one of his Pinkerton men look into Lord Grimsby's business dealings. Nothing scandalous at all, though it's clear the Dunthorpe wealth has gone threadbare over the years. But that's all right. Papa has heaps of money. Yet the moment I agreed to come to England to meet the man, practically assuring his aunt I would marry him . . . Well, one moment I'm replying to Lady Stamford's invitation and the next I hear the viscount has a mistress."

Jess imagined the viscount with another woman—kissing another woman, embracing another woman, entangled with another woman. The thought made her stop in her tracks. May took her actions as shared outrage and released her arm. The diminutive American assumed an angry stance, her lace-gloved hands settled on the curve of her tiny waist. Jess noticed the pink ribbon at the wrist of Miss Sedgwick's gloves perfectly matched the pink stripes in the fabric of her fashionable gown.

"Yes, my reaction exactly. And apparently she doesn't even have the discretion those sort of women are known for. She's a brazen thing. Walked right up to him in public and claimed his mouth. As if she had a right to do so!"

Me. She's talking about me.

Jess swallowed the words on the tip of her tongue, stifling the impulse to defend her actions or explain. There was no need. May hadn't a clue she was the woman who'd accosted Lord Grimsby, and Jess hated that she might learn the truth one day.

Should she tell it all now? Explain her reasons—motives that had nothing to do with desire.

But such a claim only explained that first kiss. How could she explain the way she'd reacted when he'd carried her to the sitting room? Did desire have anything to do with how much she'd yearned for his kiss? *Yes.*

From the moment she'd opened her eyes late in the morning, head throbbing from too much wine and the horrible things she'd blurted out at dinner, Jess had known that whatever he'd said to her, whatever had passed between, she wanted his kiss. And when the memories came back, the realization he'd not taken her lips as she'd hoped he would, the skin of her forehead, her cheek, even the tip of her nose, tingled as she recalled the heat of his mouth against her skin.

And she'd wanted his kiss in the library, when she'd glimpsed the man behind the frown, a man with nothing of the grim nature for which Kitty claimed he was known.

"To tell you the truth, I can't imagine him kissing anyone at all."

Jess tensed at May's emphatic judgment and prayed her expression gave nothing away.

"What makes you say so?"

"Well, he's very dour, isn't he? The man didn't smile at me at all." May looked at Jess expectantly. "Most men are happy to see me. Why isn't he? He should be. Don't you think? If I'm to marry him."

Jess thought back to all of her encounters with Lord Grimsby and couldn't recall a single instance of a true smile, just the grin she'd been privy to in the library. She wanted to see it, Lucius filled with happiness so immense that it burst into his expression. Then realization came, a fizzing awareness that she wanted to be the cause. But it wasn't her place. Such looks should be for Miss Sedgwick. She was certainly lovely enough to attract any man.

"I'm sure he will. I don't think he's a man who smiles easily."

"Then why would anyone wish to marry him?"

"Is smiling so important?"

May beamed at the question, the expression softening

her face, tipping her cerulean eyes, and revealing dimples on each side of her cheeks. It was a dazzling reminder of the power of smiles.

"Of course it is. Papa says laughter is the very best medicine and laughs all the time. I couldn't love a man who never laughs. And he says that a pleasant expression is a businessman's most essential tool. It can invite, convince, or reassure."

Her conviction and exuberance were unassailable and Jess imagined May could be as successful an entrepreneur as her father, if she put her mind to it.

"Do you plan to start a business?"

For a moment May's merry expression faltered, her grin fading and long lashes fluttering down as she tipped her head.

"I'm a woman. Papa says marriage is my business."

Then she lifted her gaze to look at Jess. "And I cannot marry a man who does nothing but grimace."

"I'm certain you can make him smile, May."

And Jess *was* certain. May smelled like roses and exuded an infectious liveliness. Like Kitty Adderly, she possessed a delicate beauty, the sort of porcelain perfection Jess had only ever seen in art or fashion magazines.

"Well, now I'm not at all certain I wish him to. There's worse than just a mistress."

"Worse?"

May wasn't smiling anymore.

"Madness." May whispered the word.

This claim of madness was the same Jess had heard from Tilly and Rachel in the carriage on the way to Hartwell. She wondered at the cause of the rumors. And she couldn't help but wonder about Lord Dunthorpe. She'd yet to meet him or see the man anywhere about the estate. Did Lord Grimsby hide his father away because he was mad?

"Who told you such a thing?"

"Oh, everyone. I attended a ball in London before coming to Hartwell, and the ladies were quite dire in their warnings to me. Lord Grimsby is so rarely in society and his father not at all. Not for years. And the mother, Lady Dunthorpe . . ." May leaned toward Jess, looking back and forth over her shoulder as if they might somehow be overheard, though they stood alone in a leaf strewn meadow. "She died in a quite unexpected carriage accident."

"I suspect all carriage accidents are unexpected."

Gossip was odious and Jess bristled on Lord Grimsby's behalf that the loss of his mother should be recalled for any reason other than the grief it must have caused.

Surely, it was a tragic accident and nothing more. Jess thought back and couldn't recall Lady Stamford ever mentioning her sister-in-law, but surely if there had been some crime, some suspicion, the countess would have made mention of such a thing. Lady Stamford reminisced about her family often—her brother, her nephews, and her late husband.

"I can't believe any of it, Miss Sedgwick. Rumors are insidious and we often speculate wildly about what we don't know for certain."

May reared back a step at Jessamin's formality and

perhaps at the implication that she preferred rumor to fact.

"Have you met Lord Dunthorpe during your time at Hartwell?"

"No, I'm afraid I haven't. Lady Stamford and I arrived just yesterday."

"Well, then I suppose you're as curious as I am."

Jess thought back to the moments when the countess mentioned her brother. She'd indicated that the earl was unwell and spoke of her concern for him but never offered any other details. Whatever the gentleman's illness, perhaps it explained his son's serious nature. Her father's last days were still fresh in her mind. Worry for him had certainly sapped her, physically and emotionally.

"No, I can't say that I am, Miss Sedgwick. The viscount seems a man of sound mind, and I suspect his father is simply too ill to be out and about. Rumormongers don't always get it right."

A breeze, scented with the crushed autumn leaves beneath their feet and the smoke of a peat fire, cooled Jess's cheeks as she looked out on the meadow. She took a deep breath, savoring the scents of the countryside, attempting to stem the flash of anger that made her lash out at Miss Sedgwick.

Why am I so eager to defend a man I hardly know? That kiss had surely addled her brain, not to mention what it had done to her heart.

For a moment, she almost wished to have the shop back, for a problem so immense and seemingly hopeless it would occupy her mind, use up all of her energies, and leave her with nothing left for desire and this terrible yearning for a man she could never have.

She wanted to turn away from May Sedgwick, to somehow make her way back to Marleston Hall and collect that old, tattered dress she'd worn on the carriage ride to Wiltshire. That dress, one other, and a portmanteau full of books, the photo of her father, and a few of her writings for the union, were all she had left from her life in London. Could she make a new life with such meager scraps from the old?

"Miss Wright? Jess? What shall I do?"

"You must do what you think best."

Jess needed to take her own advice. Lady Stamford could certainly find a more suitable companion, and with a bit of luck Jess could rebuild a life back in London—one uncomplicated by a viscount who kissed her and scrambled her wits. Maybe she could even rebuild a business of some sort, though the thought of it brought a mix of anxiety and fear. What if she failed again? She had to try. Leave the business of favorable marriages to women like Miss Sedgwick, who'd been blessed with all the qualities men desire.

"I'll do the same." Jess exhaled the words, satisfied with her decision. Relief heightened her senses, making her giddy, eager to begin on the path she'd chosen. "Can we return to Hartwell, May? I must speak with Lady Stamford."

"Wait. Please, Jess. Miss Wright."

May tugged at the sleeve of Jess's dress.

"I only arrived in England three days ago, Jessamin. It

would be so wonderful to have a friend, someone I could trust. Won't you help me?"

Standing in the oak leaf–covered meadow, black curls streaming out in the breeze and blue eyes shimmering as if she might let loose a tear, Jess thought May looked a good deal like a heroine in a sentimental novel, one in desperate need of rescue. It was tempting to give in to her plea, to agree to be as helpful as May asked her to be. At the bookshop and as a member of the Women's Union, Jess enjoyed being helpful. It gave her more pleasure and purpose than selling a dozen books at the bookshop. But aiding May Sedgwick meant revealing her own scandalous behavior in Mayfair, not to mention nosing into the family affairs of Lord Grimsby and his father.

She felt unreasonably protective of Lady Stamford and her family, including the viscount. If Lord Grimsby's father was ill, what business did she have exposing the fact? Aristocrats could be as contrary as they liked. Perhaps the man simply loathed social gatherings.

And while Lord Grimsby often appeared conflicted, a man whose eyes signaled desire even when his expression remained neutral, he seemed wholly sane, though perhaps not as jovial as Mr. Wellesley. Why should his more reserved nature be the cause of ugly rumors? A pang of guilt that her own actions at the gallery might have exposed him to derision made her turn away from Miss Sedgwick. Her desire to protect the viscount, to protect herself, clashed with her impulse to be helpful to May, and the decision she'd made moments before began to shift and crumble.

"Ladies, there you are. I was sent to slay the dragon and fetch you back for tea. But I see you are both well and in no need of rescue."

Robert Wellesley spoke as he ascended the small rise toward the meadow. Even from a distance, Jess could see he was smiling. The wind whipped his wavy gold-brown hair and without a jacket or vest, his white shirt shifted and billowed as he walked. But for a journal and pen, he looked like an erstwhile poet—a Shelley or Wordsworth wandering about the countryside seeking inspiration for verses about clouds and flowers.

Jess saw Miss Sedgwick turn and take in the sight of him. The American heiress made a little sound of pleasure, as if she'd just taken a bite of chocolate or something sweet.

When he stood before them, Wellesley sketched an elaborate bow, reaching his hand out as if he was a dandy doffing his feathered hat.

"Miss Wright." He spoke Jess's name, but his gaze locked on May Sedgwick. "And you must be Miss May Sedgwick. Yes, I know. We have not been formally introduced, but Miss Wright will tell you how I loathe formality."

He reached out and May met his hand by lifting her own, smiling as Wellesley bowed to kiss it.

"Then we're in agreement, sir. There is far too much formality and not nearly enough laughter here at Hartwell. But you should at least tell me your name."

"Mr. Robert Wellesley is a friend of Lord Grimsby's." Jess had no idea why she felt the need to rush in with a bit of formality.

Wellesley still held May's hand and leaned too close to her, whispering near her ear. "You must call me Rob, Miss Sedgwick, when no one else is about."

"And you must call me May."

They both glanced at Jess, as if assessing whether she counted as anyone else.

"Oh, Miss Wright won't mind. I'm already May to her, and she is Jess to me. She's agreed to be a help to me during my time at Hartwell."

May pulled her hand from Wellesley's grasp and turned to stand with Jess. Hooking her arm around Jess's, she tugged and began walking back toward Hartwell.

"Come, Rob. It wouldn't do for me to be late to my first tea."

Chapter Seventeen

"I BELIEVE THE host is an essential element at a social gathering. Or at least in the case of your betrothed's debut."

"She's not my betrothed yet. I've barely met her. You always were a man for haste."

A closed door had never stopped Wellesley. He'd pushed his way into Lucius's study and now sat opposite him, occupying Maxim's favorite chair before the fire and managing to look more comfortable in the piece of furniture than anyone ever had.

"Having second thoughts?"

Lucius arranged and then rearranged the writing implements on his desk, the blotter perfectly straight, the inkwell just at the top, and the magnifying glass and letter opener equidistant from the paperweight, a polished black stone he'd brought back from Scotland.

"I barely have any thoughts about Miss Sedgwick at

all. I only met the woman an hour ago. Quite frankly, she was more interested in the family bric-a-brac."

Wellesley was far too audacious to try concealing his mirth.

"I fetched them from the meadow, your two young ladies. Miss Sedgwick is a strikingly pretty thing, but there is something delicious about your aunt's companion." Leaning forward, he lifted the paperweight without asking, and began hefting it in his hand to test its weight. "If Miss Sedgwick is sweet, Miss Wright is rich and savory. We must ply her with wine more often."

Lucius felt a movement in his cheek. A muscle there took to twitching whenever his feathers were ruffled, which meant it always twitched when Robert Wellesley was about.

"Do you have no sense of propriety? Behave yourself, Wellesley. With both of them. And give me that rock." He settled the shiny bit of basalt back in its proper place with an inhale of satisfaction.

"Miss Sedgwick may be my countess one day." *Mercy, what a thought.* "And Miss Wright will soon be back at Marleston with Aunt Augusta or in London running a new bookshop."

It was the story Lucius had spent the morning concocting, repeating it in his mind, a makeshift tale to convince himself Miss Wright should go sooner rather than later. He had to squelch his desire for her. Convincing himself of her impermanence in his life seemed a promising tactic. At least until she'd walked into the breakfast room and he was near her again.

"Augusta tells me she lost the shop and Miss Wright doesn't speak much of going back to London. Your aunt means to raise her up from bookseller to baroness or some such."

Lucius ignored the man's use of his aunt's first name and focused instead on the notion of Augusta's matchmaking efforts. Matchmaking for Miss Wright.

He tugged at his necktie, wincing at the look he imagined Mather would have given him if he saw the mess he was making of the valet's efforts to tie the perfect knot. The notion of Miss Wright matched with some baronet turned his stomach sour. He knew the noblemen and gentry within the county. Most were married, one was far too old for Miss Wright, and the other was far too unprincipled. He'd rather see her with Wellesley. Though as he studied the smirk on his friend's face, every impulse in him denied it. No, he didn't wish to see Jessamin matched with any of them.

The very notion of her with any man of his acquaintance sparked an absurd impulse to find her, tuck her into his carriage, and set off for the family estate in Scotland, making one short stop along the way in Gretna Green. Good God, what would his aunt make of that?

Lucius laughed. Out loud. Not a long drawn-out sound, more of a brief chortle, escaping before he thought better of it.

Robert looked stunned. He blinked, then again, and sat up straight, holding himself very still, as if he feared Lucius would make more sounds, louder, and more uncharacteristically exuberant. Then the shock broke, softening his features, and his face creased into a full-on Wellesley smile.

"My God, man, you're smitten."

"I beg your pardon."

"The look on your face before you made that awful sound. I know that look. You were thinking of a woman. And since you are less than impressed with Miss Sedgwick, I can only deduce you were pondering our lovely suffragette."

"Wellesley." Lucius used his menacing tone, much like the one Robert's father had used on the two of them when they'd devised some sort of adolescent mischief.

"Sorry, old friend. Doesn't work on me anymore." His smile broadened, indicating his utter lack of repentance. "I don't blame you a bit, Grimsby. She's a fascinating creature, our Miss Jessamin Wright. She may not come on with frills and fire, our Jess, but one can tell passion is lurking just there under the surface. She's intelligent, lacks artifice, and her hair is the most fetching shade of auburn I've ever seen."

The more Robert spoke about Jessamin, that lurid smirk ever on his lips, referring to her in a nickname he had no right to use, the more Lucius yearned to yank the man out of his father's chair and trounce him as he had when they were boys. And if he called her "our" anything once more, Lucius thought he could rouse the energy to kick Wellesley all the way back to his family estate several miles away.

"And she kissed you. For a significant sum, apparently, but her actions indicate she is a woman with a bit of mettle. Although considering her failing shop and her father's debt, perhaps she was just desperate."

"You seem to have considered the whole matter a great deal."

"I have merely listened and observed. And I spoke with your aunt on the subject after you stormed away from breakfast this morning."

He'd left because he couldn't bear another second in the same room with Miss Wright, knowing the woman who might turn his life in an entirely different direction was on her way to Hartwell. Yet now, having met Miss Sedgwick, he felt certain of nothing. Except that she didn't move him. She was lovely and lively and would make an unconventional countess. He suspected most in London society, and even some here in the country, would be charmed by her American vigor.

But Lucius simply found it . . . irritating. Even if she spent most of her time in London and he at Hartwell, could he endure those moments they were, of necessity, together? He couldn't imagine producing the expected Dunthorpe heir with a woman who, in spite of her beauty, sparked nothing in him, not even a flicker of desire.

"Perhaps you should send her away."

The thought had already crossed his mind too. Yet his aunt had extended the invitation, and he suspected Miss Sedgwick would be content to spend the fortnight cataloging the Dunthorpe art collection. He just had to make sure none of it was missing after her departure. *No, it's impossible.* It would be a grave insult to Miss Sedgwick and her powerful father if he sent the girl packing so soon after her arrival.

"She obviously has you in a dither and it is clear our Miss Wright is meant for more than serving out her marriageable years as your aunt's companion. Augusta says she means to make a good match for her, yet she also says she can't do without her."

"Pardon?"

Realization seeped in, and Lucius pushed back from his desk, prepared to call Wellesley's assertion outrageous.

Robert meant he should send Jessamin away, not the American woman. Though he'd had the same thought himself just a few hours before, hearing it from Wellesley's lips rankled.

"You think I should send Miss Wright away?"

He sank back in his chair, resigned to hear Rob's arguments, though he doubted his childhood friend could convince him any better than he'd persuaded himself.

"Look at you, Lucius. You can't even carry on a proper conversation without clouding over with thoughts of the woman. How can you marry Miss Sedgwick when your mind is full of Miss Wright?"

It wasn't only his mind. She seemed to hold every part of him in thrall. He'd never been so aware of another person in his life.

"And what if Miss Sedgwick finds out that the woman who kissed you in Mayfair is living under your roof?"

He stood then, anger and frustration driving him.

"She doesn't live under my roof! She is employed by my aunt. And while my aunt may be determined to marry her off to some country squire . . ."

What? What could he do to avoid such a fate for Miss Wright? Perhaps sending her back to London with enough funds to start a new shop was the best he could do for her. At least it would spare him the agony of seeing her married off to one of his neighbors.

He covered his mouth with his hand and then reached up to pinch the skin above his nose.

"You're right."

Wellesley was a bit like Aunt Augusta, an enemy of silence, and Lucius looked up when his friend remained quiet.

"What is it? You always have something to say."

Robert snapped his mouth closed, bit his lip, and lit up with a devilish smirk. "I was simply savoring the moment. I'm not sure you've ever said those words to me before."

"Yes, well, don't expect it to become commonplace."

"No, certainly not." He reached for the paperweight again, but Lucius beat him to it and slid the stone out of his reach. "Although the victory is bittersweet."

"Is it?"

Robert tugged at his ear, a habit Lucius remembered from their youth. It was a rare outward sign of discomfort for a man who made merriment his mission in life.

"I've never seen you like this, my friend. Whatever the

expectations that are now yours instead of Julian's, you must not forfeit all of your own desires."

A knock sounded at the door of his study, though at first he thought it was his heartbeat, knocking wildly in his ears.

When he didn't respond, Robert stood and opened the door.

"You changed your dress. How lovely."

"Lady Stamford insisted."

Even before she spoke, Lucius knew it was Miss Wright at the door. Her presence had set his body on alert, as if some part of him knew she was near, even if he couldn't see or touch her.

"She sent me to find you and Lord Grimsby. More guests have arrived. I take it the party is complete now, and she wishes His Lordship to help make introductions."

Wellesley opened the door wider as she spoke and lifted his arm to indicate she should enter, but Jessamin held back, not moving from her spot just past the threshold.

Robert was right. She did look lovely. And the pleasure Lucius always felt at the sight of her was magnified by the contemplation of never having the experience again if she returned to London or married another man.

Unlike Miss Sedgwick, she willingly met his gaze. She looked at him, into him, and seemed to speak volumes with her eyes alone. She opened her mouth and he imagined words he longed to hear in her warm, mellifluous voice—words neither of them should, or could, speak.

But her words were practical, inspired by duty. What should be done. What must be done. And that was better. Those were motives he understood.

"Shall we go in to tea, my lord?"

THE PARTY HAD grown by four more guests during the morning and early afternoon. Lady Matilda Turbridge, a neighbor and longtime friend of his aunt, had arrived with her granddaughter, Miss Annabel Benson. Lady Katherine had been retrieved from the train station and Dr. William Seagraves, the village doctor, had walked over from his home several miles away. He looked wind-chafed and a bit unkempt, though his eyes lit up as he took in the collection of young women around him. Seagraves was quite vocal about his hunt for a suitable wife, though his income was far below his expectations for a fortunate match.

After introductions were made, the ladies separated into one group and the gentlemen into another, though Lucius noticed that Jessamin held back, sitting apart from the rest of the gathering with Miss Benson. The younger woman seemed to hang on Jessamin's every word, and he chastised himself for a pang of envy, the wish to take Miss Benson's place and speak privately with Miss Wright rather than engage in meaningless chatter with the gentlemen.

When Miss Sedgwick began to sing and Wellesley accompanied her on the piano, the others gathered round to listen. Miss Benson took a chair near her grandmother, finally tearing herself away from Jessamin, and Miss Wright made her way toward the drawing room door as if she meant to escape. Lucius longed to join her, wherever she might go. His head had begun to throb after twenty minutes surrounded by so many voices, and May's singing, though sprightly and melodious, did nothing to ease the ache in his temples.

Lady Katherine approached Jessamin, whispering something to make her blush. A ribbon of scarlet rushed across her cheeks and neck, and then she turned away. Jessamin glanced at his aunt once before leaving the drawing room, walking so quickly she lifted the skirts of her gown to keep from tripping.

Curious. Very curious.

The blond woman caught him watching her and approached.

"Lord Grimsby, do you remember me?"

"My aunt said we met at a ball." He didn't remember the woman at all.

"Indeed we did. You did not care to dance, as I recall."

"I rarely dance, Lady Katherine."

"What a pity, and please call me Kitty."

"Are you acquainted with Miss Wright?"

She laughed, a jarring, high-pitched sound, before lifting a hand to her mouth as if to stop herself.

"I am. I see that you are too, my lord. Though I was surprised to find her here at Hartwell." She gazed at him knowingly, as if he should take some special meaning from her words. Almost as if she believed they shared a very great secret and had agreed to keep it from all around them.

She'd piqued his curiosity.

"May I ask how you're acquainted with Miss Wright?"

She smiled again, a dazzling flash of white across her bow-shaped mouth.

"Of course, my lord. We are both members of the Women's Union. It's a charitable group for the most part, though we're also bound by a belief in the vote for women."

"Sounds formidable."

"Oh, very formidable, my lord."

Lucius had a notion Lady Katherine was speaking of herself rather than the women's organization.

"And is Miss Sedgwick acquainted with Miss Wright, my lord?"

The question, asked with a slow, subtle cadence, made his skin itch.

"Yes, certainly. They've been introduced."

She seemed to gather this information and tuck it away, an inscrutable expression on her face.

He longed to ask her what she'd said to Jessamin, what she'd done to make her distressed enough to leave the room. But he suspected he wouldn't get the truth from Miss Adderly even if he was rude enough to question her plainly.

"You seem bemused, Lady Katherine."

She tipped her body toward him, too close, and whispered so that none might overhear.

"It's just that it seems a dangerous proposition, my lord. That the wealthy American woman you plan to wed and the ruined shop owner who scandalized you in front of everyone should be socializing together. And here, at Hartwell, the very heart of the great Dunthorpes of Berkshire."

She might have known about the incident in Mayfair from her acquaintance with Jessamin, yet Lucius knew—from the glow of triumph in her eyes and her mocking tone—that Lady Katherine Adderly was the woman who'd offered a hundred pounds to humiliate him. And for just this moment, he suspected, when she might savor her victory.

He had no intention of playing her game.

"Why shouldn't she be? Miss Wright is my aunt's companion."

At least that bit of news was unexpected, judging by the way Lady Katherine's mouth dropped open and her lashes fluttered over wide eyes.

"Lady Stamford? She took employment with *your* aunt?"

A nod was all he could manage when what he truly wished to do was tell Miss Adderly just how much he'd relished Jessamin's kiss, that her attempt to mortify him had brought him nothing but pleasure. Pleasure and several weeks of sleepless nights.

When she said nothing more, he left her standing there, that shocked look still fixed on her face. He turned away from her and the rest of the gathered guests, who were too enthralled with Miss Sedgwick's performance to notice his exit.

Two maids approached him in the hallway, heads down, carrying trays with more tea toward the drawing room.

"Miss Wright. Have you seen Miss Wright?"

The one he'd mistaken for Jessamin answered. "I believe she's in the kitchen, my lord."

Chapter Eighteen

"My goodness, Tilly, you are a very fast learner."

"My mum did teach me a bit when I was very wee, miss. I remember as I go along."

Jessamin smiled at the younger woman and nodded, encouraging her to go on.

Tilly read another few sentences in a stop-and-start manner, looking up for affirmation or assistance from Jess when she came upon a word she wasn't sure of.

"And will I go next, miss?"

"Yes, James. You're next."

The boot boy, James, was as keen to learn to read as Tilly. Rachel stood nearby ironing one of Lady Stamford's underskirts. Jess knew she was listening, though she'd repeatedly declared books did not interest her at all. Only ladies' magazines, she'd insisted, and then mostly for the fashion prints. Now she just listened in, pretending disinterest.

James had heard Jess and Tilly reading together in the kitchen on Jess's first night at Hartwell. He'd been an eager student ever since, though he wasn't keen on their choice of books. Tilly wished to read one of Miss Austen's novels, but James begged to practice with a penny dreadful his brother had given him.

Tilly continued on, gaining confidence and speed. They had begun reading *Pride and Prejudice* before leaving Marleston, and Tilly read from the third chapter.

"' . . . for he was discovered to be proud, to be above his company, and above being pleased—' " she read until James interrupted her with a guffaw of laughter.

"Sounds a bit like our Lord Grim, eh?"

Jess knew it wasn't true of Lord Grimsby at all but held her tongue. He'd never spoken to her as anything but an equal, and he clearly took pleasure in discussing books.

"You shouldn't say such things, Jimmy," Tilly chastised, seemingly oblivious to her own tendency to gossip about Lord Grimsby and his father.

"Nor should you interrupt Tilly when she's reading. You would not appreciate her cutting in when you're reading about Terrible Bill Tetley and all the other scoundrels in your book."

"Yes, miss." James looked contrite, though he still held the shadow of a grin on his small face.

The sound of a man clearing his throat and heavy footsteps nearly frightened all of them off their chairs.

"I'm ever so sorry, my lord. We were just—"

The viscount held up his hand and Tilly stopped in mid-sentence, waiting with a horrified look on her face for what she seemed to think would be a terrible punishment.

"No need to apologize. Reading is a fine pursuit. Never seem to find the time for it myself anymore. James?"

"Yes, my lord."

Jessamin watched as the boy sat up straight, making him appear taller and older than his years. He looked at the viscount with a kind of reverence, despite his recent jest.

"Perhaps you could find time to read the *Times* or the *Sporting News*, and report back to me now and then."

"Yes, my lord!"

"Miss Wright, may I speak with you?"

Jessamin patted Tilly on the shoulder as she approached Lord Grimsby. The girl was still quaking in fear, though James beamed as if he'd just been elected king for a day.

Lord Grimsby walked to a corner of the kitchen, far enough away that others could see them but might not hear their conversation.

"Well done, Miss Wright."

In the few steps it took to follow him to the corner, Jess practiced justifications and arguments in her mind, expecting chastisement for wasting the staff's work time or distracting them. She didn't expect commendation, or the glint of appreciation in his gaze.

"You approve, my lord?" She'd managed to get the words out without stuttering, but her pulse stuttered, fluttering wildly in her veins.

"Yes, of course." The light in his eyes seemed to dim

and he looked a bit crestfallen that she'd expected anything less of him.

"But you don't approve of women having the right to vote?"

Jess clutched the fabric of her skirt and bit her lip the moment the words were out. She'd had the habit since childhood of blurting out thoughts in her head whenever the impulse struck. It had proved harmless when Father and shelves lined with books were her only companions. But why provoke the viscount when the man had just praised her?

"Do you truly wish to have this conversation now? Here? In the kitchen?"

She wasn't certain where the correct time or place might be, but she was quite content to let the matter rest altogether for the moment. She'd take the question back if she could, but just as she opened her mouth to speak, he heaved a breathy sigh.

"Very well, Miss Wright." He widened his stance and crossed his arms over his chest, and she longed to smile. It was the same manner he'd assumed when she first approached him in the meadow upon arriving at Hartwell.

He rocked back and forth on his heels. "To tell you the truth, I have not given the matter as much thought as I should. Certainly not as much as you and my aunt would no doubt urge me to." Looking at the floor, he clenched his jaw and furrowed his brow.

Jess realized the kitchen had gone quiet. The viscount was so tall and broad-shouldered, she had to crane her neck to see around him, and she wasn't surprised to find

Rachel, Tilly, and James with their gazes turned her way.

Lord Grimsby finally raised his head. When he spoke, his tone was measured and calm. "I would not oppose women's suffrage outright, but do women know enough about the issues they'd be deciding upon?"

Kitty really did have everything about the man wrong.

"That is it exactly, my lord. They must be educated about such matters. Anyone who casts a vote should be."

"Which brings us back to your reading lessons." He lowered his arms, and the tension in his body seemed to ease.

Jess couldn't imagine her life without the ability to read, and she'd found more enjoyment in teaching Tilly and James than she'd ever experienced selling books or managing her father's shop.

"Well, yes, I suppose it does. The ability to read would be the first step to that sort of education."

Lord Grimsby leaned in, lowering his voice. "And again I say well done, Miss Wright."

"Thank you, my lord."

A flicker of satisfaction flashed in his gaze, but he didn't smile or indicate his pleasure in any other way.

"How did you come to believe I was opposed to the suffrage?"

Like an unstoppable, onrushing tide, Jess knew the whole of it must come out eventually. And something in the way the viscount looked at her, as if he could see into her, beyond any defenses she might construct, made her wish to tell him the plain, unvarnished truth.

"Lady Katherine told me."

His mouth curved, not quite a grin, just a wry tip at the edges of his full lips.

"Did she, indeed? She is why I came to find you just now. The lady said something to you. Upset you."

Kitty's words had upset her, though she'd said nothing cruel. She'd whispered so that no one else could hear and asked how Jess had come to be at Hartwell. A reasonable question, since anyone aware of the circumstances of Jess's first encounter with Lord Grimsby would know it was the last place she belonged.

Standing in the sitting room as May Sedgwick held court and considering how to respond to Kitty, Jess had known it too. She didn't belong at Hartwell.

And yet here, with Lucius standing near enough to touch, whatever she'd known in the sitting room faded.

But what had Kitty said to him? Perhaps she'd finally confessed her role in the Mayfair incident.

"She told you, then?"

"No. She admitted nothing, but it all became clear. What did she whisper to you?"

"She only asked why I'm here, but her question did cause me to reconsider my employment with your aunt."

"Do you wish to leave?"

"I'd almost decided to do so earlier today. When Miss Sedgwick arrived."

That news seemed to unsettle him. He lifted his hands to his hips and turned away from her. Taking a few steps, he tread in a small circle and then walked back to confront her.

"But here you are, Miss Wright. What brought on your change of heart?"

There was a pause, fragile and full of meaning, between his question and her answer. Jess couldn't tell him a truth she wasn't certain of herself. She felt out of place at Hartwell and yet couldn't imagine never seeing him or Lady Stamford again. And something about May Sedgwick tugged at Jess's nature, a tendency to offer help when and where she could.

"Miss Sedgwick. She asked me to stay." It was far easier to point to May than admit any of her own unsorted feelings. "I suspect Lady Katherine would find that ironic."

He tilted his head up, examining the ceiling above him, and pursed his lips. Jess thought he might finally smile.

"I don't give a damn what Lady Katherine thinks."

And it was clear he did not. He moved a step closer, vibrating with emotion. Anger? Frustration? Jess couldn't read the expression in his gaze.

"And I do not wish you to leave. I am not certain . . ." He whispered the words, the most tentative admission she'd ever heard. Jess waited for him to finish, to say more, but he remained quiet. Quiet and tense, like a coil ready to spring.

"Certain, my lord?"

He edged toward her, his large frame blocking her view of everyone else. She expected him to answer, yet his gaze held nothing but questions and his eyes searched hers, as if she might know the answer.

But she didn't have answers, and she wasn't certain she could find her voice to speak. It was his answer she needed, longed for. Why did he wish her to stay?

She drew in a breath and held it, every inch of her body tensing. Even her heart seemed to pause, waiting for a reason to beat. It was as if he'd drawn her to the edge of a great precipice, and she wanted to know he'd catch her if she fell.

"I am only certain of this." He lifted his hand and flicked his wrist back and forth, pointing first to himself and then to Jess before lowering his arm. "Even as it confounds me."

He didn't touch her, didn't kiss her, merely looked at her, searched her. He seemed to ask if she was certain of this too—this powerful, undeniable pull between them.

His questioning gaze, the need she saw there, was enough to draw her closer to the edge.

"Yes."

Finally, and quite devastatingly, he smiled at her. Not a fleeting expression, but a broad, gleaming expression that etched lines in his face and revealed half-moon dimples on each of his cheeks. He looked boyish, joyful, as if, just for a moment, he'd left his burdens behind.

Something in her eased, lifted. To be the cause of his smile—that was reason enough to stay at Hartwell.

But what had she agreed to with her *yes*? She couldn't deny the attraction between them, but could she ignore her circumstances? Employed by his aunt, and committed to assist his potential bride during her stay at Hartwell, she couldn't envision a scenario that ended in anything other than her ruin or their mutual heartache.

He seemed to sense her doubts and moved closer, as if to shelter her, and the rest of it fell away—the kitchen, the other staff members watching, her doubts rushing in. There was only Lucius, standing so close she could feel the warmth of his body, see the stubble on his chin, study the shape of his mouth and wish he'd smile again.

Jess imagined being brave, lifting onto her toes and kissing him as she had that night in the gallery. She ached to kiss him, and what blissful relief it would be to stop denying what she wanted, what was in her heart, what her whole body affirmed every time he was near. Surely he could read it in her gaze every time he looked her way.

The latch that held her back was fragile, so easily slipped. Emotions bubbled up, ready to burst free of the constraint she'd imposed. Before she could think better of it, impulse won out. She reached up, eager to touch him, ready to kiss him again, as brazenly as she had the first time.

"What the deuces are you two doing conspiring in the corner over there? Jessamin, I've been looking for you everywhere. And Lucius."

Lady Stamford stood at the bottom of the stairwell leading from the kitchen up to the hall near the dining room. Her expression reflected more curiosity than anger, but Jess's guilt made her breathless, as if all the air had been drawn from the room.

She took a step away from Lucius, and then another, until she felt the cool tile of the kitchen wall at her back.

He held still a moment, drew in a ragged breath, and turned to address his aunt. "We were just on our way upstairs, Aunt Augusta."

Lucius didn't move away from her, and Jess was grateful for the shelter of his broad shoulders and chest, to have a moment to compose herself away from Lady Stamford's gaze. She felt the press of his leg against the skirt of her gown, and then, between them where none could see, his hand, just the edge of it, brushing against her own.

Her body thrummed with a sickening mix of desire and regret, and she wanted nothing so much as to reach for him, to borrow a bit of his strength.

Then he turned, a quick dip of his head, and spoke under his breath. "Meet me in the library tonight."

He turned back toward his aunt, giving Jess no time to answer, but he remained near as they approached Lady Stamford.

"Jessamin, would you check on our young ladies? Lady Katherine is just settling into her room. See that she has everything she needs. Then would you meet me in my sitting room, my dear? We have much to accomplish before dinner. And Lucius, my boy, you should go and see to your guests who've lingered in the drawing room."

Her tone was light, affectionate, with nothing of command in it, yet Lucius nodded his acquiescence and moved toward the stairs. He didn't look back at Jess until he'd reached the first step, where he turned a moment to gaze at her before continuing his ascent.

"Are you quite well, my dear?"

"Yes, quite. Thank you, my lady."

She'd never fibbed to Lady Stamford before, but Jess wasn't certain she'd be well again for quite some time.

WITH EACH STEP he took away from Jessamin, boot heels clicking on marble, Lucius wished to return and finish their conversation. Though filled with more intimation than words, more bold glances than explanations, it was as if they'd made a start, taken a momentous step. And he had no desire to retreat.

"My lord!"

Lucius had never heard Mrs. Ives's pleasant voice at such an emotional pitch. The older lady rushed toward him, twisting her long white apron in her hands.

"Forgive me, my lord. It's your father. He wishes to see you, and he's quite adamant on the point."

Lucius looked back toward the drawing room where he could still hear Miss Sedgwick singing. Wellesley accompanied her in his rich baritone. The pair must have presented quite a sight, so distracting, Lucius hoped, that his guests might forgive their lackadaisical host.

"Lead the way, Mrs. Ives."

Lucius followed the diminutive woman and attempted not to speculate about what might have set his father off this time. He was never certain just how to approach Maxim—straight on or sideways. When he adopted the direct approach, head up straight, confidence in his stride, meeting the cool blue eyes so much like his own, his father was variably pleased at his moxie or provoked to irritation. But approaching him otherwise, with one's head down or one's attention far too distracted with a red-haired suffragette, opened Lucius to attack, and when he was least prepared for it.

"Father, I understand you wish to speak with me."

"Speak to you! No, I wish for you to speak some sense to this woman. She's devised some ridiculous scheme to evict me."

Father was in a dither, the flesh of his face mottled in purples and reds, and his fists clenched so tight that the skin stretched across his knuckles appeared thin as vellum. Lucius had seen him in such a rage before—worse, and far more often than he liked to recall.

Calm yourself was the sentiment echoing in Lucius's head, but he knew from experience such admonitions only fanned the flames of his father's wrath.

When Lucius glanced at Mrs. Ives, she stood behind his father, biting her lip and rapidly shaking her head in denial.

Lucius spoke softly. "Mrs. Ives, perhaps you could explain."

Maxim's body trembled. Lucius saw the movement of his shoulders and watched his hands spasm against his legs.

"Have a care when you listen to her. She'll say anything to have her way, and the woman's as overprotective as a new mother."

Mrs. Ives shook her head again at Lucius, her eyes reflecting a sadness and fatigue he'd never seen in the indefatigable nurse's face.

She approached and began to whisper, though his father was close enough to hear.

"There's quite a severe leak in your father's bedroom, my lord. I only suggested that he—"

"The woman wants to separate me from all my comforts."

His father had begun lifting a few of his belongings, a framed watercolor of Lucius's mother and an ivory-handled magnifying glass he treasured, to emphasize his point.

"If I might have a word, my lord."

Mrs. Ives turned her head toward his father's bedroom, and Lucius lifted his arm to urge her to lead the way.

It was a room he'd rarely visited, the room his parents had shared, and Lucius stopped in his tracks at the sight of his mother's painted portrait. She looked down on him, cool and regal, so unlike her true character, from above the fireplace. One of her ornate perfume bottles rested on the mantel under her portrait, and Lucius knew without lifting the stopper that it would smell of lavender.

Mrs. Ives directed his attention to the water-damaged ceiling near the eastern wall. A menacing web of rounded splotches stretched all the way to the center of the ceiling, encompassing the bed, side tables, and wardrobe, though the worst damage was near the wall's edge. A series of pots and bowls were arranged on the floor to catch drips, and in some areas the water had created boils in the plaster, part of which had burst, shedding shards of paint onto the floor.

"Why has no one told me about this?"

He knew some of the eastern-facing rooms were leaking, but he'd been assured his father's rooms were not.

Mrs. Ives bowed her head a moment before answering. "His Lordship forbade me from telling anyone. He said you had enough worries, my lord."

Lucius frowned at the assertion. His father was a selfish man, rarely concerned for others, and he'd certainly never worried for Lucius's sake.

"I suspect he did not wish to move from his rooms, Mrs. Ives. I've spoken to the steward about repairs to this portion of the house, and they should commence soon."

As soon as he married a wealthy bride like May Sedgwick.

Mrs. Ives screwed up her face in a look of unmistakable distress, and her cheeks began to go crimson, as if she'd burst if she couldn't confess whatever troubled her.

"Out with it, Mrs. Ives."

"If I might, my lord, I do believe your father should be moved now." She lifted her hands before rushing on. "Only temporarily, my lord. Until the repairs are completed. With the rains this time of year, I fear mold might set in, or the damage will worsen."

She was right, of course, but as Lucius turned his head toward his father's sitting room, he could only imagine the battle ahead. He loathed the prospect of these same walls that had witnessed so many of his parents' rows rattling with shouts and denunciations again.

"Perhaps you could persuade him, my lord. He's taken against me on the matter, but surely he'll abide your wishes."

Lucius tipped his head and offered his father's nurse a rueful grin. What a fine life it would be if it was all as Mrs. Ives claimed, with a biddable father who was concerned with his welfare. It might afford him the ability to run Hartwell as he saw fit, to break with tradition and manage the estate with a mind to profitability rather than tradition. It might allow him to make his own choices.

"You overestimate my influence, Mrs. Ives."

Something in the way he spoke the words caused the nurse to cast her eyes down.

"Forgive me if I spoke out of turn, my lord."

"Not at all, Mrs. Ives."

An antique floor clock in his father's sitting room chimed. With only two hours left before dinner, Lucius wouldn't have time enough to convince his father of anything, and it seemed far preferable to allow the earl to settle his nerves before taking his evening meal.

"I agree with you, and I'll speak to Father tomorrow about moving to one of the guest rooms. Temporarily. Thank you for bringing this to my attention."

Lucius glanced at the dingy blotches on the ceiling again before returning to the sitting room.

His father sat reading before the fireplace, all the previous fuss seemingly forgotten.

"I will not be moved. And if you would carry on marrying the American girl, repairs can commence at once." After speaking while continuing to gaze at the pages of his book, Maxim finally turned his cool blue gaze toward Lucius. "I should like to meet her."

His father had always enjoyed the elaborate ritual of a full table and formal dinner, and it was only proper that he meet the woman chosen to preserve the family estate.

"Then join us for dinner, Father. As you say, you should meet Miss Sedgwick."

"My lord, if I might, I do not think—" Mrs. Ives's

objection was not unexpected, and Lucius smiled, stopping her mid-sentence. Apparently his smiles were such a rarity, they could rob women of speech. His smile broadened as he watched her expression shift from opposition to shock.

"I know it will present challenges, Mrs. Ives. Perhaps you could join us as well?"

The older woman stared at Lucius as if his question was more disturbing than his father's worst outburst. Mrs. Ives had never been asked to dine with the family before, yet despite his recent outburst, her presence usually calmed his father, soothing his frequent distemper like no other remedy. If dinner wasn't to turn into a spectacle, Mrs. Ives would be essential.

"Please join us, Mrs. Ives."

They both looked back at Maxim, who sat up straight in his chair, his eyes clear and gleaming, looking every bit a man who knew what he was about and whose mind was focused on the here and now.

"Yes, join us, Ives. I should very much like to take supper at my own table and meet this American chit who'll be mistress of Hartwell."

Lucius's pleasure at seeing the clarity in his father's gaze faltered at his mention of Miss Sedgwick as the future mistress of Hartwell. It was what was expected, and even he envisioned marriage to Miss Sedgwick as his most reasonable course. Hell, the crumbling walls around him urged him to settle the matter. But nothing about the sound of it brought contentment or anticipation. Lucius tugged at his necktie for relief from its tight embrace and realized the idea of Miss Sedgwick as his countess—a woman who had yet to look at him with anything other than bland civility—filled him with dread.

And there was more; another emotion surged clear and true above all others, one that eclipsed his dread about Miss Sedgwick and the constant worry about his father—a determination that Jessamin Wright not leave Hartwell, at least not yet.

Chapter Nineteen

"WHEN YOU SAID you'd taken a post with a noblewoman, I never imagined you meant *his* aunt. I'm shocked she would make you such an offer."

"Not nearly as shocked as I was."

Jess poured cups of oolong tea for Kitty and herself from the service a maid had delivered to the sitting room moments before. She couldn't help but think of the first time she'd met Kitty and watched the marquess's daughter do the same. What a difference a month made. That day Jess had been afraid of her work clothes dirtying the Adderlys' pristine furniture. Now she wore a gown nearly as fashionable as Kitty's.

What if she'd said no to the money? She could easily envision days still filled with worry over the shop and her father's debt, but it was harder to imagine never meeting Lucius, never kissing him, never knowing the name of his favorite book.

The thought of it brought a hollow ache to her chest.

Kitty watched her with glassy eyes, mouth slightly agape, still seemingly unable to reconcile Jess's presence at Hartwell. Then she emitted a long sigh.

"I suppose it was all for nothing. He'll never dance with me, will he?"

The tremor in Kitty's soft voice was so different from her usual confident tone that Jess glanced at her in concern.

"I don't think there'll be any dancing at the house party. He doesn't seem to be fond of it."

Kitty's mouth puckered in a moue of displeasure.

"Even if he hosted the most elaborate ball in England, he wouldn't wish to dance with me." She reached up to twist the strand of pearls at her throat around her fingers. "My little scheme didn't do any good at all. And it cost you your shop."

Jess's impulse to apologize seemed foolish. She *had* lost her shop. Kitty had lost nothing, except perhaps the illusion that men could be maneuvered through humiliation.

But she wondered about the rumors May had spoken of hearing in London.

"Did it cause a great scandal for the viscount?"

Kitty laughed, the tinkling bell sound Jess remembered from their first meeting, but it tailed off at the end into something deeper, huskier, and more than a bit mischievous.

"Scandal? Hardly. I think I actually did the man a favor." She took her first sip of tea and smiled above the rim. "The gossip rags assumed you were his mistress. It's caused the misses to think him infinitely worthier of a swoon, and thus he's far more admirable to the rakes."

Jess couldn't reconcile how by possessing a mistress a man might become more appealing or admirable, but a comic vision flashed in her mind of Lucius striding through Hyde Park as ladies dropped like flies at his feet and gentlemen doffed their hats.

"I'm sure he'll be pleased."

"Unlikely. Does anything please him? If I ever see the man smile, I'll eat these pearls."

I made him smile.

Jess pressed her lips together.

"Are you content here as his aunt's companion? I'm still willing to give you the one hundred pounds I offered. You did earn it."

Jess shook her head. She'd never take the money. The very mention of it made her fidgety, and Kitty's assertion that she'd earned the money only made it worse.

"It wouldn't be proper. You intended to assist with the bookshop, and that's impossible now."

"It wasn't proper for you to kiss a viscount, but you seemed to manage that all right."

There was nothing snide in Kitty's tone, and she leaned forward, emphasizing her point with a flash of determination in her gaze.

"I didn't merely offer you the money to help with your shop. You know I aimed to embarrass Lord Grimsby."

She seemed quite a different young woman from the one Jess had met in Belgrave Square. Though still lovely and dressed in fashionable clothing, sadness colored her gaze, even diminishing the pitch of her voice. She exuded less artifice and much more sincerity. On their slight acquaintance, Jess doubted Kitty would divulge any of her woes, but she was curious.

"Have you been well, Miss Adderly?"

The change of subject seemed to take Kitty by surprise. She shifted her body, sitting a bit straighter in her chair, and clasped her hands in her lap before answering.

"I've had a bit of a disappointment, but I shall be well. Forgive me if I'm not quite myself."

Jess saw no need for apology. This more honest Kitty was much more appealing.

Attempting a smile that didn't match the expression in her gaze, Kitty added, "I thought a bit of country air and a few days away from London would do me good."

"At the home of the man you wished to embarrass?" Her words came out harsher than Jess intended, but Kitty didn't seem to notice the rebuke.

"I didn't come to Hartwell for Lord Grimsby. I simply needed a few days away."

For the most part, Jess believed her. The honesty in her tone was unmistakable, or perhaps very well feigned.

Kitty took another sip of her tea and then pressed her forefinger against her lower lip.

"I'm still confounded by Lady Stamford offering you employment. It's clear she wishes to match Grimsby with the American. Might not your presence here endanger her plan?"

Jess hadn't ignored the mystery of it. The question always lingered in the back of her mind, and the best answer she'd devised was that Lady Stamford offered her employment because she knew the desperate nature of Jess's circumstances. And yet ascribing Lady Stamford's actions to altruism wasn't entirely satisfying. Shouldn't a titled lady loathe the woman who'd scandalized her nephew in such a very public manner?

"I believe she did it out of goodwill, a desire to help someone in need."

Kitty laughed in her high-pitched titter.

"And she selected the one woman in London who'd kissed her nephew?" Kitty continued to tap her lip thoughtfully. "Though I suspect you weren't the only woman in London he'd ever kissed."

Jess tried not to blush, closing her eyes and willing her cheeks to cool, but the heat was already winning, and Kitty read more in her ruddy face than she intended to reveal.

"My goodness, Jessamin. Are you infatuated with him?"

"No!"

Was she? Infatuation, love, they'd never been her options. The bookshop, helping to manage it and then struggling to save it—that had been her only option.

Her feelings for Lucius weren't comparable to any experience in her life. They were singular, but fragile and ephemeral. If she examined them too closely, surely they'd turn to dust in her hands. She couldn't carry on longing for a man when he was intended for a life so unlike her own, a woman so different than she would ever be. In a lifetime of reading, she'd always avoided books of fairy tales.

Kitty watched her with a narrowed gaze, a single blond brow arched over her right eye.

"All right. I acknowledge there is . . . something between us."

Jess loved the English language, appreciated the variety of words, the specificity and nuances of meaning. When she was twelve years old, Mother had given her a dictionary, and she'd consumed it with all the excitement of a page-turning novel. Words of ambiguity, the *things* and *somethings* of the world, made her skin itch. Yet she'd acknowledged it in the kitchen. *Something* existed between them. And now, some madness made her confess it to Kitty, the woman who'd set her on the viscount's path in the first place.

"I knew it." The satisfied young woman Jess recalled from their first encounter beamed at her from the opposite chair.

"How could you know what I'm not certain of myself? Did he speak to you about me?"

Kitty set her teacup carefully on the table between them before coyly tilting her green eyes up at Jess. She was enjoying herself far too much.

"He said nothing, but it was in his eyes, something in the way he spoke your name. He bristled when I mentioned you. That told me quite enough."

Jess sighed, tensing her hand around her teacup. Rather than break it, she reached out to set the delicate porcelain on the table, rattling the cup in its saucer along the way.

Did Lucius love her? Whatever his feelings for her or hers for him, what would it profit either of them?

"It's impossible."

Kitty's expression flattened, not quite a grimace, just the absence of pleasure.

"Then return to London with me when I go. If I can't convince you to take the money, perhaps I could help to find you a more suitable position."

Kitty leaned forward, shocking Jess by reaching out to pat her hand, much as Alice had in the coffeehouse. "In time, you could earn enough to rebuild your shop."

Rebuild my shop. It seemed as strange and impossible a prospect as a match with Lucius. She wasn't even sure she'd ever had a shop. It had always been father's bookshop—his idea, his dream. She'd only been a steward, and a poor one at that.

She focused on the other possibility.

"What post would I be suited for?"

Kitty sat back and pursed her lips, leaning her head to the side as if assessing her.

"What about governess? My youngest sister would love a suffragette governess with whom she could discuss books."

Kitty's words ratcheted Jess's heartbeat, but the emotion fizzing in her belly was equal parts anticipation and uncertainty. London was home, familiar, a place where she could do good and be useful. Lady Stamford would argue for her usefulness now, in her role as lady's companion. And while writing letters and arranging appointments with the dressmaker were useful to Lady Stamford, for Jess, the most rewarding aspect of living at Marleston had been her time spent teaching Tilly to read. And now James too.

When she gave no answer, Kitty smoothed down the skirt of her yellow silk gown.

"If you prefer to stay, I wish you well. Truly. And I'll do what I can to—"

"He's meant to marry May."

The truth of it burned her throat, like the time she'd snuck a sip of her father's revolting gin. Jess clutched her hands together, squeezing as tight as she could. She felt chilled, miserable. Perhaps Kitty hadn't meant to refer to Lucius at all. Just because the man lingered in her thoughts didn't mean everyone else suffered from the same preoccupation.

"My ears have gone quite pink. Grannie used to say that meant someone was telling tales about me."

May Sedgwick stood just beyond the sitting room threshold, her teal eyes glowing, and a sly expression tipping her mouth at each edge.

"Is this a private gathering or might I push in?" Even as she asked the question, May did just that, gliding into the room as her ruffled bustle and train swished behind her.

Jess stood and went to the bellpull to ring for more tea, swiping at the single tear that had escaped down her cheek. If May had overheard her conversation with Kitty, they were going to need a great deal of tea.

May took her time arranging her dress after settling into a plush chair. She'd donned an extraordinary gown of gauzy peach silk with a wave of beige lace over each puffed sleeve.

When May caught Jess studying the elaborate creation, she said, "It's a tea gown. My aunt told me to be sure to bring several tea gowns as you English so adore your tea."

Jess and Kitty exchanged a glance, but neither could refute the claim. And though Jess counted herself a novice when it came to social niceties, she knew enough to hold her tongue about her preference for coffee.

As if to prove May's point, a maid entered the room bearing a fresh tea service and placed it on the table between them. The girl began pouring, but May shooed her away and played the hostess, seeming to enjoy the formality of asking each of them their preferences.

When they'd all settled back with their steaming cups of tea, May took a single sip before plunging into the fray. "To tell you the truth, I'm not certain I wish to marry at all."

Jess swallowed her tea too quickly and coughed until the tickle in her throat eased.

"You came a long way to meet a man you did not wish to marry." As Kitty spoke the words, Jess repeated them in her mind.

"A very long way, indeed. And I did consider a match with him. Honestly, I did. But more than anything, this trip afforded me an escape from a dilemma."

"What dilemma?" This time Jess and Kitty spoke nearly in unison, the two words bouncing off the sitting room walls.

May took another deep draw of tea, setting her cup carefully on the table beside her before answering.

"My father intends to marry again." The moment she spoke the word *father*, all the joviality in May's tone fled. But despite the emotion behind her declaration, May's expression remained buoyant. Her mouth curved when Jess and Kitty exchanged confused glances before turning to her expectantly.

"I suppose that doesn't quite explain it."

She picked at one of the ribbons of her gown before continuing.

"She was his mistress while my mother lived, a greedy, selfish creature who sees none of his true merit, only what he can buy for her." She looked up to gaze at Kitty and then Jess. "Matchmaking for my sake provided a useful distraction. It was a means of securing a bit of his time and attention."

"Your father approves of the match with Lord Grimsby?" Kitty's question had May nodding vigorously, loosening a few black curls.

"Oh yes. Papa knew Lady Stamford in her youth. He adored the notion of me marrying into her family, and gaining a title to boot. He was so pleased that he even offered to escort me to London."

Lady Stamford hadn't mentioned the arrival of May's father, though Jess wasn't privy to every piece of the countess's correspondence. If he'd offered to escort his daughter, where was he?

"Unfortunately, he was detained by business matters

in New York." May sniffed before pinching her mouth into a frown. "He promised to travel as soon as he's able."

Jess didn't expect the sense of kinship that welled up as she watched May angrily flick the bows on her gown and struggle to hide her glum expression.

After her mother's death, she'd craved her father's attention with a kind of greedy desperation. Whatever the difference in their upbringing and situation, she felt for May.

"He must dote on you. My father wouldn't escort me across an ocean if I was to marry a king." Kitty spoke teasingly, and glanced at May as if to reassure her, but Jess detected bitterness in her tone.

"Oh, I'm sure he would. I met your father at a dinner I attended in London. He seemed quite charming."

"Yes, he's very good at charm." Kitty stood as she spoke, sweeping a hand down to settle her gown. "Ladies, if you'll excuse me, I should go and dress for dinner."

Jess reached down for her father's watch, easing it from the pocket of her skirt just enough to read its face. Kitty was right. There was a little over an hour before dinner, and she'd yet to return to Lady Stamford.

"We should prepare too," May said as she lifted her teacup for a final sip. "But I must request your help, Jess. You did promise you'd help me."

There had been no promises, but Jess nodded and waited. Nothing could be as odd as Kitty's request that she kiss a stranger.

"If you're able, would you go into the dining room and rearrange our place cards?"

"Place cards?" The cards to indicate where each guest should sit were sometimes used at Marleston for a particularly elaborate dinner with several guests, but there'd been none on the dining table during Jess's first night at Hartwell.

"Yes, I suspect they'll seat me next to Lord Grimsby, but I'd have much more fun near Wellesley, or anyone else."

Jess swallowed hard. "Do you truly dislike him?" The room seemed to grow quieter. Her rushing breath and the patter of her heartbeat grew louder.

May took a long moment to consider the question, reaching up to loop a finger around one dark curl, puckering her mouth.

Like a swinging pendulum, Jess's emotions tipped from hope to guilt and back again.

"I suppose I don't know him well enough to dislike him. Not really. But I haven't taken to him as I thought I might." She smiled with a childlike glee. "Perhaps I'll wait for a duke. I'd much rather be a duchess. Wouldn't you?"

Chapter Twenty

WHILE LADY STAMFORD read a telegram from May's father, Jess worked on invitations for a ball her employer planned to host in the coming season. She tried to focus on the fine stationery beneath her hand and forming words and numbers in neat, carefully formed script, but her thoughts wandered. Her mind sifted memories of Lucius—the scorching heat of his gaze the night she'd kissed him in the gallery, the tenderness of his touch after she'd made a fool of herself at dinner, the furrowed flesh between his eyebrows when he looked at her as if she was the most vexing woman he'd ever encountered.

In a few days she'd return to Marleston with Lady Stamford. Would she ever see Lucius again?

"Perhaps we can put the invitations aside for a bit. We've plenty of time. Are you up to reading to me, Jessamin? I should like a spot of poetry before dinner."

Jess pressed the cool skin on the back of her hand

against her flushed face and hoped Lady Stamford didn't notice.

"Of course, my lady." Jess never declined an opportunity to read poetry, and it would occupy her mind far more effectively than addressing invitations.

"This one?" She pointed to a blue leather-bound book of poetry Lady Stamford sometimes preferred, but the countess shook her head.

"No, would you fetch the collection of Romantics? The one I purchased from your shop."

Lady Stamford had never actually paid for the book, but Jess's salary was such an astounding sum, she could hardly argue about the cost of a single volume of poetry.

"It's in my bedroom, on the table by my bedside. Thank you, my dear."

Making her way into the hall, Jess walked in a daze, her thoughts still full of Lucius. May's dislike of him shouldn't please her as it did. It wasn't as if he would choose her if he didn't marry May. And surely a deeper acquaintance would serve to show May how kind and open he could be, much more engaging than Mr. Wellesley, though perhaps with less gloss. Jess would take the quiet strength of Lucius over the obvious charms of Mr. Wellesley every day of the week.

An image of Lucius, his cool gaze and black hair with a mind of its own, flashed in her mind. Those stray strands slipping over his eyebrow or curling across his ear of their own volition must be quite an irritant to a man so used to commanding all about him. She grinned at the thought and imagined a child, a young boy with clear azure eyes and undisciplined sooty locks, running across the lawns of Hartwell.

Jess clenched her hands. Long ago, she'd promised Father she could do without marriage and motherhood. Lionel Wright had named his shop Wright and Sons Booksellers, but there'd never been any sons. None who survived anyway. When her mother died giving birth to her third child, and the boy joined her just days later, Jess knew it meant the bookshop would be hers one day. Though just fourteen years old, she'd accepted her role—to help Father run his shop and keep it open after he'd gone. It was what he expected of her, and she could never bear to disappoint him.

Lost in her thoughts, in memories that eclipsed even Lucius's handsome face, Jess found herself colliding with a warm, hard, spice-scented wall. She looked up into the eyes of the man who'd smiled at her as no one ever had. He held her in his arms, much as he had the night they met, and a shiver danced across her skin when he slid his hand down her back.

He pulled away, releasing her, but seemed at a loss for what to say.

"Jessamin . . . Miss Wright . . ."

"Pardon me, my lord." Jess forced her legs into motion to carry on with the task of collecting Lady Stamford's poetry book.

But when she finally did move, walking around him to continue toward Lady Stamford's bedroom, he reached out to stop her, gently encircling her wrist with his hand.

"Where are you going? You haven't decided to leave after all, have you?"

"Leave Hartwell?" The words lodged in Jess's throat and she swallowed against the lump.

"Excuse me, my lord. I must fetch a book for your aunt." The physical act of pulling away from him was easy. He held her wrist lightly and released her as soon as she tugged. But the notion of walking away from him for the last time if she accepted Kitty's offer to return to London—that thought sparked a spike of pain in her chest so sharp it made her breathless.

"TELL ME YOU haven't let her go."

Lucius burst into the sitting room where his aunt reclined on a settee, feet up, her pugs settled on her lap.

She huffed a sigh at his outburst but didn't move from her comfortable arrangement. Pollux, or Castor eyed him disdainfully, letting Lucius know his shouts were not at all conducive to napping.

"Gracious. Calm yourself, my boy. Sit. Just there so I can see you. Would you care for some tea? I was just going to ring for some."

When Lucius had settled himself into the chair opposite his aunt, a furnishing far too low and petite to accommodate his long legs and arms, he rested his elbows as well as he could and steepled his fingers in front of his face. He steeled his nerves, taking a long, deep breath, and tamped down the frazzled emotions his collision with Jessamin had wrought. He could still feel her soft curves against the skin of his palms.

"Now tell me what has upset you so."

"Nothing at all." Had he really just burst into the room braying like a madman? "I wonder if you've had the pleasure of conversing with Lady Katherine Adderly since her arrival."

"Briefly, yes." Augusta didn't seem particularly disturbed by the lady's behavior.

"She came to me and confessed being the one behind the incident in Mayfair. Her apology did seem sincere, though I suppose I should write to her mother about the whole silly charade. Shall I ask her to return to London?"

He quite liked the idea, but he feared she'd simply take Jessamin with her. "No, I see no need to go that far."

"As I said, I do not think it will do you or any of us any real damage, but it was childish. Sarah must have taught her better than that." Lucius had no notion of what marchionesses taught their daughters, but he could hardly bear a grudge against Kitty. If not for her vindictive lark, Jessamin would never have come to that gallery and kissed him.

"I'm sure she did."

"There's more." Augusta took a deep breath. "She said she was shocked to find Jessamin here, and in my employ. As a means of making amends with her, she's offered Jessamin the funds to return to London. She hopes to help her find a position there."

His aunt sniffed, clutched at the neck of her gown, and sat up straighter on the settee. "But I cannot do without her."

Neither can I.

His aunt studied him, and he turned his head to examine the wallpaper. It was yellow, and his aunt always claimed the blue suite of rooms. A surge of pleasure came with the realization he sat in Miss Wright's sitting room. The room looked quite different in the light of day. He moved his gaze to the door along the west wall of the room, the door that led to Miss Wright's bedroom. At least while she was at Hartwell. He mentally charted the space between the bed where she laid her head and his own rooms.

"I won't let Miss Wright go." Augusta's tone was as fierce and emphatic as the one she'd used when he was a boy, assuring him that his father did love him.

"Nor will I." Lucius didn't realize he'd spoken the words aloud, but his aunt's wide eyes confirmed that he had.

"Does she wish to go?" she asked, twisting her handkerchief as if she might rend the flimsy fabric apart. "I would not deny her what she truly wished."

What of me? Would you deny me what I truly wish?

Lucius stilled his tongue to keep from speaking the sentiment. He was loath to allow his aunt to read the emotion in his eyes, careful not to unwittingly form some expression that would reveal the need and desire that had become his constant companions since meeting Jessamin Wright.

"Why is she so essential?" He asked himself the same question through many a sleepless night. Now he kept his tone light, his expression mocking as he spoke the words to his aunt.

"She is quite the most organized young woman I've ever met."

Lucius wasn't sure about that claim as he surveyed the

room Jessamin had inhabited for the last few days. Several books were stacked in a haphazard pile on her bedside table, and papers were scattered across the top of her desk, one piece crumpled but not yet discarded.

"She knows my schedule better than I do and has caught me up with the piles of correspondence and all of my usual visits. She manages my appointments, sees to menus, and arranges everything with the staff when I host guests at Marleston."

What a countess she'd make. He liked the image of Jessamin organizing the daily running of Hartwell as effectively as she had apparently transformed his aunt's life. But that led to other thoughts, and his pulse raced at the notion of facing each day with her by his side, of taking her to bed every night. Being the one to take the pins from her magnificent hair, to peel every layer of cloth and lace from—

"She's well read." His aunt's emphatic tone, as if she still needed to convince him of Jessamin's worth, shocked away his musings.

Lucius coughed and avoided his aunt's gaze. "She did own a bookshop. I suspect she was never at a loss for something to read."

She could read to me. Lucius had devoured books as a youth. It chased away the loneliness, allowing him a measure of comfort no matter where he was. Now, between assuming his father's role as lord of Hartwell and dealing with the demands of running the estate, he rarely turned the pages of a book for pleasure, unless it was the pages of the estate's ledger books.

"And she reads well. In fact, she is just about to read me a bit of poetry. You should stay and listen."

The pleasure of hearing her lovely voice reading poetry seemed too much, a treat he didn't deserve. What could he offer her when everyone expected his imminent betrothal to another woman?

Aunt Augusta watched for his reaction. He projected a mask of disinterest—a shield against all invaders. He'd practiced it well. Still, her perusal nettled him.

"I could only find a book of poems by Shelley, my lady."

That voice they'd just mentioned sounded in the silence that had fallen over the room. Jessamin stopped so abruptly when she saw him, he feared she might topple over. She was wearing her spectacles. He hadn't seen them since the night she'd walked up to him so boldly in the art gallery.

"I must have been mistaken. Only one Romantic poet then. But it's Shelley and that will do quite nicely. I must have left the collection back at Marleston. Thank you, my dear." His aunt gestured toward him accusingly. "As you can see, my nephew has claimed your chair. Join me here on the settee and let us hear you read."

Augusta shifted to allow Jessamin a small space on the end of the settee, and Lucius watched as she settled herself there, noting how careful she was to avoid his gaze. Her cheeks had begun to bloom into a fierce blush, and she seemed to hate that most of all. But the contrast of rosy skin against the creamy paleness of the rest of her face only made her lovelier. Still, he ached at the notion she was embarrassed and he and his aunt were the cause.

"My aunt tells me you have quite a talent for reading poetry." It was the most inane compliment he'd bestowed in his life, and he realized when she turned her dark green gaze on him that it had done nothing to give her ease.

"I have been reading for many years, my lord."

"Yes, of course. And teaching everyone else how to do so, apparently."

Lucius did not mind her teaching his boot boy to read. Indeed, every staff member ought to be able to enjoy the pleasure of a book. Heaven knew they had enough of them at Hartwell, especially considering his impulsive purchase after the bank had reclaimed Jessamin's shop. That bit of information would be difficult to explain, and he had no idea how he might tell her, or if he ever would.

"The ability to read should not be the privilege of one class over another." She bit the words off at each end, and Lucius found no satisfaction in the challenge in her eyes. He sat up straighter in his chair.

"I agree, Miss Wright. Everyone should have the right to study, as long as it doesn't interfere with their duties."

She quirked an odd expression, more scowl than smile.

"Surely educated men and women would carry out their duties far better. Would they not?"

They were sparring and he'd never intended to fire the first shot.

His aunt had apparently tired of it all. "Indeed. Well said, my dear. Lucius has a fine reading voice too, though

I haven't heard it in years. Indulge us, nephew." Augusta indicated the slim volume in Jessamin's hands.

He closed his eyes, sensing defeat before he'd even begun to fight. Miss Wright's scent tickled his nose and his aunt watched him with the look she'd give him as a boy when he'd done something utterly witless. Reaching up to settle his necktie, he ended up tugging at its constraint and forced his hands down to the arms of the chair, only to find he'd balled them into fists.

Shaking the tension from one hand, he opened it palm up and held it out to Jessamin. "Let's have it then, Miss Wright."

He tried to extract himself from the small chair to reach her, but Jessamin moved more quickly, approaching him in two quick strides. She lifted the slim volume and laid it in his hand. As their fingers touched, he felt a jolt of heat warm his body, though her fingers were cool. Their eyes met and he saw amusement in her expression. The minx enjoyed the embarrassment that had now been transferred to him. He liked seeing that flicker in her emerald gaze, that ember of joy, and he wanted to stoke it.

He opened the book, a volume of poems by Percy Bysshe Shelley. He flipped the pages to "Queen Mab," a poem he'd read at university and recalled enjoying. He cleared his throat, took a fortifying breath, and began to read.

Augusta's voice stopped him before two syllables could escape his lips. "How can you begin reading, Lucius? I haven't even told you which page."

"I had taken the liberty of choosing a poem."

Augusta made a snapping sound with her tongue. "No, I must choose. That is the way of it."

He glanced at Jessamin as if she might come to his aid. Sitting ramrod straight, perched on the edge of the settee near his aunt, she merely nodded her head. "It's true. That's the way we do it."

"What page, dearest aunt?"

"Page one hundred and three, if you please."

He turned the pages until he was near the end of the volume and landed on the one hundred and third page. A single, short poem took up the space of the folio page. It was titled "Love's Philosophy." Lucius skimmed the words he was about to read and finally felt the strands of the web in which his aunt had ensnared him. He speared her with an icy gaze above the book's edge and narrowed his eyes at the Cheshire grin sealing her lips.

The poem might as well have been written in a foreign language, so strange was its meaning to a man used to stifling his emotions. He stammered through the poem's first stanza, every line causing him to stumble. Full of sentiment and intimate meaning, the words tripped his normally steady tongue while his mind wandered into places he'd only ventured since meeting Jessamin.

Mercifully, his aunt stopped him short. "Oh, that's not right at all, Lucius. It seems the clever Miss Wright surpasses you in poetry reading after all. Do go and rescue him, my dear."

Jessamin hesitated before obeying her employer, but then he sensed her moving toward him. He couldn't look at her as she retrieved the little book from his hands. He thrust it toward her and sank down further into his chair.

Lucius had always acknowledged the beauty of Jessamin Wright's voice. It wasn't high-pitched and interspersed with giggles, nor too deep and unfeminine. It was smooth and rich, just the sort of voice for reading anything at all.

" 'The fountains mingle with the river—' "

His aunt stopped her. "Don't start again, dear. Just continue on."

Lucius knew what came next and couldn't resist watching her mouth form the words as she read. Her full lips lovingly caressed the kind of words that had caused him to stumble. He studied her neck and followed the smooth white expanse of skin that arched up across her cheeks.

" 'Nothing in the world is single;/All things by a law divine/ In one another's being mingle—/Why not I with thine?' "

As she read, her cheeks gradually flamed again into a blush as crimson as her mouth.

" 'See the mountains kiss high heaven,/And the waves clasp one another . . .' "

She spoke of kissing, and he was struck with the memory of her lips on his as vividly as if she stood before him, the taste of her fresh on his tongue. At that moment, he understood the value of that kiss. It had changed him—it had changed everything.

" 'And the sunlight clasps the earth,/And the moonbeams kiss the sea—/What are all these kissings worth,/

If thou kiss not me?'" As Jessamin spoke the last line, her voice wavered and the book started to slip from her hands. She caught it and looked up at Lucius. Her eyes glowed behind her spectacles. Her glance drew him, pulled him, as if she alone knew how reach beyond his defenses and lure him. He started to stand, but she stopped him.

"No. I . . ." For a moment, she seemed confused, disoriented. Then she approached his aunt and handed her the book. "Forgive me, Lady Stamford. I need a breath of air."

His aunt replied quietly, nearly a whisper. "Of course, my dear."

A stifling silence descended on the sitting room. Lucius slid a finger between his neck and tie, wrenching the fabric until he could breathe. The press of his clothing was suddenly intolerable, as if his apparel was nothing more than a neatly tailored restraint. He couldn't stop his foot from tapping, though the Aubusson carpet was so thick, his boot made no sound.

"Lucius?" Augusta's voice had lost its usual lighthearted tone.

"Yes, Aunt?" He stopped tapping his foot, but his fingers immediately began to trace the carved pattern in the arm of his chair.

"You are not a fool." She said the words firmly, without a sliver of doubt.

"Am I not?" Lucius didn't share his aunt's faith in her assertion.

"No. So you must go after her." He lifted his head and

met his aunt's eyes. She looked ready to command and be obeyed. But a smile softened her lips, and he knew in that moment she'd always seen through his veneer of cool detachment—always had and always would. "Only a fool would stay here with me at a moment like this. Go and get her."

Chapter Twenty-One

SHE WASN'T DIFFICULT to find. Jessamin had escaped to the second-floor balcony, a broad and shallow terrace that ran along a patch of Hartwell's west wall. It was a part of the house that was still structurally sound and one of the most appealing aspects of the west-facing façade. The sunset glow gilded her in warm hues and her hands rested on the weathered stone balustrade as she stared out on the lawns of the estate. Crimson and gold leaves dotted the green, discards of the great oaks and maple trees that formed the edge of Hartwell Woods. Those trees had thrived on the estate far longer than Lucius.

He could only guess her thoughts. Fear told him she was planning how to leave. And some part of him, a vein of honor and propriety, told him he should assist her to do just that. He could offer her nothing honorable, and while his aunt seemed to adore her, such a vibrant, intelligent young woman deserved more than a life as a lady's companion.

A breeze lifted a loose wave of her auburn hair, and the strands stroked her neck and the side of her face. Lucius flexed the fingers of his right hand. He had touched that skin, knew its supple texture, and he longed to touch her again.

She must have sensed him watching, for she turned her head, eyes widening. Stepping away from the balustrade, she tipped her chin up and folded her arms across her chest. Her expression stony and resolute, Jessamin looked as if she anticipated a confrontation.

A bit of metal at her throat caught the light and Lucius saw her spectacles hanging at the neck of her gown. Tenderness washed through him, a heat in the center of his chest that made him want to smile. They seemed such a fragile contraption for such a strong, resilient woman. And the sight of them tucked into her neckline reminded him of the night in the gallery, watching her fold them neatly, admiring her fastidiousness even as he wondered what the devil made her approach. Then the jolt of shock when she lifted onto her toes and kissed him.

Lucius opened his mouth to speak, but then sealed his lips again, completely at a loss for what to say. His emotions were at odds with his reason, and he had always deferred to reason, always trusted it over emotion. His father had been ruled by his passions—anger, resentment, jealousy, fear—and he couldn't allow himself such a fate.

Yet Jessamin provoked nothing but emotion. From

the moment he'd met her and every moment thereafter, thoughts of her consumed him, and none of them had been dispassionate. He should avoid her, stamp out this endless desire that overruled his reason. He should send her away, for his sake and her own.

Because no matter the craving that erupted whenever she was near, no matter the tumult she stirred in him, he had to do his duty and marry Miss Sedgwick, or some other woman like her. He must. Despite Father's accusations regarding Lucius's mother, Lucius had never doubted Dunthorpe blood flowed in his veins, and that meant duty, not just to his father, but to his family, to the estate.

Yet he wanted her. Lord, how he wanted her.

Like a fever, it burned him from the inside out. As he stood watching Jessamin, memorizing every angle and curve of her lovely face, lingering far too long on the seductive swell of her lips, his body began to shudder.

A battle had commenced inside him. He knew what he had to do and what he must say to her. He would send her away—allow her to rebuild her life, and carry on with his own.

But then she moved. He might have been dreaming for how slowly she approached, lit by the gloaming light, rebel strands of red-gold hair streaming around her face. She stopped just before him, looking up at him, just as she had in Mayfair. He'd read fear in her eyes that night, but now he saw something else—desire that echoed his own.

Jessamin lifted a hand and rested it on his chest, high near his shoulder, slipping it down across his waistcoat.

She would feel the tremors racking his body, sense his heartbeat banging a fearsome tattoo. He should snatch her hand away, hide his feelings—reason must conquer passion.

"This time it won't be because you're a viscount who snubbed another woman. It will be because you're the only man I've ever wanted to kiss."

Then she lifted onto her toes and her body swayed toward him. Lucius slid an arm around her waist, savoring the heat and weight of her. They had performed this dance before on the night they'd met. The night she'd delivered a one-hundred-pound kiss. But no one paid her for this moment. She chose it. She wanted him, here where no one watched, with no reward and no inducement but her own desire. The thought thrilled him, and he felt the tide of battle turn.

He couldn't walk away from her now if Hartwell crumbled around him.

Jessamin pressed her mouth to his, and his knees nearly buckled with relief. Her lips were the sweetest, richest confection. Memory couldn't compare to the raw pleasure of tasting her again.

Then he felt the tentative press of her tongue against his own and lost the battle.

He reached for her hair, allowing himself the joy of releasing a few pins. He stroked loose silken strands as he kissed her and then trailed his fingers down to explore the skin of her face, her neck. He deepened the kiss, letting her feel his hunger and need, speaking to her with the stroke of his tongue and slide of his mouth, telling her with kisses all the sentiments he couldn't speak aloud.

Jessamin released a moan, low and throaty, and he pressed her back against Hartwell's wall, cushioning her in his arms. He kissed her and touched her everywhere her blasted proper, high-necked gown would allow. His hands roved over the lush curve of her hips, the full swell of her breasts. Lucius pulled back to gaze at her, grinning at the dazed look in her eyes and the bee-stung plumpness of her mouth.

She smiled back at him and reached her hand out, tracing the tilt of his mouth with her fingers.

"You're smiling again, or very nearly." She spoke the words with a tone of wonder.

"I smile a great deal when you're about, Miss Wright."

She looked offended by his claim. "Rarely. You've only smiled at me once since the moment we met."

He ducked his head and wrapped his hands around each side of her waist. He studied the contrast of his skin against the vibrant blue of her dress. It felt right to hold her, to trace the shape of her body with his hands. He didn't wish to ever let her go.

"Perhaps smiling isn't simply the matter of flashing one's teeth and guffawing like a fool."

She continued to trace his mouth as he spoke, stroking his lower lip, then skimming her fingers across his jaw before touching his mouth again.

"You should smile more. Laugh more."

Lucius nipped at one of her fingers, and Jessamin let out a girlish squeal.

"As long as you're near, I will."

She began to pull away, but he leaned toward her, capturing her in the frame of his arms, and kissed her again, slowly, relishing the velvet warmth of her mouth. She responded by clasping the lapels of his jacket and pulling him closer.

Lucius heard another squeal, but it hadn't come from Jessamin. Then he heard women's voices and reluctantly lifted his head. Jessamin's eyes were huge as she clasped a hand to her mouth.

He looked back over his shoulder and saw them. Miss Sedgwick and his sister stood on the lawn below, staring up at them. The two women were speaking to each other, his sister patting Miss Sedgwick's arm. But then Miss Sedgwick stalked away, apparently toward the house, and disappeared under the terrace.

He still held Jessamin in his arms, but she pushed away from him, broke from his grasp, and fled into the house.

He opened his mouth to call her back, but like the moment when he'd walked onto the balcony, no words would come.

"Lucius, what have you done?" His sister still stood on the lawn below. He could hear the distress in her tone and watched as she patted at the corners of her eyes with a handkerchief.

"Go to my study, Julia. I shall be there directly."

Now it was his turn to lean against the balustrade,

sucking in gulps of cool autumn air, and struggling to tamp down the passion he'd given free rein. Control seemed so far gone, he doubted he'd ever grasp it again. His heartbeat thundered in his ears, so deafening it drowned out all other sound.

Damn it all. Painfully aroused, Lucius wanted nothing more than to send everyone else packing and hide away with Jessamin, giving and taking pleasure in her arms for as long as he was able.

He wanted her, but it was more than that. He needed her. She'd electrified his life, animating a heart he'd thought rusty and long past repair.

But would she choose a life at Hartwell? She'd tasted independence as a shop owner and knew her own worth. She was a suffragette, for heaven's sake. Her actions in Mayfair might have appeared the height of audacity, but he suspected she'd done it out of desperation. And it must have taken a good deal of brass for her to walk into that gallery and kiss him. The attraction he felt for her sparked to life in that moment, but so too had an abiding admiration for her courage and spirit. Could such a woman be enticed to become his impoverished viscountess?

And what would become of Hartwell without Miss Sedgwick's wealth? The only means of preserving the estate was to diminish it, to sell off part of the land and perhaps the family silver. Maybe Miss Sedgwick would care to purchase that vase in the entry hall she seemed so fond of.

He gripped the stone of the balustrade and huffed out a bitter laugh. Miss Sedgwick might be willing to buy half the family heirlooms at Hartwell, and investors could nip at his heels to develop parts of the estate all they liked, but his father would have none of it. The man might struggle to recall people and places, but he'd never wavered in his insistence that the Dunthorpe lands remain intact.

Squeezing the flesh between his brows didn't offer a bit of relief, but Lucius suspected nothing would until he faced whatever consequences awaited him in his study.

AT THE CLATTER of a knock at her bedroom door, Jess nearly jumped out of her boots.

She both hoped and feared it was Lucius. For the second time in her life, she'd brazenly kissed him, and this kiss had been so much sweeter than the first. This time she'd known the man she was kissing, had talked with him and seen him smile. And she'd been all too aware of the consequences. She liked May, the woman his aunt intended him to marry, and she'd experienced the luxuries of Hartwell, the world he'd been born into while she merely stumbled through hoping she didn't break anything. But knowing the consequences hadn't stopped her. Nothing could have changed her mind when he stood there looking so lost, so anxious for her reaction, and so eager to touch her.

Someone knocked again, and she prayed it wasn't Lady Stamford. How could she explain herself? Knowing the consequences of kissing Lucius hadn't prepared Jess for the look on May's face. Her guilt when she spotted May on the lawn brought a wave of queasiness that made Jess want to retch. But now, alone in her room, she couldn't resist recalling the pleasure she'd felt before that moment, and the rightness of being in Lucius's arms.

A deep-toned voice called through the door. "Miss Wright, it's Rob Wellesley. May I speak with you?"

Mr. Wellesley knew something was amiss. Jess could see it in his verdigris gaze.

"I know it's not quite proper, but might I . . . ?" He gestured toward the sitting room and then proceeded to walk in before she'd agreed.

"Did Lady Stamford send you to fetch me?"

"No. Grimsby called me into his study and asked me to come up and see that you're well."

The news that Lucius had sent him, that he was concerned about her, ignited a flutter of pleasure in her chest, and it eased a bit of the misery of whatever trouble she'd caused by kissing him on the balcony.

"Are you well, Miss Wright?"

Jessamin nodded. Her legs still trembled from the overwhelming sensations Lucius's kisses had sparked. But whatever it said about her sense of propriety—and she feared it said nothing good—the truth was that she wanted nothing more than to kiss him again.

"How is Lord Grimsby faring? And Miss Sedgwick?"

"They are all gathered in his study. Lady Stamford and the viscount's sister are there too, and his sister is carrying on dreadfully. The lady is quite inconsolable."

"She does seem to suffer from sensitive nerves."

Jess bit her lip the moment the words were out. It was hardly fair to think poorly of Lucius's sister. Considering the whole matter from Lady Julia's perspective, Lucius was sinking further and further into scandal. And Jess was the cause.

When Jess said nothing more, Mr. Wellesley took a turn around the room, glancing out the long leaded-glass windows at the view of Hartwell Woods, and then running a finger along the satiny upholstery of the desk chair before looking down to examine the papers on Jessamin's desk. "'Duty and Desire. Women's Education at Century's End.' Is this a speech for your suffrage group?"

"Yes, but it's not finished yet."

Wellesley smiled in that slow, easy way of his, his face blooming into an expression somewhere between delight and mischief.

"Sounds intriguing. Which do you choose, Miss Wright? Duty or desire?"

When he moved closer, that amused expression still fixed on his face, Jess felt the urge to let out a burst of panicked laughter to ease the tension that had her body in knots. She coughed against the tickle in her throat.

"As I argue in my speech, women should not have to choose. We must find a way for women to do their duty *and* obtain the education they desire."

For a moment she heard the same strident tone in her voice that Alice used during speeches at the union.

Mr. Wellesley was no longer smiling. He'd become pensive. "Will you give the speech yourself? Your meetings are in London, are they not? Do you think you'll ever return to London?"

He spoke the questions so quickly that there wasn't

time for answers. But his last query, whether she'd return to London, had been weighing on Jess's mind since her arrival at Hartwell. Hours ago, Kitty's offer to help her had been tempting. But now—after that kiss and experiencing how right it felt to be Lucius's arms—everything had changed. She couldn't imagine leaving Hartwell and never seeing Lucius again. Yet she couldn't fathom a way to stay.

Jess sank onto the edge of the bed and felt it shift as Mr. Wellesley seated himself too. With his long legs stretched out next to hers and his woodsy fragrance scenting the air, the impropriety of his presence in her room struck her and she edged a few inches away.

His laughter, a hoot of pleasure ebbing into a husky chuckle, made her jump.

"Don't worry, Jess. I'm not here to ravish you. I take my time and give plenty of warning before I commence ravishing a woman."

He stood, turning his back on her to look out the window facing the woods as if to prove his disinterest.

"Forgive me, Mr. Wellesley."

He turned his head, glancing at her over his shoulder. "Do you love him, Miss Wright?"

With a gasp and strangled squeak, Jess shot up from the bed. How could he ask her such a thing? If she was going to unravel her feelings and confess them to anyone, it should be Lucius.

Wellesley turned and approached. "You must forgive me. I can see I've shocked you." He reached inside his pocket and produced a square of cloth, offering it to her.

"You see, sometimes, Jess, we can't have both. We must choose between duty and desire."

Jess reached for the pocket square and dabbed at the tears she'd been unable to hold back. Her stomach no longer rolled in her belly, but a fire had started in her chest, a searing pain like she'd never experienced in her life, as if her heart might turn to cinders as it broke.

"My dear Miss Wright, I must have your answer."

His blue-green eyes had gone limpid, so clear that Jess could read real emotion in his gaze, unleavened by his usual charm. He looked as anxious as Lucius had on the balcony. And Jess felt raw, ready to confess the truth she'd struggled to deny.

"Yes."

He ducked his head, and Jess felt it must be the wrong answer, one he hadn't expected. He'd anticipated her denial. And denial was what she should have clung to. If she didn't love Lucius, it would all be so much easier.

Then Wellesley lifted his head and his smile, broad and genuine, cooled a bit of the heat in her chest.

"Very good. Then if it's between duty and desire, I suspect I know what he'll choose."

Jess nodded with a heavy sigh. Lucius was a nobleman, his father's heir. Though she'd explored only a small portion of the estate, she suspected it was vast. There would be tenants, farmers and working men and women who relied on Lucius and his father to maintain the lands and buildings on the estate. What sort of hypocrite would she be if she committed time to helping working families in

London's charities and dismissed the well-being of the people who worked Dunthorpe lands?

"Try not to fret. He'll be unbearable if you tell him I said so, but Grimsby is by far the most intelligent man I've ever known. And he's resourceful. If circumstances had allowed him to continue in his uncle's business, I suspect he'd be as well off as Miss Sedgwick's father."

Jess frowned. It was no surprise to hear that Wellesley thought Lucius intelligent, but she'd never imagined him as a man of business.

"Come, Jess, we really should go down and join the battle."

A shiver chased down her back. "Battle? What battle?"

"You have met his sister, haven't you?"

Chapter Twenty-Two

"YOU MUST SEND that young woman away immediately, Lucius. She scandalized you in London, and now here in your home. Our home. Our whole family has been put to shame. Everyone in the county will know." As ever, his sister was emphatic. Lucius had listened to her chastisement and outrage for what seemed like hours. He was on the verge of asking her whether she wished to blame Jessamin for scandalizing all of England when his aunt interjected.

"We cannot merely send her away, Julia. What of Miss Wright's reputation?"

Lucius knew his aunt would defend Jessamin and so had yet to do so himself, but he was finding it increasingly difficult to allow Julia to continue her tirade. And Julia wouldn't wish to hear about any of Jessamin's merits—her intelligence, her resilience, and her ability to remain good-natured when life dealt her losses and burdens. He'd have to convince her to teach him that trick.

"What reputation? The young woman is a hoyden who kisses men she doesn't know." Julia glared at Lucius. "And then kisses them again as often as she likes, apparently."

He'd never kissed Jessamin nearly as much as he would have liked, but judging by the mottled violet-red flesh on his sister's cheeks and the way her tone had risen to an ear-shattering screech, it wasn't what she'd wish to hear.

"Surely you aren't suggesting Lucius owes her anything out of duty or honor, Aunt Augusta. The woman has behaved abominably." Marcus spoke for the first time, and Lucius was disappointed to hear the undertone of priggish disgust in his brother-in-law's voice. He liked Marcus, respected him. He'd respect any man who could tolerate Julia and quench her temper with a few words as Marcus could. But he couldn't allow him to misjudge Jessamin or assign her all the blame for their kiss on the balcony.

"Marcus—"

His aunt's voice cut in over his own.

"Marcus, forgive me, my boy, but you hardly know Miss Wright. She is a fine young woman." Aunt Augusta waited a breath until she caught Lucius's gaze. "She would make a fine countess."

A ripple of pleasure rushed through Lucius to hear his aunt echo the thought that had chased through his mind not an hour before, but Julia huffed an outraged cry and sprang to her feet.

"Aunt Augusta, how can you say such a thing? I must put a good deal of this down to you for bringing her here. The woman has no breeding, no refinement, no sense of propriety. She is inappropriate in every way one can imagine. And might I remind you of Miss Sedgwick? You brought that poor young woman here, across an ocean, to marry Lucius. And now you mean to match him with your lady's companion?"

For a woman as prone to fainting and the vapors as Julia, she always managed to find an endless supply of air to express whatever point she wished to make. And she was almost as tenacious about battling her position as his aunt, though there was no finesse or real effort at persuasion with Julia, only a plethora of righteous indignation.

Catching her breath to continue, his sister lifted her hand to touch Augusta's arm. "She may have a few fine qualities as you say, Aunt Augusta, but one good apple does not improve the entire tree. Who are her family? She admitted at dinner last night that her father gambled his life away."

Though Julia spoke the words low, mostly for their aunt's benefit, Lucius could no longer hold his tongue.

"Surely none of us want to be judged for our father's errors, do we, Julia? How many invitations would you receive if you were known only as the Dark Earl of Dunthorpe's daughter?"

His sister and brother had always been concerned with being invited by the better families and to the most fashionable events, and even as a child he hadn't missed their concerns that Maxim's erratic behavior might cost them the most enviable invitations.

"You dare compare me to a grubby bookseller's daughter?"

And, of course, his sister would miss his point entirely.

"I think you mistake his meaning, Julia."

His aunt seemed serene despite Julia's shouting and the irritation he'd been able to curb in his own tone, and it pleased him to find that Aunt Augusta seemed equally unmoved by Julia's outrage and her insults. She'd spent more time with Jessamin and had no doubt of her virtues. In time all of them would come to see Jessamin's worth.

"May I speak to my nephew alone? Julia and Marcus, we shall see you both at dinner."

For a moment Julia considered protesting. Lucius saw it in her eyes. But Marcus stood and hooked an arm through hers, and she followed without another word as he led her from the room.

"Are you going to tell me what I must do too?"

"No, my boy. I am going to ask you what you wish to do."

It was a question no one had ever asked him before. Not once in his life.

"Perhaps it would be easier if you merely commanded me." This time, he didn't think he could abide her wishes, but he was used to having his choices and actions dictated.

"Why? It's never been effective before."

She smiled at him but Lucius couldn't return the expression.

"I have never refused anything that's been asked of me. Indeed, I usually had no choice in the matter at all."

She opened her mouth as if to protest and then lowered her head. When she glanced up at him again, her eyes shone with unshed tears.

"Many choices were taken from you."

"Many? All. Sent away as child. My work for Uncle Buchanan cut short after Julian's death. A title, this house, these burdens"—he reached for the papers on his desk, lifting them, though he knew she could have no notion what they contained—"thrust upon me. Even the choice of my life's companion is to be shaped by Father's demands and the expectations of others."

The tears came now, trickling down his aunt's cheeks, and he cursed himself as he went to her and embraced her.

"Forgive me my moment of petulance."

She reached up and patted his cheek. "It was long overdue, I think."

After dabbing at her eyes with a handkerchief, taking a deep breath, and straightening her back, she asked him again, "What is it you wish to do?"

"What if I said I wish to marry Jessamin Wright?"

He waited, expecting his aunt to protest, prepared to defend the choice his heart had made.

"What of Miss Sedgwick?" She spoke the words with a lilt at the end, with less anger than he'd expected.

What to do about Miss Sedgwick? Not only must he find a way to tell her and preserve her pride, he would have to find a way to maintain the estate without her dowry. As Lucius pondered the question, a knock sounded on the study door and a maid pushed it open.

"My lord, pardon me. Miss Sedgwick to see you, my lord."

It seemed the young woman's name was on the tip of everyone's tongue. Then the lady herself appeared. She was dressed for dinner in a stunning gold beaded gown. Sapphires glittered at her neck and dangled from her ears, and blue sparks flared in her eyes.

"May I have a word, my lord? It is a matter of some urgency."

Lucius gestured to the chair in front of his desk, ignoring the twitch in his jaw and the roiling in his belly. He'd made his choice, and disappointing Miss Sedgwick, or facing her wrath, was part of the price.

Just as Miss Sedgwick moved to sit, Wellesley led Jessamin into the room and closed the door behind them.

"Jessamin. Robert. My dears, if you would just give us a few moments." His aunt's gentle tone revealed nothing of the tension in the room.

May replied instantly. "No, I wish them to stay. This concerns all of us. Well, except for Rob, perhaps, but I am content to have him here too."

May folded her hands primly in her lap, lifted her chin, and rolled back her shoulders, as regal as a queen on her throne.

"I mean no offense when I say that I do not wish to marry you, Lord Grimsby."

She pressed her lips together a moment before continuing. "I am my father's daughter, and I am well aware that ours was to be a fair exchange, my dowry for a title."

She turned and glanced back at Jessamin. Lucius eased forward in his chair, prepared to defend her if Miss Sedgwick's intention was to rebuke. Instead, May turned back and faced him, her eyes glistening.

"I saw you kiss Miss Wright."

Lucius was prepared to take every ounce of blame, and heaven knew May Sedgwick deserved an apology. "Miss Sedgwick, I'm—"

"No, please, my lord. I do not say it to accuse. It only helps me make my point. After seeing that kiss, how could I wish for a marriage that's nothing but a business transaction?"

She sighed and sank deeper into her chair. "Goodness, never let my father hear me say such a thing."

Her expression lightened into a smile that seemed to ease the mood of everyone in the room. Wellesley grinned and Lucius was relieved to see color rush back into Jessamin's cheeks.

"To be frank, I feel at ease knowing your heart is engaged elsewhere." May glanced back at Jessamin. "I wish you both all the happiness you can bear. But for my part, I'll be leaving Hartwell tomorrow. My father has arrived in London." At that pronouncement, May dipped her head left to peek at Aunt Augusta and his aunt nodded, as if the news was no surprise to her at all. "I will join him there and convince him to stop for a while. I do love London."

She spoke the last with the same enthusiasm she'd gushed on her first day at Hartwell when she'd twirled around the entry hall and cooed about the art and decor. She was an irrepressible young woman. Nothing seemed to daunt her, and Lucius suspected she could convince her father to relocate to London permanently if that was her desire.

She stood and Lucius followed suit. "My best wishes go with you, Miss Sedgwick."

May reached across his desk and offered her hand, not for him to kiss, but to shake as men of business did when sealing a bargain. When he accepted, she smiled. "I suppose it's too late to ask you to call me May."

She stopped a moment, whispering with Aunt Augusta and embracing Jessamin before sweeping from the room. Without a word, Wellesley followed after her.

Lucius inhaled deeply as his eyes sought Jessamin. She stood near the fireplace, her green gaze locked on his. The way she looked at him made his breath catch in his throat and every worry over the future, all the resentment of what had been heaped on his shoulders, the endless concern about his father and the future of Hartwell—it all fell away. Whatever came next, whatever challenges they would face, he could accept anything as long as Jessamin looked at him that way each and every day of his life.

AFTER MISS SEDGWICK'S unexpected—at least to Lucius—declaration that she planned to leave Hartwell and his sister's quarter-of-an-hour diatribe in the study,

Augusta suggested an hour's delay before serving dinner, and the kitchen staff seemed grateful for the reprieve.

It didn't seem nearly enough time for what he needed for achieve, and he'd told himself that convincing his father of anything a couple of hours before dinner was futile, but something had changed. Some lock had been opened, a barricade breached. His mind was no longer clouded with fantasy, but filled with plans.

A single knock on his father's door brought Mrs. Ives to the threshold and she admitted him with an odd mixture of eagerness and anxiety. When he saw his father, he understood. Mather, who'd served his father as valet for years before tending to Lucius, was gathering towels and shaving implements, and his father appeared quite a changed man for his efforts. Clean-shaven, hair trimmed, and partially dressed in his evening trousers and white shirt, he looked much as Lucius remembered him from years past.

"I'd like a word with my father, Mrs. Ives." His father's nurse began following Mather out of the room but then stopped and spoke to Lucius quietly.

"I should take your father down to the drawing room early, my lord, to give him a few moments to settle in. He needs a bit of time to adjust whenever his situation changes."

Lucius nodded and waited until Mrs. Ives departed before reaching up to settle his cuffs, adjust his waistcoat buttons, and turn to his father with his fists clenched at his side. Change was precisely what Hartwell needed. Change was what Lucius would insist upon—from how they managed the lands, to how they managed the finances, to whom his father expected him to marry. Change was in order. He could give his father time to adjust to it, but he would not waver in his insistence.

Choices might have been taken from him in the past, but, in truth, his goals had been damnably ambiguous. After two years of work in his uncle's London investment office, he hadn't convinced himself to stay on. Not to mention the ambiguity of his heart. For years it seemed as cold and barren as the Arctic tundra and he'd been content to leave it unexplored.

Until Jessamin.

"Father."

Lucius waited, judging the look in his father's eyes. These days he couldn't be certain if the earl would know him. Tonight he did. Lucius recognized the look Maxim invariably gave him—an assessing squint of one eye that somehow conveyed judgment and disappointment in one glance.

"Tell me again about this American you plan to marry."

Lucius took the chair next to his father's and turned so that he could face Maxim.

"I'm not going to marry her. She's returning to London tomorrow."

Maxim squinted at him again, then his gaze darted uncertainly from Lucius's face to his mother's portrait. His father's hand began to tremble as he clenched the arm of his chair. Lucius moved forward, on the verge of calling Mrs. Ives to help calm Maxim.

"But what of Hartwell? What of the estate's repairs? What of your duty to this family?" Shouts echoing off the walls, Maxim dug his fingers deeper into the chair's arms, clutching as if he were falling and the furniture's solid frame represented his grip on safety, solidity.

His fingers were thin, almost fragile, a spindly pattern of sinew and bone, but even as he studied his father's hands, Lucius couldn't imagine a more stubborn, unbendable man. And yet, despite years of enmity and distance between them, Lucius had never truly considered defying his father's wishes. Now he realized that trusting his own judgment and defying Maxim were the only way to truly do his duty—to Hartwell and his heart.

"I take it you mean to marry another young woman."

His father's voice had calmed and he loosened his grip on the chair, though he kept his gaze focused on his wife's portrait rather than face Lucius.

"Yes."

"Rich?"

Depending on one's currency, Jessamin was wealthier than most. She certainly had more good humor than he'd possess in her situation.

"She has no dowry."

His father's cool gaze raked him from head to toe while each side of his mouth turned down in a frown.

"What to do you intend to do?" Maxim flicked a hand out to encompass his peeling ceiling and water-damaged walls.

Fear of his father, a muted echo of the terror he'd felt as a child when Maxim would rage and rampage through the house, stirred in the back of his mind, tightening his chest, but Lucius swallowed it down. He'd never be that cowering child again.

"I plan to manage the estate, as you've asked me to do. Difficult decisions must be made, but they will profit us all in the end. I will not debate the matter."

Maxim squinted at him with both eyes, frowning as he sometimes did when a moment of forgetfulness descended. Then the frown melted, the cloudiness in his gaze seemed to clear, and his lips spread in a grin.

His father thought he was Julian. He'd mistaken him for his elder brother dozens of times since Lucius's return to Hartwell. When his father smiled, Lucius knew he must be mistaking him for Julian.

"It's Lucius, Father."

"I know who you bloody well are. Julian was never half so stubborn or imperious. But I wager when it comes to finances, your uncle taught you better sense than Julian ever possessed."

Lucius sank a bit deeper into his chair, letting a sigh of relief hiss through his teeth. Then he leaned forward.

"And this woman, this penniless creature you intend to marry? No doubt your decisions about my estate will profit her too."

The plan to sell off part of the estate had been percolating in his mind for months, but now Lucius hoped every judgment he made for Hartwell's future and his own would benefit Jessamin. Providing for her happiness and the health of the Dunthorpe estate—those were his goals now, clear and unambiguous. And if he could manage both, he'd finally grasp a bit of happiness of his own.

"Yes, she will benefit, of course. As my wife." *If I can convince her to marry me.*

"Is she beautiful?" Maxim turned his eyes back to Lucius's mother's portrait. "She must be if she's turned your head."

"She's an extraordinary woman."

His father's brow arched far too high to indicate anything but doubt. But then he crossed his gnarled hands over his stomach and sighed in a long deflating breath, and all the fight seemed to seep out of him too.

"Very well."

"Very well?" Lucius squinted and suspected he looked a good deal like his father. Could it truly be as easy of telling the man of his intentions and then praying they went to plan?

The floor clock chimed the half hour and Lucius decided to leave the unexpected accord with his father to solidify over dinner and broach the details in the morning. But as he rapped on the door to signal Mrs. Ives should reenter, a chill of doubt settled in.

"I'll see you at dinner, Father."

"A lack of dowry might be forgiven if she's of a decent family. I presume she has that at least."

"No." But that didn't matter. The list of a woman's qualities or lack thereof, the weighing of one woman against another, one title against another—none of it had ever interested Lucius before becoming heir to his father's title.

"Is it Augusta's companion with the auburn tresses?"

Hand tensed on the door handle, back stiff, Lucius turned back to face his father. He dipped his head once and then started out the door.

"Infatuation is well and good, but you can't marry the girl."

Lucius stopped but didn't turn back. "I'll marry Jessamin, or I won't marry at all."

Jessamin was a fine woman, certainly, but even if Miss Hobbs or whatever her name was had possessed her intelligence and countenance, he suspected he'd still long for Jessamin Wright. Her essence, her elemental nature, whatever substance set her apart from every other woman he'd ever met called to that same essential part of him. Whatever the equation or alchemy of it, and he was convinced he could never explain it as clearly as he felt it, she was the only woman he'd ever wish to marry.

Chapter Twenty-Three

He left his father's room no less determined on his course, but Lucius feared his brief discussion with Maxim had been an uneventful skirmish in what could become a long drawn-out battle. And he was no longer convinced of the wisdom of his father's presence at dinner. If their conversation had riled him, any of the guests might be caught in Maxim's wrathful crosshairs, and he could be more biting and disparaging than Julia on her worst day.

With the prospect of Maxim shouting at the dinner guests and his head full of what he would say when he finally proposed to Jessamin, Lucius needed a finger of whiskey to settle his nerves before dinner. It didn't help. Drink never did. It warmed his body but turned his thoughts cloudy until the only impulse he could sort out was the desire to see Jessamin. After he allowed Mather to help him into formal evening wear, that desire propelled him down the stairs and into the drawing room.

When he crossed the threshold, he saw that his worries about the evening had been unfounded. Miss Sedgwick held court and the rest of the guests formed a semicircle around her, except for Wellesley, who sprawled carelessly on the arm of a divan. The group appeared completely in thrall to a story that made even his sister smile. And seated beside Julia, his father sat tall and august. In his finely tailored suit of evening clothes, Maxim's thin frame looked almost robust.

Lucius breathed a sigh of relief and scanned the room to find the only person he truly wished to see. But Jessamin was nowhere in sight, and a sense of dread skittered across his skin, raising gooseflesh. Only one other person was missing from the assembled guests—Lady Katherine Adderly. Lucius clenched his jaw, curled his fists, and tried to stem the panic. Had Kitty convinced Jessamin to leave Hartwell after all?

He turned back toward the hall and noticed Melville directing a small troupe of servants away from the dining room. As a footman passed, Lucius turned toward the young man.

"Jeffrey, please have a maid sent up to Miss Wright's rooms. She is overdue in the drawing room."

"She is already in the dining room, my lord."

Before the footman could finish speaking, Lucius was on his way to find her. The sight of Jessamin stopped him short on the threshold. She was wearing a green gown again, this one with billowing satin ruffles and a neckline that made his mouth water.

Her surprise at finding him watching her made her

bite her lip, and he wanted nothing so much as a taste of her.

"I-I was just looking for place cards. May asked me to, though I suppose it doesn't matter now." Her words rushed out as she pointed to the table. "But there aren't any. Place cards, that is."

He moved to stand next to her, savoring her look of anticipation. He resisted touching her, but barely. Standing near enough to feel her skirts pressing against his legs, he turned his attention to the table and tried not to imagine lifting her onto it.

"We don't use them at Hartwell. My mother disliked them. She was conventional in many ways, but she had the radical notion that meals should be enjoyable and our guests should sit wherever they liked, rather than being bound by order of rank or status."

That pleased her. Out of the corner of his eye, he saw the flash of her smile and couldn't resist turning and giving her all his attention.

"Tell me about your mother."

Lucius swallowed, and then again, but emotion blocked his throat and stilled his tongue.

"Based on her books in the library and her egalitarian views about the rules of the dining room, I think I would have liked her."

He managed a nod, though he found it difficult to meet her gaze. He stared at the skirt of her gown, the lavish arrangement of crystal, silverware, and porcelain on the table, anywhere but at her face.

Then he saw her hand easing over his where he gripped

the back of a chair. Her warmth seeped into his skin, and he looked up to face her.

Softly, tenderly, she said, "It's difficult. I know. I miss my mother too."

He nodded again and found his voice. "Every memory I have of time spent with her is a happy memory. I realize now she wasn't content here at Hartwell, and with my father. But she rarely let me see that."

The affection in Jessamin's gaze encouraged him to continue, and now that he'd started, he found there was much more to say.

"She was clever and strong and she knew her own mind. Like you. After she was gone, all the happiness went too."

Lifting his head, Lucius glanced at the high ceiling and studied the elaborate chandelier, adapted for gas now, though it had blazed with dozens of candles when he was a boy.

"My father sent me away after she died. I suppose I look a good deal like her. Perhaps I reminded him of her. He said he couldn't bear the sight of me."

She squeezed his hand and he turned his to clasp hers, their fingers threading together like puzzle pieces slipping into place.

"I was only in Scotland a few years before going away to school and then university. When my brother died and my father called me back to Hartwell, I doubted I could ever be happy within these walls again."

Tipping his head down, he saw Jessamin had turned her attention to the chandelier too. The creamy expanse of her neck lured him and he couldn't resist reaching for her, slipping his free hand around her waist and pulling her near.

She gasped but leaned into him, lifting her clasped hands between them.

"And then you came to Hartwell, and I found that I could."

He dipped his head to kiss her and she lifted hers to let him, but they paused and pulled apart at the sound of Kitty Adderly's unmistakable singsong voice.

"I suggest you two stifle that urge. Although I decided to break with tradition and come in unescorted, the rest of them are close on my heels."

JESS WASN'T CERTAIN she'd make it through her second dinner at Hartwell. The tension in the room was so thick, it would surely choke her by the third course. Nerves kept her from eating or drinking much, and all she truly wanted was another moment, or several, alone with Lucius.

Only his presence kept her from being rude, excusing herself, and leaving the room. When she felt the point of his sister's glare, Jess turned to focus on Lucius, and he offered reassurance. Nothing as obvious as a smile, just a quirk of his mouth or the softening of his gaze. He conversed with those around him when questioned, but he'd glance at her now and then, as if to ensure she hadn't bolted.

May and Kitty sparred playfully with Mr. Wellesley,

and the village doctor attempted to join in, but Dr. Seagraves seemed destined to offend, though it was clear his real intention was to charm.

"Ladies, your tresses are lovely. I meant no offense. I was merely saying that there is something particularly lovely about auburn hair." He gaped at Annabel Benson as he made the pronouncement. The poor girl had become the object of his wooing efforts, though anyone could see her hair was darker, more mahogany than auburn.

Wellesley cut into the conversation to say as much.

"You're barking up the wrong tree, Seagraves. I've known Annabel all my life, and her hair is decidedly brown. An extraordinary brown, I'll grant you. Like chocolate with a dash of a cinnamon." Wellesley turned to gaze at Miss Benson and color blossomed on her cheeks, the same shade as the bowls of hothouse peonies dotting the table and perfuming the air. "Yes, chocolate and cinnamon and a splash of almond when you least expect it. But not auburn. Definitely not auburn."

"Auburn hair?" Lord Dunthorpe, who seemed as intimidating as Jess imagined he'd be, if a bit forgetful, spoke up above the din of cross table chatter. "Who has auburn hair?"

As if the lights of the chandelier and wall sconces had been funneled to shine a blinding beam in her direction, Jess sensed the heat of a dozen gazes turned her way.

She'd been careful to refrain from taking too much wine so there was a possibility she might make an intelligent contribution to the conversation, or at least avoid saying anything terribly embarrassing. Sitting up straight, she acknowledged, "I have auburn hair, my lord."

"Oh yes, so I see. You're the one, then." He squinted at her as he spoke, and Jess wasn't sure if he meant to inspect her or intended to glare.

"I-I . . ." She tried to form a sentence, but her throat fluttered as if a bird was thrashing its way out. So much for intelligent conversation.

"Miss Wright has beautiful hair. What of it?" Lucius's deep voice was firm, as if he wished to put an end to the ridiculous topic.

His father grumbled a moment before declaring, "I prefer raven hair, like my dear wife. And you, Miss Sedgwick. Very fine, indeed. Between you and Lucius, I suspect we'll have a few black-haired bairns, as Isobel would say, running around Hartwell soon."

Conversation ceased and the guests stilled in their seats. Jess noted shock on May's face and a frown on Kitty's. Even Seagraves looked glum to find his ardor for Miss Benson derailed.

"Surely there is more to consider than hair color when choosing a wife. In the sum of a woman's qualities, I suspect the shade of her hair counts very little." After moments of struggling to find her voice, the words were out before Jess thought better of it.

"Indeed." Aunt Augusta lifted her glass up and toward Jess as if to toast her.

"Hear, hear." Wellesley pounded his fist lightly on the table, making the crystal nearby shudder.

Jess looked to Lucius and his grin and the gleam of pride in his eyes made everything else fade away.

"Yes, one must consider whether a lady comes from a good family, whether she has the sort of upbringing and breeding to be a countess. And whether she will bring honor to one's family." Julia's shrill voice was as sharp as shattered glass, and her words cut as she'd no doubt intended. "A man should consider if she's a lady at all."

In gazing at Lucius, Jess had opened herself bare and allowed his sister the perfect moment to attack. Like little knives, each of Lady Julia's words hit their mark, and the wound was so intense, Jess feared she might bleed inwardly if she moved too quickly.

But she had to leave. She lifted her napkin with trembling hands and placed it on the table.

"Julia, what nonsense you speak. Surely we needn't worry on that score where Miss Sedgwick is concerned. You are most welcome at Hartwell, Miss Sedgwick." Lucius's father's voice was almost as deep as his son's, though roughened with age, and he spoke of May with warmth, a certainty that she would soon be his daughter-in-law.

"Yes, Father. If Lucius does his duty, none of us need worry," Julia agreed.

Jess pushed back in her chair, not bothering to wait for one of the footmen to assist her, the screech of the chair's legs on polished wood drawing the attention of those seated nearby.

"My dear, are you all right?" Lady Stamford's hand

on her arm and whispered words of concern brought no comfort.

"No, I must leave."

On her other side, Wellesley rose from his chair and moved to help her. Standing despite a wave of nausea, Jess reached out and Wellesley tucked her arm in his as if they were preparing for a pleasant stroll through the park.

As they drew near Lucius, he stood and threw his napkin on the table, nearly upsetting his wineglass.

"I'll take her." The deep rumble of his voice was a balm, but Jess couldn't look at him. Not yet. If she looked at him, she might break into pieces or begin sobbing, and she couldn't bear to let his sister see her tears.

"Lucius, don't you have guests to attend to?" Julia's voice hadn't dulled and the sound of it made Jess wince.

"Don't, Julia. You've said quite enough. Please excuse me, everyone, and do continue to enjoy your meal."

Jess felt his hand on her right arm, though Wellesley had yet to let go of her left.

Lucius leaned toward the woman who'd been introduced as his father's nurse and spoke in a near whisper. "Mrs. Ives, would you see that my father gets back to his rooms safely?"

Moments later, and without entirely recalling the journey from the dining room, Jess stood at an open window in Lucius's study. She drew in gulps of fresh air while Lucius and Mr. Wellesley spoke together near the fireplace.

When she turned toward the two men, Mr. Wellesley approached and reached out to take her hands. Though she'd met the man only the day before, the familiar gesture felt natural, comforting.

"Please give no mind to Julia. She's always been sharp-tongued. It's all she has, really. She wasn't gifted with Julian's wit or Lucius's cleverness."

No one in her life had been cruel, unless one counted her father's negligence at the end as cruelty. She'd never been the object of the kind of loathing Lady Julia clearly felt toward her. Yet, in the space of a few sentences, Robert Wellesley managed to stoke Jess's sympathy, and she found herself pitying Lucius's sister as much as she disliked her.

He gripped her hands more tightly. "Did you fight very hard to keep your bookshop, Miss Wright?"

"Yes, of course. It was what my father asked of me."

He glanced back at Lucius. "How well matched you two are."

When he turned back to Jess, he'd drawn his usually smiling mouth into a grim line. He leaned toward her and spoke quietly. "You'll need that mettle to help him through this."

Jess expected him to say more, but after releasing her hands, he strode to Lucius, offered him one firm pat on the back, and departed.

Lucius stared at her with a stark expression.

When she wrapped her arms around herself, he took a step toward her.

"Are you warm enough?"

The chill causing her to shiver had nothing to do with the room's temperature. It was deeper, under her skin, bone-deep.

"Why did you plan to marry May?"

He cocked his head at the question, as if he wasn't sure he'd heard her correctly. Then he lifted a hand toward one of the chairs before the fire.

"Come away from the window and get warm."

Jess's legs felt as tense and tight as her chest, but she managed to seat herself in the chair he indicated.

Lucius closed the window behind her and then settled a blanket over her lap before taking the chair next to hers.

"First, know that I intend to speak to Julia—"

Jess rushed to stop him. "I want to forget all of it."

"I can't forget."

The memory of the first time he'd spoken the three words were in his mind. She could see it when she gazed at him and saw the tremulous curve of his mouth. Jess reached for him and he lifted his hand to meet hers.

"What of my question? Can you tell me why?"

He stroked a thumb across the back of her hand as he spoke. "I suspect my aunt has warned you away from the eastern wing of the house."

Lady Stamford had mentioned it once, indicating that portion of the estate was undergoing renovations.

"My parents used to share those rooms, and now my father refuses to be moved. He was quite . . . obsessed with my mother. Perhaps he remembers her best in those rooms." He closed his eyes a moment before continuing. "He's not well, you see. His emotions run riot and his memory often fails him completely."

It explained why his father avoided public gatherings, why he preferred to keep to his rooms and required a nurse to accompany him to dinner. Suddenly, the aristocratic older man who'd struck her as intimidating seemed human, vulnerable. He needed Lucius, not simply as his heir, but as his steward, a man with the will and strength of character to take on the challenges of running the estate. And, apparently, repairing it.

"The renovations are extensive?"

Lifting his free hand, Lucius pinched the flesh at the top of nose, and Jess longed to reach a finger up and smooth the lines of worry creasing his brow.

"The renovations haven't truly begun. The cost is . . . extensive."

"And May is rich."

He nodded and reached for her other hand.

"Very. And yet I have no more interest in marrying her than she does in marrying me."

His words warmed her more effectively than the fire, but Jess knew May's wishes and Lucius's weren't the end of the matter.

"But it's what your father asked of you." Jess tightened her grip on his hands as she echoed the answer she'd given Mr. Wellesley. She understood duty to one's father. It had driven the last twelve years of her life.

"My father does not ask. He expects. He insists."

Jess knew the sadness in Lucius's gaze, knew the weight of a father's expectations. She pulled her hands from his, but he held tight, only letting her go reluctantly.

Standing before the fire a moment, heart sore and mind muddled, she willed herself to turn to him. There was a truth they were both avoiding, and it was what mattered most.

Taking the few steps toward his desk, Jess took care not disturb to any of the implements on top, recalling Lady Stamford's story about how very particular he was about arranging them.

"Even if you don't marry May, you'll have to marry someone like her. A lady with the dowry you need."

She'd managed to say the words, but he didn't give her time to dwell on them before approaching in three determined strides. Standing behind her, he rested his hands on her waist and pulled her in close, fitting her body against his.

"There's something I need more than a rich girl's dowry."

His fingers brushed the nape of her neck, sliding stray tendrils of hair aside. Then he kissed her, a warm, firm press of his mouth that reverberated through her body, fizzing down her spine, and lower, until she felt it to the tips of her toes.

"I need you."

Moving to her side, Lucius reached out to tilt her chin gently, just enough to meet his gaze.

"What sort of man did your father intend for you to marry?"

"He never expected me to marry at all. I told him I would keep the shop instead." Now that she did consider it, now that she sometimes allowed herself to dream of the joy marriage could bring, it hurt to recall how easily her father had allowed her to renounce the notion. Shouldn't he have wished for that kind of happiness for her?

Lucius looked contemplative before reaching up and stroking one finger down her check, skimming it along the edge of her chin.

"It seems we've found in each other what neither of us expected but always hoped for."

Pleasure expanded in her chest, warm and sweet, filling every hollow space, every painful corner. Jess embraced it. No thoughts. No doubts. Just the love she'd kept locked away, waiting for Lucius to set it free.

She reached for him, but he'd already gathered her near, kissing the tip of her nose, each cheek, even the curve of her chin before taking her lips. He tortured her with slow, drugging kisses when she wanted to pull and press, to get as close to his body as she felt to his heart.

When Lucius lowered his head to kiss her neck, Jess made the mistake of opening her eyes, of taking in the polished wainscoting, the elaborately carved fireplace, and the glinting silver-framed photographs on the mantel.

Doubt seeped in, fears and uncertainties. Lucius lifted his head as if he could sense the tumult in her mind.

He reached up, cupping her cheek in his palm. "What is it?"

Jess took a breath to express her worries and ruin their blissful moment, but the clicking patter of canine paws on the main hall's marble floor drew their attention to the study door.

Lady Stamford swept in and Castor and Pollux ambled along behind her.

"Oh . . ." The countess looked momentarily abashed, and then lifted her chin. "Lucius, Miss Wright has had a most trying evening. I assumed you'd had a maid help her to her room."

She lifted her arm toward Jessamin. "Come, my dear, let's get you to bed. We should all get a sound sleep so that we may face the challenges ahead."

Jess shifted her gaze from Lucius to his aunt and then back to the man she loved. She nodded to let him know she'd go with his aunt, but when she took a step to move from his side, he slid his hand down to grasp her wrist.

"Rest well, Jessamin. I spoke to my father last night, but I intend to speak to him again in the morning, and then I'll have a rather important question for you." He smiled, a quick, easy dip of his mouth and flash of teeth, as if he did it all the time.

Jess's heart flipped and swelled in her chest.

As she preceded Lady Stamford from the study, the pugs trotting ahead of her as if to lead the way, Jess heard Lucius's aunt whisper to him.

"Speak with me in the morning before you approach Maxim again. We must formulate a strategy."

Chapter Twenty-Four

JESS WAS WELL practiced at sleepless nights. She'd found no rest for days upon first arriving at Marleston, and back in London, living in the cramped rooms over the shop, she'd lain awake many a night worrying over her father and money— always money. If not the root of *all* evil, it had certainly shaped her life. Her parents had constantly fretted over sales and debts, even before Father's vices had begun whittling their funds.

And now she found herself in love with a man who said he needed her when she did not have the one thing he needed most—the wealth to help him repair his estate. If she'd learned anything from her parents' marriage, it was the nature of partnership. They'd been true helpmates, allied in every trial, assisting each other with every task. It was no wonder her father had been so lost after losing his life's partner.

Could she be that to Lucius? To be his wife—*could there be a sweeter notion?*

But could she take what she wanted—his love, his name, his heart in exchange for hers—and fail to give him the dowry he'd sought in a bride? Could she consign him to a life of worrying over money and watching his grand estate crumble around him? The love she'd seen in his eyes tonight had warmed her from the inside out, but what if some future day came when he turned on her with resentment in his eyes? The thought made her clench the blanket and bite her lip until she tasted blood.

Turning onto her belly, Jess buried her face in the plush pillow and concentrated on any other thoughts than worry over money. She silently recited poems she'd memorized as a child. Recalling favorite novels, she repeated whole paragraphs in her mind until coming to the edge of what she remembered. Finally, she turned to Shakespeare, grasping for a dark play, as somber as her mood, and began reciting lines from *Macbeth*. These she couldn't resist speaking aloud and turned her head so that her voice was only half muffled by the pillow's bulk.

"'The night is long that never finds the day.'" That seemed particularly fitting. She repeated it until drowsiness drew her down into near sleep. When she heard the pitter-patter of raindrops beating at the windowpanes, a comforting sound that reminded her of the bookshop and London, she finally gave in and slept.

But a moment later, or so it seemed, she squinted one eye open.

"Drat!" A housemaid stood by a chair, bending down to rub her shin.

Jess usually woke to the sight of Tilly, who'd tended to her since their arrival at Hartwell, and she didn't recognize the young woman grimacing in pain.

"Are you all right?"

"Oh yes, miss. Ever so sorry. I'm not familiar with this room to cross it in the dark. Shall I turn the up the gas and open the curtains?"

The room was unusually dim for morning, and when the maid drew the drapery back, Jess saw why. Storm clouds hovered, darkening the sky.

The ominous weather matched her mood, and the murky state of her mind.

"Is Tilly unwell?"

"No, miss. She's helping in another part of the house. The storm last night caused some damage, or so I heard."

The maid turned her attention back to sorting out Jess's clothing, but news that the estate had suffered damage during the night had Jess out of bed and rushing through her morning tasks and pinning her hair. The maid huffed with frustration, so Jess accepted her help to dress, but then sent the girl on her way.

She needed to see Lucius, to know that he was safe and well, but when she reached the ground floor, Jess found herself in the midst of chaos. Maids and footman scurried past in both directions, some carrying furnishings, others weighed down with piles of folded linen.

When Tilly emerged from the far end of the hall, Jess

rushed toward her, only to find the girl wide-eyed and frazzled, arms full of bloody clothing.

"It's His Lordship, miss. There was an accident in that part of the house."

Tilly cocked her head back to indicate the eastern portion of the house, and Jess moved past her to follow a maid carrying more clean linens.

Dirty, wet footprints provided a trail up a winding staircase that opened to a hallway. Most of the doors along the wall were closed, but outside one open door, two maids knelt on their hands and knees sopping up water.

Jess stepped between the young women and heard the rough voice of Lucius's father.

"Then leave me here, damn you. Let me die here. I won't leave this room."

Mrs. Ives stood near the threshold, blocking the way, but Jess could see over the woman's shoulder to the scene inside. Lucius's father lay in the middle of an elaborately carved four-poster bed, and Lucius stood at his bedside. A blood-soaked bandage covered part of the earl's head and dark stains marred his pillow and bedclothes. Chunks of plaster littered the floor and a gaping hole in the ceiling revealed the rafters above. Water ran down the walls, and nearly everything in the room looked wet or dusted with plaster.

Mrs. Ives stepped aside to allow a footman to carry a chair past her and out of the room. Turning, she caught sight of Jess.

"Careful, miss. The floor is still quite slippery."

"Jessamin."

The warmth in Lucius's voice as he moved around his father's bed and approached made her heart ache. But the sight of him, whole and safe, was such a relief Jess almost reached out to embrace him.

"I'm glad to see you." Despite his earnest tone and the way he gazed at her as if she was the most appealing woman he'd ever seen, Jess didn't believe him. She'd seen the dark half-moons under her eyes in her looking glass and noted the sallow tint of her skin.

Lucius looked exhausted too, and bloodstains marred his white shirt.

"Dr. Seagraves says Father will be fine. It's a slight cut, but head wounds bleed quite a lot. Seagraves doesn't think it will even leave a scar." He leaned in and spoke low. "My main objective is to get him out of this room."

"Your objective should be to marry that American and repair this bloody house." His father's call from the bed made Lucius wince, but then he looked at her and took a deep breath, as if preparing to reenter the fray.

"Can I help?" She itched to do something to aid him, to care for him, the man who seemed to be responsible for everyone else. She'd help his father too, if she could, and if the earl would let her.

He reached out to rest his hand on her upper arm. She could feel the chill in his fingers through the fabric of her dress.

"Would you wait for me downstairs in my study? Or the library, if you like."

Jess peeked around at his father. Mrs. Ives was urging the earl to get up from his sodden bed.

"Can I do nothing here to help you?"

Lucius shocked her by stepping closer and kissing her forehead—one quick press of his mouth before pulling away.

"You help me more than you know." He looked back at his father too. Mrs. Ives and two maids were easing Lord Dunthorpe into a simple wooden chair.

Lucius rubbed her arm gently and she hoped some of her body's heat seeped through to warm his fingers.

"We must move him, and I suspect the less of an audience he has, the smaller the fuss he'll make. At least I pray that's the case."

Judging by the scowl on his father's face, Jess wasn't certain anything would prevent a fuss, but she turned to leave, glancing back at Lucius when she reached the threshold.

"I'll come to you as soon as I can."

The promise in his gaze and tone reassured her. She would do as he bid her and wait for him in his study, but she knew Lady Stamford would be in a dither over her brother's injury and sought her out first.

She found the countess in a spacious upstairs guest room.

"Jessamin, there you are, my dear. Would you come help me organize this room?"

The room was meant to house Lord Dunthorpe until his portion of the house could be repaired, and Jess directed the placement of furniture and arrangement of the earl's possessions. It seemed the only personal item he'd have to do without was his enormous bed.

Seeing that Jess had the room preparations well in hand, Lady Stamford headed downstairs to reassure the other guests at breakfast and see May Sedgwick off to the train station.

An hour later, the room looked ready. The earl's belongings and furniture lent it a comfortable, lived-in air, and Jess thought Lord Dunthorpe might end up enjoying the move after all. After sending one of the maids up to tell Lucius and Mrs. Ives the room awaited its occupant, Jess made her way to Lucius's study.

It seemed cavernous and hollow without Lucius's presence, but hints of his spice scent lingered in the air, and that soothed her. She considered reading while she waited for him and entered the library through the connecting door. Selecting *The Count of Monte Cristo*, Jess curled up on a settee near the windows and watched as dark clouds swept across the sky. They churned and twisted, much like the thoughts in her head, but there was a glimmer of clear sky on the far horizon. And there was a single beacon in her mind's chaos too.

I love him. Nothing else was as clear as that single thought, that unwavering feeling, that absolute certainty. *I love Lucius.*

JESS WOKE TO the sound of Lucius's deep voice carried through from the study. "We should speak elsewhere. Jessamin's asleep in the library."

"She should hear this, Lucius." At Lady Stamford's reply, Jess sat up and almost knocked Lucius's favorite book onto the floor. She reached out to grab it as he spoke again.

"Yes, but I hate to disturb her. She looked peaceful."

Jess walked over to replace Lucius's book, careful to tuck it in as neatly as she'd found it. When she turned back to the connecting door, Lucius's voice rang through it.

"I can't marry her. I won't."

At his emphatic declaration, Jess's heart stalled. She gripped the edge of the bookcase, unable to catch her breath.

"You heard her. The woman has no interest in marrying me. And she's halfway to London by now."

Jess inhaled and then gasped air into her lungs. May. He was talking about May.

"He'll continue to insist."

"He insisted he wouldn't leave his rooms and now he has a gash on the head for his stubbornness."

Lady Stamford's voice turned quiet, tentative. "We could consider other options."

"If you mean to show me that list of eligible women again, I'll be tempted to wreck the other half of the house."

"I have only one woman in mind. As I'm guessing you do. A dowry is the issue we must conquer." Lady Stamford's voice held the same tone Jess had heard every time the countess set out to overcome a dilemma.

"Damn a dowry! There are other means of raising money."

Jess heard Lucius's footsteps approach the door between his study and the library and she sank back against the wall. What a coward she was to eavesdrop rather than join the battle, as Mr. Wellesley would no doubt urge her to do.

"How much does the estate require?" Lady Stamford asked.

There was a pause, a long drawn-out silence, and then Jess heard Lucius retreat across the room. "More than you can imagine."

A rustle of papers followed.

"Good heavens."

Jess approached the door and turned the knob, stepping into Lucius's study.

He leaned against the front edge of his desk, arms crossed, head down, and his shoulders slumped. She hated the defeat etched in every line of his body.

When he heard her footsteps and looked up, a light lit his eyes.

"Jessamin, I'm sorry we woke you." He approached and reached for her hands, seemingly unconcerned that his aunt witness the action, but Jess still considered Lady Stamford her employer and held back.

"Aunt Augusta, would you mind if I have a word alone with Jessamin?"

Lady Stamford assessed them a moment before acquiescing. She called to the dogs, who'd settled near the fireplace, and then turned to Lucius.

"I'll grant you a moment, my boy. That is all. Then I have a proposal both of you should hear."

She laid a sheaf of documents on a side table before departing and Jess stepped away from Lucius to retrieve them.

"You needn't—"

"May I?"

They spoke over each other, but Lucius nodded as if he'd heard her request.

"It's not happy reading, I warn you."

They appeared to be invoices, with descriptions of work and associated costs, from masons, bricklayers, carpenters, and smiths. The figures on the documents added up to an astounding sum, more than her father had ever dreamed of earning in his life. More than most men could fathom.

"They are estimates. But the work is all necessary if we're to restore the eastern walls and renovate the tenant housing."

Jess lifted the papers out to him, and Lucius took them, returning the documents to a precisely arranged pile on his desk. She'd been eager to get them out of her hands, and yet he couldn't ignore them so easily.

"This has been hanging over you. I'm sure it weighs on your mind. It must be difficult to think about anything else." Jess realized she wasn't just speaking of Lucius, but of her own preoccupation with bills that couldn't be paid, money that was nowhere to be found.

He lifted off the desk and stalked toward her, reaching out to grasp one of the ribbons at the neck of gown. Jess's breathing hitched and she edged toward him. Being near him felt so right, she could almost forget the rest.

"That was true until quite recently." He wrapped the length of ribbon around his index finger. "Until a night in Mayfair when I met the most extraordinary woman." He reached a hand up to the curve of her waist, urging her closer. "And she has so completely taken hold of my mind that I have few thoughts about anything else."

He lowered his mouth to hers and Jess kissed him with all the passion, all the love she felt. She gasped when he palmed her breast with one hand and reached around with his other to cup her backside. Light-headed, breathless, she pulled back to gaze at him, imprinting the image in her mind. His lips trembled, and his eyes shone with the same need that made her body ache. A lock of hair curled down onto his forehead, and she reached up to stroke the silky strand.

"I love you."

She'd finally said the words to him, and he smiled. She wanted to remember that too. A pain, that searing burn as if her heart had turned to a glowing coal, made her gasp. But it was right that it should hurt. She knew her next words would be the most difficult of her life.

"I love you, but I cannot give you what you need."

He tensed and his body went hard in her arms, stony and still, as immovable as the statue she'd imagined him to be the night they'd met.

"*You* are what I need."

Jess pushed gently at his chest. If she was to do this, she could not bear him so near.

"Those estimates on your desk say otherwise." When Lucius released her and she stood two steps away, Jess chafed her hands together, suddenly cold. "I don't mind talk of money. I was raised in a shop, after all. You need money, and I haven't even earned my first month's wages from your aunt."

For several minutes, Lucius stared at her blankly, as if was looking through her, past her. Then he lifted a hand and scrubbed it across his face.

"I don't need your wages, Jessamin. Only you."

His words, so heart melting the first time she'd heard them, sounded now like an unbearably great responsibility. As if he believed her merits outweighed the enormous sums owed to the repairmen. As if she was more valuable to him than a grand estate. As if his desire for her negated his duty to his father. But was she that much of a prize? Jess wasn't convinced her worth could compensate him for all that he might lose if she became his wife.

"What if I'm not enough?"

He tipped his mouth at that, though the expression was more sardonic than pleased. "For a taciturn man with an irascible father and a crumbling home?"

Biting her lip, Jess weighed the various arguments she'd been having with herself all morning.

"I love you enough to wish for your happiness more than my own." She'd repeated the thought in her head, but her voice trembled when she expressed the sentiment.

"Me too, but I believe they are one and the same."

Jess shook her head. That couldn't be. Happiness couldn't be so easily grasped when it had eluded her for so long.

Lucius crossed the space she'd created between them before she could rally another argument.

"My darling Jess, trust me to find the money."

The moment the words slipped out, Jess clasped a hand to her mouth and began to shiver. Her body went hot then cold and her pulse slowed to a sluggish thud.

"What is it? Tell me."

"M-my father used to say that."

She heard it then, similar words but in her father's London accent. She no longer saw Lucius but Lionel Wright's beseeching face. *Trust me to find the money, love.*

"I take it your father couldn't be trusted." Despite Lucius's gentle tone, the words were hard to hear. The truth was hard to hear.

"Not with money, no. Not after Mother died. He only knew how to make it disappear."

Jess didn't have the will to resist when Lucius gathered her near, resting his chin on the top of her head. He rubbed his hands down her arms, and drew delicious circles across her back. The urge to melt into him, to reach out and grasp whatever future he offered . . . She'd never known a greater temptation.

He drew back and assessed her. "You've stopped shivering, but I suspect you didn't get a bite of breakfast. Let me speak to my aunt, check on Father, and see to the remaining guests. Then we can talk."

Exhaustion made the few steps across the study seem like a mile, and when Jess heard Lucius's footsteps behind her, she half hoped he might offer to carry her up the stairs.

"Jessamin, if not trust, then time. Give me that and I will sort this out."

His confidence was palpable, like a current of energy she could draw from to fuel her hopes. But hopes weren't certitude, and Jess still wasn't certain Lucius might not be happier with a wealthy wife, a contented father, and an estate with ceilings that didn't collapse when it rained.

Chapter Twenty-Five

THOUGH IT WAS early evening and most guests had retired to their rooms, Lucius knew returning to his own room wouldn't bring any rest. After speaking to Jessamin in the morning and dealing with his father's ire much of the afternoon, he'd overseen the departure of nearly all the houseguests. Only Kitty Adderly and Wellesley remained, and Lady Katherine promised to make her way back to London on the first morning train. He'd sought Jessamin out before luncheon, but a maid informed him that she was resting and he hadn't the heart to disturb her. Still, he longed for nothing more than to spend the night in her arms, to hold her and love her, to pleasure her with every ounce of energy he had left after a day that had upended his life in the most fortuitous of ways.

Somehow he had to convince her to stay. He had to convince her to be his wife.

His body protested with every step he took past her

bedroom, but he willed his heated thoughts to cool and turned toward Aunt Augusta's door. He'd yet to find an opportunity to speak with her and formulate a plan to deal with the estate's finances.

Fatigue and worry for Maxim had painted dark shadows under his aunt's eyes, but her mouth still curved up when he stepped into her sitting room.

"Nothing douses a house party like a flood."

Lucius chuckled, finding that particular sound quite easy all of a sudden.

Augusta looked as shocked by the sound as he was by the realization.

"Hardly a flood, Aunt Augusta, just a minor torrent."

Castor and Pollux were sprawled in a heap on the settee, and she nudged one dog's rump to make a place for him.

"Thank goodness Maxim wasn't severely harmed."

"Yes." If anything, his father's injury made him more indignant than usual, but it was a relief to know his wound would heal quickly. No doubt his anger over being removed from his usual rooms would take longer to cool. While his father had finally relented and agreed to relocate temporarily, Lucius had yet to further broach the topic of Hartwell's future and his own. Though he hadn't witnessed it, his father had apparently spent the better half of an hour complaining to Augusta about Lucius's mismanagement of the estate and his desire to marry to suit his whims rather than as duty dictated.

Settling himself in a chair across from his aunt, Lucius was uncertain how to begin. All his hopes rested on his ability to find a way out of the estate's financial troubles.

Augusta generally loathed silence and often jumped in to fill the quiet with a quip or platitude. Tonight she simply watched him with an inscrutable expression.

"I plan to ask Jessamin to be my wife."

His aunt sniffed and fussed with the folds of her gown. "I take that as a given. I did allow you two more than a moment unchaperoned. I thought you might have asked her then."

"No. I can't ask her until the rest is settled. She trusted her father to overcome their financial difficulties, and he failed her. She needs to *see* that I can find a way." Lucius eased back in his chair, letting a deep breath whoosh through his lips. "But you approve of the match?"

"How could I not? You seem set on it, and you know my feelings for the girl. I consider her a treasure."

Lucius opened his mouth, snapped it shut, and then began to speak again, only to find his aunt had left him at a complete loss for words.

"She's a quite singular young woman, and I can only take pleasure in losing her as a companion if I will gain her as a niece."

"Father—"

"—will come to admire her as we all do. Don't worry yourself on that point, my boy."

With a moment's reflection, Lucius wasn't truly surprised by his aunt's approval. She adored Jessamin. But he felt none of Augusta's certainty about Father blithely accepting Jessamin as his bride.

"Did she often speak of returning to London?" Lucius fisted his hand as he asked the question. A nagging fear had unsettled him throughout the day. What if Jessamin's resistance to their match had as much to do with the kind of life she preferred as the sort she thought he needed? Perhaps he'd presumed too much. Surely she missed her shop and the ladies of the Women's Union Lady Katherine mentioned. He didn't even know if she had family in London who might be missing her as fiercely as he would if she left Hartwell.

He wouldn't be a man who suffocated his wife with demands, jealous of every moment she spent out of his sight, so possessive that all she longed for was escape. He wouldn't be his father.

And yet, what if he was like him? He'd never wanted anything as he wanted Jessamin. He did long for each moment he could have her to himself, and all morning he'd feared nothing so much as the possibility that she would leave.

His aunt considered his question a long while before tilting her head and replying. "No, my boy, she never did. She mentioned a friend called Alice and a coffee shop she used to frequent." A devout tea drinker, Augusta shivered at the mention of coffee, but Lucius had rather enjoyed a hearty cup of it on his occasional visits to London. He made a mental note to have Hartwell's cook order coffee.

"And she did mention the desire to visit London, just a day trip, perhaps in the spring."

Relief deflated and buoyed him all at once. The tension in his body eased and yet he leaned forward, eager to attack the matter at hand.

"I have an idea, Aunt Augusta. Several, actually, about how we might address the repairs to the estate and secure its future financial health."

Augusta moved so that she truly faced him on the settee, her eyes alight with eagerness. "I also have information that might prove useful to you, but carry on and tell me your plans first."

"Information?" He could see she was bursting to divulge it. "Perhaps you should share your information first. Particularly if it involves knowledge of a hidden treasure buried on the estate."

"I'm afraid not, my dear. This concerns my own contribution to your happiness, and Jessamin's." She puffed out her chest, inhaling deeply, as if preparing herself for a momentous declaration. "I will, of course, release her as my companion."

Lucius leaned forward and lifted a hand. "Now, wait. I haven't asked her yet. She hasn't agreed to be my wife. I don't wish to coerce her into that choice."

"Of course not! I will wait for the proper moment. However, I wish to give her something, and I fear she won't accept it if she views herself as my employee."

Knowing his aunt, her history, and her affection for Jessamin, Lucius guessed what she might be planning.

"I would like to provide her a dowry."

Lucius didn't care if Jessamin brought a farthing into their marriage, but he could see in Augusta's face that she was determined. She'd lost a daughter, his cousin who'd only lived long enough for her christening, and he hadn't missed the maternal care his aunt had shown Jessamin. Gratitude made it difficult to speak and certainly impossible to say all that he wished to, but he managed to dip his head and reach for his aunt's hand. "Thank you."

"You may have to help me convince her to accept it. Did you know she returned Miss Adderly's payment for kissing you?"

The news burst in his heart like fireworks, shooting hot sparks through his veins. He gripped the back of the settee and shivered, not from chill, but from the force it took to stay seated when all he wanted was find Jessamin and kiss her senseless. Had she given back those sorely needed funds because she'd felt in their kiss what he had, a strange alchemy of need and desire, a sense that whatever he'd been seeking might have finally been found? He hoped that impulse had driven her.

"I can see that pleases you."

"Immensely."

Augusta smiled, a flash of pleasure, and then turned on him with a serious expression he'd rarely seen on her face. "Good. Now tell me your plan."

He reached up to run a hand through his hair in a Wellesley-like manner, reaching back to rub the nape of his neck. But the tension he expected to find wasn't there. He'd considered this plan for months, long before Jessamin Wright kissed him in that gallery. But thank God she had. It had been a catalyst to push him beyond his father's expectations.

"Part of the estate must be sold." He saw his aunt's throat working and the pained look in her eyes, but he rushed on. "We are fortunate that a portion of the estate was not included in the entail. Clever forefathers, or foremothers, I suspect. And some acres were acquired later."

Augusta began shaking her head, a slow back-and-forth movement of denial or dismay, but Lucius expected resistance. He'd learned young, with the loss of his mother and his move to Scotland, that change inspires resistance. He'd been fighting change and scrabbling for control all of his life.

"I don't simply propose diminishing the estate. Mr. Leighton, a land developer and entrepreneur, plans to purchase our acreage near the village and use a portion for housing and a portion for manufacturing. And I plan to invest in his ventures."

She frowned at that. "Invest? I thought the objective was to find money, not spend it."

"As Uncle Buchanan taught me, one must invest to earn."

Augusta narrowed one eye at him, clearly unconvinced.

"Tenants have abandoned our land to seek manufacturing jobs in the cities. Agriculture alone won't support Hartwell. We must invest. Wisely, yes. But we must invest."

Lucius waited as his aunt cast her face down and examined the carpet, pursing her mouth and scrunching her forehead in apparently deep contemplation.

He wanted her support and would likely need it to

bring his father around, but he would approach Maxim without her backing if necessary.

A scratching sound drew his attention to the door, and Lucius expected to see one of the pugs seeking a way out. Instead he looked down to see a shiny shoe and dark trousers attached to the lanky figure of Rob Wellesley emerge through the doorway.

"I couldn't sleep and had a wander. Then I heard voices and thought I might join in."

"Why?"

His aunt mistook Lucius's tone and shot him a chastising glance.

"Don't be rude, Lucius. Most of our guests have departed. We should be grateful we haven't frightened Robert off too."

"I don't frighten easily." Wellesley beamed a charming smile.

"We should carry on our discussion tomorrow. Give me time to consider your plan." His aunt spoke the words quietly as if she thought Wellesley might not take notice, but the man was as alert as a terrier.

"What plan is this? Please tell me it involves Miss Wright. Have you asked the woman to marry you yet? The suspense is doing my head in." Wellesley turned toward Augusta and then looked at Lucius.

"Your discomfort has not quite found its way onto my list of current concerns."

As ever, Wellesley seemed impervious to Lucius's sarcasm and settled into a chair, stretching his legs out, crossing them at the ankles, and then folding his hands over his stomach.

"So, what's the plan?"

Lucius rarely rolled his eyes, but few people exasperated him as effectively as Robert Wellesley.

"I must speak to my father about some changes in the way we manage the estate."

One of the pugs jumped down to sniff their visitor and Wellesley reached a hand out to give it a scratch behind the ear.

"You mean to sell Dunthorpe lands."

Lucius glanced at his aunt, who looked surprised by Wellesley's deduction.

He chuckled when he saw their faces. "Oh, I'm not Sherlock Holmes. I was listening at the door."

Resisting the urge to roll his eyes twice in the space of minutes, Lucius moved forward on the settee, resting his elbows on his knees. "My father will be resistant, to say the least."

"How old is he?" Wellesley asked the question in a light tone, almost flippantly.

"Though I'm not sure how it signifies, he'll be eighty come May."

Robert sat up in his chair and leaned forward, mirroring Lucius's posture by placing his elbows on his knees.

"Don't you see? Your father has seen wars and revolts, the deaths of three English kings, survived the loss of his wife and eldest son. The man endures change better than you allow."

He was right. Lucius didn't know if he could bring himself to admit it to him, but the reassurance in Rob's words settled his mind.

"Tell him your decisions, Lucius. He's put you in charge of this estate, so take it. Don't ask him or cajole him. Just tell him what must be done."

Aunt Augusta opened her mouth but then closed it without uttering a sound.

Wellesley reached a hand up to muss his hair and sighed in frustration. "Does it never strike either of you that the one person he loved most in this world was the only one who ever stood up to him? From what I recall of your mother, she was never afraid to tell him the truth." He grinned at his own declaration, as if utterly pleased with himself. "Our suffragette reminds me of her a bit."

My suffragette. Lucius didn't say the words, but he allowed himself a moment of the possessiveness he'd never understood in his father.

"I'm astounded." Lucius infused his tone with as much seriousness as he could manage. It was a challenge considering how much lighter he felt, and how effectively Wellesley's arguments had bolstered his confidence.

Wellesley returned a rare frown. "Why?"

"To realize that under all that disheveled hair and charm, you've been hiding a bit of good sense and cleverness."

His smile broke slowly, glacially considering Wellesley's usual mirthful manner, but when it finally came, followed by a low chuckle, neither Lucius nor his aunt could resist smiling too.

"High praise, indeed. Then shall I expect an invitation to the wedding?"

Chapter Twenty-Six

THE PATH TO Lucius's bedroom was the matter of a few steps down the hall, far easier than it had been to force her way through the crowd in the gallery that first night she'd met him. But Jess's legs trembled in much the same way, and, standing outside his chamber, she needed a moment to draw in a few deep breaths and will her pulse to stop hammering in her ears. When she finally raised her hand to knock, the sound of voices on the other side caused her to hesitate. She leaned in to listen, and in the same moment the door swung open and Lord Grimsby's valet, Mr. Mather, exited with an empty tray thrust out before him.

"Pardon me, miss." The valet expressed no surprise at finding her on Lucius's doorstep so late at night. He merely maneuvered around her in a precise, steady manner, never allowing the tray to shift in his hands.

Inside the room, Lucius stood next to a small table covered with food and a steaming teapot in the center.

The valet had clearly been busy. Lucius looked immaculate, his tamed black hair and elegant clothes presenting an orderly contrast to his disheveled state when she'd seen him in his father's room.

"I'm interrupting your meal."

Her words seemed to ignite him, and he stalked toward her with a hungry gaze that had nothing to do with food.

An answering pulse began in her body, thrumming in her chest and down into her belly. She needed him to touch her, kiss her, do all that his heated gaze promised. But he brushed past her, wrapping one large hand around her upper arm, and reaching out to close the door with his other. When he stepped close to her, sliding his hand down her arm, teasing her palm open with his fingers so that he might grasp her hand, Jess moved toward him as she'd done the first night they met.

"I was told you were sleeping and didn't want to disturb you. Did you have dinner? If not, please join me?" His voice, deep and low, melted her with a flush of warmth.

"Food is the last thing on my mind." It wasn't what she'd meant to say. She wasn't even certain how she'd formed the words, seeing as his voice, his scent, his nearness had turned her mind to porridge.

He chuckled, a delicious rumble bubbling up and echoing through her. He did it well, as if laughter came as naturally to him as it did to May or Wellesley.

Jess pulled back.

"What? I did promise to laugh more."

His gaze held the promise of laughter and much more, and when he dipped his head as if he meant to kiss her, Jess ducked away only because she knew if he put his mouth on her, she wouldn't be able to say any of what she'd come to say.

"I've come to a decision."

He took a step back, giving her space to breathe, but he continued to clasp her hand tightly, as if he had no intention of letting her go.

For the first time in her life, Jess spoke of a decision that had nothing to do with money, and nothing to with what she should do, what her father expected of her, or what she must do. She spoke the truth in her heart.

"I want to be with you tonight."

His tug nearly pulled her off her feet, but Lucius caught her, wrapped her in his arms, and lowered his mouth to hers. She'd tasted his kiss before, but not like this, not when she pushed away doubt and opened herself to him. She lifted her hands to his chest, hooking a finger into the front of his waistcoat, pulling him that single breath closer. Slipping a button, she could just press her hand inside, across the starched linen of his shirt, close enough to feel the tripping thump of his heartbeat. He deepened the kiss, reaching up to sink a hand into her hair, working pins free, and stroking down each strand he loosed.

Then he drew back, as breathless as she. The look he gave her, so full of love and admiration, soothed her, assuring her this—this precious connection that had been between them from the first—mattered most.

"I want you for more than tonight. I want you to be my wife."

She'd promised herself she wouldn't blush, but relief rushed through her veins, a melting sweetness, an incandescence of heat and pleasure and such happiness she couldn't manage a reply.

"I will do that again properly, knee bent, ring in hand. I promise."

Jess reached for his hand and lifted it to her breast, placing his palm over the point at which her heart seemed to determined thrash out of her chest.

"Only you." She repeated his earlier words, tenderly, as solemnly as she'd utter any vow. "I only need you."

When he pressed his lips to her cheek, it wasn't enough. Jess wanted more. Turning her head, she sought his mouth, and kissed him deeply, exploring, teasing him with her tongue as he'd taught her to do.

He wanted her, needed her. It made her bold, and her boldness seemed to thrill him. He pulled her closer, he explored with his hands, caressing her flesh where he could, dragging his fingers down her back in a delicious stroke. But he let her explore too, tipping his head when she moved her lips to his neck, moaning appreciatively when she nipped at the flesh of his ear, and emitting a low growl when she slid her hand down to tentatively stroke the hard length of him through this trousers.

The primitive sound set off an answering pulse in her center, and Jess pulled back, frightened at her own hunger and need, so fierce it made her quiver.

He cupped her cheek. "We can take it slow."

Slow wasn't what she wanted, but it was likely what she needed.

"Wh-what does your aunt say to all this?" Grasping for any thought other than the need to mold her body to Lucius's, Jess latched on to her one lingering concern.

Fearful she'd doused all the passion of the moment, she couldn't quite meet his gaze.

"She's pleased. Thrilled, I suspect. You'd only agreed to be her companion for a year, but now she'll get to keep you as a niece forever. You know she can't do without you."

He reached his hand to around to grasp her nape, and the slide and heat of his palm on her skin made her moan.

Dipping his head, he hovered over her mouth, lips brushing hers, breath gusting against her skin. "Neither can I."

When he finally kissed her, pressing his mouth to hers, Jess opened to him, urging him to plunder, and reached up to his waistcoat, freeing more buttons until she could press her palms against his chest. But it wasn't enough. She needed to be closer, needed to feel his heated skin against her own. Tugging his shirt, she pulled until she felt the edge of it slip from his trousers. Lucius gasped against her mouth when she slid her fingers underneath, finally touching the firm, supple plain of his chest. His skin was so warm, heated velvet, even across the muscled ridges.

Breaking their kiss, Lucius gazed at her a moment before lowering his head again and kissing her neck, lifting to skim his mouth over the curve of her ear and then laving the skin below it. When he dipped his head, pressing his mouth to the skin just above the neck of her gown, a warm syrupy heat melted her inside and a craving, deep and profound, took hold.

She lifted her hands to front of his waistcoat, peeling the garment back and pushing it from his shoulders. He released Jess long enough to lift his arms and pull his shirt over his head. Having seen the male form only in sculptures or paintings, Jess found Lucius's chest a revelation and ran her hands over his skin, amazed by the contrast of soft flesh and hard muscle, the smooth expanse of his stomach and the dark patch of hair forming a trail to the edge of his trousers.

He allowed her explorations only a moment before reaching for her again, grasping her waist, then sliding his hands up over the swell of her breasts, lifting a finger to the button at the top of her bodice. He paused, a flash of uncertainty in his gaze. But Jess wanted more—for him to touch her as he'd allowed her to touch him, to shed every barrier between them, to know him as she'd never known any man.

She reached up to slip the top button on her bodice herself, and he reached for the next, and the next. Once freed, Jess slipped the front hooks of her corset, and Lucius pulled at the bowed ribbons to release her chemise. As soon as the cotton slipped from her breasts she reached out to embrace him, sighing with pleasure at the slide of skin against skin.

He pulled away just enough to take her hand, leading her through the sitting room to a doorway and his bedroom beyond. Without his heat warming her, his chest covering hers, Jess felt a moment of embarrassment and lifted a hand to cover her breasts.

A fire burned in the bedroom hearth, heating the air and filling the room with an amber glow. Jess could just make out the details of a grand four-poster bed with a deep blue counterpane.

Lucius released her hand and closed the space between them, pressing his body against hers and reaching up to free the rest of the pins from her hair. She watched his eyes, and then the seductive grin curving his mouth, as he threaded his fingers through the strands, drawing them down across her chest and over her breasts. He tilted his head back and smiled, as if pleased with the sight of her taut nipples peeking through the waves of her hair.

"You're magnificent."

Before she could respond, speak, or reach for him, he dipped his head and drew a nipple into his mouth. She arched back and he wrapped an arm around her waist to steady her. He licked and teased until she moaned and reached up to dishevel his silky black hair as she'd longed to do every time she looked at him. Then she pulled back, afraid she'd scratched him or grasped him too roughly.

"Did I hurt you?"

He lifted his head, giving her a chance to breathe.

"It will only hurt if you stop," he rasped before taking her other nipple between his lips, treating it to the same loving, delicious attention. His hands were as busy as his mouth, and she felt her skirt loosen, her petticoat slip over her hips, and the ribbon lacing her drawers drawn free.

When he moved his hand between them, pushing her drawers over her hips, and then sliding his fingers down, skimming them across the flesh at the apex of her thighs, Jess bucked against him and her legs turned to jelly. He eased her back, lifting her onto his bed, staring down at her with awe and adoration as he reached for the buttons of his trousers. She saw his hand shaking and reached up to help him.

Jess watched, enthralled as Lucius slipped out of the last bit of clothing between them, pushing his trousers and drawers over the chiseled edge of his hips, lower, revealing his impossibly hard length. She lifted a hand to touch him there, but he eased her back instead, lifting his body over hers and easing down gently until their bodies melded—chest to chest, thigh against thigh, his stiffness teasing at her damp cleft.

She lifted her mouth to his, eager to be joined in every way. She took the lead, grasping his head in her hands, slipping her tongue into his mouth, and he groaned, grinding his hips against hers. His cock pressed deeper, sliding in the moist heat between her thighs, and she lifted her hips, needing him closer, aching for a release she could not name.

Lucius turned his head, pressing kisses to her neck, then whispering in her ear. "I need to taste you."

She thought he meant to kiss her again. Yes, she needed to taste him too, but she emitted a little whine of protest when he pulled back instead, easing his body off hers and sliding down. She opened her mouth to ask him to kiss her, beg him if necessary. But then he did, pressing his mouth to the cleft between her breasts, trailing his lips down her belly, dipping his hot tongue into the hollow of her belly button, and then moving lower. When he pushed her thighs apart, gently, stroking his fingers over the sensitive inner skin of her legs, Jess bit her lip to stifle a cry—of pleasure, embarrassment, need. Then his tongue, the hard pointed tip of it, eased her open, tasting her, savoring her, lapping at her body as if she was the sweetest delicacy he'd ever known.

Jess couldn't hold back her cries. They rang out of her as she clutched at his shoulders, sank her fingers into his hair, and bucked against his mouth. Sensation seized her, drawing her tight, to the sharpest point of pleasure. Just when she thought it too much, thrashing her head side to side against the bed, pushing then pulling at Lucius's head, a wave of sensation broke over her. She opened her mouth to cry out but heard nothing but the violent pulse of her heartbeat in her ears.

When she opened her eyes, Lucius was there above her, smiling at her as if she was precious and loved. Then he eased against her again. *Yes.* She'd never known pleasure like the heat and slide of his body as he molded it to hers.

She lifted her knees, urging him closer, and felt the length of him lunging inside. *Yes.* She needed him closer, deeper. He tensed, controlling his movements despite her attempts to draw him near.

"Easy, love."

He kissed her then, and she reached down to stroke his back, his arms, his hair, every part of him she could touch and caress. He stroked her with his tongue and matched the motion with his hips. Jess gasped as he thrust in to the hilt, then deeper, faster, drawing her into pleasure so complete that she forgot the flash of pain.

As he drove into her, kissing her mouth, her neck, the skin above her breasts, he whispered to her between kisses. "I love you. I need you. Stay with me."

"Yes." It was all she could manage, that and the way she bucked against him, tugging him closer, needing him as she'd never needed anyone before.

When she drew near the unbearable point of pleasure again, he came too, flooding her with sensation as he groaned into her mouth.

Afterward, lying sated and tangled together in the firelight, they exchanged more kisses and precious promises.

"I love you."

"I need you."

"Nothing will part us now."

Chapter Twenty-Seven

JESS WOKE TO find herself in a warm, masculine cocoon, Lucius's arms wrapped around her, his body spooning hers. The fire in the grate had faded to embers and she could see dark skies through a slit in the drapes. It wasn't easy to pull away from him, to exchange the delicious heat of his body for the chill in the room, but she could only imagine the apoplexy they'd cause his elderly valet if the man found her in His Lordship's bed come morning.

She kissed him gently on the curve of his shoulder, unable to leave without capturing the taste of him on her tongue. Then, after lifting the counterpane to cover him, she dressed and returned to her room, holding her breath as she tiptoed down the hall, afraid to make a sound that might wake Lady Stamford or, heaven forbid, Kitty Adderly.

Her bedsheets were cold and the bed itself far too large and lonely, but Jess closed her eyes and replayed the happiest moments of her life.

Then Tilly nudged her shoulder.

"Good morning, miss. Don't want to be late for breakfast. Miss Adderly will be taking her leave soon, and I hear Mr. Wellesley will return to Granby, his family's home nearby. Seems the house party is over almost before it's begun."

Jess washed and dressed quickly, grateful for Tilly's assistance. Beyond the intense desire to see Lucius, she couldn't miss the opportunity to speak to Kitty before her departure. Though theirs was a strange and short-lived acquaintance, she suspected a marquess's daughter might be just the person to advise her on the most challenging undertaking of her life.

However much she loved Lucius, nothing in her life prepared her for the role of viscountess. Lady Stamford and Marleston's staff had patiently instructed her in rules of etiquette, but Jess knew there was more, a world of expectations and traditions she'd only read about in books. Her teachers had been Dickens and Austen, who were as likely to satirize the aristocracy as paint them with accuracy.

When she entered the breakfast room, hoping to find Kitty, her breath wisped between her lips and she beamed like a child on Christmas morning. Lucius sat at the head of the table but stood the moment he glimpsed her. He smiled too and then strode forward, embracing her and lowering his mouth to hers. Before Jess could protest that a maid or footman might see them, Lucius pulled away and led her to the chair next to his.

"I woke to a very empty bed," he whispered.

She leaned toward him, only just resisting the urge to touch him. "As every bachelor should."

"We must rectify that as soon as possible. Don't you agree?"

He handed her a plate of eggs and toast, and she noticed her teacup was already full, but it was dark. She'd never seen tea so dark.

"It's coffee. Aunt Augusta mentioned your fondness for it, and Cook apparently likes it too. She was happy to share."

Jess lifted the cup to her lips and sipped the warm brew, wondering how quickly they could reasonably marry.

"Thank you. And, yes, I agree." Now that she'd decided, she didn't wish to wait another moment to be his wife.

"I checked on my father this morning. He's settling into his new room remarkably well. I'll inform him about my detailed plans for the estate after breakfast."

When a footman entered the room, Jess pulled her hand from Lucius's reluctantly.

"My goodness, aren't you two up early?"

Lady Stamford swept in as she spoke and then stopped, tipping forward as if she might fall over. "Oh. Oh, I see."

Jess wasn't certain at all what Lucius's aunt saw, but it seemed to please her. She broke into a beaming smile and her gaze turned glassy. "I am so happy for you, my dears."

"Happy about what?" Mr. Wellesley strode into the room, glanced at each of their faces, and then stopped short, much as Lady Stamford had. "Oh, I see."

His grin was more mischievous than usual, and that was a good deal of mischief. What could everyone see? Happiness? Joy? Perhaps lovemaking tinted one's skin or put a sparkle in one's eyes. It made sense to Jess that an experience so extraordinary should leave its mark.

"I hear you're returning to your family home, Mr. Wellesley," Jess asked as he seated himself directly across from her and began heaping marmalade on a slice of toast.

"Yes, without May to flirt with and Annabel to tease, what's the point in staying?" Chomping down on a bite of toast, and then closing his eyes a moment as if to savor the marmalade, Wellesley reached down to his napkin and leaned toward Jess with a glint in his eye. "I'd stay for you, of course, Jess. But I trust you've already been taken."

Lady Stamford choked, coughing as little droplets of tea dribbled onto her plate. Jess rushed to pat her back and offer a fresh napkin as Lucius glared at Wellesley.

"How soon are you leaving?"

Wellesley rose and moved to Lady Stamford's side, kneeling by her chair and looking up at her with all the remorse of a naughty puppy. "Forgive me, Augusta. You know my tongue is forever getting me in trouble."

Lucius's voice cut off the absolution Lady Stamford appeared on the verge of offering. "Perhaps you should keep it in your mouth more often."

Lifting his hand to his lips, Wellesley pinched his fingers together and twisted, as if turning a key in a lock.

When Lady Stamford seemed recovered, Jess returned

to her chair and relished a few more sips of coffee. Their small group continued in companionable silence. Wellesley's silence was particularly impressive, and Jess found herself almost missing his irreverent quips. He brought out a teasing, sarcastic side of Lucius that she quite liked.

It was odd not to hear Lady Stamford's voice too, though she did glance warily at Wellesley now and then between bites of egg and toast. And once she looked on the verge of commenting when she caught Jess and Lucius gazing at each other too long.

If nothing else, Jess expected Kitty to sweep in and spark conversation.

"Miss Adderly hasn't left yet, has she?"

"You're keen to speak with her?" The concern in Lucius's tone surprised her. Surely he couldn't doubt her desire to stay after what they'd shared.

"Yes, I would like to speak with her before she goes."

Lady Stamford directed a footman to refill the teapot as she replied, "She asked for a tray in her room, my dear. She wished to oversee the preparations for her—"

A sound, a hammering shudder as loud as cracks of thunder, rumbled through the room.

"What the devil was that?" Wellesley asked around a mouthful of crumpet.

Lucius stood, not bothering to straighten his waistcoat, and started toward the breakfast room door. A red-faced footman rushed in at the same moment, nearly colliding with his much taller master.

"Forgive me, my lord. Mrs. Penry's asked me to come and say we have an unexpected guest." The lad laid a hand on his chest and sucked in gulps of air, trying to catch his breath.

Lucius waited with admirable patience, and the young man finally rewarded him with the answer they all sought. "It's Mr. Sedgwick, my lord, and Miss Sedgwick too. Mrs. Penry sent them to the drawing room."

Jess twisted her hands together under the table. When she looked up, Lucius was watching her. As he had in the dining room two nights before, he made a slight, tiny movement with his mouth, not quite a grin but a softness meant for her alone. Then he dipped his head in a subtle nod, reassuring her, comforting her, signaling that all would be well.

He turned to his aunt and Wellesley. "If you'll excuse me."

When he was gone, silence fell in the room and everyone's appetites seemed to wane. Jess couldn't rouse herself to take another bite, and Lady Stamford kept turning her gaze in Jess's direction rather than attending to her breakfast plate.

Wellesley broke the silence. "Do you know what it's about, Augusta?"

"No, my boy, but I should go and find out." She stood, prompting Jess and Wellesley to do the same. She embraced Jess and then pulled back to pat her cheek. "Wish Lady Katherine a safe journey for me. And try not to fret."

JESS MADE HER way to Kitty's room and tapped lightly on the door. She expected a maid to answer, but Kitty pulled the door open and gasped.

"Heavens, what's happened? You're positively peaky," Kitty said. She reached for Jess's hand and pulled her inside. "With all the guests gone, I didn't think I'd miss any excitement at breakfast."

Jess slumped down on a chair, but popped up again when Kitty squealed. Reaching behind her, Jess slid a fur-lined velvet traveling cloak out from under her backside.

"I'll just lie that over here." Kitty placed the garment with care, seated herself opposite Jess, and rested her hands in her lap. "Tell me everything."

"May has come back with her father."

"Mmm." Kitty pursed her mouth and reached up to tap her lower lip. "I thought she might. Well, I thought he might insist on it."

"Why?"

"I suspect he's offended, or simply doesn't wish to see his plans overturned." She leaned back and settled her skirt around her. "From what I hear, he is quite like my father. Charming, affable, and utterly ruthless in his business affairs."

"Is the marriage of his daughter a business affair?" Jess's father had been obsessed with money—losing it, winning it—but he'd never been cold. He never would have bartered her. Then again, he'd never expected her to marry at all.

"Even May said he saw it in that light."

Jess breathed in deep, longing for strength, longing as she hadn't since childhood for her mother's embrace.

"Do you remember when we met at your home in Belgrave Square? I asked for us to speak plainly with one another. Will you speak plainly with me now?"

Kitty tipped her head. "Yes, of course."

"You're a marquess's daughter. No doubt you'll marry an aristocrat yourself."

Kitty surprised Jess by grinning. "I wouldn't count on that, but go on."

The next words stuck in Jess's throat, like a miserably tough piece of mutton at the Frog and Whistle that she'd happily spit out if no one was looking.

"Can you imagine me as a viscountess? Would you accept me among your noble friends?"

Kitty's bow-shaped mouth dropped open, and then she snapped it shut, nibbling at her lips, but made no reply.

Jess took it as a sign of the worst. "It's impossible, then?"

"Oh, Jessamin, a viscountess is not imagined or conceived. She simply is. If he marries you and makes you a viscountess, then that's what you shall be. I would accept you, of course."

Kitty grinned again, but there was no pleasure in it. "Most will accept you. Outwardly. It's how they snipe about you behind your back that will keep you awake at night."

Reaching out, Kitty flicked at her skirts, as if she'd just been showered with invisible bits of debris.

"But to be honest, to speak plainly, as you say, they would snipe about you even if you were born with blue blood in your veins. That's the nature of an insular, backbiting group." She titled her chin high. "You simply learn to rise above it, and give them something else to talk about. You're clever and passionate about your politics. That's enough to win you a few allies."

Jess took comfort in Kitty's words, and more so because it was clear Kitty wouldn't simply tell her what she wished to hear. As Kitty spoke, Jess allowed herself to imagine life as Lucius's viscountess, managing the staff at Hartwell and interacting with well-bred ladies like Kitty, who'd no doubt wish to speak of fashion, of which Jess knew little, and their ladylike accomplishments, none of which Jess possessed.

Surely stamping a title on her stationery or having her name inscribed in a great book next to Lucius's would not make her a success in his world. And what of her world? Would she be able to continue her work with the Women's Union? Speeches could be written anywhere, but she longed for the camaraderie of the meetings and her discussions with Alice.

Would Lucius ask her to give up her interests to be his wife? No, she couldn't imagine it. Yet she could imagine, with absolute clarity, her own faux pas at social gatherings—saying the wrong thing, reaching for the wrong bit of silverware.

"I would never wish to bring him shame."

"We all make mistakes, Jessamin. Just look at my little scheme at the gallery. I thought I'd humble him and have him on his knees. Instead, you have him enthralled."

She laughed as she said it, her pitch rising in a soprano titter, and then stood.

"I must go if I'm to catch my train, but let me do this."

Turning to a satchel on the bed, she reached inside and pulled out two bits of paper.

"Take this and don't say no."

Jess reached for the offerings.

"It's a ten-pound note and my calling card."

Jess lifted the money out to her. "Kitty . . ."

Kitty put her hands up, palms out. "No, I insist. It's enough to get you back to London if you wish. You can call on me or leave a note with my card and I'll come to you. My offer to help you find a position still stands."

Jess followed Kitty into the main entry hall and waited as a footman and maid bustled about them, assisting Kitty into her traveling coat, hat, and gloves, and tucking her bags into the Dunthorpe carriage for the journey to Newbury station. After a final round of well wishes and watching the carriage roll out of sight, Jess stepped back into the hall, fighting the urge to stop and listen at the drawing room door.

Chapter Twenty-Eight

IF THE MAN hadn't come to Hartwell to spoil each and every one of Lucius's plans and force his daughter into a marriage she didn't desire, Lucius might have found Seymour Sedgwick amusing. He smiled a great deal, a broad toothy expression that he managed to infuse with merriment and charm. And though he was a man of small stature, he seemed to command the room. Like his daughter, he exuded a kind of palpable energy and spoke each word as if he equated communicating with convincing. He would have made a fine actor on any stage.

"May is my only child, you see." He turned toward May, mouth quivering, gaze earnest, but May didn't return one of her sunny expressions. Her full mouth remained immobile, and Lucius noted faint shadows under her eyes and a few tears still tangled in her lashes. She looked young, and it struck him that the girl was a dozen years his junior and half that number of years younger than Jessamin. Her confidence and charm seemed excessive for one so young, and yet none of it seemed to have any effect on the man she'd clearly inherited it from.

"Her happiness, the prospect of seeing her settled. Well, nothing is more important to me than that, Lord Grimsby."

And nothing is more important to me than getting you out of my home.

Though Sedgwick had indicated a chair for Lucius to take a seat, seemingly oblivious to the outrageous rudeness of the gesture, Lucius continued to stand, and at a distance from Sedgwick. There was such intensity around the man, it seemed as if he might burst into flames if he moved too quickly or scraped against anything, and Lucius wanted him away from Jessamin and the rest of his family.

"I hope Miss Sedgwick knows that I wish her all the happiness she can bear."

Lucius met May's gaze when he repeated her words to him. Her quick nod seemed indication that she'd meant what she'd said and this unexpected visit came at her father's instigation, not hers.

"I'm glad to hear it, Grimsby. Then perhaps we should discuss dates, May's dowry, and your future as man and wife."

Perhaps it was one of the strategies the man employed in business—the impervious wall, unchanging and immovable, regardless of his adversary's responses or denials. And it was clear they were adversaries, no matter how wide Sedgwick's grins.

"Mr. Sedgwick, May and I cannot marry. And I am only content to say that in her presence because she assured me—"

"She was mistaken."

May turned away to look out the window as her father continued.

"Whatever she said to you before she departed for London, put it out of your mind, Grimsby. She now tells me she was overwrought and has had quite a change of heart. Women are such changeable creatures, are they not?"

It was the first moment Sedgwick let the mask slip, and as his glamorous outer shine faltered, Lucius glimpsed fury, resentment, bitterness, every ugly impulse that could twist a man. He'd seen it in his father's eyes.

Sedgwick's smile suddenly seemed reptilian.

And he continued smiling, impervious even to interruptions, after a maid knocked at the drawing room door and requested Lucius's presence in the hall. He excused himself, relieved to close the door behind him.

"He wants you to marry her." Augusta stood just beyond the threshold, looking as distraught as when they'd found his injured father after the storm.

Lucius kept his voice low. "Yes. Are you coming in? Perhaps he'll listen to you." He wasn't sure anything he'd say would make its way past Sedgwick's impenetrable wall of confidence, and with each breath he wasted, the temptation rose to simply throw the man out bodily.

"How's Jessamin?" She'd looked heartbreakingly uncertain when he'd left her in the breakfast room, and he wanted to see her, touch her, reassure her. If not for Sedgwick storming in, he might have already spoken to his father and been planning how to ask her to marry him.

"I asked her to see Kitty off."

His stomach writhed at the mention of Kitty Adderly. She'd offered Jessamin a means to leave Hartwell and rebuild her life in London. He wouldn't keep her from that choice, but he could no longer imagine his future without her.

When Lucius turned to enter the study, expecting Augusta to follow, she reached for his arm.

"I knew Seymour Sedgwick many years ago."

His aunt had as sharp a mind as anyone he'd ever known, yet he couldn't help frowning at her admission. It was a story she'd mentioned to him on more than one occasion.

"I refused him, Lucius. He asked me to marry him and I refused him."

"Pardon?"

She rushed through her explanation in a panicked whisper.

"My father wanted to marry me to an ogre, a truly dreadful man. Sedgwick was the most audacious of my suitors, forever asking me to elope." She drew in a deep breath and raced through the rest. "I agreed, but even as I said the words I knew I couldn't go through with it. The shame, the scandal, and I know now I was already half in love with my Edward."

Augusta glanced nervously at the study door as if Sedgwick might materialize from the other side, but

Lucius stood stunned a moment, letting the whole of it sink in.

"I fear it may color his treatment of you and his determination that May not be refused."

"She refused me." Surely May would affirm her conviction that she did not wish for a blatantly practical marriage.

"He's a very difficult man to convince."

Lucius had sensed it after a few seconds in the man's presence, but it didn't signify. He only intended to marry one woman, and it wouldn't be May Sedgwick.

UNABLE TO KEEP still and listen to the ticking of the mantel clock a second longer, Jess stood a few paces outside the drawing room door arguing with herself about whether to stick her nose in or head back to her rooms.

As she approached, loud voices emanated from the room.

She and Lucius belonged to each other now. Could she really let him face this trouble alone?

Then she heard him shout, his low bass rattling the wall. "What if I do marry your daughter? What then?"

A wave of nausea swept through her and she gripped her stomach, closed her eyes, and willed it away. Drawing near the door, Jess lowered her head to listen.

"Am I to forget your threats?" Lucius made a tsking sound of disgust. "A breach of promise suit? Try to make that ship sail when no promise was ever made."

"That ship sailed, Lord Grimsby, when my daughter

left New York harbor." Mr. Sedgwick's voice cut like a knife, crisp and sharp, his American accent much more careful and precise than his daughter's.

"Father . . ." In one word, Jess heard May's distress and fury. Her father spoke over her, and Jess imagined his dismissal incensed her more.

Swallowing hard, Jess reached out to knock on the door's top panel. Nervousness made her legs shudder, but she couldn't spend her life with Lucius listening at keyholes, forever on the wrong side of the wall.

After a moment, the door swung open mere inches, and Lady Stamford stood in the gap, her face drawn, eyes stricken and distressed.

"I'm not sure you should be here now, my dear."

May's voice carried from inside the room. "Let her come. Father, this is Lady Stamford's companion."

When Jess stepped into the room, she swiveled her head for a look at Lucius. He sat at his desk, arms clasped across his chest, and his mouth as firm and tight as the first time she'd seen him in the Mayfair gallery. He looked more ill-tempered than he had that night, but his gaze, a little release of tension in his shoulders, indicated her presence was not wholly unwelcome.

Mr. Sedgwick, a dark-haired and immaculately dressed man, sat straight and tall in the chair in front of Lucius's desk. He barely grazed her with his gaze before turning his attention back to Lucius.

Jess approached May, who sat on a settee along the back wall, and May stunned her by lifting a hand to touch her. She clasped Jess's hand and tugged her to take the space on the settee next to her.

Once Jess was seated, May leaned in to whisper. "He's truly not as fearsome as he seems. He thinks he's defending me, and doing so always gets his back up."

"Marry her, Grimsby, and you can enjoy life within the walls of your lavishly restored home. And please your father, and keep your promise to my daughter."

"There was never any promise." May's voice sounded small, childlike, almost plaintive, but her father spoke again as if she hadn't said a word.

"In addition to May's substantial dowry, I would like to offer that sum again as a wedding gift. Come, Grimsby, you must prefer that to breaking up your family's estate."

"My nephew's heart is engaged elsewhere." Lady Stamford spoke with the same tremor Jess heard in May's voice. Jess didn't look her way, but her declaration made Jess hold her breath.

Then a bark, a sound Jess thought might be one of the dogs, rattled through the room. When it split the air again, she realized it was Mr. Sedgwick's strangled laughter.

"You dare speak to me about love, Augusta? I don't think I'll hear you on that count. You, a woman who never kept her own promises."

"Sedgwick . . ." Lucius's ominous tone, a more serious version of the mocking one he often used with Mr. Wellesley, set off goose bumps on Jess's skin.

"Yes, yes. My daughter mentioned a woman who kissed you in a far too public display."

May didn't react to her father's pronouncement, and it struck Jess that May might still be unaware she was the woman who kissed Lucius in Mayfair. What a muck-up it had all become. One kiss, one scandalous, wonderful kiss had turned all their lives upside down.

"It would be a shame to see that woman named in the lawsuit. You'd both be outcasts."

He thought her a woman concerned with her place in society, one who worried about her reputation and status. As a woman who'd presume to marry a viscount should be.

But Jess wasn't that sort of woman. She didn't move in his society. Hers was much more circumspect. Who would cast her out? Ousted from the Women's Union would be a blow, but she doubted the ladies of the group would be so quick to cast judgment.

"That sounds delightful. We can live out our lives in the countryside in peace and quiet."

Lucius glanced at her as he said it, one touch of his gaze on her face. Jess had never heard such wistfulness from him, and it made her ache to hold him.

"You are an astoundingly selfish man. Scorn my daughter, ruin another woman, and then turn exile with her here in your moldering heap." That sound shot from the man again—a short burst of barking laughter.

"Exile doesn't frighten me. I've been exiled before."

"Yes, a sojourn in Scotland. Yet all the Scots I know are quite practical men. Carnegie is as solid as his steel. Didn't you learn any of that Scottish practicality, Grimsby?"

Jess clenched her free hand into a fist against her thigh. She'd never been tempted to strike another human being in her life, but she suspected Mr. Sedgwick had inspired the urge in many.

"If you care nothing for your reputation or this woman's, what would become of any children you might have?"

Children. Jess rarely imagined that blessing for herself. In her future as bookshop owner, motherhood seemed an unlikely fate. But she'd read enough books to know that she and Lucius might have started on that path last night.

Would their children carry the stigma of scandal? Rejection, solitude, loneliness—she couldn't relegate a child to that. She couldn't consign Lucius to it either. Would he become an outcast for choosing her as his wife?

If she loved him—and she did, with all her heart—she had to spare him that.

Standing and pulling away from May, she stepped close to Lady Stamford.

"Perhaps you're right," she whispered, "I shouldn't be here."

"Of course, my dear." Lady Stamford cupped her cheek, a comforting gesture her mother had used to soothe her a thousand times. "Go up and have some tea. We'll sort this out."

Mr. Sedgwick continued talking, May was still beseeching, and for all she knew Lucius remained at his desk, inert and angry. Jess couldn't look at him. If she did, she wouldn't have the strength to go. So she kept her eyes on the door, made her way through, and forced herself to take the stairs back to her room. She was tempted to look back at path she'd taken. Surely all the blood was being drained from her body. She grew colder, emptier, with every step.

Chapter Twenty-Nine

"WHAT THE BLAZES are you doing?"

Jess reached back into the depths of the tall oak wardrobe in her guest room and had just skimmed her fingers across the beveled face of her father's pocket watch when she heard Robert Wellesley's voice. Grasping the cold metal disk, she pulled the watch out and emerged to look at him.

"I thought I'd lost my father's watch."

She had none of her own clothes and didn't mind leaving without any other possessions. Only the watch seemed essential. After cupping it in her palm a moment, she dropped it into the small travel bag Lady Stamford had given her.

"You're packing. Where on earth are you going?"

"Back to London." Jess carefully folded papers containing Alice's upcoming speech and placed them inside one of the books she'd brought with her from the shop before adding it to the bag.

"Why? What are you thinking?"

Miserable thoughts with no easy resolution, no happy ending whichever way she turned the matter.

"That I'm not meant for this, nor prepared for it. I'm not what Lucius needs." Jess sank onto the edge of the bed, pointing at herself. She'd read in one of Lady Stamford's etiquette books that it was terribly indelicate for a lady to do so. "How can I be a viscountess? I'm a bookshop owner's daughter and a writer of speeches and political articles. I'm a suffragette and . . ." That was the end of the list. What were her other accomplishments? "Nothing more than that."

"You're the woman he loves."

Jess narrowed her eyes at Wellesley. His confidence filled the room. No wonder Lucius found him such an irritant.

"Sometimes duty is the right choice, Mr. Wellesley. I chose it most of my life, and I did it well. Duty seems the right path."

Wellesley leaned a hip against the door frame, crossed his arms, and smirked at her as if all the words that had just taken so much effort to speak were the most absurd he'd ever heard in his life.

Making him understand felt as necessary as convincing herself. She'd need that conviction to force her legs to carry her out the door.

"Lucius was willing to do his duty before he met me. Maybe I've set him on the wrong path. I shouldn't have kissed him. I shouldn't have taken that money. None of this should have happened." Placing her hands on her hips, she nearly screamed in frustration. Her mind had gone sluggish and slow. "We're like two planetary bodies that spun into a strange orbit and should never have crossed paths."

Wellesley seemed truly confounded by her analogy, and he mimicked her stance, lifting his hands to hips.

"I don't know a damn thing about astronomy. I admit it. But I do know Lucius, and he's been changed by you. For the better. The man loves you, completely. Being a viscountess, it's . . . Trust me, Jess, you can carry it off. It mustn't be difficult. You should meet some of my aunts and uncles with titles. Fools, bloody fools."

"Are you saying I'm a fool?"

"You're a fool if you get on a train and leave him." Wellesley rushed forward and grasped her upper arms, his gaze earnest and intense. But the fire in his expression didn't warm her. She wasn't certain she'd ever truly feel warm again.

"I told you that you'd need mettle, and that you would need to fight. I never thought this would be easy."

His admonition didn't bolster Jess as he'd intended. It cut her, drained her, and she sensed herself falling, all the air escaping, like an aeronaut's balloon crashing to the ground. Wellesley held her up and led her to a chair, but she refused to sit. This was no time to faint and fade. This was when she most needed strength, if only to admit her weakness.

"I don't think I have it in me." He shook his head, unable to hide his disappointment. "I'm afraid I'm not the heroine you think I am, Mr. Wellesley."

He lifted his head, gaze fixing on hers, and broke into one his charming grins.

"Oh, you are, Miss Wright. You have *heroine* written all over you. I've seen it from the day I met you."

He was dogged, indefatigable, and Jess couldn't detect a trace of sarcasm in his tone. But she couldn't believe his claim either.

"I'm not the woman you imagine me to be."

His shoulders sagged and for a moment he looked as deflated as Jess felt.

"No, Miss Wright, you must take your own measure. Choose who you wish to be. If you choose to be Lucius's wife, and for his sake, I hope you do, you'll be glorious at it." He held his hands out, measuring an invisible object in one and then the other. Perhaps he was teasing her for the astronomical analogy. "Because you love him and he loves you."

From Mr. Wellesley, it all sounded terribly simple. The man seemed to see the world as velvet lined, gilded, every trouble easily resolved. But Jess knew difficulties came by the dozen and not all could be tucked away and decorated with a pretty bow.

"And it will cost him his father's love, his father's approval. It will cost him the destruction of his home."

Wellesley had the temerity to chuckle. "This old pile won't be fall to pieces. Lucius has a plan. He's going to sell off part of the estate and—"

"No! He shouldn't have to do that."

"Of course he should." Wellesley raised his voice to match her tone and Jess stepped away from him.

After a gusty sigh and a few moments ruffling his bronze hair, Wellesley approached her again.

"We are careening toward the twentieth century. Times have changed, Jess, and we must change with them. Wheat and barley will no longer support a house like this. Lucius wishes to invest in manufacturing and it seems a brilliant idea, though I admit to as much knowledge about investing as astronomy."

He shrugged and sighed again. "You should trust Lucius. I've known the man all my life. He can be a bit of an overbearing bastard at times, but he's a good man. And he's never wanted anything as much as he wants you. Anyone can see that."

Jess chewed on her thumbnail—another unladylike habit that even her mother had tried to break her of—and shook her head in denial.

"Sometimes what we want isn't what we need."

Wellesley spun on his heel, turning his back on her, and Jess thought he might walk away and leave. Instead, he whirled around with a desolate expression on his face, as if she'd smashed his illusions as effectively as she'd shattered her own.

"If you must go back to London, Miss Wright, if you miss your city and friends, your Women's Union—that I can understand. But don't leave him. You should come back for him. Fight for him."

Her father had implored her with the same look she saw now in Mr. Wellesley's eyes. He'd besieged her with assurances, promises of future glory, and guarantees that the tide was just a hairsbreadth from turning. *Our luck will change.* But it never did.

"Lucius is a fighter. Look, I still have a scar here." Wellesley lifted his head to indicate a faded white inch-long scar at the under edge of his chin. "He'll fight for you. Problem is, he's never known what he wanted until now. He's been told what he must do, should do, and now he knows what's possible. That he must make his own choices."

Choice. Perhaps she and Lucius had too few of them in their lives, but that only meant it was essential they make the right ones now.

"I want him to be happy, but I'm not sure I can make him happy."

Wellesley reached for her hand and Jess reluctantly allowed him to take it.

"You already have."

She pulled away from his grasp. "I don't mean for today or tomorrow. I am looking ahead to the rest of his life." Looking ahead to children born under the cloud of scandal, to a day when Lucius might gaze at her not with love but with resentment.

Like a clear bit of sky breaking through and sweeping away the clouds on the horizon, Wellesley lowered his head with a frown but looked up at her with a beaming smile.

"I can see your mind is set on going, but allow me to hope you'll come back. Are you going to leave a note for him? Or for Lady Stamford?"

Jess shook her head. She'd tried, but her own hand

betrayed her, shaking furiously every time she put pen to paper until she'd scratched out and splattered, finally crushing two sheets of precious paper and tossing them in the bin. She'd always trusted words, loved them, memorized them, but they'd failed her today. None seemed sufficient to describe her reasons and rationales. Those were all about emotion, feeling, and all the feeling words seemed pale, too feeble to explain her agonizing choice.

"Rob?" It seemed so long ago, that first night they'd met at Hartwell, when he'd asked her to call him by the diminutive. "Would you tell him that I love him?"

Tears slid down her cheeks as her voice broke, and a slashing pain ripped her, not just an ache in her heart but an agony so complete it seemed to wind its way into her arms, her legs, into every fiber of her form.

As she lifted her bag and turned to leave the room, Wellesley moved as if to stop her.

"I must go now." Now or she'd falter, now or she'd forget all her reasons and rush downstairs to find Lucius, and let duty and dowries be damned.

"What if the carriage hasn't returned from delivering Miss Adderly to the station?"

Jess moved around him. "Then I'll walk."

"It's nearly six miles."

Jess took one step over the threshold. "That's nothing to me. I'm a Londoner, Mr. Wellesley. I'll walk."

And she did, mechanically forcing her feet into motion. Behind her, she heard Wellesley mutter.

"That's just the sort of thing a heroine would say."

Chapter Thirty

"ARE YOU GOING to tell me the rest?"

Jess sat with Alice McGregor at the back of Bourne Street Hall. Alice was due to give Jess's speech at the top of the hour, and they'd gone over notes and main points so many times the words had begun to blur.

It was her fourth day back in London and much had started to blur. Depleted of tears and exhausted, Jess had lost the ability to concentrate or take pleasure in anything, not in food, not even in books.

She'd been living off the charity of Kitty Adderly and had yet to find employment. Lady Clayborne, Kitty's mother, tolerated her temporary presence in their household but had refused the suggestion she stay on as young Violet's governess. Not well-bred enough to teach a marquess's daughter, apparently.

"I'm not sure there's enough time for the whole story."

Jess's voice sounded hollow to her ears, and that was fitting. It matched the hollowness in her heart.

"Indulge me. Distract me. I don't admit this often, but I have a wee tickle in my belly before each speech." Alice turned in her chair, nudging Jess with her arm. "Besides, we still need to fill more of these chairs before I begin."

The group of women was sizable and growing, and Alice expressed hope more would filter in as the morning progressed. As it wasn't a regular Women's Union meeting, they'd secured a more spacious venue and invited guest speakers to draw a larger attendance. Kitty had accompanied Jess to the event but disappeared among the crowd the minute they'd walked through the door.

"As I said, the role of lady's companion didn't suit me."

"Yes, you did say that, several times. But why? I know the decision to work for Lady Stamford was a difficult one, but you said she seemed kind and extremely generous."

Alice turned in her seat to look at Jess directly. "Were the duties very challenging, then?"

Alice's teasing undertone was impossible to miss, but Jess couldn't blame her. Thinking back to her time at Marleston, Jess recalled her first days filled with dress fittings and selecting sumptuous fabrics for gowns, and later days writing letters, walking the dogs, and teaching Tilly to read. None of it had been onerous or difficult. She'd slept in a luxurious room and had it all to herself. Aside from the few hours a day Lady Stamford required her assistance, she'd been given time to read and write, more hours of leisure than she'd ever known in her life. And then they'd gone to Hartwell.

"No, it wasn't the duties. Though you can't imagine the rules and things you must remember. Points of etiquette most people never dream of worrying about."

"Oh, do tell?" The mockery was thick now, but Alice's dimpled grin lessened the sting.

There were so many rules of propriety. How could she pick just one to illustrate their collective ridiculousness?

"How about this? On the table at formal dinners, they have multiple glasses at each place setting. There are multiple spoons at each setting too, a separate spoon for soup, another for fruit, and even a tiny one just for salt. Multiple forks and knives too. There's even a fork that's just for fish!"

Alice stared at Jess as if waiting for more, distinctly unawed.

"What if you didn't have fish?"

"Then they wouldn't put that fork on the table."

"But then you wouldn't have to remember it."

Jess huffed at Alice's refusal to agree with the silliness of multiple forks for a single meal. "But you still needed to know what to do with it."

"I see. That does sound terribly taxing." Alice said the words in her best aristocratic accent and it was the worst Jess ever heard.

"Oh, all right. The work itself wasn't difficult. I suppose I could have gotten used to it eventually, but I don't fit in that world. Lady Stamford is a countess, her brother is an earl, and her nephew's a viscount. And look at me."

Jess lifted her skirt, a simple black bombazine handed down from the Adderlys' lady's maid. There was a slight tear in the skirt Jess had only just noticed and had yet to repair.

"I see that you're showing me your skirt that needs mending, but I suspect you're attempting to make a different point."

"I'm making the point that I don't belong in that kind of society."

"Because you need to mend your skirt?"

"Because I wasn't born with blue blood."

"But there've been other people who entered into the aristocracy and weren't born to it. The man that you . . . you know . . . at the gallery. You said he was planning to marry an American."

"Whose grandmother was a viscountess. She knew the rules."

"But you just told me the rules can be learned. I now know fish forks are an essential part of a formal dinner."

Oh, she was infuriatingly literal. Jess knew it was a strategy she often employed to draw others around to her point of view.

"Learning it and being it are two different things." Jess uttered the words emphatically, but they sounded silly echoing in her mind.

"Well, of course you can't go back and be born under a different sun, but you can marry into it. You could be a viscountess."

She really needed to introduce Alice to Mr. Wellesley. They seemed possessed of the same vein of unshakable confidence in her ability to step into a role she was woefully ill-prepared for. As if being a suffragette and a viscountess were compatible.

"When would I come to meetings in London or write speeches?"

Alice looked at Jess as if she and her question were well and truly daft.

"When do you do it now? I suspect you'd find the time or you make it. Don't most lords and ladies have homes in London and spend part of the year in the city?"

Jess hadn't given it much consideration. Lucius never mentioned a home in London, and yet it wasn't as if they'd taken the time to converse about the list of Dunthorpe family holdings.

"Lady Stamford has a London home. That's where you went before departing with her to Wiltshire. Does her nephew have a place here too?"

"I don't know. Why do you ask?"

Jess had never truly argued with Alice. They debated, and she enjoyed the back-and-forth tussles of intellectual discussion. But this was different. She felt pursued, routed, as if Alice was strategically knocking down each of her defenses.

"Because I suspect the point you're making with your skirt and excuses is that you can't marry him."

Alice turned away and sat quietly for a moment, as if she knew her mention of marriage would set Jess on edge and send her pulse galloping.

Then she turned back. "Did he ask you, Jess?"

She nodded, but that didn't seem sufficient. Alice

loved words as much as she did, and she'd always told her the truth.

"Yes. Not formally, but he said the words."

"If he said the words, then he asked you."

Alice was merciless, and Jess felt exposed, as if it wasn't just her skirt that was torn, but the flimsy bulwark of excuses she'd erected around her heart.

"Yes, he asked me."

Alice's tone was less strident, but no less persistent. "And did you answer?"

There had never been a simple *yes* but she'd told him, as he'd assured her that he was all she needed. She'd laid her heart open and let him in, shared her body with him, and wanted nothing more than to spend the rest of her days by his side.

"I gave him an answer. He knew I wished to marry him."

"And you left? He asked you to marry him and you left?" Alice reared back and stared at Jess. "To come here to Bourne Hall and listen to a speech you wrote? You already know everything I'm going to say!"

Jess stood, too full of emotion to contain it.

"It's not that simple. There were very practical reasons for him to marry someone else. He needed money. He needed a rich wife, one who understands the role of viscountess. He could find that in any number of women, and none of it in me."

Alice listened to her shout, ignoring the women who turned to listen nearby.

Jess slumped back down in her seat, drained and depressed by her own excuses.

After a moment, Alice nudged her arm gently. "And yet he asked *you* to marry him."

He had. He'd said he wished to marry her and asked her to give him time to make all the rest right. And she'd up and left. She hadn't given him the trust he deserved, and she hadn't trusted herself. That confounded her most of all. She'd relied on herself from the age of fourteen, even run a shop, however ineffectually, on her own.

Why hadn't she trusted herself? Trusted him?

"Yes, he did."

Alice crossed her arms across her chest. "Surely there are ways for a rich man to find more money."

Jess was almost afraid to tell Alice the rest. She could already see what her friend would do with it, how Alice had very neatly pulled all her fortifications down.

"He did have a plan."

Victory lit Alice's eyes and she turned on Jess with a satisfied grin. "Then there's no real impediment, except your torn skirt and doubts about yourself."

Alice was good. So good that Jess allowed hope to tremble into life, to spread its leaves and bloom in her mind. She'd been a fool. A good, strong, honorable man loved her and wanted her, no matter the challenges. He wasn't her father, with vices and false promises. He was like her. He'd done his duty all his life and she was his heart's desire, as he was hers.

The only weakness had been on her part, giving in to doubts and fears, rather than relying on her strength and good sense as her mother had taught her to do.

Jess turned to Alice. "When I a little girl, if I would

cry over something silly or have a tantrum, my mother would take me by the arms, look me in the eyes, and tell me that I was made of sterner stuff."

Grief, a familiar pointed ache, surged up, but Jess swallowed it down.

"Sometimes, when things were difficult and I could see that they were both worried about money, I would hear her tell my father to be strong. And he would be. She had magic in her words, I think."

Alice reached out to pat her hand, the same gesture of reassurance she'd offered when Jess lost her shop.

"Once she went, Father didn't try to be strong. Maybe he tried. I don't know, but he wasn't strong anymore. I tried to tell him once, in the way that she did, with that fierce and loving look in her eyes, but it just made him cry. I reminded him of her, I think. It didn't make him strong."

Alice edged forward in her seat and turned so that she could look Jess squarely in the eyes.

"Do you need me to tell you?"

Jess nodded. "Maybe I do."

Reaching out, Alice took her by the upper arms and spoke, her tone both gentle and firm.

"Jessamin Elizabeth Wright, you are made of sterner stuff."

Looking down, Alice continued, "I suggest you mend your skirt, if it bothers you so much. Though you can hardly see it." Then she looked up to meet Jess's gaze again. "And then get yourself on the first train back to Berkshire and the man who wants to marry you. It's clear you can't stop thinking about him. And I bet he misses you too. Don't you think?"

"Yes." Those were questions she'd tried to hold at bay. Did Lucius miss her? Did he hate her for abandoning him? If he did, would he ever forgive her?

"You did your best for your father and his shop. You proved your mother right. You are made of stern stuff. Don't forget it again. If you do, send me a telegram and I'll come and remind you."

Jess couldn't keep a few tears from escaping, but she swiped them away. It seemed incongruent to blubber while Alice insisted on her strength.

"Thank you, Alice."

Her friend nodded and grinned. "Wish me luck with the speech."

"Of course I do. Good luck."

"I'd wish you luck too, Jess, but I don't think you need it. You have all the makings of a happy life. You just have to grab it."

"Thank you, Lady Katherine Adderly, for your generous donation of fifty pounds!"

At the sound of the announcement, Alice and Jess exchanged a wide-eyed stare, as if recalling how this had all begun with a "generous donation" in Kitty's drawing room.

"Kitty's mother gave her a check to donate," Jess explained. "The marchioness says she loves being charitable."

"And we welcome that sort of charity any day," Alice

said through a smile, still clapping with the crowd to acknowledge the noble lady's donation.

"Well, well, look at us. It's our own little reunion. Hello again, Miss McGregor." Kitty joined their group. "What's the goal today? How much have we to raise for the Union?" Kitty asked.

Always blunt, Alice said, "We'll take as much as we can get, though we did set our goal at two hundred pounds. I thought it quite ambitious, but your donation will help immensely. Thank you, my lady."

Kitty's mouth flattened, her pleasant expression fading, and she stared with wide eyes at something behind Jess. Before Jess could turn, a deep, familiar voice rumbled at her back.

"I think you'll make your goal, ladies. I've just put a check for one hundred pounds in the donation box."

Jess closed her eyes, breathed deep through her nose, and prayed for the bravery her mother and now Alice claimed she possessed. Then he touched her, resting his hand on her upper arm, and electricity zinged through her—reigniting her heart, sending her pulse galloping and her head spinning.

"Jessamin?"

He'd leaned in, speaking behind her ear, tickling the hair at her nape with his hot breath.

She whirled on him. He was breath-stealingly beautiful, and yet far too pale. The dark shadows beneath his eyes made her ache, and the days they'd spent apart, all the frustration and pain, welled up to choke her.

"One hundred pounds."

Those who saw her kiss him in Mayfair thought her the kind of woman to be bought for a sum, and on that night she was. Kitty Adderly had bargained for her actions with one hundred pounds. But she wasn't for sale anymore. She wasn't desperate anymore. There was no bookshop to preserve. Just her heart.

"It seemed fitting. My aunt told me you returned the money to Lady Katherine."

Kitty cleared her throat and turned away at his words, as if too embarrassed or displeased to hear more.

But the knowledge that Jess gave back the money clearly pleased him, the satisfaction of it softening his eyes and tilting the edges of his mouth until Jess thought he might smile. She realized she was holding her breath, eager for the sight of it.

But he didn't smile, and Jess feared she'd broken the easiness and trust between them.

"I did give it back. I couldn't take money for kissing you. It wasn't appropriate." She ducked her head. She didn't mean kissing him. It certainly hadn't been proper, but it never felt anything but right.

She reached out her hand and he grabbed it fiercely, grasping so tight that he whispered an apology and loosened his hold. But only a fraction.

"I didn't want kissing you to be about money, as everything else in my life had been."

Jess leaned in, close enough to catch his scent and wish they were alone, far away from the curious gazes of dozens of women.

She whispered, "I hope you felt that each time we kissed."

He dipped his head, speaking low, though the women around them leaned in to catch every word.

"I did."

She looked up and then it came, breaking over his face and setting off his dimples, a smile of amusement that kindled a warmth deep in Jess's breast, chasing away the chill that had been with her since leaving Hartwell. Leaving him.

"I'm sorry I left."

He reached up to cup her cheek, then slid his long fingers down to stroke her neck. Jess trembled and the heat in her chest spread, flames licking at every inch of skin he touched.

"Are you?"

Jess nodded, tongue-tied, brain addled, her mind focused as intently on his lips as she'd been the first night she kissed him.

Then he pulled away and she gasped at the shock of it, the loss of his heat.

But he continued to watch her, his gaze locked on hers as he slipped his hand inside his coat and retracted his closed fist. Then he took one step back, glanced at the ladies nearby pretending not to gape and failing miserably, and bent his tall frame down on one knee.

Time stopped, her pulse chugged slower, and surely her brain had gone on a holiday to the coast. She remembered breathing was very important, but only managed to do it in a stop-and-stutter manner, sucking in a breath, and then forgetting to exhale until it whooshed out in a most unladylike manner.

Lucius dipped his dark head once and then looked up at her with another easy smile as if he was so full of joy, they were easy to spare.

"I did promise to do this properly. Will you marry me, Jessamin?"

Jess opened her mouth, but the only sound she managed was a broken sob. Her heart beat *yes, yes, yes* in a steady tattoo. It echoed in her mind and she felt it there, just on the tip of her tongue. She nodded her head until she felt pins coming loose. He had to know she wanted this, even if she couldn't manage to make her stubborn tongue obey.

"Yes." She heard Alice's voice behind her. "The word you're looking for is *yes*."

He didn't glance at Alice but kept his eyes on Jess, pinning her with his gaze, waiting for her words, just hers. For her heart.

"Yes!" It finally came, bubbling up and overflowing, and suddenly she couldn't stop saying it. "Yes, yes—"

"Our sincerest thanks to Lord Grimsby for your most generous donation of one hundred pounds! Ladies, we've reached our goal for today's fundraiser."

A cheer went up, then another, and the assembled ladies broke into applause, every pair of female eyes seeking the man who'd made the day a success.

He'd taken Jess in his arms, gathering her close and dipping his head as if to kiss her, but then he pulled back and lifted his fist, unfurling his fingers to reveal a band encrusted with a row of seedling-shaped diamonds and tiny pearls.

"It was my mother's and all the Dunthorpe countesses before her. Now it's yours."

Jess had never owned a piece of jewelry in her life, and never dreamed of a possession that linked her to generations of nobility, but as he lifted the ring to place it on her finger, there were no twinges of doubt, no flash of uncertainty. She would be his countess, his viscountess, whatever title men could bestow. She could bear all the duties and tackle every challenge, as long he was hers and she was his wife.

When he reached for her, Jess went into his arms and fit against him as easily as the first night they'd met. She lifted her face for his kiss and Lucius gathered her so close she could feel every breath as the buttons of his overcoat dragged against her shirtwaist. He lowered his head, mouth hovering over hers a moment, and then pulled back.

Reaching up, he gently removed the wire-rimmed glasses Jess forgot she was wearing and tucked them into his upper coat pocket with care.

"Let's keep these safe. I've grown rather fond of them."

Lucius kissed her then, in front of every member of the Women's Union, its donors, and the ladies who'd come to hear Alice and others speak. Someone coughed, one woman sighed, and then a few more clapped and giggled. Jess wasn't sure if she was behaving very much like a freethinking woman or scandalizing every female in the room. She only knew she loved the man whose mouth moved over hers in a familiar dance of love and desire, and she leaned into him, letting him take her weight, allowing the comfort of his embrace to soothe away the pain of their separation. He reached up to caress a strand of her hair that had fallen loose and then rested his hand on her neck, his warm palm pressing against the frantic beat of her pulse.

"We promised never to part." Jess whispered the words. She'd broken their promise, but she wouldn't allow doubt and fear to defeat her again. "We'll keep that vow." And all the vows that would come after.

Leaning in, Lucius rested his forehead against hers. "Promise." And in that word, she knew that he was not just renewing all the promises they'd made by firelight, whispered words and solemn vows. With that word, he was assuring her that their future itself would be filled with promise.

Epilogue

After what the gossip rags referred to as an o'er-hasty marriage in London, Lucius and Jess returned to Hartwell and began planning repairs that would be undertaken with proceeds from the sale of several acres near the village. Lucius's father's rooms were to be tackled first with the dowry money Aunt Augusta had provided for Jessamin.

Augusta extended her stay at Hartwell, and though Jessamin was no longer her lady's companion, she continued to read to Augusta in the afternoons, and on some days her audience grew by one more. Maxim occasionally confused her with the American his son was *supposed* to marry, but more often he came to listen to her read to Augusta, though he preferred adventurous tales to the poetry his sister favored.

The Christmas holiday was to mark Lucius and Jess's first dinner hosted as man and wife. They'd invited a small group of friends, including Mr. Wellesley and Annabel Benson, and Jess convinced Alice McGregor to take the train up from London. All of the loved ones who'd championed their union and were most pleased by their happiness would spend their holiday at Hartwell.

"But Christmas isn't for days, and I've already received far too many wedding presents."

Lucius smiled, raking Jess with a smoldering gaze. He wanted to kiss her, touch her, make love to her until she only had the breath to whimper his name. But it was time to show her the books. He should have done it months ago.

"Yes, I know. Now come with me."

One of the dogs followed them. He'd become attached to Jess, so much so that he was content to abandon his twin for hours at a time.

"Castor, careful my husband doesn't trip over you."

Lucius had come dangerously close on more than one occasion, as the pug had a terrible habit of melding into the train of Jessamin's skirt.

"You can tell them apart?"

"Of course."

He suspected it was a spot of brown fur among the beige or the curl of one of their ears, but he'd yet to discern it.

Noting his studious examination of the dog as Castor stared up at him impatiently, Jessamin grinned. "Don't worry, I'll teach you."

Lucius led her down the hall, past his rooms and the suites staff were preparing for their guests, to a door near the end. The room had been used as a catch-all for broken furniture in need of repair, old estate ledgers, and the family's outmoded or out-of-season clothing. Now it also included crates full of books Lucius hoped Jessamin would be pleased to see.

"We have plenty of rooms. This is used for storage. Do we need it for the guests?"

She was already unbuttoning her cuffs and rolling up her sleeves as if he was going to ask her to help him clear out the family's discard room.

He reached for her arm to stop her, and then stroked his fingers along the inside of her wrist, holding back a moment before turning the knob and opening the door.

Doubt niggled at his mind. He'd purchased the books months before and considered giving them to her every time he'd had the agonizing notion of sending her back to London. Would she be angry that he'd kept them from her?

She had his aunt's uncanny ability to divine his thoughts.

Reaching up, she smoothed the lines furrowed in his brow. "What is it, love?"

"I have something to show you."

Jess seemed to read the seriousness in his tone and her mouth went tight, concern dimming her eyes.

He didn't want that. He had to show her.

The moment he opened the door she grinned, though it was impossible to make out anything in the darkened room.

"It smells like a bookshop." She grasped his arm,

squeezing tight and then tugging like an excited child. "Do you have books up here?"

In the short time they'd been married, Jess had already made more use of Hartwell's library than Lucius or any of his siblings had. Only his mother had loved the estate's library as Jess did.

"Yes, many books."

He went to the wall and turned up the gas, lighting up the crowded space.

Jess lifted both hands to her mouth, one clasped over the other, and her green eyes went wide above her fingers.

Lucius waited, clenching his fists, balanced on tenterhooks, praying he hadn't caused her pain.

Then she was in his arms. "Oh, Lucius."

He buried his face in her neck, soothed by her violet scent, at home in the comfort of her embrace.

When she pulled back, she beamed at him before turning to approach one of the open crates. She reached inside and lifted two volumes, sliding her fingers over them gently, worshipfully, tracing the embossed elements on the cover, stroking the spine.

"Mr. Briggs planned to auction them. I offered for them first." He shrugged as he spoke, attempting to keep his tone cool and emotionless. At the unpleasant pull of his coat across his shoulders, he realized he'd never shrugged in his life. At least not on purpose.

"But why bring them here?"

Because they were some part of you I could have.

"I don't understand." She sounded dazed.

"Neither do I, to be honest."

Nothing about transporting her books from London to Berkshire made sense. He'd simply given in to an impulse, as he'd done every time he'd touched and kissed her. It didn't bode well for his reputation as cool, calculated Lord Grim, and he was pleased at the prospect of discarding the moniker once and for all.

"Before the day I met you, I would have sworn that I don't have an impulsive bone in my body. But you . . . you seem to have found it, and given it free rein."

"You bought *all* of my books?" Despite the evidence before her, her voice hadn't lost its incredulous tone.

"Yes, every single one of them."

"And you brought them here?" She pointed down to the ground at her feet, but he knew she meant to Berkshire, to Hartwell. Though she clutched a book to her chest, he wondered how long it would take her to feel it, the tangible evidence of his impulsivity, and believe it.

"Yes. As you see. They're all here."

He gestured toward the books around them, spilling from crates and stacked in piles. He shook away the discomfort that disorder always inspired in him, attempted to embrace the clutter that made her happy, and focused on the woman who made him happy, staring at him, eyes still wide in wonder.

"But you didn't know if you'd ever see me again. Did you?"

"No. I knew my aunt was concerned about your situation. I thought she might offer you money or a position, but I never dreamed it would be in her own household. I never dreamed she would bring you here."

He didn't like to think of what his future might have been if she hadn't.

"I'm glad she did."

There was no mistaking the thrill she took in examining the books. A kind of light had come into her eyes and a glow lit her skin. It was a look he'd only glimpsed when he'd find her in the library. Something about books brought her more fully alive, and he felt like an ogre for having kept them from her an hour, let alone months.

"Perhaps I should have given them to you sooner. But I couldn't bear the notion of you leaving. I should have given you that choice. I would never wish to trap you here."

The words were bitter on his tongue. And bitter memories sprang up too, all the misery his father had caused his mother when he'd tried to tether her to him and Hartwell.

The look of awe and delight slipped from her face and she whirled on him, two books clutched in her hands.

"I did leave, but that was to do with my own fears. These books wouldn't have made me go or stay."

She approached him, reaching a hand out and tucking it into his waistcoat, pressing it over his heart.

"Do you still think I'm going to leave?" She laid the books aside and bit her lip, looking up at him with enough love and tenderness to reassure any man.

He shook his head. He trusted their bond. Trusted in her love. "No, but I would like it very much if we are never apart again."

He reached for her, pulling her in close, filling his

hands with the curve of her hips as she reached up to grasp his lapels.

"Yes. Me too. Didn't we make that our vow? I did readily agree to it."

He kissed her, a soft brush of his mouth on hers. When he pulled back, she turned to trail her gaze over the piles of her books.

He couldn't resist asking, "Do you ever miss your shop, Jessamin?"

She looked at him, a sly twinkle in her green eyes.

"Can I tell you a very great secret? An awful truth about me."

Lucius assumed as mock-serious tone.

"Yes, but I think you should have done it before I married you."

Her low voice went whispery soft, as if she truly was relating a terrible secret.

"I never felt that it was my shop. I never embraced it fully. It was my father's shop, what he wanted. And I so wanted to please him, especially after Mother died. I know it's not true, but when I was a girl, I thought I was the only thing he had to make him happy. Me and the shop. He made me promise I would care for it, that I would keep it going. On his deathbed, he asked that of me. I couldn't say no. I didn't have a choice."

She turned her gaze toward the crates of books and deflated on a sigh.

"When Mr. Briggs wouldn't take my payment, and I knew the shop was closed and it was over . . . I couldn't admit it to myself, but I felt relief. A lightness, as if a weight had been lifted. And I felt guilty for that relief, but not guilty enough to want to go back and recreate a bookshop that I never truly wanted."

Tipping her head, a lighter a lilt in her voice, she nodded and said, "I do love books, but I have no desire to be a bookshop owner."

Lucius drew her body against his, and she returned her attention to him with a grin full of promise.

"But you will be the lady of Hartwell? I believe you have agreed to that."

Her grin bloomed into a smile, a beautiful, easy expression of joy that lit up the room and sent spirals of warmth through Lucius's chest.

"Yes."

He ducked his head, needing to see her eye to eye.

"And you'll be my wife. I think perhaps you've agreed to that too."

She giggled, a deliciously low, seductive sound that drew an answering rumble from his throat.

"Yes."

Keep reading for a sneak peek at Christy Carlyle's next breathtaking Accidental Heirs novel,

ONE TEMPTING PROPOSAL

Becoming engaged? Simple.
Resisting temptation? Impossible.

Sebastian Fennick, the newest Duke of Wrexford, prefers the straightforwardness of mathematics to romantic nonsense. When he meets Lady Katherine Adderly at the first ball of the season, he finds her as alluring as she is disagreeable. His title may now require him to marry, but Sebastian can't think of anyone less fit to be his wife, even if he can't get her out of his mind.

After five seasons of snubbing suitors and making small talk, Lady Kitty has seen all the ton has to offer . . . and she's not impressed. But when Kitty's overbearing father demands she must marry before her beloved younger sister can, she proposes a plan to the handsome duke. Kitty's schemes always seem to backfire, but she knows this one can't go wrong. After all, she's not the least bit tempted by Sebastian, is she?

Available November 2015

About the Author

Fueled by Pacific Northwest coffee and inspired by multiple viewings of every British costume drama she can get her hands on, **Christy Carlyle** writes sensual historical romance set in the Victorian era. She loves heroes who struggle against all odds and heroines who are ahead of their time. A former teacher with a degree in history, she finds there's nothing better than being able to combine her love of the past with a die-hard belief in happy endings.

Give in to your Impulses . . .
Continue reading for excerpts from
our newest Avon Impulse books.
Available now wherever e-books are sold.

An Excerpt from

RIGHT WRONG GUY

A Brightwater Novel

by Lia Riley

Bad boy wrangler Archer Kane lives fast and loose. Words like *responsibility* and *commitment* send him running in the opposite direction. Until a wild Vegas weekend puts him on a collision course with Eden Bankcroft-Kew, a New York heiress running away from her blackmailing fiancé . . . the morning of her wedding.

"ARCHER?" EDEN STARED in the motel bathroom mirror, her reflection a study in horror. "Please tell me this is a practical joke."

"We're in the middle of Nevada, sweetheart. There's no Madison Avenue swank in these parts." Archer didn't bother to keep amusement from his answering yell through the closed door. "The gas station only sold a few things. Trust me, those clothes were the best of the bunch."

After he got out of the shower, a very long shower which afforded her far too much time for contemplating him in a cloud of thick steam, running a bar of soap over cut v-lines, he announced that he would find her something suitable to wear. She couldn't cross state lines wearing nothing but his old t-shirt, and while the wedding dress worked in a pinch, it was still damp. Besides, her stomach lurched at the idea of sliding back into satin and lace.

She'd never be able to don a wedding dress and not think of the Reggie debacle. She couldn't even entirely blame him, her subconscious had been sending out warning flares for months. She'd once been considered a smart woman, graduated from NYU with a 4.0 in Art History. So how could she have been so dumb?

Truth be told, it wasn't even due to her mother's dying wish that led her to accepting him, although that certainly bore some influence. No, it was the idea of being alone. The notion didn't feel liberating or "I am woman, hear me roar." More terrified house mouse squeaking alone in a dark cellar.

She clenched her jaw, shooing away the mouse. What was the big deal with being alone? She might wish for more friends, or a love affair, but she'd also never minded her own company. This unexpected turn of events was an opportunity, a time for self-growth, getting to know herself, and figuring out exactly what she wanted. Yes, she'd get empowered all right, roar so loud those California mountains would tremble.

Right after they finished laughing at this outfit.

Seriously, did Archer have to select pink terrycloth booty shorts that spelled *Q & T* in rhinestones, one on each butt cheek? And the low-cut top scooped so even her small rack sported serious cleavage. *Get Lucky* emblazoned across the chest, the tank top was an XS so the letters stretched to the point of embarrassment. If she raised her hands over her head, her belly button winked out.

As soon as she arrived in Brightwater, she'd invest in proper clothes and send for her belongings back home. Until then . . . time to face the music. She stepped from the bathroom, chewing the corner of her lip. Archer didn't burst into snickers. All he did was stare. His playful gaze vanished, replaced by a startling intensity.

"Well, go on then. Get it over with and make fun of me." She gathered her hair into a messy bun, securing it with a hair elastic from her wrist she found in her purse.

"Laughing's not the first thing that jumps to mind, sweetheart."

Her stomach sank. "Horror then?"

"Stop." He rubbed the back of his neck, that wicked sensual mouth curving into a bold smile. "You're hot as hell."

Reggie had never remarked on her appearance. She sucked in a ragged breath at the memory of his text. *Bored me to fucking tears.*

"Hey, Freckles," he said softly. "You okay?"

She snapped back, unsure what her face revealed. "Tiny shorts and boob shirts do it for you?" She fought for an airy tone, waving her hand over the hot pink "QT" abomination and praying he wouldn't notice her tremble.

He gave a one-shouldered shrug. "Short shorts do it for all warm-blooded men."

"I'll keep that in mind," she said, thumbing her ear. He probably wasn't checking *her* out, just her as the closest female specimen in the immediate vicinity.

He wiggled out of his tan Carhart jacket and held it out. "You'll want this. Temperatures are going to top out in the mid-forties today. I've stuck a wool blanket in the passenger seat and will keep the heat cranking."

Strange. He might be a natural flirt, but for all his easy confidence, there was an uncertainty in how he regarded her. A hesitation that on anyone else could be described as vulnerability, the type of look that caused her to volunteer at no-kill rescue shelters and cry during cheesy life insurance commercials. A guy like this, what did he know about insecurity or self-doubt? But that expression went straight to her heart. "Archer . . ."

He startled at the sound of his real name, instead of the Cowboy moniker she'd used the last twenty-four hours.

His jacket slipped, baring her shoulders as she reached to take one of his big hands in hers. "Thank you." Impulsively, she rose on tiptoe to kiss his cheek, but he jerked with surprise and she grazed the appealing no-man's land between his dimple and lips.

This was meant to be a polite gesture, an acknowledgment he'd been a nice guy, stepped up and helped her—a stranger—out when she'd barreled in and given him no choice.

He smelled good. Too good. Felt good too. She should move—now—but his free hand, the one she wasn't clutching, skimmed her lower back. Was this a kiss?

No.

Well . . . almost.

Never had an actual kiss sent goose bumps prickling down her spine even as her stomach heated, the cold and hot reaction as confused as her thoughts. Imagine what the real thing would do.

An Excerpt from

DESIRE ME MORE

by Tiffany Clare

From the moment Amelia Grant accepted the position of secretary to Nicholas Riley, London's most notorious businessman, she knew her life would be changed forever. For Nick didn't want just her secretarial skills . . . he wanted her complete surrender. And she was more than willing to give it to him, spending night after night in delicious sin. As the devastatingly insatiable Nick teaches her the ways of forbidden desire, Amelia begins to dream of a future together . . .

WHY HADN'T SHE just stayed in bed? Instead, she'd set herself on an unknown path. One without Nick. Why? She hated this feeling that was ripping her apart from the inside out. It hurt so much and so deeply that the wounds couldn't be healed.

Biting her bottom lip on a half-escaped sob, she violently wiped her tears away with the back of her hand. Nick caught her as she fumbled with the lock on the study door, spinning her around and wrapping his arms tightly around her, crushing her against his solid body.

She wanted to break down. To just let the tears overtake her. But she held strong.

"I have already told you I can't let you go. Stay, Amelia." His voice was so calm, just above a whisper. "Please, I couldn't bear it if you left me. I can't let you leave. I won't."

Hearing him beg tugged at her heart painfully. Amelia's fists clenched where they were trapped between their bodies. There was only one thing she could do.

She pushed him away, hating that she was seconds away from breaking down. Hating that she knew that she had to hold it together when every second in his arms chipped away at her control.

"You are breaking my will every day. Making me lose myself in you. Don't ask this of me. Please. Nick. Let me go."

If she stayed, they would only end up back where they were. And she needed more than his physical comfort. He held her tighter against his chest, crushing her between him and the door like he would *never* let her go.

"I told you I couldn't let you go. Don't try to leave. I warned you that you were mine the night I took your virginity."

Tilting her head back, she stared at him, eyes awash with tears she was helpless to stop from flowing over her cheeks. "Why are you doing this to me?"

The gray of his eyes were stormy, as though waiting to unleash a fury she'd never seen the likes of. "Because I can't let you go. Because I love you."

His tone brooked no argument, so she said nothing to contradict him, just stared at him for another moment before pushing at his immovable body again. Nick's hand gently cradled her throat, his thumb forcing her head to lean against the door.

"I've already told you that I wouldn't let you walk away. You belong to me."

Her lips parted on a half exasperated groan at his declaration of ownership over her.

"How could I belong to you when you close yourself off to me? I will not be controlled by you, no matter what I feel—"

Before she could get out the rest of her sentence, Nick's mouth took hers in an all-consuming kiss, his tongue robbing her of breath as it pushed past the barrier of her lips and tangled with her tongue in wordless need.

Hunger rose in her, whether it was for physical desire or a need to draw as much of him into her as possible was hard to say. And she hated herself a little for not pushing him away again and again until she won this argument. Not now that she had a small piece of him all to herself. Even if it wouldn't be enough in the end.

Without a doubt in her mind, she'd never crave anything as badly as she craved Nick: his essence, his strength, *him*.

Her hands fisted around his shirtsleeves, holding him close. She didn't want to let go . . . of him or the moment.

His touch was like a branding iron as he tugged the hemline of her dress from her shoulders, pulling down the front of the dress. The pull rent the delicate satin material, leaving one breast on display for Nick to fondle. His hand squeezed her, the tips of his short nails digging into her flesh.

Their mouths didn't part once, almost as if Nick wanted to distract her from her original purpose. Keep her thinking of their kiss. The way their tongues slid knowingly against the other. The way he tasted like coffee and danger. Forbidden. Like the apple from the tree he was a temptation she could not refuse.

His distraction was working.

And his hands were everywhere.

An Excerpt from

MAKE ME

A Broke and Beautiful Novel

by Tessa Bailey

In the final Broke and Beautiful novel from bestselling author Tessa Bailey, a blue collar construction worker and a quiet uptown virgin are about to discover that the friend zone can sometimes be excellent foreplay . . .

DAY ONE HUNDRED and forty-two of being friend-zoned. Send rations.

Russell Hart stifled a groan when Abby twisted on his lap to call out a drink order to the passing waiter, adding a smile that would no doubt earn her a martini on the house. Every time their six-person "super group" hung out, which was starting to become a nightly affair, Russell advanced into a newer, more vicious circle of hell. Tonight, however, he was pretty sure he'd meet the devil himself.

They were at the Longshoreman, celebrating the Fourth of July, which presented more than one precious little clusterfuck. One, the holiday meant the bar was packed full of tipsy Manhattanites, creating a shortage of chairs, hence Abby parking herself right on top of his dick. Two, it put the usually conservative Abby in ass-hugging shorts and one of those tops that tied at the back of her neck. Six months ago, he would have called it a *shirt*, but his two best friends had fallen down the relationship rabbit hole, putting him in the vicinity of excessive chick talk. So, now it was a halter top. What he wouldn't *give* to erase that knowledge.

During their first round of drinks, he'd become a

believer in breathing exercises. Until he'd noticed these tiny, blond curls at Abby's nape, curls he'd never seen before. And some-fucking-how, those sun-kissed curls were what had nudged him from semierect to full-scale Washington-monument status. The hair on the rest of her head was like a . . . a warm milk-chocolate color, so where did those little curls come from? *Those* detrimental musings had led to Russell questioning what else he didn't know about Abby. What color was everything else? Did she have freckles? Where?

Russell would not be finding out—ever—and not just because he was sitting in the friend zone with his dick wedged against his stomach—*not* an easy maneuver—so she wouldn't feel it. No, there was more to it. His friends, Ben and Louis, were well aware of those reasons, which accounted for the half-sympathetic, half-needling looks they were sending him from across the table, respective girlfriends perched on their laps. The jerks.

Abby was off-limits. Not because she was taken—thank Christ—or because someone had verbally forbidden him from pursuing her. That wasn't it. Russell had taken a long time trying to find a suitable explanation for why he didn't just get the girl alone one night and make his move. Explain to her that men like him weren't suitable friends for wide-eyed debutantes and give her a demonstration of the alternative.

It went like this. Abby was like an expensive package that had been delivered to him by mistake. Someone at the post office had screwed the pooch and dropped off the shiniest, most beautiful creation on his Queens doorstep and driven away, laughing manically. Russell wasn't falling for the trick, though. Someone would claim the package, eventually. They would chuckle over the obvious mistake and take Abby away from him because, really, he had no business being the one whose lap she chose to sit on. No business whatsoever.

But while he was in possession of the package—as much as he'd *allow* himself to be in possession, anyway—he would guard her with his life. He would make sure that when someone realized the cosmic error that had occurred—the one that had made him Abby's friend and confidant—she would be sweet and undamaged, just as she'd been on arrival.

Unfortunately, the package didn't seem content to let him stand guard from a distance. She innocently beckoned him back every time he managed to put an inch of space between them. Russell had lost count of the times Abby had fallen asleep on him while the super group watched a movie, drank margaritas on the girls' building's rooftop, driven home in cabs. She was entirely too comfortable around him, considering he saluted against his fly every time they were in the same room.

"Why so quiet, Russell?" Louis asked, his grin turning to a wince as his actress girlfriend, Roxy, elbowed him in the ribs. Yeah. Everyone at the damn table knew he had a major thing for the beautiful, unassuming number whiz on his lap. Everyone but Abby. And that's how he planned to keep it.